Crooked Love

A Novel

Heidi Ferrer

To my own Mama, Nancy,

to Nick,

and especially to our brave son, Bexon.

You are the light of my life.

Mommy loves you forever.

ISBN-10: 0615732127

ISBN-13: 978-0615732121

Author's note: While this book is a work of fiction and memory is of course, imperfect, it was inspired by my family's own medical journey. I tried to get the medical facts of my son's experience as correct as possible, in the interest of telling the story and passing the information along to other families. In other words, the medical stuff is mostly true, but of course, I'm not a doctor and I'm also human. If I made any factual mistakes in that or any other area, my apologies, my intention is to entertain and hopefully to help other families facing this and other challenges: You are not alone. The emotions are real and I lived them, here is a piece of my heart.

1
Tracks

The monster came to take not one life, but two, with no conscience or concern for human suffering, not even that of an innocent child. It was the worst nightmare Kai had ever experienced, worse than anything she could ever have imagined. She was standing in a large crowd of people, in front of commuter train tracks at a modern metro station, and everyone was staring at an eighteen month old baby boy. The baby was uncomprehendingly tied to the tracks, as the powerful train thundered towards his small, wriggling, terrified body. It cast a shadow like a futuristic, menacing metallic robot on rails.

The tracks curved and corkscrewed, like a sadistic theme park ride, but the twists didn't slow it down. It hurtled ahead at what seemed like light speed, on a collision course to crush him, and *no one was doing anything to stop it*. The baby was crying, hysterical, as the crowd looked on—concerned, but bizarrely unmoving. Kai was paralyzed by fear—*why was no one untying this baby boy*? Her mind raced—SAVE HIM—PLEASE—HELP!!!

It was like an old fashioned melodrama, with a victim lashed to the tracks in a dusty, sepia toned town, but these were modern times, and Kai knew that this was very, very *real*. This was *happening*. She opened her mouth to scream, but nothing came out, as if the terror had sealed off her throat. She tried to move, but she was locked—frozen—with searing fear and horror coursing through her veins.

Her desperate eyes saw several doctors in white coats at the front of the crowd, looking on, even one doctor in light blue surgical scrubs, holding a shiny scalpel. That doctor looked concerned, caring, even, but what was he going to do, *operate on a baby on the train tracks*? The sunlight glinted off the scalpel as the train's blaring whistle pierced her mind, and everything started to spin.

Suddenly, she noticed a very handsome, dark haired young man in the crowd, with a small cleft in his chin. She looked back at the baby boy, crying hysterically. He had this man's jaw line, but he had honey blonde hair and green eyes.

Kai looked at the man pleadingly, begging him with her eyes to help, "*Save him—*" but he slowly shook his head, backing away.

"*It's not my baby,*" he said sadly, disappearing into the crowd.

The way the handsome man looked at her struck her as odd, surreal. This man, this dark stranger, *knew her*. And the way he looked at her told her something else—it hit her like a punch in the stomach. This baby no one was saving was *hers*. He had her wavy honey blonde hair, her green eyes. *Hers*.

The fear and pain was overwhelming, she desperately fought the urge to pass out, her dizzy, reeling mind was threatening to close down. She was only twenty years old; she had never had a baby! She had never even been pregnant. But she knew—she now knew in her very cells that this baby was *her son.*

Suddenly, she could move her legs, and she dashed to the baby, lurching, then staggering forward and falling to her knees, struggling to untie the ropes with violently trembling hands. No one stopped her and no one tried to help her. She couldn't untie him; it was too complex, too twisted—wrapped around the metal tracks in complicated loops and knots...

NO NO NO NO NO NO NO, this couldn't be happening. The crowd just looked on silently, shaking their heads, as the sunlight danced like daggers off the metal of the charging, thundering train.

She was sobbing, now, realizing in that instant it was too late to save him. The doctors were giving up, walking away, and the malevolent train was almost upon them, an unstoppable beast. The engine roared, the wind created by the machine's force nearly blowing her away from the child, nearly knocking her away from her son. No, she had to be touching him. She *had* to.

She had time to escape, to leave him there, to live. That was no option.

Kai lay down on the tracks beside her baby and put her arms around her boy, holding him and starting to sing the only song she could think of, *Three Little Birds*, by Bob Marley. "*Don't worry...about a thing... 'cause every little thing's...gonna be alright...*"

The baby stopped crying as the train bore down. His big green eyes were trusting, now. They were flecked with bits of gold, exactly like hers, but hers were filled with terror. They locked eyes for a long moment, and he looked at her as if they were one, as if she was his safe place, she was his *home*. Her heart ached and guilt surged through her body like a knife, as she looked to the sky. It was a sunny, blue-skied day. Palm Trees waved, dotting the horizon. How could anything bad ever happen to an innocent?

"*Please, God,*" Kai prayed, "*take me, not him.*"

Just before the train hit, Kai closed her eyes. The cruel tracks shook violently and she whispered "*Mama.*" The baby's tiny, warm hand touched her cheek, and everything became enveloped in an inky ocean of black.

2
Before

Once, Kai had nearly died. Once. Now, whether she was riding the wave or just paddling out, she knew she had led a mostly charmed life. She took deep, cleansing breaths, soaked in the brine of the surf, and thanked God and the universe for every single, amazing day she got to be alive, alive, *alive*. The tide cleaned the darkness away. It always would, wouldn't it?

A California beach girl with a natural, bohemian style, one event had scorched a permanent hole in Kai Weston's sand dust, barefoot world. That was the day her beautiful mom, her best friend in life, walked out the door and never came home. A phone call on her cell, from a stranger. Blood clot to the brain. She never felt a thing.

Kai was twenty years old when her mom died, and now, at twenty three, she honored her mama's life by being grateful for every moment. It's what her mom would've surely wanted. Not that she didn't grieve—oh, she crumbled like one of those thin papers that cover Italian amaretti cookies, the kind you light on fire and it disintegrates, just poofs into thin air. She dropped the phone, then smashed it against the wall, dropped out of UCLA and went inside of herself for a year; crawled inside a pit she never knew existed, the kind of place where hope rots and your insides liquefy. Now she didn't talk about that time, to anyone. It was Her Dark Place, and she never wanted to face that kind of pain and fear again, *ever*.

She wanted to, no; she *would* radiate *light* and *joy* into the world, into the universal energy where her mama's soul still surely dwelled. People said that Kai's mother, Beka, was an angel on Earth, the kind of person who didn't have a mean bone in her body. Kai wanted to be exactly like her mom, or at least to try.

Besides that one very bad thing, Kai had always been pretty lucky and she didn't know what she had done to deserve it. Maybe she was a good person in a past life?

A lot of her daily luck was the kindness that comes to attractive girls, although Kai never *felt* beautiful, in that way that girls can be damaged when their own father deserts them young. Her self-esteem deeply bruised, her insides felt plain and emotionally paper thin, a house of straw, not bricks.

It was as if her own mirror was permanently cracked; because apparently, the rest of the world saw her differently. If she walked into a sub shop for a sandwich, ordering just the sandwich, the skinny teenager behind the counter would throw bags of free chips and cookies in with it. If she walked past a rug dealer, the owner would step outside and hand her a free, burgundy Persian throw rug. If she went to a five star restaurant, heads turned, and the plump, ruddy faced, normally irritable chef personally shuffled out from the kitchen, to bring her table an amuse bouche, on the house.

Her friends would call her every time they wanted to go to the hottest new club, because even if she didn't know the owner, when she smiled, the ropes would part and they would glide right in. A heavily tattooed rock star would send them a round of free drinks and then invite her to his house for an after party. It was embarrassing, she didn't want to be rude, but she always declined.

The truth was, she had never not had a boyfriend, in fact, not since preschool, when Billy Kellan proposed to her on bended knee, holding his late grandmother's antique wedding ring. Five other boys were in line behind Billy, all with treasured family diamonds clutched in their small, hot, sweaty palms, some of them stolen from their very own mothers. One curly dark haired boy, Bradley, brought his grandmother's Tahitian black pearls. Four year old Kai wanted those, to be truthful, but she told him she couldn't accept a family heirloom.

Her older sister Janie resented Kai's good fortune to be born both pretty *and* smart, with that laid back sensibility that drew people to her like magnets. Janie didn't "get" Kai's deep seeded insecurity, she thought her sister had it made. Janie was not quite as tall, she was pretty, but in more of an average way, she was not quite as bright in school—everything was more of a climb for Janie. Kai's teeth came in straight; Janie needed both braces and a jaw expander. Kai's eyes looked like emeralds, Janie's were blue clouded with gray, as if they were your dream trip to Fiji—ruined by a gloomy rainstorm.

Kai had those breasts that were on the small side, but looked like they were saying "*Hello, World!*" Janie's nipples were larger and flatter, her hair just a bit thinner and more coarse, Janie often thought she looked like God had tried to make Kai and she, Janie, was the dough that didn't rise. The dough the baker threw away so he could make the really *good* bread.

Kai had big feet and long toes, but boys, and later men, mostly found that adorable. She decided to accept her weird feet, declaring at age thirteen "I think I love my big boats, because they sail the rest of my body where I need to go."

Kai joked that she loved getting sand in her butt crack, it was "exfoliating"—Janie declared it "gross," then upon turning eighteen, promptly moved as far away from the ocean as she could get. She now lives in Hays, Kansas, where she's a stay at home mom of three little

6

girls under the age of five, with a sweet, preacher husband. Since their mother died, the two sisters had drifted apart. Janie homeschooled her kids and she was always too busy to visit California. The pain Kai went through following their mom's death was something Janie couldn't, or wouldn't stand to hear about—she was pregnant when it happened, and said she had to protect her emotions in order to protect the baby.

To Kai, it appeared Janie had no grieving phase, but who was she to say? Everyone grieved differently, and their lives couldn't have been much more different in the years that followed. *"Save the drama for your mama,"* wasn't that the old expression? If Janie wasn't gonna grieve for their mom, Kai wondered if she had shut down her emotions completely.

When her mom died, she broke up with her college boyfriend; she couldn't feel any love or joy through her grief. Kai eventually took the small amount of money her mom left her, and bought a teeny tiny, rickety ass little beach shack from a nice old man named Gus, with red surf shorts, white hair and a bristly beard—a beach Santa Claus. She hand painted BEACH MAMA across the front of it and started sewing handmade sarongs, weaving beach sandals from rope, and using beach glass and shells to decorate handmade bikinis. It was her therapy, the first glimmer of hope that began to bring her out of her depression and grief.

It was like she was slowly, painstakingly pulling herself up a rope, clawing herself back from a deep, dark pit of nothingness and despair. She would sleep there, in the hut alone at night, feeling the salty breeze of the ocean, aware that she could be harmed by some crazy stranger, some drifter or maniac, but *needing this*, on the deepest level, to save her. To stop her from going over the edge of the boat, back into the deep end.

While she was hanging on, barely hanging in, the craziest thing in the world happened. A young female celebrity from a reality TV show wandered into her hut and the paparazzi took a million pictures of her trying on Kai's stuff. The next week, the photos were in *US Magazine* and on PerezHilton.com, the popular gossip site. Every photo had the "Beach Mama" sign in the background, and Kai had a gazillion customers before she could blink.

That was just the kind of thing that used to happen to her, that was her "old good luck" before she lost her mom, and she had to admit, it was *fantastic*. Just six months before, she had wanted to walk into the surf on a moonlit night and just *disappear*. Thousands of times, she had imagined how drowning might feel: cold, wet, panic and unbearable pressure, then nothingness. No more loss and *no more pain*. Now *hope*, that thing with feathers, began to fill her patchwork heart again.

Maybe she could have an actual future, even an actual *career*.

Other celebrities started coming by to check her stuff out, and they began inviting her out to their parties and the hippest bars in Hollywood. Real actors intermingled with reality stars and musicians—there were different levels, but the young and famous seemed to be in some kind of "celebrity club," and she was given a pass inside their rarified, gilded world. It was not a bad world to be in—everyone was nice to you, and a lot of things were free. She went out on dates with a guitar wielding rock star that had just broken up with an actress who was America's latest romantic comedy sweetheart. She was hit on by "A" list actors, producers, film directors and drop dead gorgeous male underwear models, who appeared on billboards in Times Square—displaying all of their *bidness* to billions.

It was a whirlwind, fueled by mojitos and champagne, as everyone told her she should be an actress/model/whatever…but no one felt like *the one*. No one felt like her future husband, or the future father of her child. No one felt like *home*—until she met Teddy.

Teddy Verona was a walking dream, when he strolled into her shack one day, his surfboard casually slung under his muscular arm. He wasn't a typical surfer type, but he was damn good at it—he was damn good at a lot of things. Kai had always been drawn to thick dark hair and big brown eyes with heavy, Bambi lashes. It was her physical opposite, and she also liked a quick wit, with a bit of a potty mouth. A good/bad boy, he had to want to pull up her skirt in the elevator, maybe even sneak a finger up under the edge of her panties…but not pull her hair and certainly not strangle her in the corridor. Was that too much for a good/bad girl to ask?

Teddy put her into his palm and gently held her. The Verona family was wealthy with vineyards in northern California—Verona Vineyards, of course—but even they had been hit by the economic downturn, their rare varietals and five hundred dollar bottles of wine couldn't be sold at many restaurants, since people had learned to watch their dollars a little more closely. Teddy had enough money to be more then comfortable. He owned a mansion in Beverly Hills and had started a production company with two close friends, as he told Kai; he "wanted to produce films he believed in." Kai respected his taste. His favorite film was about an old jazz musician in Paris, called "Round Midnight." It was beautiful and sad and had a lyrical winter beach scene that cracked her heart wide open like an egg.

Kai tasted a bottle from Teddy's best vineyard and nearly cried…it felt like red, warm heat mixed with velvet, melting down her throat. He grinned at her reaction and declared, "You're a *beach girl*, Kai, you have to experience the great beaches of the *world*!"

So off they went, on a magical mystery love tour: first to Bora Bora, where they swam with swirling stingrays and black tip sharks, without a cage, and made love in the beach hammock beside their private hut over the pristine, jewel colored waters. Every morning, they watched the fish swim under the glass floor of their hut, then took their rolls from dinner the night before with them under water snorkeling, feeding a swirl of multi-colored fish by hand. Hundreds of them—yellow angel fish—even one school of fish with iridescent scales the colors of a pastel rainbow…

Some of these particular fish, had they looked upwards while swimming with their little fins beneath their romantic over water hut, may have just seen the underside of Kai's perfectly heart shaped, tan booty through that glass floor window.

Fiji…the Virgin Islands…the South of France…the Italian Riviera…Ibiza…Greece…they danced and partied and made love. They ate like kings, Kai was brown and happy and her belly started to swell just a bit…too much delicious food, she thought.

But no, it was even *more* joyful.

A *baby*!

It was a miracle. She had almost died, and now *life* was growing inside her. She stared at the stick and screamed and jumped up and down and hugged Teddy, then called Janie, who said "God is good." Kai thought, God is *great*.

A part of Kai, that damaged part that was her long gone father's daughter, still couldn't believe that someone like Teddy loved *her*, had picked *her*. But she tried to stop looking at her own mirror as cracked; she tried to see herself now as Teddy saw her.

He proposed just days after they found out. On the moonlit beach, right beside her shack, with a four carat, antique cushion cut ring set in platinum, from the '40s. She said "*Yes!*" but asked him if they could have the wedding after the baby was born. Teddy said, "Whatever you want, babe." She always felt like she was a person who did better with less on her plate, she didn't want to be planning a wedding and preparing to be a new mother at the same time. There was time for everything; she was not in a rush to get a wedding band on her finger.

Teddy wasn't famous, and Kai was glad about that. Nothing against the talented and famous…she just wanted to be happy. *An uncomplicated life.* Family and relationships, *love*, that was what truly mattered. And she wanted to be a good mama, like her mama was. At least she would give it everything she had.

She moved into Teddy's mansion in Beverly Hills, a little bummed that it wasn't on the ocean, and the décor was a little sleek and state-of-the-art modern for her taste. He promised they'd get a place in Malibu that was all her style; he was trying to be smart and pace out the real estate market. They were only a twenty minute drive from the ocean, he reminded her, which was true, and they had a pool, but she missed the charm of her tiny shack. Teddy said she could start a line of beachwear, he knew so many designers personally, which he did. There was no huge hurry, they had their whole lives ahead of them.

There was something else they needed to attend to, first, and that was Kai's growing belly. They had an ultrasound, where the baby was the size of a kicky *gummy bear*! There was actually a *person* in there! It blew her away—she cried large, hot, waxy tears, right there in the doctor's office.

At her five month ultrasound, they had decided they wanted to know: It was a *boy*! A baby boy. She had grown up with a sister; she had never seen a boy become a man.

"Your baby is perfect," those were the exact words her Ob/Gyn, Dr. Wallace, said after the ultrasound, "he has good lips!"

Kai beamed as Teddy squeezed her hand. They wanted to name him before he was born, Kai had read it was a good way to help them both bond with him in the womb. "He has his beautiful mother's lips," Teddy

11

smiled, kissing Kai's own pink, cupid bowed pair. "Of *course* he's perfect," the proud daddy-to-be said. *"I don't live a wrinkled life."*

They named him Fin, with just one "N"— because of their mutual love for the ocean and because he just might have been conceived with fishies swimming beneath them, right under that over water hut in Bora Bora, beneath his beach mama's booty.

JOY, the joy of all joys, filled her spirit—where there once was despair, there now was *endless possibility*. Who would he be? What would he teach her? What kind of love could she give him? The unconditional love her own mama had given to her, she hoped.

And to be honest, Kai was also scared. She didn't play the lottery, what bigger lottery could you play than having a baby? What if she lost him, before he was full term? What if he got sick? What if he died? She had some deep seeded guilt about her luck—*why her*?

She wasn't blind to the dark side of life. Why bad things happened to good people is something she could not fully comprehend, but she believed in God. Kai believed there must be a universal order to things; maybe it was a cosmic plan that humans weren't meant to know the meaning of their lives, until they passed on from this world. She tried not to think about it too much, it terrified her to know that children got diseases, that children were abducted. How could there be a meaning to *that*? She had to shut out those thoughts, she realized it was irrational. Most kids grew up healthy and just *fine*! *She* was still here, and she had made a ton of stupid mistakes in her life, especially as a teenager. She had actually *hitchhiked* once—her poor mother! Her kid was never hitchhiking, yikes.

Kai believed deeply in gratitude, and tried to keep her focus there, she didn't want to put out any negative energy into the universe, especially not with her little one budding inside her belly.

12

Kai's sister Janie believed that God controls everything that happens in a person's life, and that you do not have any control *whatsoever*. If something is God's will, it will happen, no matter what you do, for good or ill.

Kai wasn't sure she believed that entirely, but it did take some of the guilt off of her shoulders. She wasn't choosing her good luck; *God* was, so she shouldn't look at God's gifts as a burden. She once saw a man on TV, a guest on *Oprah*, who saw many people die in a plane accident. The man survived, but he witnessed these people perishing, burning up in their seats in flames. It was a horrible story, but the beautiful part was that this man who survived said he could actually see the people's auras, or souls, leaving their bodies, and that some were much brighter than others.

Kai decided in that moment that she wanted her aura to be very, very bright, and every day as she got out of bed, she said a little prayer, asking God to help her achieve it. She wasn't going-to-church-every-week religious, but she felt like she had a special relationship with God, her whole life. They just talked, kinda hung out; the whole world was His church, in her humble opinion. Being in nature, whether you were by the ocean, in the lush forest, taking in the majestic, snowcapped mountains or witnessing a hummingbird suspended in flight, those experiences were akin to being in one of the most holy chapels on Earth.

Kai loved being pregnant. Eating pregnant was *fabulous*. Every time she ate healthy food, she felt so good about doing it for two. One day, she thought, she would tell Fin he was mostly made of organic salads, vanilla buttercream cupcakes and daydreams.

She was high on pregnancy hormones—she felt like she could take on the world! Sure, she had a few emotional moments, some normal teariness and irrational worry, what pregnant woman didn't? You know, when you read you could lose the baby if you eat unpasteurized cheese, or cold cuts that could have listeria on their surface— *innocent cold cuts*! Well, it's hard not to have a few worry filled moments, she figured that was normal.

Overall, it was the happiest she had ever been. She played classic rock and felt her little boy kicking to the drum beats of The Beatles and The Stones, who *says* you can't get no satisfaction? Her baby just *loooved* Bob Marley, of course, he already had excellent taste. Kai and Teddy went to a big summer action movie and their little guy kicked through all of the action scenes—Kai worried that he thought all those gunshots and explosions were real. *Noooo* more action fare, she decided after that, she wanted to do absolutely everything right for this kiddo!

She took her pregnancy vitamins with folic acid every day, ate a healthy, balanced diet, devoured every pregnancy book she could get her hands on, and took every class on babies and motherhood in the greater Los Angeles area. The women who worked behind the counter at The Pump Station in Santa Monica, a place where Kai took prenatal classes and dragged Teddy along, got to know her on a first name basis. She asked so many questions in class, Teddy joked that he, "Didn't realize he was having a baby with the annoying student who sat in the front row and always has her hand raised."

When they were walking down the Santa Monica shopping street called 3rd Street Promenade, one day after a class on breastfeeding—enjoying street performers and creamy light green pistachio gelato—a distracted, pimply faced teenage boy nearly ran directly into her swollen belly. Without thinking, Kai swerved and drop kicked him to his bony knees.

Preggo *Ninja*!

Teddy thought it was hilarious, saying, "That progesterone kickin' in, babe?" but Kai would drop kick Jesus Himself if he ran smack into her uterus. She wasn't gonna let anybody, not even the son of God, hurt her angel.

14

3
Born

Kai gave birth the natural way, of course she did. She had nothing against drugs on principal, but she wanted to experience this, this feeling only a woman can have, warts and all. She did do it in a hospital, just in case there was an emergency, she wanted the best possible care for her baby. There was no emergency, just hours upon hours of the *worst physical pain* she'd ever experienced…next time, to be honest, she would go for the drugs…but in the end, it was *sooo* worth it. Little Fin *was* perfect: 7 pounds, 13 ounces, perfect ears, perfect eyes, perfect nose—and yes, *great* lips.

He looked a lot more like Kai then Teddy, but he was a "mix tape." He had Kai's green eyes and her nose, but he had Teddy's strong jaw line, with an adorable little cleft in his chin. He had Kai's honey blonde hair, a tiny, wavy tuft. He also had the cutest little dimple, right above his butt crack.

Kai thought of that as his "birthmark," something that made him special. Just something that made him, *him*.

Kai called her sister to tell her. Janie was genuinely excited for her, she would have preferred her nephew be given a Biblical name, but she thought his name should at *least* have two "Ns." She said to send pictures; they couldn't fly the whole family out, right now. Her husband Joseph had a whole congregation counting on him; there were severely ill cancer patients in the local hospital he had to visit. Kai could hear Janie's kids yelling in the background, "Those are MY bubbles!!" "I want some cheese!" and "Give *me* the baby Jesus! He goes in the *manger!*" Kai said she understood why they couldn't fly out right now, and she did, but she was sad to not have family there with her. She thought about her mom a lot—she would've been there.

A bunch of their friends came by the hospital to congratulate them, some famous. A couple of them were young parents, but most of their twenty something friends didn't have kids, yet, they were among the first of their group to enter this strange new land.

One young celeb mama who was married to a short statured rock star gave Kai a darling white gold charm necklace with Fin's name carved in it. They were completely showered with flowers and adorable, if sometimes over the top, baby gifts. *Cashmere* baby clothes? Wow, this child would live in the lap of luxury. Kai thought she wouldn't mention the cashmere to Janie; she would turn down her nose at that concept. When it's your new baby, though, nothing really seems too good for them.

Friends of Teddy parents sent all of the old school classic gifts, a silver baby brush and comb set from Tiffany's, silver spoons and first baby cup, all engraved with his monogrammed initials. It was all so sweet and so traditionally beautiful. Kai thought about how funny and odd it was that childbirth can be, and usually is, full of blood and pain, and then you get all of this fluffy/shiny stuff as a reward for going through it. Well, that and the baby, *that* was the real prize.

Teddy's parents came to the hospital with a bottle of fine champagne, happy to be grandparents, but fighting over what they would be called. Grandma and Grandpa were apparently *out*, that sounded too "old" in their view. The top picks were "Popo" and "Nonny," or "Papa" and

"Glamma," but Kai's head was spinning and she needed sleep, so they left, slightly buzzed and still bickering about it. Teddy said it was typical his folks would make it all about *them*. "*Welcome to my childhood,*" he said, shaking his head.

The first night they brought Fin home, Kai stayed up all night long, watching him sleeping. She couldn't believe someone so small could breathe on his own. She was afraid if she slept, she'd wake up and he wouldn't be there—but each morning that came, he was still there. It was a *miracle*, every single morning! She hoped she wouldn't mess this up; this was officially the Big Leagues.

His nursery was the palest sea green, an underwater theme, naturally. Kai hand painted fishies and a crazy legged octopus and sea turtles, a friendly ocean wonderland. When Fin napped, she held a small mirror to his tiny lips, to see it steam up and make sure he was still breathing. Each time she watched him sleep, she hoped her own Mama could see him, from wherever she was, right now. Somehow Kai just knew she could.

Breastfeeding was a *lot* harder than Kai thought, the little guy would take a few sips and then pass out on her breast, but she slowly got the hang of it. Her nipples ached at first—stung and bled, even. She pumped later on, to have some extra milk to freeze, and felt like a milking cow being hooked up to that wretched machine every two to three hours, even in the middle of the night. She wanted to do it, because the baby gets immunities from the mother's breast milk, she knew it was the best thing she could do for her baby. Sometimes it really "sucked," both literally *and* figuratively.

The lack of sleep and the incredible demanding need of an infant wore her down at times, wore her down to *Chinatown*. Sleep deprivation *is* used as a torture device in war, after all, and sometimes it was no fun at all to be spacey and feel her feet and very bones aching, as she rose from bed at 3am, *yet again*. This was a *lifelong* commitment, being a parent—completely intimidating, to be honest. Sometimes she thought, what the *hell* had she gotten herself into??? Maybe skydiving without a parachute would've been less dangerous? They already swam with sharks. Maybe shotguns at twenty paces?

Still, every day, there were moments filled with light. Fin's first smile, first laugh, first bite of solid food (baby rice cereal—organic, of course), every new thing was a true joy to behold. The first "MA-MA" was like a large red balloon inside her very heart; it swelled as if it would burst out of her chest, and lifted her up in the high blue sky. Who needs sleep, anyway? Sleep is overrated, she had an *angel* to raise!

The wedding plans kept getting pushed back, Kai couldn't decide on a date. She still had an extra ten pounds of baby weight left to lose, what was the emergency? They were young; they were madly in love, and still getting this new parent thing down—everything in good time.

Looking back, she felt she should have known. Looking back, she blamed herself.

She could pinpoint the first time her maternal instinct kicked in that something was not totally "right." Something was "*off*." But she thought she was being paranoid, maybe even melodramatic. She was a new mother; it was her *job* to worry, right?

Fin took his first glorious, shaky steps at eleven months. He had been "cruising," walking while holding on to something like furniture or Kai's jeans, but the first time he walked without holding on to anything, he leaned to his right side, ever so slightly.

She noticed it, but blew it off. He was just learning to walk, for heaven's sake; of *course* he was wobbly and unstable! She couldn't believe she would turn such a joyful moment into worry, it was ridiculous.

18

"Don't *catastrophize,*" she told herself.
Sometimes she felt she had post-traumatic stress, from the sudden way her mother died. She needed therapy, probably, but Fin's laughter was the best therapy on Earth.

"YAYYYYYY!" she yelled, "Teddy, come fast, he just WALKED!"

She got so excited that Fin stumbled and fell down from the commotion, but when Teddy ran in from the other the room, he walked again, all three of them over the moon with this huge milestone. Fin giggled and beamed, he was already a little showboat and a flirt.

"*Marry me*, babe, come on. We have to finally set a date!"

Teddy was already down on his knees, and so was Kai, and now they were all three laughing and then crying and poor little Fin didn't know what the hell was happening to his crazy, sleep deprived parents. Kai swept the baby up and hugged Teddy, whispering "*Yes yes yes yes yes yes...*" as they kissed and hugged. *Bliss*.

She had her two boys, one a man, and one who would grow to be one, some day. And she would get to witness it, his first steps, his first words, the first time he swam in the ocean, the first time he *danced*.

She looked up, silently thanking God for her good fortune, for this opportunity to witness miracles firsthand. For this second chance.

4
Curve

"Beware of the UNDERTOAD!!!" Kai cried to Fin, who giggled and tried to say toad, but it came out as "toe!"

She was giving him a bath, he *loved* being in the water, they had that in common. She knew the term was "under tow," she was already trying to teach Fin about ocean safety, perhaps a tad (overzealously?) early.

Her own mom had teasingly told she and Janie there was an *actual* toad deep in the water who would pull little girls under, if they swam out too far. Kai had imagined a big, fat, warty green toad on the ocean floor, sort of a Jabba the Hut toad, wearing a crown like he owned the sea, his slimy tongue flicking out— ready to suck little girls under—into the waters dark and deep.

Kai washed Fin with a soft froggy bath sponge and enjoyed him splashing around. She had tried on her wedding dress that day. Actually, she had tried on two dresses; she was still trying to decide between them. Part of her wanted to wear a '70's style, white crocheted mini dress, a lot like the style Raquel Welch once wore, and part of her wanted to be classic in a long, ivory silk sheath with spaghetti straps and fresh wildflowers in her hair. For sure, she would be barefoot and on the beach. She didn't have any desire to go poofy princess, no tiara for her.

Teddy already made her feel like a princess, jeez, they practically lived in a modern castle. She could afford almost anything she wanted. It was beyond bizarre to walk into Barney's or Saks and be able to walk out with a pair of six hundred dollar, hell, thousand dollar designer shoes, that was *not* what her childhood was like *at all*.

Her mom Beka was a single mother and a part time domestic airline attendant, they weren't starving, but money was tight. It was crazy fun to buy beautiful things, but Kai didn't shop that much, she always wanted to be with Fin. He was the coolest little dude to hang with, and she still didn't have anything against shopping at Target. They didn't carry diapers at Barney's, anyway. Her dirty little secret was that she thought Target was kind of a blast.

Teddy wanted to go out more to the old clubs they used to hang at, but the "mommy hangover" didn't sound so hot to Kai. Teddy said, "We're still in our twenties, we're *allowed* to have fun!" but to Kai, being with Fin *was* fun, the most fun she'd ever had.

They did have one big BBQ pool party with all of their friends over, swimming and sunning and cooing over Fin. That was sort of the extent of their social life in the baby's first year, except when one or two friends would pop by and hang. Teddy would meet his friends out for drinks once in a while, but he couldn't drag Kai along. He accused, "You're tied to that baby like the cord is still attached!"

Teddy kept saying they should take another big trip, to Venice and Rome, Florence and Milan, all places Kai hadn't been, yet. He wanted to show her the great cities of the world, but she couldn't bear the thought of going without Fin. Teddy said it was crazy to bring the baby, they would get the best nanny in town and his parents would visit, but he didn't get it. She didn't want to drag a less than one year old on germ infested planes, through crowded airports and across time zones. There

would be plenty of time for travel when Fin was a little
older. She couldn't wait to show him Bora Bora and
watch him snorkel and feed the pastel rainbow colored
fishies.

Kai smiled, soaping up her almost one year olds
little body, it was so sweet how soft and silky his skin
was, with the organic baby wash she liked to use. She
loved the scent. Fin was splashing and playing in the
water with his bath toys, frogs and yellow ducky's, when
Kai noticed something weird—he was leaning to one side.
She soaped up his back and belly, noticing that one side
of his ribs stuck out ever so slightly.

"TEDDY!" she called, "Honey, can you come in
here a sec?"

Teddy came in from the bedroom; he had been
reading a screenplay in bed. "Bath time, huh?" he smiled.
"Little boys like to be dirty! Mud pies for everyone!"

"Do you see how he's leaning to the right in the
tub?" Kai was a little worried, now.

Teddy looked at Fin's back as he splashed. "No,
not really."

Kai wrinkled her nose. "*Seriously*? You don't see
it?"

"No, I see a normal baby boy, babe." Teddy
ruffled the top of Kai's hair. "You worry too much." Kai
rubbed her hands gently down Fin's sides. "I think I feel a
slight...hump...or something."

Teddy furrowed his brow. "A *hump*? You think
our baby is a *hunchback*?"

Kai winced at the word and at his angry tone; she
had clearly hit a nerve. "No," she said, "it's more in the
front...on the side, here." Fin looked worried, sensing
"mommy's upset" in that way kids do.

"*Hey*, don't get all Quasimodo, Notre Dame on
me," Teddy forced a grin, trying to lighten the mood. Kai
splashed in the water to distract Fin, and he squealed with
happiness. "Hon, we go to the best pediatrician in Beverly

Hills," Teddy said, "At every one of his check-ups, Dr. Edelstein says he's a *perfect child*. He's hit all of his milestones on time, the Doc would've noticed if something was wrong. Do *you* have a medical degree?"

He was right, Fin had the "pediatrician to the stars," he had been on *Larry King Live* and the *Today Show*, talking about his method of doing "slow and steady" vaccinations, rather than multiple shots in a single day. Kai had read a lot about Autism and she wanted to be as safe as possible. She believed in doing vaccines, just not overloading a little baby's system all at once, with four to six doses in a single day. Her doctor also never, ever gave vaccines if the child was sick, Kai appreciated the logic of that. She trusted him.

Kai exhaled, smiling at Teddy, "You're right, we have his one year check-up in a week, I'll ask the doctor then." Her dashing fiancé kissed her on top of the head, walking out.

Kai took Fin out of the tub, drying him off in a plush yellow baby towel with a hood that looked like a duck. She kissed the little dimple on top of his tiny, perfectly round butt—she loved that, his little unique birthmark. She had asked Dr. Edelstein about that, too, and he said just what she thought, "That's just Fin. That's just part of what makes him, *him*."

And boy oh boy, how she loved her boy.

"Fin-Again, *begin again*!" she called to him, as he giggled and raised his arms to the sky— it was a play on the fact that most people thought his full name was Finnegan, it was one of their favorite mommy-baby games. He was delicious and an *outrageous* flirt, she could barely get out of the grocery store without him making eyes at the check-out lady. He flirted with them all, no matter if the woman was young or old, regardless of race or physical appearance. They would always ask if his full name was Finnegan, and she would smile proudly, "No, it's Fin, just three letters, like those things on fish.

She hugged her sweet baby. Of *course* he had hit
all of his milestones on time—raising his head, smiling,
rolling over, crawling, beginning to talk—and now
already walking, at less than a year old. Still, it was
normal to worry, right? Was she a big worry wart, an
Undertoad, bringing everybody down? Was she
catastrophizing, again?

Teddy didn't seem to have the same level of
bonding with Fin that she did, but maybe those
expectations were too high. It was different for dads than
moms, right? Their bonding often happened later, like
when they can play ball, was that how it worked?

Kai honestly didn't know from her own
experience, her own dad had abandoned them when Kai
was just four. He had a gambling addiction, along with
liquor and women. "*Addictive personality,*" her mom had
said, when they were old enough to understand, "I
should've known what I was getting into." Sometimes her
mom would say, when she was really tired, "I had *no idea*
what I was getting into."

Teddy was a loving father, but he often only
played with Fin for an hour a day or less, he was always
in his home office on the phone or reading screenplays.
He had a lot of "meetings" with writers, people in
Hollywood had *endless* meetings, it seemed. Kai knew he
was trying to create a new business, a production
company, but sometimes she walked into his office and he
was playing video games. Killing aliens or zombies. How
many times could you shoot something before it became a
bore? Could video games *seriously* be more interesting
than his own child, saying his first words?

Kai looked down at her body, taking inventory.
Pretty good, her skin still tan and creamy, but she still had
seven pounds of baby weight to go. Her boobs were still a
little veiny from the pregnancy, but it was going away,
they would be back to normal, eventually. They still had a
good shape, she got lucky in that department. Maybe they

24

weren't having sex enough? She had been extra horny while pregnant, maybe she had slacked off with being sleep deprived and all, baby spit up in your hair is *soooo* sexy.

She didn't want to irk Teddy by suggesting something could be wrong with his son. She just prayed her little fishie would make it safely through the beautiful, but sometimes treacherous ocean of this thing called life.

Her eyes misted over as she looked into Fin's green ones with his thick blanket of long, dark lashes. She had never felt this kind of love in her life; she didn't even know it existed. It was the mythical love a mother had for her child. You know, it got a lot of "press," but she had always wondered, was it *real*?

It was, Kai now knew. It must've been how much her mom had loved her. She would do *anything* to protect him, to ensure his safety and happiness. She never wanted him to feel any pain, *ever*. She knew he would, some day, and the thought of that broke her heart into sharp, jagged pieces that shattered on the floor. Becoming a parent made her vulnerable in ways she *never* wanted to feel, but the yin and yang of it was that the joy also knew no bounds.

"Swim to where it's warm," she whispered into her little fishie's ear, nuzzling him and gently kissing his nose as she cuddled him in the yellow duck towel.

"Always swim to where it's warm."

5
Watch and Wait

Two new parents trying to take a baby's rectal temperature, groggy at four in the morning, is an un-delightful comedy of errors. Fin was wriggling and crying hysterically, he had the worst fever of his young life that night, 103 degrees. Kai had read in her motherhood books that rectal temperatures were more accurate. Fin cried and Kai fleetingly wondered why she had wanted to have kids in the first place.

Remember sleep? Sleep was *fun*. A full night's sleep was *rejuvenating*. Kai realized wistfully she'd probably never experience it again. *The things we do for love.*

It wasn't much of a blast for the doctor on call or his wife, either, who they phoned and woke up to find out if they should take Fin to the E.R. He was just over a year old and had only had some simple colds and mild teething fevers before this, Kai thought her attempts at breastfeeding and pumping all those exhausting hours and months may have helped give him a strong immune system. She was proud of that, but now she was a little scared. At what point was a high fever damaging to an infant? Oh, *crap*.

Dr. Edelstein, their regular pediatrician, was on vacation, so the person they woke up was his colleague, Dr. Schmidt. The doctor said to give Fin infant Tylenol and see if he felt better, he said it was probably just a virus. Kai measured out the dose in the dropper and because she was so tired, her hand trembled as she squeezed it in Fin's screaming mouth. *Oh crap, oh crap, oh crap…*

What if she got the dosage wrong? What if she accidentally *overdosed* her own baby?

Skydiving without a parachute, was that still an option?

Fin stopped crying and gazed up at his twenty something parents with his serious, long lashed big green eyes, he could tell something important was "afoot." These two looked like a couple of wild haired, junior mad scientists, praying they didn't screw this up.

The infant Tylenol worked and Fin went back to sleep. The next day was his one year "well baby" check-up, which now was basically a "sick baby" check-up. Dr. Schmidt looked a little tired himself, and Fin was cranky and feeling pretty funky in the exam room. They were talking about his fever and the vaccination he was set to get today, which now would have to be put off until he was well. Dr. Schmidt was sweet with Fin and tolerant of his crabbiness. He did the basic exam, but he didn't take off Fin's clothes, because the room was chilly and he was, well, sick. He said they could just pop Fin back in for his next shot when all of his symptoms went away.

It wasn't until they got home that it occurred to them that they hadn't asked about the slight curve in his back. "*CRAP!*" said Kai. "I can't *believe* I forgot to ask him!"

Teddy lifted up Fin's t-shirt and they both checked out his back again. There it was, the slightest curve in his little spine, but it was still almost undetectable to the naked eye. It was the type of thing you wouldn't even notice, unless someone pointed it out to you.

Teddy said he wasn't worried. "Everybody has some quirk of their body, like I have one leg a half centimeter shorter than the other, and you have those *freakishly* big feet."

Kai shoved his shoulder, "You said you love my feet."

"Look," Teddy smiled, "We'll show the doc when we pop him back in for the shot in a few days or so. I bet he's gonna say it's nothing."

Kai nodded, it probably *was* nothing. She put it on the mental back burner, the kiddo needed a diaper change, a bottle and his nap. *No rest for the weary!*

The next few weeks passed by and Fin's virus got better, but he had a slight cough and his nose kept running on and off. He was acting perfectly healthy, but there was no way Kai was going to have him get an inoculation when he had signs of a cold. She wouldn't even let her kid eat non-organic strawberries, because she read that kids living near the crops in California had a higher percentage of Autism diagnosis. True or not, she figured, why take the risk?

A whole month had passed before it occurred to them that he still needed the shot. Kai called the doctor's office and the receptionist said, "Sure, come by this afternoon." Kai mentioned that she needed the doctor for just a second, to check out Fin's back, "Although it's probably nothing." The slight curve didn't look any worse to her or to Teddy since the last visit to the pediatrician, when he had the fever.

She and Teddy both took Fin to the doctor's office, quickly getting the shot from the nurse and then running into their regular doctor, Dr. Edelstein, in the waiting area on their way out. They chatted with him, while Fin occupied himself with a wooden toy kitchen set for toddlers. Teddy casually mentioned they wanted him to take a look at Fin's back, and the doctor lifted his t-shirt, suddenly looking a bit concerned.

Kai instantly got butterflies in her stomach, asking, "Do you see that little curve, to the right? Is that just *him*?"

She nervously tried to make light of it with a dumb joke, "You know, how everybody has some body quirk, like a mole in some weird place or one boob slightly bigger than the other?" She cringed, that was *so* unfunny, had she actually *sexually harassed* her baby's pediatrician? Another mother in the waiting area with her three year old, frizzy haired hyperactive boy rolled her eyes at Kai's spazzy comment. Teddy shot her a "*Really?*" look, but the doctor, mercifully, let it go.

"I do see something. It's probably nothing to worry about, but just in case, I'm gonna send you to my colleague, Dr. Conroy. He's one of the best orthopedists in L.A. In fact, I'll call him right now." The doc walked down the hall to his office, and Kai and Teddy sat with Fin, on the couch next to the woman who Kai had irritated. The crabby woman proceeded to let her three year old, snotty nosed little monster run riot around the waiting room, yelling and banging the toy pots and pans. If that kid hit her baby with one of those pans, Kai thought, she was gonna freak.

Dr. Edelstein poked his head back in the room a minute later. "You know what, guys? He has a cancellation and could see you in ten minutes, if you have time right now."

"Really? *Great*, thank you!" Kai hopped up, holding Fin on her hip. Fin cried out "We did it!" which he had learned from the cartoon "Dora the Explorer." Dr. Edelstein smiled, "I'll call him and let him know you're on your way."

Dr. Conroy was a pediatric orthopedic surgeon with a Chi-Chi office, filled with dark brown leather chairs, magazines for tired parents, and puzzles and colorful stacking blocks for the kids. Kai was enormously relieved when they were summoned to a small exam room and on the way there, she noticed dozens of photos of happy children he'd treated, pinned on giant corkboards on the walls, along with notes like: "I can do my ballet again! Thank you, Dr. Conroy!" and "You saved my arm. You are the nicest doctor I've ever met. Love, Ethan, 6."

It was so sweet, and there were even a bunch of photos of celebrities with their kids, Dr. Conroy was clearly on their family's Christmas card lists. The short and balding, friendly Dr. Conroy swept into the exam room minutes later, shaking their hands with great cheer. He checked out Fin's back and he didn't look worried at all.

"Yep, we should do an X-ray today, but it doesn't look too bad."

Teddy smiled at Kai, "*See?*"

Kai wasn't too thrilled to have an X-ray done on her one year old, but she guessed she had no choice. She asked the doctor about the radiation risks. He shook his head dismissively, "It's less radiation than what he would get flying from L.A. to New York."

That didn't sound so bad at all. She bent over to pick Fin up, noticing the doc checking out her cleavage. Oh, well, he was a male whose face came to the exact height her boobs were, she chose not to let it bug her. She carried Fin back to the X-ray room and the nice red haired female technician said "*This* little guy?" in that tone of, "*Oh, no.*"

Kai nodded and got a sudden lump in her throat. The male technician asked her if there was any chance she could be pregnant. She said "No," and they gave her a heavy gray, protective vest to wear, so she could be in the room with Fin.

They laid him on the enormous table and Fin got scared, squirming and starting to fuss, crying "*Ahhh...MAMA!*" Kai began to sing the song that always seemed to soothe him from birth, Bob Marley's *Three*

Little Birds. "*Baby, don't worry...about a thing...'cause every little thing's...gonna be alright...*"

Like magic, it worked, like it almost always did, and they took the image of his spine.

Back in the exam room, Fin toddled around, looking for trouble, as Dr. Conroy came in and put the X-ray up with the screen light glowing behind it to show them.

At the first sight of it, Kai's heart nearly stopped.

Wow. His little spine *did* have a curve. It looked *much worse,* when you could see the bones actually curving in a slight "C" shape, to his right. She knew this much, a human spine isn't supposed to look like the letter "C". Crap. *Crap crap crap.*

Kai fought back tears. "What does this mean? Is that really bad?"

"Bad," Fin repeated, exploring the exam room and realizing the small metal trash can lid could be banged on like a drum with his hands. *Bang bang bang.*

Teddy seemed stunned, he didn't say a word, but his knee started bouncing nervously up and down. The doctor took some manual measurements on the X-ray and turned back to them. "No, it's not that bad, it's 25 degrees. You don't have to even do anything if it stays below 34 degrees," he said casually.

These numbers didn't mean much to Kai. "What's a normal spine number...or, er, degree?"

"Well," the doctor said, "perfectly straight is zero." The doctor glanced at Fin banging on the trash can, trying not to look irritated, which he was. *Bang bang bang.*

Kai and Teddy were both too stunned to focus on the noise. Kai felt sick. There was a *big* difference between twenty-five degrees and *zero.*

"Will it cause him any pain?" Kai asked, suddenly realizing the sound was irritating the doctor, and quickly scooping Fin up to stop the drumming.

31

"Will his back look weird?" Teddy chimed in.

She suddenly felt embarrassed that Teddy asked that—it sounded a little shallow—but the truth be told, she didn't want her little boy to get made fun of when he was older, either.

"No, no, no," the doctor assured them, "It won't cause him any pain, and it very likely will straighten up on its own. I've seen hundreds of these self-resolve. Just come back in a month and we'll do a follow-up X-ray to check it."

He was still acting like this was *no big whoop*. Kai was so relieved; she wanted to hug the man. It would probably *just go away*! It was *painless*! They thanked the doctor and he walked out of the room like a hero.

"*YAY!*" she said, and Fin cried "Yay!" back. Kai hugged him, kissing him all over his gorgeous little face. Teddy stood up. She could tell this had shaken him; the image of the glowing, curved spinal X-ray was still a little shocking.

He tried to play it off, "See, babe? I told you it was probably nothing. Now stop worrying, you have a *wedding* to plan."

She took one last look at the scary, lit X-ray, promising herself not to worry about it until the next appointment. Why worry if it might just go away? It would be a total waste of energy.

What was that quote she once read, about worrying? "*Worry is a prayer for something you don't want.*"

She wasn't gonna put that kind of bad mojo out there. She did have a wedding to plan, even though it was still eight months away. In L.A. you had to book all of the vendors like the flowers, catering and musicians, months and months—if not well over a year—in advance. It was crazy stressful, part of her wanted to do it by themselves, with just Fin there and a minister, but Teddy wanted a big wedding and his parents did, too. They had a lot of friends

and business associates to invite. There was talk of a
private fireworks display over the ocean, they had to book
a barge and get the permits, the whole nine. She wanted to
make everyone happy, it wasn't a lot of laughs being
around Teddy's mom when she wasn't happy—she was
pretty high strung and high maintenance about the
wedding plans.

One month later, they brought Fin back for the
check-up. Kai sang Bob Marley's *Three Little Birds* again
for the X-ray, and then they waited anxiously in the small
exam room for the results.

Her palms were sweating when Dr. Conroy
walked in; putting up the new X-ray beside the first one,
with the light ominously glowing behind their son's
crooked little bones. Kai's heart sunk. It looked *worse*.

She instinctually reached for Teddy's large,
masculine hand, clutching it for comfort, as Fin squirmed
on her lap. Teddy's knee started jumping like mad as the
doctor took his manual measurements on the new X-ray
and then turned around, facing them. "It's a little worse,"
he announced, "28 degrees instead of 25, but like I said, if
it stays like this or straightens up on its own, you never
have to do anything."

Kai sat forward, "Is this common in kids his age?
What is the diagnosis?"

"Oh, it's scoliosis," the doctor replied bluntly. He
was devoid of any emotion.

Kai blinked. This was the first time the word
"*scoliosis*" had even been mentioned.

"Oh, I know what scoliosis is!" she blurted out
awkwardly, "You mean, like in that Judy Blume book,
Deenie? You have to wear a brace, right?"

"Not always, it depends," the doctor replied,
"Approximately three percent of the population is
affected by scoliosis."

Everyone had at least one student with a scoliosis brace in their junior high or high school. Kai had no idea it could happen to babies or toddlers.

"There's no scoliosis in my family," Teddy said, shocked, "We met with a genetics counselor when Kai got pregnant. She had the amniocentesis, all the ultrasounds, there was nothing—how could this happen?"

"It may be genetically related and it may not be. It's nothing Kai did or didn't do during the pregnancy, it may be idiopathic. Idiopathic just means '*no known cause.*' We like to joke that term means us doctors are idiots, because we can't figure out the cause." He chuckled to himself, as if this was the most hilarious thing ever.

Kai wasn't finding the humor, "So, what's the worst case scenario?" she asked. She didn't want cheesy jokes, she wanted to know the facts.

"Well, like I said, it could still self-resolve, or stay as it is. This degree of curvature won't even be noticeable in a grown man; he'll look completely normal once he grows up and fills out. If it got over 34 degrees, I would send you to my colleague, who's one of the best orthopedic surgeons in the country. He would probably recommend a brace, and maybe years down the road, you might have to consider surgery."

"How would that affect his life? Could he still play sports?" Teddy asked.

Kai felt sick to her stomach, asking, "Would he be in any pain?"

The doctor walked over to the exam table, beginning to draw something with a pen on the thin white paper covering it. "No, scoliosis doesn't cause any pain," he answered matter-of-factly.

Kai exhaled, "Wow, I didn't know that, thank God."

"He can play sports and do everything. I realize that when you mention to parents the words 'spinal

34

surgery' they think, there's *no way* anyone is going anywhere near my child's spine, but if he has to get spinal fusion surgery in high school, his back will be even stronger playing football than if he hadn't had it."

Kai looked at what the doctor was drawing; it was a crude sketch of a tube of toothpaste. "See, it's like a tube of toothpaste," the doctor said, "once the paste is coming out in a curve, the more you squeeze the tube, the more curved it comes out."

This made no sense to her; this was about bones, a child's spine…why was this man casually talking about *toothpaste*? But Fin was all over the room, babbling and trying to get into the small metal trash can in the corner. Great, there were probably some bloody, infected needles in there, Kai worried as he began to open up the lid.

"No!" Kai shouted, swooping him up in her arms, as Teddy vigorously shook the doctor's hand in that "man-to-man" way that salesmen in the 1950's did, selling their smiles to each other.

"Come back in three months, we'll do another X-ray, and see where we are," the doctor said, then he grabbed Fin's file and walked out of the exam room.

Kai was dumbstruck. *Her baby had scoliosis*? But it still may be nothing and just *go away on its own*? The doctor was so casual about it, and they did have access to the best doctors and medical care possible. They were doing all the "right things."

The X-rays looked bad, especially with that wall backlight glowing through them, but to the naked eye, Fin's back *still* didn't look *that* crooked. It just looked like he had the slightest little curve. Three months was a long time to wait, but the doctor was the expert. What did they know? She didn't want to expose Fin to any more radiation from multiple X-rays than absolutely necessary.

It was October, now, so they'd come back at the end of December. Kai promised herself she wouldn't worry herself sick about something they couldn't do anything about. Just as Teddy had said, *she* wasn't a doctor; *she* didn't have a medical degree. These people were *specialists*, she had to trust them. Besides, Fin *deserved* a happy mama, not one who was constantly stressing and depressed.

"It's gonna be okay, it's gonna go away on its own!" Teddy declared brightly, as they walked out of the office. "Did you see the photos of the kids he's treated on his walls? How many celebrities take their kids here? They can afford to go *anywhere*; he has to be the best in the West."

He was right, "The best of the best," "the best in the West." *That* was the kind of medical care her child was receiving, and Kai reminded herself to be grateful for it.

They dived into the holidays, full force. They took pictures of Fin in his very first Beverly Hills pumpkin patch, the one called Mr. Bones on Doheny Drive that many celebrities went to for fun and photo ops. They were probably the only two parents in the hay filled, happy sea of orange pumpkins having this discussion:

Kai: "There's no scoliosis in my family, either, not that I know of. Now, if he becomes a gambling addict like my father…that's *all me*. Do you think it could have anything to do with the mojitos I drank in French Polynesia?"

Teddy: "Honey, the doctor told us the fetus, or zygote, or whatever, wasn't even attached at that point. You could've shot up *heroin* before it was attached, those were his exact words."

He was right, not that Kai would've been shooting up heroin pregnant or not, but the doctor assured her she was safe. Besides, scoliosis wasn't fetal alcohol syndrome, which was a crazy thought; she was just trying to wrack her brain to see if it was something she had done wrong.

She tried not to think about it constantly, to keep the holidays fun. They dressed Fin up as a green pea pod and a sock monkey for his first Halloween, attending a friend's "Teeny Halloweeny" party for babies, and ordered a hundred Christmas cards with Fin's sweet smile under a "Baby's First Christmas," red velvet Santa hat. Kai even convinced Teddy to fly out to Kansas for Christmas, so Janie could finally meet Fin in person, and the little cousins could all be together. Now *this* required some major negotiating techniques, on par with those mastered by world leaders.

First, Kai had to promise to spend Thanksgiving with Teddy's folks, and swear they'd spend Fin's 2nd Christmas in Northern California with his family at the vineyard. Then, she penciled in a *lot* of sex with her fiancé—hey, his mother could wield a lot of weapons, not the least of them guilt and a very fat wallet, but she couldn't compete with Kai's beautiful vagina. Well, Kai certainly *hoped* not!

They'd always had incredible chemistry, she had dropped the rest of the baby weight, and she broke down and wore some *actual lingerie* for the first time since giving birth. She was bringing it to the *mat*, baby! She even researched babysitters and hired one for a night, so that they could go out together like grownups, after grilling the poor babysitter with every question in the "paranoid mommy" rule book. "Have you been trained in infant CPR? What if he starts choking?" etc. She hired a registered nurse who had raised six kids of her own, and she *still* left her a long list of detailed info, just in case.

They went out until two in the morning that night, and Kai had fun, although she did feel a little out of place amongst all of their single friends who didn't have kids, yet. It was great to see everybody, and to be reminded of their pre-baby life, but she thought about Fin *constantly*. The next morning, waking up at six AM with him wailing, she wished the house had black-out curtains and sound proof walls, and that they had bought stock in ibuprofen.

At Thanksgiving dinner in Napa Valley, as they dined alfresco on the Verona's massive stone patio that overlooked rows of grape vines, Teddy's mother Wendy actually said this to Kai, "Darling, do you think the scoliosis is from putting the baby in that horrible *swing* so much? I mean, in my day, we just rocked our babies in our arms, or in a cradle. That constant mechanical motion of those things you kids use nowadays is a *horror*."

Kai had used the same type of baby swing nearly every modern mother does, did *all* of their kids develop scoliosis? Uh, *no*.

She bit her lip and explained that it might self-resolve, that their next X-ray for Fin was set for December 29th, then she sipped her Syrah and choked down a bite of turkey with the sweetest smile she could muster.

That night in bed, Teddy was already asleep, when Kai started softly crying, worrying about that stupid ass *swing*. Maybe she *had* used it too much? Fin *loved* the swing, he loved napping in it, but she *did* move him around! She carried him on her chest and put him on his back in the crib, like all the books said to do, for safety. Maybe she had an extra small uterus and poor lil' Fin was squished in there. *Intrauterine molding*, she had read about that somewhere. *Crap*, maybe it *was* her fault?

Christmas in Kansas was a world away from L.A., it felt like it was possibly on an entirely different planet. Hays has a really small airport, so they had to take one of those tiny, rickety propeller planes into town, which scared the hell out of Teddy.

Kansas has that vast, flat landscape that you think wouldn't be pretty, but it's actually quite beautiful, with a stillness and majesty to its miles of clear blues skies that seem to go on forever and ever.

Hays is a sweet Midwestern city of about 20,000 residents, the kind of town where the main street is actually named "Main Street." They have an Applebee's restaurant, so you know, they're big time. That was their big dining out adventure, the first night they arrived, the whole clan piled into a giant Applebee's booth with two high chairs for Fin and Janie's youngest girl, Ruth. Teddy, accustomed to five star restaurants, discovered that boneless buffalo wings are not bad—*not bad at all*.

Janie's house was light yellow and two stories, Kai and Teddy stayed in an upstairs guest room with Fin in a portable crib. Janie's husband, Preacher Joe, was the strong, silent type, which was funny for a guy whose job is to talk and preach, but he was kind and seemed solid. Janie's three kids, Micah, 5, Sarah, 4, and Ruth, 2, were adorable—full of energy—with excellent manners and bright eyes. Janie hand made a lot of their clothes, and they were always impeccably dressed in lots of frilly dresses, ribbons and bows.

They didn't get snow on Christmas, but it was cold and the kids had a blast running around Fin, who giggled and laughed the whole time, he adored being around his cousins. They all got *tons* of toys, Teddy and his parents had boxes delivered, and Janie kept complaining it was too much. After they opened all of the presents and cleaned up the wrapping, Janie roasted a big, juicy turkey with all of the fixins, and it was a festive time, until Kai showed Janie Fin's back by lifting up his Christmas sweater.

Janie took a long look, and then said solemnly, "We'll pray for you and make sure to add Fin into our church's prayer circle. Whatever God's will is *will be*."

That was sweet and all, but to be honest, it pissed Kai off. Whatever *God's will* is? Okay, she didn't want to get blasphemous on Jesus' birthday and all, but what the *hell*?

"Are you saying that if my child needs spinal surgery, that's God's will? Why would God want my child to have to go through that? What if the surgeon made a mistake and Fin was paralyzed? Why would God want *any child* to suffer *at all*? I mean, I'm sorry, but why are children starving in the world, right now? I just don't believe in that kind of God." It all came out of Kai in a rush. She sucked in a breath, surprised by her anger.

Janie sighed, "This is what always happens whenever we get together, Kai. You either have faith in His plan or you don't."

"Why can't I believe in God, but not believe that everything that happens in the world is His plan?" Kai's face was hot, this oversimplifying about the bad stuff, things like hurricanes or earthquakes with people buried in the rubble, drove her *nuts*. Her sister had pushed her buttons from the moment she was born, and now her eighteen month old child, her *baby*, may have a serious *health problem* and Janie couldn't just be *supportive*? How about "I'm sorry, this is scary, this *sucks*, I pray the next X-ray is good news?"

Little Micah, Sarah and Ruth all came running into the room in their matching plaid Christmas dresses, red velvet with bows in their hair, dancing around Fin, who started giggling at their antics and jumping in excitement.

"Yeah!" Fin yelled, "Oh, *yeah!*"

Children were so innocent; it took Kai's breath away. She exhaled; she really didn't want to fight. She'd been fighting with her sister her whole life, and she didn't want a family blow up on Christmas, especially not in front of the kids.

"In our church, we just consider the 'differently abled' kids to be souls God chose to make *extra* special," Janie smiled, looking at Fin. He was running and playing right along with the other kids.

40

"Does he look *differently abled* to you?!" Kai blurted at her sister, furious, "We don't even have a full diagnosis yet, the doctor said he may be just FINE!" She grabbed a bottle of red wine from the counter and poured herself half a glass. *Great*, she thought, she was turning to the bottle. Well, Jesus turned the water into wine, it's in the Bible.

"I realize that, Kai, I was just saying I'll pray for you. If you had a child with a cleft lip or a club foot, I would pray for you. I always keep you in my prayers, even when we disagree. You're my sister."

Kai was ashamed she had yelled in front of the kids, she realized she was touchy, but she could not *believe* the things that Janie said—on *Christmas*, no less!

Of *course* there was nothing wrong with any differently abled child, or any child with a health problem, but why was she comparing apples to oranges?

They avoided the subject the rest of the trip. The next morning, they visited the main town park, which was officially called Frontier Park, but the locals nicknamed it "Buffalo Park," because it had real live buffalo grazing in it. They flew out later that day. The kids had a great time at the park, but Kai had never been happier to leave anywhere.

Why had she wanted to go visit her sister again? It always ended like this, with hurt feelings and weeks or months of not speaking. What was it about family that pushed every single one of your buttons like an age-old bruise?

"Do you think boneless Buffalo wings are made of *actual* buffalo?" They were sitting in the plane about to take off and Teddy was trying to cheer her up, "I mean, the trip *did* have a theme, you have to give it that," he added. Kai couldn't muster any humor, she was emotionally spent.

Teddy wasn't giving up. "Next Christmas, we can go to my folks' place and have the annual holiday fight. I

gotta warn ya, though, my mom can pack a punch—
especially when she's drunk."

Kai looked at Teddy and grinned as the rickety
little plane took off, with only ten people on board,
including the pilot. Fin was sound asleep in his travel car
seat, which was strapped on to his own plane seat, his
Bambi lashes resting against his chubby little, pink
flushed cheeks.

"Do you think it was God's plan for Janie to be a
pious *bitch*?" Teddy grinned at Kai and she laughed, she
loved him for that one.

It's just like they say, there's the family you're
born into, she thought to herself, the one you don't get to
choose, and there's the family you *make*. She reached for
Teddy's strong, comforting hand. Together, they had
somehow made an angel.

This much, she knew, was true.

6
Train

"*Huh.* Well, yeah…I think I'll refer you to my colleague at Angels Mercy Children's Hospital, Dr. Lowther. He specializes in scoliosis in children."

It was December 29th, between the Christmas and New Year's holidays. They were looking at Fin's 3rd X-ray glowing from the wall in Dr. Conroy's office. It was *definitely* worse, the curve of his little spine in a more pronounced "C" shape than three months ago. They had celebrated the happy holidays, obediently "watching and waiting," while their child was *bending.*

Teddy's knee started jumping up and down. Kai was speechless, they were already at a specialist, a pediatric orthopedic surgeon—*an orthopedist for children.* Why had they been going to him for three months if he didn't specialize in scoliosis? There was a *specialist above the specialist?*

"What is the degree, or um, number, now?" Kai asked in a hushed tone.

"34 degrees, so it's on the edge, but it's close enough that I'd like you to see Dr. Lowther and see what he says. You'll be in excellent hands; I can't recommend him highly enough."

So that was it. The once cheerful Dr. Conroy was done with them; he was *kicking them up* to a higher level of doctor. No parting gift, just "*See ya! Good luck with your next dealer.*" It flashed through Kai's head that he always checked out her cleavage. She had a crazy thought about smacking him across his bald head with his own tiny shoe, but she controlled herself.

"I'll ask Dr. Lowther to get you in as soon as possible, hopefully within a week." Kai thanked him and shook his hand. She didn't really know what she was thanking him *for*, but it seemed like the polite thing to do. He told them they could collect Fin's three X-rays from the front desk, each one worse than the last.

Teddy was silent. His jaw got tense, it seemed like he couldn't even look at Kai. Fin babbled as she picked him up and put him in the stroller, and they left the exam room and walked into the hallway, both stunned. On the way out of the office, Kai impulsively grabbed a cherry Dum Dum lollipop off of the counter, unwrapping it and letting Fin have it. He was a trooper to keep going through all of these X-rays and doctor visits, he deserved a treat.

Hey, if he couldn't have a straight spine, he could at least have some sugar and artificial red dye number forty! She guessed *that* was the parting gift. The fortyish woman with graying hair in a bun behind the front desk gave them a kind, but pitying look, like she knew the people who had to take their X-rays to the next doctor might have a serious problem. The broken arms and legs get fixed *here*.

Kai realized they just had left the group they wanted to be in, the group that *doesn't* have to visit the specialist who performs spinal surgery on children. They left the "*It's probably nothing*" group. Now they were in the group you didn't want to be in, the "It *might* be something bad" boat. Kai didn't want to be in that boat.

She was baffled as she walked beside Teddy outside the building, pushing the stroller down the palm tree lined sidewalk as he fiddled with his cell phone, their reflections fluttering in the giant, opaque glass panes of the medical tower. "I thought he *was* the specialist. Why were we going to a doctor who doesn't specialize in scoliosis? Because it wasn't *serious* enough, yet? And now it is, or it might be? Is Fin's toothpaste squeezing out the wrong way?"

"Let's *not* freak out, okay?!" Teddy blurted, getting out his keys as they reached their car and Kai opened the back door, strapping Fin into his car seat. Teddy got behind the wheel of his BMW and started the engine, exhaling. "Let's just have the appointment with the other doctor and see what he says!"

They got in for the appointment the following Monday, less than a week later. They barely talked about it in the days that passed. Teddy buried himself in screenplays and videogames, spending a lot of time in his home office, shooting aliens and zombies fifty thousand times in the head.

They celebrated a very un-festive New Year's Eve at home with Fin, ordering in some Chinese take-out and half-heartedly having a single glass of champagne, before both falling asleep at ten PM. Fin woke up at six, what was the point of watching the ball drop in Times Square as other people partied on TV?

It was hard for Kai not to compare it to their pre-pregnancy New Year's Eve, eating ridiculously pricey sushi, drinking cold dry sake and dancing on the tables at the hottest club in Hollywood. Not that she wanted to be there now, but she knew Teddy wished they were. She didn't blame him, but she just wanted to be in a place where her baby was safe.

They were both hoping for the best, trying not to assume the worst. Scoliosis *was* treatable after all, Kai told herself, Fin might have to wear a stretchy brace for a few months. Hopefully not.

She held out hope that this new doctor would say he was improving on his own, no treatment needed at all! You are free to go and live a happy, perfect life. *A wrinkle free life*, like Teddy once said.

But what if the doctor *didn't* say that? What *then*?

"Don't assume anything until you see this new doctor," she kept repeating to herself, "*Don't catastrophize!*"

That was easier said than done. Dr. Lowther's very beige office was chock full of patients. *Happy New Year.* It was in a very nice red brick building in Beverly Hills. This was his private office; he did his surgeries at Angels Mercy Children's Hospital, in downtown L.A.

Kai had done her research on him on the Internet, and he did seem to be the "best of the best" in this major, metropolitan area. He had two kids of his own, she read in his hospital profile, and boasted degrees from top schools. Kai made eye contact in the waiting room with a mom in her thirties who was holding a baby girl, who wore what looked like a brace on her hips and legs. The mother seemed scared, looking at Kai with sad, wary dark eyes.

Kai smiled at her kindly. She felt badly for this tired, worried mom, but what her daughter had was *not* what Fin had, if he even had anything they'd have to treat. She thought about asking this mom about her experience with Dr. Lowther, but there was no time. Fin happily wriggled off her lap and started walking around the waiting room, flirting with all of the women, saying "Hi!" with his adorable smile and big green eyes. Kai was occupied by chasing him, and as usual, he charmed everyone in the room, until they were called in to the exam room by the nurse.

Dr. Lowther looked non-threatening and had a warm smile. He greeted Fin in a friendly manner, like a cheerful, distant uncle, and asked if he could watch him walk across the room. Fin was shy, but he finally came walking to mommy part of the way on his tippy toes. The doctor asked "Does he do this all of the time?"

Kai replied, "Sometimes, does that mean anything?"

"It...*can,*" was all he said. The doctor checked Fin's back, and noticed the dimple above his butt, the one that Kai considered his cute little birthmark.

"He has a sacral dimple," the doctor noted.

"What's that?" asked Teddy, worried.

"Some babies have it and it means nothing, but it can be connected to other things..." the doctor explained. Kai was stunned. She had asked their pediatrician about it months ago, he had said it was nothing—"Just *him.*"

Months ago, she had noticed something that could mean something important regarding her child's health, had pointed it out to their excellent pediatrician, and was told it was *nothing*? How could that *happen*?

"I showed that to our pediatrician, he thought nothing of it. What can it mean?" Kai asked, her nerves fraying.

"Well, there are things that can contribute to the cause of scoliosis that can only be found on an MRI. Before I make a diagnosis, I'll need you to have an MRI done on Fin's spine."

Teddy's leg starting nervously jumping again, "When—where should we have it done?" he asked.

This was *not* a wrinkle free life.

"I'm going to have my assistant contact Mercy Children's. If it were my child, I'd only have it done there, they're the most experienced in the city in doing anesthesia on infants."

Kai's head was starting to spin. She wanted to ask the right questions, but she didn't know what they were. Of *course* they wanted to go to the hospital that had the most experience in doing this, of *course*. But she had just been told her eighteen month old baby was going to have to have an *MRI with full anesthesia*. People sometimes died from anesthesia. She was scared to death.

"What could be causing the scoliosis?" she asked. "What would they be looking for in the MRI?"

"Well, it could be that the spinal cord is tethered, I really can't say. If that's the case, it would have to be untethered surgically, and that might cure the scoliosis on its own. See, your spinal cord should normally be floating freely in the spinal fluid, but it can be tethered or connected to the bone, which could cause pulling as the child grows. That surgery would have to be done by a neurosurgeon; I wouldn't perform that for you."

"So, you're saying we could have one surgery, and he'd be cured?" Teddy seemed very interested in this. One little spinal surgery on their baby, Kai thought, oh, *just that*.

"One surgery, possibly," the doctor replied, getting a touch impatient, "Again, I can't really discuss the treatment until we have a correct diagnosis."

"What's the best and the worst case scenario?" Kai wanted to know what to expect, to prepare herself as well as she could.

The doctor actually seemed a little uneasy in answering this, like he didn't want to freak them out. He took a long pause.

"Well, the *best* case scenario is that the scoliosis is idiopathic—meaning no known cause, no bone deformities or tethered cord, or anything directly causing it, and it spontaneously straightens on its own. If you want to pray for something…that would be the best outcome."

Teddy appeared to relax a bit, leaning forward, "So, that could still happen, right?"

"It…*could*," the doctor smiled, "then you wouldn't have to do anything."

"And the worst case is spinal surgery, right?" Kai asked anxiously, as Fin started getting restless, beginning to whine softly. *"Want to go,"* he begged, tugging at Kai's jeans. She didn't blame him; she wanted to go, too.

"Listen," the doctor said, "I do what my 'tummy' tells me to do. You know, I won't even do surgery on older kids, if they say they don't want to do it. I had one

patient I asked, a little girl, and she said "No, Dr.
Lowther," and I refused to do the surgery until she felt
comfortable with the idea. A few weeks later, she sat on
my lap and said 'Dr. Lowther, I want to do the surgery,
now.'"

Dr. Lowther smiled, proud of his moral policies.
He seemed like a good guy, Kai thought, a guy who
follows what his "tummy" tells him to do.

She had Googled scoliosis on the Internet the
night before, unable to sleep—and she had seen some
things about kids being put in braces, and also something
about plaster casts. It was all so much information to take
in at once. "What about braces and casts?" she asked.

"Yes, I do bracing myself. I also do the surgery."
He looked like he got a bad taste in his mouth. "Casts—
that is *not* what I do. They don't even do it in Los
Angeles. If you wanted that, you'd have to go out of
state."

Teddy and Kai looked at each other. Teddy
furrowed his brow, "We live in a major metropolitan city
with great doctors and hospitals, why would we go *out of
state* for anything?"

The doctor smiled, "I know a doctor who does
casts, but it's…kind of like *religion*. You either believe in
it or you don't."

Well, that solves that, Kai thought. It sounded like
something kooky, crazy parents do, not people with
excellent health insurance, who live in a major city. No,
Teddy was right, why would they want to go out of state?
They were staying right *here*, going to the hospital that
treats the most children. Fin was getting the *best*.

The doctor stood up and his perky female
assistant, Jill, came into the room, holding a clipboard.
"Jill, these nice folks need to get an MRI scheduled at
Mercy as soon as possible," he shook both of their hands
firmly, and Teddy and Kai both thanked him as he ruffled
Fin's honey blonde hair and left to see his next patient.

Jill smiled at them kindly, "It can, unfortunately, take up to two months, on average, to get an MRI appointment at Mercy, they're so busy there. I'll call you as soon as I contact them and feel free to call me, too. Here's my card. We'll stay in touch."

Kai stood up urgently, "Thank you, Jill, listen—we'll take *any appointment* they have, I mean, two months is a long time to wait and worry, can we ask to be put on a cancellation list?"

"I'll let them know that when I call. I understand." Jill obviously had to deal with a lot of worried parents, probably many of them falling apart in the office.

Kai thanked her profusely; she didn't want to make her job any harder. These people felt like the lifeline to getting Fin well. And the doctor *still* said it may resolve, just go away on its own. That's what she would focus on, just getting this MRI scheduled and praying it was clear. Fin could be the miracle child. He *would* be the miracle child, Kai just knew it.

You could trust a doctor who is only giving you the medical advice that he would give for his own child, if they were in the same circumstances. You could trust a man who followed what his tummy told him. Right?

They got a call a few days later from Jill, who said they should be hearing from the hospital about their MRI date for Fin.

After another few days of tense waiting—days that felt like years—Teddy got a message on his cell phone that the hospital was calling to schedule Fin's procedure. He was hanging out on the beach with some friends when the call came, he didn't feel his phone vibrate and didn't notice there was a message until he was almost back in Beverly Hills.

He was listening to the message as he walked into their house, yelling "Kai, the hospital called!"

"WHEN? What did they say?" she suddenly was on her feet, nervously pacing the living room. Fin was in the middle of a nap in his nursery.

"The beach was noisy from the traffic on PCH, and some surfers having a BBQ. I guess I didn't feel it vibrate in my pocket," Teddy shrugged.

"They called *forty five minutes ago*?" she was freaking out, "Teddy, call them *right now*! What if we missed getting the appointment?"

"Relax, they book two months in advance!" he was annoyed now, dialing. "Hello, this is Teddy Verona, you called about scheduling my son Fin's MRI appointment..." he paused, looking up at Kai. She had forgotten to breathe. "You do? Kai, they had a last minute cancellation, they can do it tomorrow at 6am."

Kai nodded wildly, *take it*!

Teddy paused, considering the early hour, "Do you have anything a little later in the morning?"

Kai knew he was thinking of *his* sleep, that he, Teddy, could get a little extra shut-eye. She started jumping up and down like a maniac, "TAKE THE APPOINTMENT! WE'LL BE THERE!!!"

"*Okay, okay*, we'll take it. The nurse will call us later today with instructions? Okay, thank you."

Teddy hung up his phone, looking up at Kai. "You were right, the woman said they just got this one cancellation, because they can't put a kid under anesthesia if they're sick. They didn't have anything else until mid-March."

Mid-*March*—it was January 5th today. Kai closed her eyes, feeling grateful, grasping at the hope that her luck just might be coming back.

Angels Mercy Children's Hospital in downtown Los Angeles accepted their insurance, but Kai knew that Mercy was the L.A. children's hospital where most of the low income families, or those without insurance went. Still, the doctors who practiced there were supposed to be top notch in their fields—which, of course, is what *all* children, all people deserve.

It was like entering another universe when they took their sleepy little boy the next morning, driving to downtown L.A. while it was still dark outside. They passed graffiti covered billboards, little no-name chicken joints, even a depressing, low-rent strip club on the way. The hospital had instructed her by phone that she couldn't give Fin any milk before the procedure, only clear liquids after midnight the night before, and no juice or water after 6am. Fin hated juice anyway, so Kai knew he'd get hungry soon and crabby, but at least they had an early appointment.

The hospital was eerily quiet and nearly empty that early in the day. It was a nice facility, with lots of colorful decorations for children on the walls, donated by patrons of the hospital, but it still felt like a place Kai never, ever wanted to be in her life. They passed other worried looking families in the corridors with children in hospital roller beds and wheelchairs with I.V.s hooked up to them. Some of them clearly had severe, lifelong conditions. One little girl on a gurney and her mother walking beside her both wore surgical masks. Kai knew there was a chance that this would be their only visit to this hospital, and there was also a chance they'd have to bring Fin back here for surgery. She prayed this was the only time she'd experience walking through these halls. It was certainly scary, but it wasn't that depressing to be here *once*, for something they might escape. She couldn't imagine how it would be to nearly move in to a place like this, if your child needed endless surgeries or treatments. Actually, she didn't *want* to imagine it. She told herself she had to try to turn her brain off.

Teddy was tired and even more out of his element than she was. With his privileged background, he didn't spend a lot of time in places like this, amongst immigrant families without insurance or means. Kai could see how uncomfortable he was, this just didn't *happen* to kids from families like his. This kind of thing didn't happen to *"people like us."*

"Some of these people are probably not even citizens," Teddy whispered. It sounded like a hiss.

Kai shot him a look, was he being classist or *racist* about sick children getting medical care? No, she reminded herself, he was under immense stress, she wasn't going to pick a fight about it. "I'm sure they have to be citizens to go to a city hospital," she said, trying not to have an edge in her voice or to glare at him. She wasn't sure she succeeded.

She wondered if his mom was still blaming her for the use of the electronic baby swing. She, Kai, was the low class girl who was fortunate to meet a guy like him; maybe it was *her* flawed womb, *her* mistakes of young motherhood that brought them here? *Her* fault? Maybe Teddy and his parents were pissed that Fin looked too much like her.

"Stop it," she scolded herself, *"stop* beating yourself up! You have to be strong for your baby."

They checked in at the Radiology desk and a nice, middle aged nurse asked them a bunch of questions. Fin was put into a tiny hospital gown and Kai tried to distract him with some colored plastic blocks. He looked at her and said *"Want to go,"* in a small, worried voice. That broke her heart. She swallowed a sob, saying "We can do it! Fin can do it!" in an upbeat tone. That seemed to help, and Fin responded "We did it!" It was one of his favorite phrases from the "Dora the Explorer" TV cartoon. She knew he was hungry and scared, of course he didn't understand where they were or why.

They were told only one of them could go into the room as Fin was put under for the MRI. Kai quickly replied "I'll go!" before she had even asked Teddy if he wanted to. She knew he wouldn't volunteer.

They asked her to take off any metal she was wearing and she removed her jewelry, handing it to Teddy to hold and carrying tiny Fin cradled in her arms, down the hall and into the MRI imaging room.

The technicians laid Fin down on the table with an IV inserted in his foot, the anesthesia dripping into his veins, and they were putting wires on his chest for monitoring, as they told her to say goodbye. "Ma…" he said weakly, he was going under. She gently kissed him, softly singing Bob Marley, *"Don't worry…about a thing…"* and she fleetingly thought that *some people never wake up from anesthesia.* He was just a *baby. Her baby.*

What if this were the last time she saw her baby *alive?* It was too much, too surreal, she couldn't comprehend it.

Fin was sleepy from the drugs and began to pass out, his little head lolling back, with his pale pink lips wide open just like someone passing out from illicit drugs. The technicians told her she had to leave the room now, and she was surprised that she wasn't crying or passing out herself. She backed away from her boy and somehow found the exit doors and the hallway back to the room where Teddy had to wait, a room with toys and books and a TV for the sick kids to watch. As she walked, partially stumbling into the doorway of the Radiology waiting room, Teddy got up and walked to her and she finally began to softly cry. She thought he would put his arms around her, hold her, but he just looked rigid and tense, handing Kai back her jewelry as he dug it out of the pocket of his pants, including her engagement ring and the necklace engraved with "Fin" on a charm.

They moved together awkwardly back into the hallway. Kai instinctually didn't want to upset the other kids there; the waiting room had started to fill up with other families waiting for X-ray and MRI appointments.

54

What *was* this world? This world where so many kids were ill? What was the *meaning* of this? Kai felt like she was in a bad, cruel dream.

They had been given a beeper so that they would know when Fin woke up, but they were told they wouldn't get the results of the imaging until a day or two later. The beeper allowed them to go to the hospital cafeteria and get something to eat or drink. They sat down at a booth and Teddy choked down some overcooked scrambled eggs, barely speaking to Kai, who felt numb as she gripped the hot cup of coffee in front of her.

About an hour and a half later, as they paced the hospital hallways, walking past a gift shop selling soft pillows, stuffed animals and even a miniature grand piano, they were beeped. Kai raced back with Teddy at her heels to find Fin in his hospital bed in the recovery room, being watched by a nice Latina woman, who Kai assumed was a nurse. Fin was groggy, but he was *fine*! He was actually smiling and flirting sleepily with the nurse! *HURRAY*!

Kai stroked his tiny warm back and kissed him, and after he drank some apple juice and ate a cracker, waking up a bit more, they were free to get him dressed and go home. The nurse said just to watch him that day, for falls and things, as he might still be groggy from the after affects of the drugs.

They called Janie and Teddy's parents from the car, everybody was relieved Fin came through it so well. Janie proudly said her prayer circle was on top of it and Kai gratefully thanked her sister. She would take any and all prayers for her brave little guy—yes, *indeed*!

Fin played the rest of the day, running around just like normal. His back was still crooked, of course, but he was acting like his usual charming, adorable self, happily yelling "Yeah!" and "We DID it!"

Sometimes he pronounced "Yeah" like "*Yeh*," sounding like a laid back surfer dude, and sometimes he said "*Yeh, B,*" which sounded kind of like he was saying "Yeah, baby." Fin had recently seen a Halloween themed cartoon with ghosts in it, and he starting saying "Boo!" That had transitioned into "*Boo, yeah!*" and any day now might turn into "Boo B." That kid was a crack up—even on a day like this, he made his Mommy smile.

Teddy took off that night to go out drinking with the boys and blow off some steam. When he got home at 2am, Kai still wasn't sleeping. He slipped into bed and she reached for him, maybe making love was what they needed to bring them closer. She tried to kiss him—his mouth smelled of cigar smoke and expensive scotch—but he pulled away.

"I know this is scary…I just want to feel close to you," she whispered.

"The pill's not a hundred percent protection," he mumbled, "no birth control is."

She pulled away, hurt. "What, you don't want to have sex with me because I made you a *flawed baby*?"

"No, Kai, I'm just not feelin' it right now." Teddy rolled over, and minutes later, started to loudly snore.

The next day, they got the call from Jill at Dr. Lowther's office. Jill's voice wasn't so perky as it had been before. The radiologist's report had come in, she told them, and Fin's scoliosis appeared to be *idiopathic*, meaning there was no known cause and no bone deformities. If the scoliosis had been congenital, it may have required spinal surgery to remove bone deformities. Jill said the good news was that there also appeared to be no tethered cord.

"*But*," Jill said, "They found something in Fin's spine that isn't supposed to be there, something called a *syrinx*. You'll need to meet with the neurosurgeon at the hospital to have him take a look at Fin's MRI, and get his opinion on whether Fin would require surgery to remove this."

Teddy slammed his fist against the table. Now there was something *else*, besides the severe scoliosis. Something else *wrong*.

Kai's head was spinning, her mouth suddenly dry. "What is a syrinx? Can you sp-spell that?" she stuttered.

"S-Y-R-I-N-X," Jill said, enunciating each letter.

Kai wrote it down with a shaking hand on a piece of scrap paper, feeling like her beautiful world and her beautiful relationship and her beautiful baby boy were all London Bridges.

Falling, falling down.

7
The Special Hell

Kai stayed up all night online, alone, researching the syrinx, in a panic. She read that it was a fluid filled cyst inside the spine. The full name for it was Syringomyelia (sih-ring-go-my-E-lee-uh). She read on, clicking around between websites. CNNhealth.com said that the majority of the cases are associated with Chiari malformation, a condition in which *the brain protrudes into the spinal canal*.

Did Fin have a Chiari malformation, too? Was there something wrong with her child's spine *and* brain? Was his brain *leaking down* into his spinal column?

Other causes of the syrinx could be spinal cord injuries and spinal cord tumors. Fin had never had a spinal cord injury, he had never been in a car accident, never been dropped. She had *never* dropped her boy, Kai had always worried about that...babies are so tiny and so fragile, and tired, addled parents are carrying them in the middle of the night. Since becoming a mother, she had a terrible fear that she would drop him, but she never had. *Never*, not once. She always kept one hand on his wriggling body when he was on the changing table.

Spinal cord *tumors*? Now a *tumor* was a possibility?

My God. *God, please, no.*

Even if there was no tumor, she read that the syrinx may have to be operated on. That would mean spinal surgery on her less than two year old baby boy. What if the surgeon slipped? They lived in California, earthquake country. Isn't the spine very fragile? Couldn't even the slightest damage to the spinal cord be paralyzing for life?

She kept reading on, going from website to website, in a panic. Teddy was sleeping snugly; she wouldn't wake him up to tell him this. She felt like he couldn't handle it, so he was emotionally escaping, but she also felt like *she* couldn't handle it. She was trembling, she felt alternately dizzy and nauseous—with each new frightening piece of information, she felt like she might pass out. She didn't want to read any more, but she had to. She got a glass of cold chardonnay from the kitchen, filled to the top, and went back to the computer.

Basically, she found out that the syrinx could grow rapidly at any time, pressing on the spinal cord from within. It could cause *permanent nerve damage,* if it grew. It could even grow when Fin was a teenager or in early adulthood, and the only way to monitor it was by MRIs. By the time symptoms were felt, they were usually irreversible nerve damage, which could mean anything from numbness, weakness or tingling, to pain and even possible paralyzation.

According to the website Merck.com, "A neurosurgeon may make a hole in the syrinx and drain it, to prevent it from expanding, but surgery does not always correct the problem. Even if the syrinx is drained, the nervous system may be damaged irreversibly. Symptoms may not be relieved, or the syrinx may recur."

What? Was she getting this right? The syrinx could grow rapidly *at any time*. Even if it were operated on, it may recur. And the only way to know is by repeated MRIs, or if Fin experiences symptoms, which by that time may already be *irreversible nervous system damage*? Her eighteen month old boy could not even *talk enough* yet, to tell her if he felt any symptoms! How would she even *know*?

The neurosurgeon at Mercy Hospital could see them this Friday, in three days. She would have to wait until then to get more answers. It was excruciating.

She went into Fin's sea themed, pale green nursery, and watched him sleeping like an angel, holding her breath. A thought caught in her throat, *"He doesn't deserve this."*

Kai walked into the master bedroom, seeing Teddy in a deep sleep. She noticed he had a bottle of prescription sleeping pills, Ambien, by his the side of the bed. She didn't blame him for having trouble sleeping— she barely slept herself, these days—but Kai knew she couldn't afford to be "out of it" if Fin woke up crying, needing her.

She wanted to call someone, she needed to talk to somebody, but she couldn't think of a single person to reach out to. It was the middle of the night, two in the morning. Janie and her family would be sleeping. She knew what Janie would say, anyway. She couldn't call any of their twenty something club friends without kids, they wouldn't get it, and she had lost touch with her friends from college, after she dropped out when her mom died. Kai had always had boyfriends before that; they had been her best friends at the time. She couldn't exactly call them now, about this.

She had always been a person who was happy with just one or two close friends in her life, and her mom had long been her very best friend. She had most recently thought that closest person was Teddy, the man she intended to grow old with. Maybe she had made a mistake, a huge, *horrible* mistake. Maybe she was engaged to a shallow, heartless man? Maybe she was a terrible judge of character, in choosing a man like him to be the father of her child.

Maybe it was her fault she was totally alone. She wanted to scream, to cry, to sob, but she knew she'd wake the baby.

She impulsively grabbed the video baby monitor and walked outside to their pool. She didn't even turn on the pool lights; she just stood there in the dark, watching the still surface of the water. She set the monitor by the side of the pool, the volume turned all the way up, ripped off her clothes and dived into the dark, warm water, leaving on her white cotton bra and panties, in case any neighbors were still up.

"Hello darkness my old friend..." the words of the Simon and Garfunkel song seeped into her mind, despite the fact that the most recent movie she'd seen with that song in it was one where it was used to silly, comedic effect. This was no comedy; there was *nothing* funny about her life, right now. She began to sob under the water, where no one could hear her, screaming a silent scream and letting the chlorine sting her eyes and the back of her throat, along with her tears.

She bobbed to the surface and floated for a moment, listening for Fin on the monitor. He was sleeping silently, she could hear the soft intake and exhale of his breath. She thought of the time after her mom passed on, when she used to dream of drowning in the ocean, going under and never coming back up. That was before she had a baby, another life she was responsible for. She stayed in the pool until she was all cried out, until her fingertips puckered and her throat ached from her underwater wails.

She finally dried off with towels and curled up on the floor of Fin's nursery with a spare pillow and blanket, drifting off around 5am, as she listened to his tiny chest and delicate lungs rise and fall. Was the curve on his spine pressing on those tiny lungs?

Kai had an appointment to make a final decision on her wedding dress that Thursday, and an appointment

with a florist on Wednesday. She cancelled them both,
she didn't mention it to Teddy.

It was a particular, special kind of hell to know
that your child has a serious health problem, and not even
know for sure what it is yet, or how to properly treat it. At
the same time, her terror was juxtaposed with watching
her joyful, innocent little boy laughing and running and
playing, completely oblivious to what was happening in
his little back. He was so happy, and she was so filled
with fear, she was sinking, into the waters dark and deep.

"He's *right there* in front of you," Kai kept telling
herself, "he's *still here. Enjoy* him. He can't see his
Mama depressed or crying all the time, you have to pull it
together! For *him! Just pull it together!*"

Once, she caught herself looking out the window,
in a daze, and she suddenly saw Fin looking at her, then
gaze out the window with the same, faraway stare that she
had.

It jolted her, it was as if he was thinking to
himself, "Oh. *This is what we do.*"

She tried to tell Teddy what she had found online,
but she could sense him shutting down each time. He kept
saying, "Wait until we hear what the doctor has to say."
He was spending even less time with Fin, they were
becoming like strangers living in the same house. Teddy
asked their cleaning woman, Lupe, a quiet, squat
Guatemalan woman in her fifties, to come in every day to
cook and clean, so they were rarely alone together.

The week dragged by until the day of their
appointment with the neurosurgeon. Kai dressed up a
little—irrationally—as if the doctor would give them
better news if she looked polished and pretty. Polished
and pretty women didn't have children with serious health
problems, did they?

She took a long look at herself in her full length
bedroom mirror. She had chosen nearly all black,
including shiny black patent high heels. This was not the

natural beach mama, freewheeling Kai in cotton miniskirts and rope sandals. She had inadvertently dressed as if she were going to a Beverly Hills funeral—or to her own execution.

She walked into the kitchen to grab Fin and get him dressed. He was toddling around in just his diaper, lately he had decided he wasn't crazy about pants. Lupe was washing off the kitchen counters and skeptically looking at Fin's very obviously curved spine. Lupe spoke very little English and rarely spoke to Kai since she'd been hired. Now, she furrowed her brow at Fin's back, clucking her tongue.

"Mr. Ted say you used swing too much when he growing."

Kai felt her comment like a knife in her stomach. She grabbed her child and looked Lupe straight in the eyes, "Don't you *ever say that again.*"

Lupe glared back at her, "You will have me fired?" It was a challenging tone, a threat.

Kai felt an eerie calm come over her, with Fin perched on her hip, "No. I'll have you *killed.*"

Lupe blanched and gasped as Kai turned in her shiny black high heels and walked out. This was not like her at all, to threaten people. This was not her beach mama vibe of travelling through life barefoot, wishing everyone good energy, peace and love.

She willed herself not to cry as she dressed Fin in one of his very best outfits, ivory linen pants and a dark button down shirt. He looked like a little man, her *little guy.* She brushed his soft, wavy honey blonde hair and kissed his sweet angel face.

They drove to the hospital in silence: Teddy-Ken-doll, the man who wanted a wrinkle-free life, baby fishie Fin and Kai— Executioner Malibu Barbie. She would've laughed if it wasn't so messed up and stupid and scary. What was *happening* to her?

Dr. Becket's office was on the L.A. Mercy Children's Hospital property, in a separate building. The utilitarian waiting room had a fish tank and was filled with more tired and worried looking parents and their kids. They checked in at the desk and were taken for their appointment with the doctor twenty minutes later. He was a young doctor in his thirties—handsome—with light brown hair, longish and floppy in the front, hazel eyes and a kind, intelligent manner. Kai thought he looked tired, she wondered how many sad cases he saw daily. She hoped they weren't one of the sad ones.

The doctor greeted them, shaking both of their hands, "Hello, I'm Dr. Becket. You can call me Jack."

Kai smiled as brightly as she could muster, "I'm Kai, this is Teddy, and this is Fin."

Dr. Becket smiled warmly at Fin, who surprisingly beamed back at him, Fin didn't often smile at men he didn't know, only women. The doctor put up Fin's MRI image on the wall to take a look. There were toys in the room for Fin to play with, and he went for them, happily occupied for a few minutes. Kai sat on the edge of her seat, waiting for the neurologist's opinion.

"Yes, there is a syrinx…it's small, though, only two millimeters," he said, "I don't see a tethered cord, no, the cord appears fine…and yes, I see the scoliosis, however, that is not my field of treatment." The doctor turned to face them, "I would not operate on a syrinx this small."

"So, what do we do? I read that it can grow, and if it did, it could cause permanent damage," Kai stated anxiously.

"Yes, but it also may never grow. It could be an incidental finding, something you never would have known about, if you hadn't needed the MRI for the scoliosis diagnosis."

Kai and Teddy exchanged a look. Teddy looked enormously relieved. "So, we just would have to do a brace, or whatever, to fix the scoliosis and that would be it?"

"Well...no. I want to order a second MRI for Fin, of the full brain and spine, with dye contrast. This would mainly be to rule a few other things out."

Kai's heart sunk, but she realized she had to stay focused. He was just being careful, to rule stuff out, after all. "The first MRI was just of his spine. Why would you do his brain now?" she asked.

"There are some things that can occur along with a syrinx and scoliosis, including Chiari malformation. I don't see that on this MRI, he doesn't have Chiari, but there are other, rare things..."

"Like...?" Kai was afraid to ask, but she had to.

The young doctor looked pained to say it, "Now, I don't want to scare you, because I don't expect to find this, but a brain tumor can be dripping down tumors into the spine. It's unlikely, but I feel it's wise to rule any other conditions out."

Tumors—d*ripping down into the spine. No, no no no...*

"Can we get this MRI done as quickly as possible?" Teddy blurted. Kai was slightly stunned that he sounded this involved.

"I'll order it immediately and you can ask to be put on a cancellation list, but it can sometimes be a two month wait," the doctor was already holding up a hand held recorder, preparing to record his audio notes from their appointment. Kai was slightly shocked by the two month wait, but struggled to maintain her composure.

"We'll ask to be put in for a cancellation, of course. Thank you, doctor." Kai got up to pick up Fin, as Teddy shook his hand vigorously.

Dr. Becket began recording his verbal notes, as they left the office. "Well, it's been a pleasure to meet with Fin Verona and his parents, Teddy and Kai, and my findings and recommendations are as follows..."

Starting the car, Teddy was tense, but in better spirits. "When this next MRI comes back clear, we can do a brace or whatever and this is *over*."

Kai was sitting in the back, with Fin in his car seat, "Yes, but he still has the syrinx. And the scoliosis braces…he may have to wear one for a few months or longer, maybe a year, God forbid. We don't know yet."

"Did you hear him; he said the cyst thing may never grow! An *incidental finding*, that's what he said." Teddy was driving a little too fast in city traffic, getting agitated.

"I heard him, Teddy, but they're looking for brain tumors…dripping down into the spine…I'm sure he doesn't have that, but we have to get this second MRI, we *have* to, to rule that stuff out."

"Of *course* we have to get it, let's just do it and get it *over with*!" Teddy barked—he just wanted this problem *solved*.

"I truly, in my heart, don't think they're gonna find anything else wrong, Teddy. I think this next MRI is just something we have to do, to be thorough. To cross our "T's and dot our I's."

Teddy stopped at a red light on Sunset Boulevard, turning around and very purposefully forcing a smile at Kai. It wasn't lost on her that they were right near the clubs in Hollywood where they had partied before parenthood, when they were free of these medical fears, when they were *happy*.

"They're not gonna find anything else. We'll do a scoliosis brace for two, three months if we have to, fine. We'll *fix him*, and this will be over before the wedding!" Teddy grinned, gunning the engine as the light turned green.

Kai was thrown. It was like Teddy was seeing the light at the end of the tunnel, even if his grin was painted on. She had to do that, too, she told herself. Assume only the best. They were gonna *make it*, even after all of this.

Should she tell him about Lupe, what she had said? No, she wasn't vindictive. She was just being a Mother Tiger, in that moment, protecting her baby and herself. Lupe probably didn't mean it, maybe she was superstitious, one of those people who needed a reason why something bad happened to a child?

No, she wouldn't fire her. *No* bad karma, things were looking *up* for their little family. Now, they just had to wait for the second MRI, and pray, pray, *pray*.

That day, Teddy played with Fin more than he had for weeks. Kai wanted to cry with happiness when she saw him wading Fin's little feet in the pool, then putting on his water wings and helping him practice swimming. It was a beautiful day in Southern California, with bright, sunny, clear blue skies. She had been taking Fin to infant and toddler swimming lessons for months, he just adored the water—he was a natural, of course. Her little fishie Fin—playing and splashing in the water with his Daddy. He was giggling and yelling "I did it!" and "We did it!" He was the most positive baby, she was *so* proud to be his mom.

This was a family. This the way it *should* be, they *had* to make this work.

Once Fin was asleep in his crib, and they were lying side by side in their king sized bed with its pillow topped mattress and plush, expensive bedding, Kai tossed and turned. A million thread counts couldn't make her comfortable, right now. In the dark, Teddy reached for her hand. She was exhausted, she had only slept a few hours the night before.

"Hey," he said softly, "I know I haven't been myself, these last few weeks…"

Kai tentatively held his hand. "We've both been under a lot of stress."

"I don't know what else to compare this to, I mean, everything has been such a shock. I don't know anybody who anything like this has ever happened to." He clutched her hand, turning on his side to face her and stroking her cheek. "I'm sorry."

She really didn't want to cry, but she felt the emotion rising in her. "Thank you, for saying that. It's…it's scary…it's been so scary…"

"Yeah," he said, "I kind of freaked out. But it's gonna be over soon, I know it. It's gonna be *over* and we can go on with our lives like it never happened."

Like it never happened. But it *did* happen. Kai didn't want to contradict him, she didn't want to fight. He gave her hand a final squeeze and leaned over, gently kissing her lips. She kissed him back, a light, sweet kiss. She was so, *so* tired.

"He's really a swimmer, huh?" Teddy said.

"Yeah, he sure is, he's a natural," she smiled. It was easy to be proud of her little boy. It felt so good, to be sharing those feelings with his father.

Teddy rolled over, saying "Good night, babe."

It struck her that he hadn't called her "babe" since December 29th, the day they met with the second orthopedic surgeon. It was now February 14th. It suddenly dawned on her that in the midst of all of this, they had both completely forgotten it was Valentine's Day, *love day*. She didn't care; all she cared about was that Fin would be okay. Everything else was so small, in comparison to that.

As she finally drifted off to sleep, she thought about their upcoming wedding day, their future as a family. She allowed herself to think about her dreams of designing, for a brief moment. She had a fantasy of creating a line of relaxed, cool beach wear for kids and their moms, made of all organic fabrics, with natural dyes and details.

Maybe this could all be behind them in a few months, like a bad dream in a beautiful love story. Maybe the fairy tale could come true, after all. Her prince was lying right beside her, he just needed the white horse, and she just needed a little more faith.

She closed her eyes and decided to believe.

8
Bent

The next morning, the hospital called, with the date for Fin's second MRI: March 30th. Six weeks, a month and a half away; that seemed like an eternity to wait. Kai immediately asked for Fin to be put on a cancellation list, saying they would take any earlier date and time that opened up.

They had finished a light breakfast of toast, cheese and fruit, and were checking emails in the late morning, Kai in the living room while Fin played and Teddy in his office, when the phone rang again. Kai answered, it was Jill, the assistant from Dr. Lowther's office. "TEDDY!" Kai yelled, "PICK UP THE OTHER LINE, IT'S DR. LOWTHER'S OFFICE!"

"Hello?" Teddy was on the other portable phone now, they were both on the call. "Hello," said Jill, "I understand you got the results from Fin's first MRI reading."

"Yes, we met with Dr. Becket yesterday morning," Kai replied, "We have one more MRI scheduled for March 30th, but the doctor said it was mostly to rule some things out."

"Great," Jill said.

"Does Doctor Lowther want us to make an appointment in the meantime?" Teddy asked tersely, "To do a brace or something?"

"Um, yes, with Fin's last curve measuring at 34 degrees, I assume he's going to want to do *something*." Jill sounded polite and professional, Kai thought, but it seemed like she was holding something back.

"So, the bracing for scoliosis, is it for a few months, or..." Kai trailed off, not wanting to say what she envisioned as the worst case scenario, a whole year of her little boy having to wear a stiff, tight body brace. She had read online that they were commonly worn 23 out of 24 hours a day.

"Well, depending on the individual case, it could be until adolescence," Jill replied, almost offhandedly.

Silence. Kai's mind was reeling, *what did she mean, until adolescence?* Fin was only *eighteen months old*. Teddy walked out into the living room, holding the other portable phone pressed to his ear. He looked just as shocked and stunned as Kai.

"When is that?" Kai dumbly asked, all she could think was that an adolescent was a pre-teen or a teenager. Her baby wasn't even yet two.

"Possibly as young as 11 or 12 years old, for other kids older...when the spine reaches full adolescent growth, or maturity, the doctor can perform the spinal fusion surgery."

That would mean Fin would be in a body brace 23 hours a day *for a decade or longer*. Kai didn't know what to say. Teddy just looked at her, his eyes were huge.

"Th-thank you, thank you so much for calling, um, Jill, we'll uh...we'll call back to set our next appointment." Kai was sputtering, stuttering. She hung up the phone as Teddy clicked the button on his.

"*Why didn't anyone tell us this before?*" he asked.

Kai shook her head, it was spinning again. "We need to go online right now," she insisted, "we have to research this."

"Why, what's the point?" Teddy asked her. His chiseled face looked lost, deflated. Superman stripped of his powers.

"Because there has to be a better answer than bracing until he's 11, 13 or 15, and then *major spinal surgery!*" Kai was already at her laptop, going into a Google search for "Infantile scoliosis."

What she read absolutely floored her. She darted with her mouse, clicking between websites, and began reading aloud to Teddy, paraphrasing the important parts, while becoming increasingly dizzy, faint and sick to her stomach:

"Progressive Infantile Scoliosis can be potentially *FATAL* in babies and young children."

"The severe rapid curvature of the child's own spine *can literally crush their vital organs, their heart and lungs.*"

And

"This condition can be PAINFUL, SEVERELY DEFORMING, and lead to a SHORT, PAINFUL, CRIPPLING LIFE. It's potentially *FATAL BEFORE THE AGE OF THREE!*"

She realized she was shouting, almost screeching, and she looked up at Teddy. His jaw was slack and his face was white.

"Why didn't any of the doctors *tell us this*—because they didn't want to *alarm us*?" Kai was really shaking now, trembling from head to toe. She was *alarmed.*

She choked back hot tears, seeing Fin was still playing happily with his toys, thank God. She looked at Teddy, "I need to research more. I need you to call the babysitter to watch Fin."

"Fine," he said "Kai, I...need some time." Teddy staggered out of the room.

She knew what he was thinking, "*Why*? Why was this happening to *Fin*, to *them*? *WHY*? What did we *DO*?" She knew he was thinking that, because she was thinking the same thing.

And she also knew what else he was thinking. That he didn't sign on for this. They were both still only twenty five years old. Teddy wanted to travel the world. He wanted a glamorous life, the life they had before. He could meet another "hot" young woman, one who could bear him a healthy, perfect child. Maybe even one who looked more like him.

Well, she didn't sign on for this, either, but she was Fin's mother and *he needed her*. Now, more than *ever*.

"*Baby, don't worry...about a thing... 'cause every little thing's...gonna be alright...*" Her song for Fin, their special song. She felt like maybe she couldn't sing it to him anymore, because she couldn't promise him that everything would be alright. The monsters in their closet were real; the monster was inside his little body. *Her baby's own spine was trying to kill him.*

Kai wanted to crawl into a hole, she wanted to crumble. She simply felt like *she could not handle this*. She wished she were a better mother. She wished she were stronger.

She had never missed her own mama more than in this moment. She called on her for strength, "Mama, *help me*, I'm so scared. I need you, Mommy," she sobbed. Her tearful prayer sounded like the voice of a child, which is what she felt like, a frightened little girl. She got down on her knees and prayed to God to save Fin, to heal him, and to give her strength.

She slowly rose and sat back at her computer. She kept forgetting to breathe. Hands trembling, she managed to input another Google search. On the first page, there

was a website listed, www.infantilescoliosis.org. Kai
reminded herself to breathe again as she clicked on it.
It was a website for a non-profit organization called
I.S.O.P., the Infantile Scoliosis Outreach Program. It had
a sweet, crooked little purple flower at the top of the page.
She began to read:

      "Welcome! The Infantile Scoliosis Outreach Program
(ISOP) is pivotal in connecting families of children with
Progressive Infantile Scoliosis to resources and information
needed to make the best choices possible in the care of their
child."

      Kai read on, then clicked on the "Stories" section,
and started reading amazing stories of other children with
Fin's condition, and these stories were all saying the same
thing: Their child was significantly helped and even *cured*
of Progressive Infantile Scoliosis, by wearing *casts*. Not
braces, not surgery, but a series of non-surgical *plaster
casts*. There were photos of adorable children next to their
success stories, many of them wearing the casts that
looked sort of like plaster "vests," made of the same
material as for a broken arm or leg. They all had a big
mushroom shaped cut out in the front where the child's
tummy expanded, and a smaller cut-out in the back. She
read on, finding that many of them were *cured without
surgery*, by preschool age or even younger.

      Could this be true? Weren't things that were too
good to be true—exactly that?

      This was the Internet, the modern Wild West.
Crazy, unstable people were *everywhere*. In fact, if you
want to find crazy people nowadays, you may have more
luck online than in a mental institution. Kai knew this, she
was no fool. Was this a load of B.S.? *Medical witchcraft?*
Were these those types of religious people who would
never take their child to a doctor or give them medicine,
even if the child was dying of a curable, fatal condition?
Kai had seen news stories about people like that, was *that*
what this was? That was not her. She believed in modern
medicine and medical advances, for the most part.

How could one of the best orthopedic surgeons in a major metropolitan city, at a major, renowned, respected hospital, *not* suggest this treatment, if it actually worked? Dr. Lowther had said casts for scoliosis were "Like *religion, you either believe in it or you don't.*" He had told them it wasn't even done in Los Angeles, that "*You'd have to go out of state.*"

This was the "*my tummy tells me*" doctor, the one who wanted to try bracing her child for a decade or longer, followed by spinal fusion surgery.

Kai saw there was an online support group called C.A.S.T., which stood for Casts as an Alternative for Scoliosis Treatment and was connected to the Infantile Scoliosis Outreach Program she'd just found. She signed up for the Yahoo medical group, it was free to join. She sent out an email post out to the group, with the title line of **New Here with Questions**.

She typed: "Hello, my name is Kai, and my eighteen month old baby boy has Infantile Scoliosis. We've been advised to try bracing, possibly until adolescence, following by spinal surgery. I've seen on the ISOP website that there is this treatment with casts. Can anyone share their experience/advice with me on this? My little boy's last X-ray had a 34 degree curve, but that was over two weeks ago and his back already looks worse. To be honest, I'm scared to death."

She pressed "SEND" and waited. Within minutes, someone replied:

"Hello Kai, welcome to C.A.S.T.! So glad you found us."

Kai could barely read on because her eyes were flooded with grateful tears.

"My son David was cured of Progressive Infantile Scoliosis by a series of EDF casts, Early Treatment done in the Mehta Method. I can't recommend it highly enough, it saved my child's spine and his life. I know it's scary at this point, we've all been there. Please ask any and all questions of this great group."

-Amy, David's Mom, 3 years old, started casting at 41 degrees, now measuring zero degrees in a brace!

Kai clicked back to the ISOP website, scanning the photos of the kids in casts. She suddenly felt a presence—she was already so jittery, the hair on the back of her neck stood up.

Teddy was standing right behind her.

"The babysitter came; I let her take Fin to the park. What are you looking at, not that crazy cast thing?" She turned around to see him furrowing his brow at her. "Putting babies in *body casts*? That's *barbaric*."

"Maybe it is, I don't know. It says on this website it can be a cure, without surgery."

"Dr. Lowther said it was like some nutzo religion," he muttered dismissively.

"Doctor *my tummy tells me* wants to brace my child for a decade, and then slice into his *spine*. Sorry if I'm not more *psyched* about that." Kai found herself unable to keep the anger out of her voice.

"If he had a malignant brain tumor, wouldn't you want it removed? What do you have against surgery, Kai? If they could have removed the blood clot before it killed your mom, I bet you would have wanted them to slice it out." He knew that would sting; and it did. "If they could do surgery and fix him tomorrow, I'd sign the papers right now."

"I'm sorry. I'm not against surgery, I just don't think you should do it unless it's absolutely necessary," she said, "If surgery would save Fin, if it was the best option, of *course* I'd do it. I'd sign the papers this minute. Please, Teddy, let's not fight…"

"Yeah, let's not," he looked away, the edge still in his voice. "I have a business trip, for a potential film. The financier wants to look at locations before he commits." Teddy looked like he was lying, but she didn't know for sure. He *did* have several projects in the works he was always talking about. "I have to travel to Canada and Utah for a scouting trip with my partners, we have to leave tomorrow."

"*Tomorrow? Seriously?*" Was this Teddy's way of running, fight or flight syndrome? She suddenly noticed the décor of the house, for the first time in a long time. It was cold, sleek and modern, state-of-the-art emotionless. It was Teddy, it was *him*.

"I know, I know, I just got the call. This guy's a Russian billionaire, Russian oil money, he can finance a seven million dollar independent movie out of his own pocket like it's nothing, like it's fifty cents to most people. This is the window we have to close with him, there are three other filmmakers trying to woo him at the same time."

"How long would you be gone?" she asked softly.

"A week, maybe two. Look, I can get you a full time nanny from the best agency, you won't have to be alone. I know it's terrible timing, *horrible*...but...it's my career, our future. It's the culmination of what I've been working towards. And the MRI's not scheduled for six weeks, I'll be back long before then." His anger had faded and he looked contrite, or pleading...like he was guiltily asking for her permission to go.

"If you have to," she murmured. She knew he *would* go, regardless of what she said. She couldn't forbid him from traveling; after all, it was business.

And it was. The next day, Teddy packed and quickly kissed her on the cheek goodbye, before leaving for LAX. About an hour after he was gone, Lupe, their housekeeper, approached Kai at her computer as she researched more about Progressive Infantile Scoliosis. Lupe looked like the cat who had gutted the canary and was now enjoying watching it writhe in pain.

"Mr. Teddy has changed the locks. Your things are outside," Lupe sneered.

Kai looked at her, unsure she heard her right. Lupe's eyes glowed with enjoyment as she slowly repeated her words, savoring each syllable, "*Mr. Teddy has changed the locks. Your things are outside.*"

Recognition, in the form of shock, began to seep through her. Kai slowly stood and walked outside to the front lawn, where her suitcases were packed, a yellow cab awaited, and a Jamaican nanny she had never met, a tall, regal woman in her late forties, held her child.

Lupe shuffled behind her, smiling, "Wedding off. He say he want paternity test, child does *not* look like Mister. You stay in hotel."

Fin started crying, confused by what was going on. The stranger nanny tried to shush him and he just shrieked louder.

It dawned on Kai that Teddy had her things packed overnight, while she slept. Teddy was evil. Kai had suspected he was shallow, but *nothing* compared to this. He had even kissed her on the cheek goodbye.

"I need my computer," she said softly, almost in a trance. Shock was a blessing, sometimes; the brain protects itself from imploding.

Kai waited while Lupe returned inside and brought out her laptop. Kai took it, walked over, and handed it to the Middle Eastern cabdriver in his 60's, who was putting her bags in the trunk. Then she turned, walked back, and punched Lupe in her smug, squat, self-satisfied face, knocking her with considerable force to the ground. Red blood splattered on the marble walkway, and Kai vaguely thought of a Jackson Pollack painting.

"*Give me my baby*," Kai said calmly to the stranger nanny, taking her crooked child into her broken heart and arms. Into their broken future, where everything, she feared, even the purple flowers, were bent.

9
Spinning Upside Down

Kai sat in the back of the yellow cab with the stranger nanny and her crying child beside her. The dark featured cabdriver kept looking in the rearview mirror to check out the crazy lady who had just punched her housekeeper—former housekeeper—smack in the face. He furrowed his one long, connected brow—he looked genuinely afraid of her.

One thing that is really messed up about living in California, Kai thought, is that most of the time, those palm trees are swaying, the sky is blue, and the days are sunny and temperate, and it doesn't feel like a place where people's lives can really get screwed up, yet a lot of twisted, ugly things happen here. Take this, for example.

She was still in shock and it suddenly occurred to her that she had *no idea* where they were going. She looked at the stranger nanny, who read her mind and answered "The Four Seasons Hotel."

Say *what*? A *five star hotel*? Is this what one did when one dumped one's fiancée and mother of one's crooked child into the street? Teddy had taken her to Maui once, where they stayed at The Four Seasons there. The décor, the food, the service, the beds—it was all luxurious and wonderful. Say *what*?

"Mr. Verona paid for me and the hotel for two weeks, while you transition." The stranger nanny was calmly, politely answering her questions before she asked them.

While she *transitioned*? Into what— a *werewolf*? Kai considered taking Fin to her beach hut, but no…the walls were paper thin, the hut was built on sand. Just like her relationship, she thought, although that was actually *quicksand*.

The cab pulled up to the Beverly Hills Four Seasons Hotel valet parking. Kai got out in a daze, carrying Fin. Porters took her suitcases and the stranger nanny checked in for them, and then they were in their beautiful suite with a balcony, two queen beds and a crib between them. *Fin's crib, from their house.* Teddy had already had it moved here. How long had he been planning this?

Kai put Fin in his crib with some toys and sat on the edge of one of the beds. She looked at the minibar fridge. Was everything paid for, for two weeks? How much could they rack up in charges, to *really* piss him off?

The stranger nanny sat on the other bed. She had a very small roller suitcase with her, which she had propped upright. "My name is Doris. It's a pleasure to be of service to you and your child." She said.

"*Doris*? No, that can't be right. That's an old white lady name," Kai blurted out. She was, perhaps, not at her best at the moment.

"It was actually Veruca in Jamaica, but when I moved to this country ten years ago, I chose to change it to Doris, to blend. If you must know." Doris seemed perturbed; she probably had to answer this question a lot, because she certainly didn't look like a Doris.

"I'm sorry, Doris, uh….nice to meet you," Kai mumbled, distracted.

Doris looked at her, then said in a flat tone, despite her Jamaican accent, "No it is not nice, for you. That is fine, I am paid and I will do my job…" she paused for a long moment, then said stiffly, "May I have a drawer?"

Kai was baffled by this question, until Doris gestured at the dresser. "Oh, a drawer…yes, uh, of course, take as many as you need."

By the grace of God, Fin has fallen asleep in his crib. Kai sat frozen on the bed and tried to process all of this, as Doris carefully unpacked her small suitcase, fitting everything neatly and precisely into two lower dresser drawers.

"He paid for two weeks, is that exactly fourteen days?" Kai asked.

"Yes, Ma'am," replied Doris.

"No, no 'Ma'am,' please. I'm Kai."

"I know, Miss Kai." Doris started attempting to clean the already immaculate room.

"No, not Miss, please call me Kai, thanks. You don't have to clean, it's already clean…they have housekeeping, here."

"It is in my job description, but I follow what you say." Doris stopped dusting, folding her hands at her waist.

Something suddenly occurred to Kai, something that her mother often said when people asked her how she raised two daughters as a working single mother. Her mom said, "I'm like a duck. It looks like I'm gliding smoothly across the surface of the water, but underneath, I'm paddling like hell." She thought about the fact that she was a sitting duck, but Teddy had already fired the gun, now she had to do what her mother did. She had to make it look to Fin like everything was okay on the surface, and she had to *paddle like hell*.

"Is there anything else he told you that I should know, Doris?" she asked.

Doris looked apprehensive. "He told me not to give it to you until tonight…but, there is a letter."

Kai felt her throat constrict and go dry. A "Dear John" letter.

"Can I have it, please?"

Doris sighed and pulled it out of one of the drawers, from under a folded pair of her neatly ironed pants, it was a simple white envelope. She handed it to Kai, "I would want to read it immediately, if I were you, but please don't tell him I gave it early."

"I won't." Kai was already ripping the letter open and reading:

"Kai,

If you're reading this, I am already on my production scouting trip and we have separated. I realize this is sudden, but we are not married yet, and therefore my house is my own. You were my invited guest and I was happy to have you there. We had only been in a relationship for a matter of months when you became pregnant. I had taken you on all-expense-paid trips around the globe, and we had both enjoyed ourselves immensely. However, love is blind, and it did not occur to me to request a paternity test, even when the child did not look like me. I am obviously open to one now, or at some point in the future.

After we became engaged, I felt our relationship changed, in many ways, for the worse. I wanted to continue to enjoy a certain lifestyle, while you refused, wanting to stay almost exclusively at home. I felt we were drifting apart long before this health news came about Fin. After that point, I felt you became unloving and unhappy in my home, the home that I had hoped to make ours.

We are two very different people, Kai, and I think in the long run, we will both be glad we realized this

82

sooner, rather than later. Break-ups always cause pain, and that is inevitable in this case. That is why I chose to ease the split for you by paying for a five star hotel, a nanny, and your expenses for a period of time. You may feel free to keep the ring, it's worth quite a bit of money.

I do not know for sure if Fin is my child. I do know that I disagree with the concept of putting him or any young child in a restricting and painful body cast. I think it's cruel, if not outright barbaric. I'm sure that any reasonable person will understand that no man would want to sign on for years and years of health treatments for a child who is not definitively their own blood.

I'm sorry that it had to be this way, but I am not good at goodbyes, I admit that. That is just me. I wish you the best and we will be in touch.

Sincerely,
Teddy Verona

Doris watched Kai as she read the letter, first fighting the tears and anger, then finding herself unable to stop them from streaming down her face. There were just too many things wrong with this letter to even begin. He wrote it like a lawyer ending a business deal: cold, unfeeling, bizarrely formal. He was pulling the rip cord like a complete freakin' *coward.*

Production scouting trip? He was probably partying in Vegas. She was *his invited guest*? They were *engaged* to be married! *All-expense-paid trips*? They were *his idea*!

She became *unloving and unhappy in his home*? Her child developed a fatal condition and he shut down emotionally! Yes, love *is* blind, he got that right, and they *were* two very different people. One of them had a soul and one didn't.

How could he not even ask for visitation, or to be involved in Fin's health care? If the inevitable paternity test comes back positive, which it will, because he was the only man she had sex with in *three years*…how could he live with himself, knowing he deserted his son when he needed his father the most?

"THAT *PRICK*!!!" Kai yelled, quickly glancing to make sure she hadn't woken the baby.

Fin stirred, but he was still asleep. Kai wiped her eyes and folded the letter, looking up at Doris, "Can you just watch Fin if he wakes up? And order some whole milk from room service for his bottle?"

"Yes, Ma'am," Doris answered, trying to look away, to give her some privacy. Kai ignored the Ma'am and jumped up, grabbing her computer and setting it on top of the desk in the room, plugging it in the outlet. She turned the power on and quickly typed in www.infantilescoliosis.org.

There was the curvy purple flower on the screen again. She found a phone number and a name: The founder of ISOP, Heather Hyatt-Montoya. She grabbed the hotel pen and wrote it down on the notepad they provided, scrawling a number on a second sheet of paper and tearing it off. She jumped up again, getting her cell phone out of her purse and handing Doris the piece of paper. "This is my cell number; call me if you need me. I'm gonna make a call, I'll be right back."

In the hallway, Kai breathlessly dialed the number and nervously paced as she waited for it to ring. "ISOP, how may I help you?" a friendly woman's voice answered.

"Hi, my name is Kai and my baby has Infantile Scoliosis. May I speak to Heather Hyatt-Montoya?"

"Oh, yes," the woman responded, "Please hold a moment." Kai waited breathlessly, continuing to pace the elegantly decorated hallway, as another woman's voice came over the line, "This is Heather."

"Hi, Heather, thank you for taking my call, my name is Kai, my eighteen month old baby boy has Infantile Scoliosis…his name is Fin…he had one MRI and he has a small syrinx cyst…they want us to do another MRI, but it looks like his back, the curve is getting worse, every day…and my fiancé, well, *Ex PRICK* fiancé, just kicked us out of his house…I'm babbling. I know it. I'm sorry; this is not my best day."

Heather paused a long time. "Nobody is at their best when they're scared. I know *I'm* not. Do you know your child's Cobb angle from his X-rays? That the degree of the primary or main curve."

"It was 34 degrees on December 29th, but it already looks worse, to my naked eye. It was 25 degrees, then 28, then 34; within just 4 months…they're recommending bracing and eventually spinal fusion surgery at adolescence."

"Okay, do you know Fin's RVAD?" Heather said.

"No, they only gave us one number…what's that?" Kai asked.

"It stands for Rib Vertebral Angle Difference, it's measured to determine whether or not a curve will progress or resolve on its own. RVADs of 20 degrees or more have an 80 percent chance of progression, and if an orthopedic surgeon doesn't know what it is, you may just want to walk out of their office," Heather said. Her tone was dead serious, she was no bullshit. "This is my advice. I would get an appointment with a Mehta Method trained orthopedist as soon as possible, just in case Fin has Progressive Infantile Scoliosis, which it sounds like he does. If it *is* progressive, it can worsen rapidly and dangerously, so time is *vital*, you *must act fast.*"

"Okay," Kai said anxiously. She stopped pacing and sank down to the floor in the hall, her back to the wall. "What should I do?"

"The closest Shriners hospital near you is in Salt Lake City. There is an excellent orthopedic surgeon there,

Dr. Jacques D'Astous, who I can't recommend highly
enough. He does this method of casting; in fact, he was
the first doctor in the U.S. to practice it. Shriners is a
charity hospital, so you have to be accepted to go there."

Kai absorbed this—a *charity hospital*, when she
had excellent health insurance, at least at the moment, and
was currently sitting in the lap of luxury in Beverly Hills.
A million thoughts rapidly flooded her mind, she thought
about those commercials for St. Jude's Hospital, all of the
incredible work they did for sick kids…very sick kids,
kids with cancer or rare conditions…her child was now
one of these kids. Those kids she made donations for at
the movie theater, ones who have ongoing or even
potentially fatal health problems. She lived in a major
metropolitan city, with some of the top doctors and
medical care in the world, and she had to fly to Salt Lake
City, to a free charity hospital, to get proper care for her
child. How could this *be*? Which way was *up*?

Heather continued, "First, get your child into the
Shriners' system as soon as possible, you can apply by
phone or fax or online. Then, gather all of your child's
pertinent medical records and copies of his films, the X–
rays and MRIs. Put together a package with those, a short
letter to the doctor telling your child's story so far, and
photos of his back without a shirt on…and one of his cute
face, it's nice to put a face to a name. Fed-Ex it overnight
if you can to the hospital, addressed to the doctor and the
Care Coordinator there, Angie Livingston."

Kai was writing all of this down on her little
notepad in her lap. *Shriners*, she thought…the men who
wear the funny red hats? The red *Fez*? She didn't have
time to think about it, not if they could help her child.
"Okay, got it. The neurologist said the cyst in his spine is
too small to operate on right now…but he wants us to do
one more MRI to rule some other things out. Should I still
contact the Shriners Hospital right away, or do the MRI
first?"

"If I were you, I would contact Shriners right away; it can take a couple of weeks or even months to get an appointment. In the meantime, try to get your MRI moved up if you can. Request to be put in for a cancellation slot, because a cancellation may open up in Salt Lake City for casting." Heather sighed, "This method of casting was not available in the U.S. less then ten years ago, most orthopedists, unfortunately, do not practice it, many do not even know about it. But there is a window in which you have the *best* chance for a non-surgical cure, and that window is generally to begin proper treatment under 50-60 degrees curvature, and under age two."

Kai's head was spinning. *Under age two*. Fin was eighteen months old; he'd be two in less than six months. The second MRI wasn't scheduled until he would be over nineteen months, and then it could take a couple of months to get an appointment at Shriners…who knew how high his curve could be by then? Could he have *vital organ damage* by then, *permanent lung damage*? Would he be in pain for the rest of his life?

Kai asked, "Are these casts painful? My Ex thought it sounded…barbaric."

"No, a Mehta Method EDF cast should *never* be painful, *ever*. It's a non-surgical, slow and gentle process, like the redirection of a growing vine up a wall. Most of the parents say it's much harder on the parents than the child, because of the emotions they go through—having a child with a serious condition—and especially the fear of the unknown."

"I can already relate to that," Kai admitted, almost in a whisper.

"It takes the babies and young kids a little getting used to, at first, a couple of weeks or maybe a month, but kids are incredibly resilient. You should *only* go to a doctor who is properly trained in Mehta's Method, and has the proper child size casting frame."

"Uh-huh…okay…"

Heather continued, "And the surgeries, Kai, if Fin misses the window to be cured...I mean, thank God we have them if needed, but they have a *lot* of complications. I know. I'm a single mom, and my daughter Olivia missed the window to be corrected by Early Treatment casting...what she has been through...*so much...*" Heather's voice trailed off for a few long moments, her silence speaking volumes. "She is a *brave, strong girl.* That's why I started ISOP as a mother, I've been in this battle to bring this cure to other children for going on ten years, and I'm *not done yet.*"

"Your daughter *is* a brave, strong girl and she has a brave, strong Mama!" Kai exclaimed, becoming choked up.

"So are you," Heather replied, "I won't say what I think of your *Ex.*"

Kai was shocked to hear a laugh escape from her throat. Seconds later, her voice was breaking again. "Thank you, Heather, I...really...*can't thank you enough.*"

"You're welcome. I'm sorry about what you're going through. Please keep me posted on how Fin is doing."

"I will," Kai promised, choking back a sob as they said goodbye. She clicked "end" on her phone, exhaling. One mother to another, one in Colorado and one in California, both of them just wanting their children to be well and to live normal lives. To not be in pain, to not be deformed, to not have to suffer. She couldn't believe the kindness of this woman, a complete stranger reaching out to help her, someone who actually *cared.*

It was one of the darkest moments of her life and she was yet *not totally alone.* She was scared to death of what was to come next, but she was truly grateful for that.

She slowly got up and walked back into the suite. Fin was still sleeping and Doris had unpacked much of Kai's stuff and was putting it away in the closet and the dresser. Kai smiled at her, "Thanks, Doris," she said, going to sit at her computer. She filled out the online application for Shriners Intermountain Hospital in Salt Lake City and sent it by email. Oh, the power and wonder of the Internet! She exhaled, hoping and praying that the right person would read it there, and not let Fin slip through the cracks. She would call them in the morning to make sure they got it, but now she had to gather all of Fin's medical records and the other stuff she needed for the Fed-Ex package Heather had advised her to send.

"Doris, how much do you know, about what Teddy...*Ugh*, you know what? I'm not gonna say his name anymore. I'm going to call him "Bastard"—no, "*Douche Bag,*" from now on."

Doris blinked, trying to stifle a smile, "Mmm-hmm. *That* is a new one."

Kai pressed forward, "What did Douche Bag give us to work with? He paid for this room for two weeks, I assume he paid for the cab here. Did he give us a credit card for the hotel food bill, or any money for food? Milk for his child?"

Kai had some money from her sales at Beach Mama, but it was not a fortune, she had slowly made every item by hand. She didn't have time to attempt to manufacture anything on a grander scale, Teddy had swept her up and taken her travelling before she could map that out...and then she was caught up in being pregnant, and being a new mother and planning a wedding...and she *thought*, being in love.

She needed to figure out what she *really* had to live on as a single mother, now. She looked down at her hand—yes—she still had the ring. It would be going to a pawnbroker, soon. "*What a difference a day makes...twenty four little hours...*"

"I really need to know what he gave us to work with here, Doris," she sighed.

"There's a credit card at the front desk, but Mr.—
Bag gave the hotel a limit."

"Don't shorten it, call him by his full Christian
name," Kai quipped.

Doris cleared her throat. "Mr. *Douche Bag*
allowed you two hundred dollars a day."

"*Big* of that asshole!" Kai trilled sarcastically,
beginning to calculate.

Okay, they had to afford three meals a day plus
tips, and room service was pricey at any hotel, especially
one as chi chi as this. They would have to order carefully
or get take-out from less expensive joints. "I have to run
some errands, are you okay with Fin here for a couple
hours?"

"Of course, it's my job," Doris replied stiffly,
sounding a little offended. Kai looked at her, thinking she
was *really* gonna have to remove that stick from her ass if
they were gonna co-habitate for two weeks.

"Just change his diaper when he wakes up, and
give him a bottle of milk. I'll stop at Whole Foods and
buy some groceries and snacks for him while I'm
out...and he loves books, they're in my suitcase, I
hope...please read to him...and he's very into
music...you can sing songs...do you know any Bob
Marley?" Kai realized she was starting to panic at the
notion of leaving her child with someone she had just
met.

"I do, and I'll provide him with a fat spliff, as
well..." Doris replied, tongue firmly in cheek.

Kai blinked, surprised. Doris had told a risqué
joke. "I like you," Kai smiled.

Doris smiled back with a wink. "Don't worry, we
will be fine."

Kai called the hospital and asked for a copy of
Fin's first MRI on disc, and the radiologist's printed
report. They told her they could put the MRI on a CD for
her for ten dollars, and that they could mail it, or she

could come by and pick it up. Of course, mailing would take longer, so she said she'd pick it up as soon as it was ready. In the meantime, she called Fin's first orthopedist, Dr. Conroy's office, to ask how she could get copies of Fin's three X-rays. The woman at the desk said they could make copies right there in the office, no problem. Kai didn't want to send the original copies of the X-rays to Shriners Hospital, in case she needed them in the future.

She called a cab and got the same guy who drove her to the hotel, the Middle Eastern man in his 60's, who had furrowed his monobrow at her from his rearview mirror in distrust. Both of them were *not* extremely happy to see each other, but she needed a lot of rides today, and he needed the large fare. When he pulled up in front of the hotel, she thought she heard him mutter under his breath *"Allah hates me,"* but she couldn't be sure.

Kai went to Mercy Children's Hospital and found the records department, where a nice woman gave her what she needed. She got back in the cab, and they drove in silence from downtown L.A., past the strip clubs and the greasy hole in the wall chicken joints and the homeless people, to Beverly Hills. Kai looked out the window at the homeless people pushing grocery store carts, and found herself thinking wistfully that even though she was sleeping at a fancy hotel tonight, those homeless people might be having a better day than she was. Not that she'd trade places, not that her heart didn't break for them, but still.

When they got stuck in traffic on Wilshire Boulevard, the cab driver looked at her in the rearview mirror, where she was anxiously chewing on her nails like she did as a kid.

"Nice hotel you're staying at," he observed. Kai nodded. "Is that your only child, the little boy?" he asked, trying to make conversation.

"Yes, he's my only one," she was pensively staring out the window.

"I have four," he said, "all in college, now. It's hard, but you *love* your kids. Oh you *love* your kids."

"Yes." Kai felt tears brimming in her eyes against her will.

"Something is wrong. Is something wrong with your child?" he asked.

"Yeah, he has scoliosis."

"Oh, *scoliosis!*" the cab driver looked relieved, smiling, "I know scoliosis. He needs massage, that will fix him."

Kai forced a polite, thin smile.

"*Good* massage. My cousin had scoliosis, and he is cured by this massage. Took two weeks." The man seemed quite proud of his advice. She didn't want to get into a longer conversation, Kai told herself it would take too much to explain.

"Thank you—this is the building, can you wait out here for me for a few minutes?" she was already getting out of the cab as he nodded.

Inside Dr. Conroy's office, she waited at the desk for the X-ray copies. The woman with the salt and pepper hair in a bun smiled at her sympathetically again. Just as the receptionist handed her the X-rays in an envelope, Dr. Conroy approached the desk from the inner office. He saw Kai and smiled, he always *had* been happy to see her boobs.

"Hello, Kai! Did you go to see Dr. Lowther about your boy's scoliosis?" he asked cheerfully, walking out the door to the waiting room and reaching out to shake her hand.

Kai avoided his hand awkwardly. "Can I ask you a question, Dr. Conroy?"

"Sure," he replied.

"What is an RVAD angle?"

"Uh...not sure, I don't think I've ever heard of that," his smile disappeared.

"It stands for *Rib Vertebral Angle Difference*, and it's a good indicator of whether or not scoliosis in a young child will be progressive and dangerous."

He just looked baffled, now, not sure why this young woman was trying to "school him" about his 30 year orthopedic practice. For the briefest moment, Kai felt a surge of anger at this man's ignorance, ignorance and arrogance that had already cost her child valuable time, while his spine kept dangerously curving. Wasn't it his *responsibility as a physician* to stay on top of the latest cures for a baby's *potentially fatal spinal condition*? Isn't a doctor's moral and ethical standard "First, do no *harm*"? She thought of his idiotic *tube of toothpaste* reference, and again imagined smacking him hard, over his bald little head, with his own tiny shoe—which might have a good impact—because she was certain he wore lifts.

"Maybe you should spend a little more time deepening your medical knowledge in order to help children with *life threatening spinal deformities*, rather than searching for the answers between my *tits*," she announced.

Then she turned on her heels and walked out of the office, leaving him standing there with his mouth open and a dumb look on his face, right in front of the patients who were waiting to see him next.

She didn't feel proud of herself; she just felt mad, mad and scared. She walked back to the waiting cab, thinking she was really going to have to buy a car at some point—this could get expensive, but she had to get that package in the mail as soon as possible.

On the way back to the hotel, she asked the cab driver to quickly stop by Whole Foods, so she could get some organic milk and fruit and snacks for Fin to have in the room. When he dropped her at the hotel and he was helping her to take the groceries out of the cab, the driver smiled at her.

"You have troubles, if you don't mind my saying
so, but remember you are *very* blessed. Children are the
joy of the world. They are a blessing."

"Yes, they are," Kai smiled through her worry,
and she meant it.

"If not massage, *dance!*" he suddenly exclaimed.
Kai looked at him, confused, clutching her grocery bags a
little more tightly.

"You take your child to dancing lessons, that will
straighten out the body!" he smiled, then did an
impromptu little dance for her, spinning around on his
heels and doing some form of a Fred Astaire slide, with
his arms spread out. The hotel valets and other hotel
guests waiting for their cars looked on in disbelief. *Jazz
hands*, Kai thought, *really?*

If it hadn't been so bizarre, it would've been very
funny. Her life had been turned upside down, and now
this sixty year old Middle Eastern man was doing a jig for
her in front of the Four Seasons Hotel in Beverly Hills.

Strange world.

"Thank you, I'll consider that," she replied,
handing him some money with a generous tip. "I'm Kai,
what is your name?"

"Fadi, my name is Fadi."

"I'll make sure to ask for you, Fadi, the next time I
need a cab."

He smiled, "Please," and nodded goodbye, as she
turned and walked into the hotel.

She realized he was trying to help. It was sweet,
but misguided. Massage and dance could do a lot of
wonderful, healing things, but it was not going to stop her
child's spine from aiming to crush his vital organs.

She took the elevator up to the room, clutching the
X-rays and MRI and bag of groceries, thinking that she
really had to buy a car. The cab fare and tip had cost
nearly all of her money allotted for that day. She had
owned a clunker car, before she met Teddy, but he

insisted she get rid of it when she moved in with him—he said it wasn't safe—it could break down on the freeway. Kai had donated it to a charity that supported AIDS research, it still ran fine. She had meant to buy a new car, but since Teddy mostly worked from home and she was always home with the baby, they hadn't had a strong need for it—she just drove Teddy's BMW for small errands.

She tried to control her rage at the concept that he had now dumped her, both she and their child on their duffs, Fin with a serious health problem—*without a vehicle*! What a winner she had picked in Teddy, what a champ of a father. How could she have put her trust in him so completely?

She glanced down at her large engagement ring again. She wanted to do something very violent to Teddy with it, but no—murder was out of the question—Fin depended on her. To the pawn shop it would go tomorrow. She hoped she could get a lot of dough; they would need to live on it for the foreseeable future while she got Fin's health care figured out. She didn't know how much he paid for it, but it was a pretty big ring—three carats.

God, it *better* be real, she hadn't even *considered* that! No, no, Teddy Verona had far too big an ego to get engaged with a cubic zirconia. For once, his pompous ego would help her and Fin, instead of hurt them.

The paternity test would have to wait, beyond these two weeks in the hotel with Doris, she didn't want his help right now. If he didn't want to be with his son when he needed him the most, she certainly didn't want to be around him. It was his loss, and it was a big one. She wondered if he even realized that he was missing the chance to try to save his own son's life.

With that kind of a man, that lack of character, she wasn't sure if she *ever* wanted the paternity test done. She didn't want his child support payments, begrudgingly sent only because it was the law. Not that women shouldn't take those child support payments, she knew many single mothers had to fight tooth and nail for them, but right now, she wasn't sure if she wanted Teddy's dirty money in Fin's life at all.

She entered the hotel suite and saw a note from Doris that read, "Kai, I took Fin for a stroll. We'll be back by 6."

Kai looked at the handwritten note, suddenly feeling paranoid. Could Doris be taking Fin to see Teddy? No, no way…should she be upset that Doris took him out without asking her first? No…babysitters did that all of the time, toddlers get restless without a change of scenery.

It was actually for the best, because she needed to write the letter to the doctor in Salt Lake City about what had happened so far. She put the milk in the minibar fridge, taking a couple of things out to make space. Hmmm…it was tempting to have a cocktail to relieve the stress, but no, she had work to do.

She sat down at her computer and wrote about Fin's curve progressing to 34 degrees, his MRI and syrinx cyst, and how she had spoken to Heather at ISOP and that she said that he, Dr. D'Astous, was the most experienced doctor in the U.S. doing this treatment. She asked him to please, *please* consider accepting Fin for casting, and thanked him for taking the time to read the letter and to take a look at Fin's X-rays and his first MRI. She explained that they were waiting on the date for the second MRI, but she had done her research and knew in her gut that this casting was the right choice for her child. She wrote that the curve appeared to be getting worse, and she knew the window to get him in for treatment under two years of age was narrowing dangerously fast. She tried to be polite and grateful and not to sound like a crazy person, because she knew her baby's life was on the line.

She finished the letter and took her computer drive down to the hotel front desk, where she asked them if they would be willing to print the letter up on their printer. They happily obliged, and she was already back in the room when Doris returned with Fin, who was happy as a clam from his outing in the great outdoors of Beverly Hills' Doheny Drive.

"Mama!" he cried happily, and she took him out of the stroller and kissed and hugged him on the bed joyously. "Oh, well," she joked, "I guess I'm the first woman he'll roll around on a bed with! Probably not the last, with these flirty eyes and this grin!" Doris smiled, going to wash out his bottle in the sink. Fin giggled as she did raspberries on his stomach, and they played patty cake and peekaboo, two classics that *never* go out of style. He then wriggled on to the floor and ran to flip through his favorite books.

Kai swung her legs off of the bed as Doris dried the bottle with a washcloth, "Hi Doris, I didn't mean to ignore you, I just missed him."

"No problem, he needs his mother's love and touch…there is no substitute for that," Doris replied.

Kai lowered her voice to make sure Fin couldn't hear her, "What about his father's love?"

Doris tuned to face her, "Ideally, he needs both…but many a mother has done it alone. In many countries, mothers wear multiple hats. They are the breath of the world, the feet upon which society stands. The mother's heart can contain the pain and the love of entire universe."

Kai looked up at her and nodded, moved.

"In my humble opinion, *Douche Bag* is not necessary for Fin to lead a happy life."

Kai started laughing and almost crying at the same time. How had Teddy The Prick hired such a great lady?

"Doris, I think we are gonna get along just *fine*. And I need your help on something. We have to take some photos."

"Photos?"

"Of Fin's back, his spine, without a shirt on—to send to the hospital in Salt Lake City. Do you know if Teddy had somebody pack my camera?"

Doris walked over to a drawer and took out a basic digital camera. "Even a fool can get things right a small percentage of the time. The law of averages," Doris smiled.

They spent the next hour taking pictures of Fin's back, with Doris keeping him happy and occupied with toys and books as Kai played amateur photographer, trying to get the best images she could. She finally got two that she liked—or more accurately, hated, because he was so obviously in trouble. One photo was in just his diaper or "nappy" as the Brits say, and one in his birthday suit, cutting it off just before his butt, so the doctor could see the small, sacral dimple just above it.

The scariest thing, the visual truth that lacerated her heart, was that the photos looked *much worse* than just looking at his back with the naked eye. It was as if the pictures captured what Kai didn't want to see, what her brain was partially protecting her from—her child already had a pretty severe deformity, and it was clearly getting worse by the day. It was certainly Progressive Infantile Scoliosis, because it was rapidly progressing at an astonishingly terrifying pace.

They put Fin to bed by seven and ordered some sandwiches from room service. Doris was quiet and had a book to read, which was a relief for Kai, she was exhausted from the long, emotional day.

Tom Petty had it right when he sang "*The waiting is the hardest part...*" Waiting to find out if Fin would be accepted to Shriners Hospital, waiting for the second MRI, where they'd be looking for brain tumors *dripping down into his spine*...she couldn't even think about that right now, she was so tired. She had to turn off her brain to sleep, she *had* to. By ten o'clock, she finally curled up, falling into a fitful sleep, despite the luxury bed she was lying on.

That night, she dreamed of the monstrous train. It was coming for her boy on a collision course, and it was, in fact, his very own spine.

10
Mother Fire

The nightmare was agonizing, and she was in it. The baby boy was tied to the tracks, crying hysterically, as a twenty year old Kai stood in the crowd of onlookers at the metro station, frozen in place.

She suddenly noticed the very handsome, dark haired young man in the crowd, with a small cleft in his chin. Teddy, of course, but in that way of dreams, the "her" in the dream didn't know it was him. It was as if they hadn't met, yet. Teddy was his current age, 26, but Kai was younger, the age she was just before her mother died—before tragedy had struck her life the first time.

She looked back at the baby boy crying. It was Fin, but since the Kai in her nightmare was the college age Kai, she didn't recognize him as her child.

Kai looked at the man, at Teddy— pleadingly— begging him with her eyes to help, *"Save him"*—but he slowly shook his head, backing away.

"It's not my baby," he said sadly, disappearing into the crowd.

The way the handsome man looked at her struck her as odd, surreal. This man, this dark stranger, *knew her*. And the way he looked at her told her something else—it hit her like a punch in the stomach. This baby no one was saving was *hers*. He had her wavy honey blonde hair, her green eyes. *Hers*.

The fear and pain was overwhelming, she desperately fought the urge to pass out, her dizzy, reeling mind was threatening to close down and black out. She was only twenty years old, she had never had a baby! She had never even been pregnant. But she knew—she now knew in her very cells that this baby boy was *her son.*

Suddenly, she could move her legs, and she dashed to the baby, lurching, then staggering forward and falling to her knees, struggling to untie the ropes with violently trembling hands. No one stopped her and no one tried to help her. She couldn't untie him, it was too complex, too twisted—wrapped around the metal tracks in complicated loops and knots…

NO NO NO NO NO NO NO, this couldn't be happening. The crowd just looked on silently, shaking their heads, as the sunlight danced like daggers off the metal of the charging, thundering train.

She was sobbing, now, realizing in that instant it was too late to save him. The doctors were giving up, walking away, and the malevolent train was almost upon them, an unstoppable beast. The engine roared, the wind created by the machine's force nearly blowing her away from the child, nearly knocking her away from her son. No, she had to be touching him. She *had* to.

She had time to escape, to leave him there, to live. That was no option.

Kai lay down on the tracks beside her baby and put her arms around her boy, holding him and starting to sing the only song she could think of, *Three Little Birds*, by Bob Marley. *"Don't worry…about a thing… 'cause every little thing's…gonna be alright…"*

The baby stopped crying as the train bore down. His big green eyes were trusting, now. They were flecked with bits of gold, exactly like hers, but hers were filled with terror. They locked eyes for a long moment, and he looked at her as if they were one, as if she was his safe place, she was his *home*. Her heart ached and guilt surged

101

through her body like a knife, as she looked to the sky. It was a sunny, blue-skied day. Palm Trees waved, dotting the horizon. How could anything bad ever happen to an innocent?

"*Please, God,*" Kai prayed, "*take me, not him.*"

Just before the train hit, Kai closed her eyes. The cruel tracks shook violently and she whispered "*Mama.*" The baby's tiny, warm hand touched her cheek, and everything became enveloped in an inky ocean of black.

Kai woke up in the hotel room, screaming.

Not the best situation, when you have a baby fast asleep in the crib next to you. Doris bolted up from bed as Fin began crying. Doris got to him first, and then Kai came to her senses and took him gently from her arms, softly singing Bob Marley's *Three Little Birds*, which helped calm him. Doris made a bottle of milk and Fin stopped crying.

Kai realized she had to pull it together, she had to get the package out by FedEx this morning. She got dressed quickly and called a cab, asking for Fadi.

Fadi pulled up and Kai met him outside, jumping in and asking him to take her to the CVS drugstore on Doheny and Wilshire, so she could print out the photos of Fin's back on their digital machine.

Fadi smiled, raising his single dark brow, "No dancing this morning?"

"No, Fadi, there's no time for dancing," Kai sighed wearily.

"There is *always* time for dancing," he insisted, as he pulled out from the hotel, on to Doheny Drive.

Kai printed out the photos at the drugstore and asked Fadi to take her to the nearest FedEx location. She went in and put everything in an envelope—the letter, the X-ray copies, the MRI on a disc, and the photos of Fin. She added in one of his cute face, too, as Heather had advised her to do. She addressed it to Shriners Intermountain Hospital in Salt Lake City and put attention to the Care Coordinator there, Angie Livingston, and the casting doctor, Dr. Jacques D'Astous. Once everything was in the envelope, she sealed it and kissed it and said a little prayer that Dr. D'Astous would help them.

"This must be important," said the young black women behind the desk, as she marked it overnight mail.

"It is..." Kai was holding her breath.

"We'll make sure it gets there safe and sound," the young woman replied with a smile, then she glanced down at Kai's hands, her eyes widening. Kai realized she was gripping the counter, white knuckled with fear.

Back in the cab, Fadi asked her what she was mailing, so she explained it to him in brief. He was fascinated.

"It's like applying to college," he said, "So much work and worry, and ultimately, it's out of your hands."

"No, we're a long way from college...I'm just trying to save my boy," Kai sighed.

"You are a very good mother. I think so. I am never wrong, about people. Cats, I cannot figure out, but people—I have a seventh sense."

"It's a sixth sense, isn't it?"

"Mine goes one greater. Seven is lucky, and my sense is lucky, too."

"I don't know if I believe in luck anymore, Fadi." Kai pressed her back against the seat. "I'm kind of in a crap storm right now."

"There is more than one kind of good luck. People miss this. If you are in a crap storm, perhaps you can still grab some corn."

It was too silly and far too gross to even laugh, but she did. These were her new friends, Doris and Fadi. She was begging to be accepted to a charity hospital. There was no room for snobbery or highfalutin judgement in this new world of hers.

"You know what, Fadi?" she smiled, "There *is* always time to dance. And you should always dance like the whole world is blind."

"Oh, I *do*!" he grinned.

"I know, I've seen it," she laughed. Was there laughter in a world where kids got sick? Yes, she thought, it was the very essence of survival. "Do you know a good pawn shop around here?"

Fadi did. He drove her to the nicest pawn shop in Beverly Hills, where she walked in and saw many people's former treasures in the display case: engagement and wedding rings, diamond chandelier earrings, sapphire bracelets, ruby necklaces and baubles of all kinds, gems that would take you over the rainbow of jewelry lust and desire.

Kai looked at these beautiful things and thought of the pain that people went through, bringing them here. People like her, or much richer, who lost their marriages, their homes—their lives as they knew them. That was certainly a price above sapphires.

A middle aged Persian man came out to the counter and smiled at her, "May I help you?"

"Hi, I have an engagement ring…" she held it out to him. She had brought the official papers, certifying the diamond's nearly perfect color and clarity.

He looked it over, nodding. "It's gorgeous," he said, "three carats, from the nineteen forties."

Kai nodded and smiled, "My relationship was not as gorgeous."

"When you come here with the ring—that is usually the case," the man replied simply, but not unkindly. He examined it with a jeweler's loupe, declaring, "I'm the owner. I can give you thirty thousand dollars for this ring, today."

Kai sighed, relieved. She had read online that it could be anywhere from seventeen to fifty thousand, and thirty was not bad—considering it was not being sold at

Tiffany's. She noticed a shiny white baby grand piano in the back of the shop, wondering who had to hock their baby grand and why. Too many stories in this place, it was overwhelming to think about. She had enough of a story on her own plate, right now.

"You, sir, have a deal," she said, shaking the owner's hand.

Fadi drove her back to the hotel She kept touching her ringless finger—it suddenly felt naked, vulnerable.

Fadi was watching her in the rearview mirror. "You are very young. You must go forward and love as if you've never been hurt before."

"Fadi," Kai smiled, "are you my Yoda?"

"No. I am your Fadi," he said, quite seriously, "and that is a quote from Souza. I hope your boy gets into this special hospital, this health college application...I will pray to Allah."

"Thank you, I'll take it. I'll be praying a lot, too," she said.

He dropped her back at the hotel and she suddenly realized that the waiting was now to really begin. She tipped Fadi and kissed him lightly on the cheek, he smelled earthy and sweet. She was swimming to where it was warm, and right now it was warm with Fin, Doris and Fadi. Strange life, strange world.

Back in their suite, Fin was happily jumping on the bed, while Doris stood next to him, holding her arms out around him, ready to catch him if he stumbled. "Don't worry, he is in the circle of safety," Doris said.

"Today we're going to the pool!" Kai announced, grabbing her little boy and hugging him as he giggled. "Teddy is paying for it, we may as well enjoy it."

The Four Seasons' pool was lovely. They women sat on lounge chairs and let Fin splash around, while they both ordered salads and iced teas, and took turns holding him in the water. While in the pool with Fin, Kai thought for a moment about going under in the dark pool that night at Teddy's house, when she felt like she was drowning. She still felt scared to death for Fin's future, but he was so happy in the water, she couldn't let on to him how it was crushing her inside. "*Smile…though your heart is breaking…*" as Charlie Chaplin sang, that was the appropriate song for her life, right now. Fin was innocent to her pain, and he should stay that way.

One thing she had read about the casts was that kids couldn't get wet in them, of course, because they were made of plaster. Well, fiberglass and plaster and padding, but mostly plaster, and plaster can melt. The two big "play" things kids couldn't do in the casts were swim or play in sand, because sand could get inside the cast and irritate the child's skin, or worse, cause a dangerous cast sore that could become infected.

It wasn't lost on her that she had named her baby Fin, her little fishie, because of her love of the beach and sand and the ocean, so she tried to soak it in, this moment, watching him have fun splashing in the pool. She didn't tear up or cry, she was *so* sick of crying—she told herself that she had to be a *warrior* for her child—she was the only advocate for his health and safety. His dad didn't want that role, and there was nothing she could do to force him to be here. His loss, but also Fin's….

She would not, *could not* think about that, right now. Sometimes she just had this overwhelming feeling of panic when she let herself live in her fears for Fin. She knew what it felt like to grow up without a dad, to be abandoned by your biological father, both physically and emotionally. For one, it affected your self-esteem, because that small child in you can't help but think, *If my own dad didn't love me, maybe I'm not really lovable? Maybe I did something to make him want to leave? Maybe I cried too much as a baby, maybe I was too difficult, not cute enough? Flawed in some way.* And wasn't Teddy running away from Fin because he perceived him as flawed, an unwanted wrinkle in his perfect life that he couldn't iron out?

Maybe this hole in your heart doesn't show on the outside, but it is a deep, deep wound, Kai knew that firsthand. Your mom can be a lot of things, but she can't be your father figure, there for you day in and day out, listening to your problems and worries, helping you with your homework, telling you that you're special, even when the boys at school make fun of you because you're too short or too tall or you have big feet. Besides surfing, Kai didn't play sports, she wouldn't know how to teach Fin how to throw a football or play soccer or hit a home run.

Later, back up in the room, Kai put Fin down for his nap, and as he looked up at her with total love and trust in his eyes, he said, "*Best.*"

"Yes," she beamed, her heart swelling with love, "You're my baby and you are my *best* friend."

Fin snuggled up to go to sleep and Doris went to take a bath, while Kai went online to do some more research about his condition and the ISOP organization. What she found out absolutely blew her mind.

Heather Hyatt-Montoya founded ISOP as a single mother who was desperately searching for a cure for her own child's rapidly progressing scoliosis. Her daughter Olivia's curve had reached an extremely dangerous 100 degrees by age two and a half. Her doctors in Denver had tried bracing her curve, but she continued to rapidly get worse in the brace, as often happens in progressive cases. What was medically offered for Olivia's future was deterioration and ultimately, fusion of her young spine, long before her torso was fully grown, which meant certain lifelong deformity and severe lung problems.

Heather began researching the globe for a better answer for her daughter. Only one doctor out of at least twenty orthopedists in her home state of Colorado suggested serial plaster casting for Olivia, but it was not even available in U.S. hospitals at the time, back in 2000. This one doctor who suggested casting did not personally practice it, and said that U.S. doctors back then generally considered casting to be archaic and ineffective—like Teddy accused, a "barbaric" thing to do to a baby or young child. In the past, some doctors who saw children with curves of 90 degrees or above were told to simply *"Take their child home to die."* Kai shuddered in horror, imagining the mothers holding their precious babies and being told this, by so-called "trusted" medical professionals.

After reaching out to doctors in England, Scotland, Spain, Holland and France, Heather reached a French doctor who was close to retirement, who agreed that Olivia needed treatment immediately and that her scoliosis could no longer be ignored by the medical community. The French doctor recommended halo gravity traction with a turnbuckle cast, which would correct her scoliosis gently and could buy her valuable growth time for her chest cavity before she needed any surgical intervention.

Heather considered moving to France to get help for Olivia, but Dr. Jacques D'Astous, who she had been conferring with at Shriners Hospital in Salt Lake City, informed her that this French doctor would be visiting Salt Lake before he retired. This pioneering doctor at Shriners Hospital, D'Astous, agreed to apply Early Treatment with a Mehta cast on a young twin boy whose family had contacted Heather for help, and the child miraculously grew straight!

After doing that first successful cast, Dr. D'Astous agreed with the French doctor's recommendation for treating Olivia and proceeded with a complicated procedure to save Olivia's spine, applying halo gravity traction combined with a turnbuckle cast, but her curves had gotten too severe to be cured without surgery.

Heather had missed the window to save her own daughter from multiple invasive and complicated surgeries, and now she *damn well* didn't want that to happen to anyone else's child.

She began the ISOP website in order to reach other families and share information about this condition. Then Heather heard of and connected with Dr. Min Mehta, a female doctor born in India, who had practiced for many years in the U.K.

Dr. Mehta had recently retired from The Royal National Orthopedic Hospital in London and Stanmore, and she had already straightened over 100 infants and young children by treating them in her Early Treatment method of EDF serial corrective casting. Kai couldn't believe what she was reading: Dr. Mehta followed the progress of her patients for over ten years, finding they remained straight—*CURED*!

Kai had to remind herself to breathe as she took it all in. So many people with diseases are desperately searching for a cure, and this potentially fatal and deforming condition in babies and young kids *had one*. And somehow, most of the best doctors and hospitals in Los Angeles and the world did not practice it, know about it, or believe in it? How was this even *possible*?

Stunned, but energized, Kai's eyes flew across the screen. EDF stood for Elongation, Derotation and Flexion, which is a technique of using a three dimensional table to correct scoliosis, which is a three dimensional problem—a complex "corkscrewing" of the spine, rather than a simple curve. U.S. doctors had generally only been taught Risser casting, which is done on a basic, two dimensional flat table. Two French doctors in the 1960s named Morel and Cotrel improved the traditional Risser casting technique by adding a third dimension of correction called *Derotation*. This technique was first invented to be used only on adolescents and adults, in order to obtain and maintain correction of scoliosis post a surgical operation, or to try to halt a severe curve from getting worse.

Dr. Mehta's pioneering breakthrough was in using this method on babies and young children with progressive scoliosis with the goal not to just *hold* a curve, but to actually *cure* it. She realized that by applying three dimensional casting to babies early, she could harness an infant's rapid rate of growth and literally "train" their young spine to grow straight, gently and permanently.

Mehta modified the EDF casts to fit the bodies of infants and children, she was a scoliosis sufferer herself and discovered she could use a smaller version of the Cotrel table; a child sized one, and cure kids with a quite simple solution for what has been the most horribly difficult pediatric orthopedic condition to treat *in human history*.

Dr. Mehta was brilliant and *right*, it worked, especially if the treatment was begun before age two, beginning with a 50-60 degree curve or less.

Kai felt her heart palpitating in her chest. Fin's X-ray had already measured in the 30s at only 18 months. What if he got much worse before he received his first cast? Kai steadied her breath and reminded herself that in this moment, she couldn't control that, but she *could* educate herself.

She dove back in, reading that the reason starting early was so vital was that the human spine grows 50 percent in the first two years of life, so that is the best time to harness the child's own natural rapid growth with this gentle, non-surgical method.

Mehta also added a uniquely large, "mushroom" shaped, open window cut-out in the front of the casts, to allow for room for the kid's lungs and stomachs to be comfortable, to be able to expand to breathe and eat. She designed front and back cut-outs to prevent rib deformities that had sometimes happened with the much smaller, circular, "front only" cut-out of old fashioned Risser casts. The strategically placed cut out in the back of her cast design is to help correct the child's rotation/spinal twisting with the expansion of their every breath.

It took training to learn to do the method right, and each child was unique, but it was and is a cure made of something that costs almost nothing, and that most people played with as kids: *simple plaster*. The basic idea, it seemed to Kai, was almost like braces on teeth, or the re-direction of a vine growing up a wall, a slow correction to becoming as straight as possible.

She sat back in her chair at the hotel room desk, blown away. Dr. Mehta had been doing this practice, this cure, for decades; she had even published a respected medical paper in the U.K. documenting her findings. Even with all of that proof, doctors had flat out told Heather that Mehta's style of casting did not work and continued to offer only ineffective bracing and painful, deforming surgeries to these kids.

Kai went on the C.A.S.T. online support group and learned even more from the other parents there. These spinal surgeries have a very high complication rate when done on young children. This could result in grisly consequences- Kai saw several photos of kids with severe deformities that had received spinal surgeries, (medically called "surgical intervention with distraction rods") as toddlers. Years later, at age 7, 8, 9 and 10 they were experiencing pain and still undergoing procedures like Halo traction, that metal halo with bolts in the child's small skull that Kai had seen in the movie "Fight Club."

At first, Kai recoiled at the image of the metal halo, with an increasing weight that is lifting the child's head to the sky, a weight that older children have to pull around behind them on a bulky wheeled contraption when they walk. It was a frightening looking thing, but then she found out that in cases where the child is not cured by casting in time, if they miss that crucial window, the halo can buy very valuable growing time for the child—in a desperate effort to save their lung function and to put off spinal surgery for as long as possible.

In other words, that horrible looking contraption was a *good* thing, if things got that bad. Kai could never imagine, in a million years, that she would have thought of something like that metal halo on a kid as a good thing, but now with what Fin was potentially facing—she understood why a parent would choose it. They simply were making the best choice for their child's health that was available to them at the time.

Her research brought her to another extreme looking thing some parents chose to stave off spinal surgery and give their child more time to grow, something called VEPTR rods, which are expandable rods, surgically implanted inside the kid's body, outside of the child's rib cage. These rods didn't touch the spine and had a similar function to the halo, to provide structure and growing time, to prevent the child's spine from compromising, crushing or collapsing their lungs. They had to be surgically expanded as the child grew, involving more cutting, more hospitalization and more painful surgical procedures.

Even scarier, surgical "hardware" like VEPTR and growth rods are only able to be used for approximately three and a half years of the child's life once the first surgery has begun, with surgical "lengthenings" done every six months. So let's say, the first surgery takes place at age three- after 6 or 7 surgeries, by age six, the child is out of options! And what happens then?

Kai found out from Heather Montoya that the medical community is now finding these surgeries can lead to the child's spine spontaneously fusing prematurely, meaning stopping growing for life. *Fin could be full height by age 6, 7 or 8 years old*. He would be like a dwarf, or at least deformed, never growing to his full height. And the pain, the back pain, what would he experience? It sounded like torture…

Of course, Kai didn't blame any parents for making the best choice available to them, if surgery were the best option for Fin, she knew she would do the same in their position.

Spinal growth rods with magnetic expansion were on the medical horizon, but it was still unknown when they would be widely available, or how safe they would be in the long run. It was still pretty experimental, which was obviously scary when it involved metal and magnets going into your child's back or spine, not to mention the extreme pain and recovery from the initial surgery. Kai had seen photos and read stories on the support group about a child's recovery from the surgery, too, firsthand accounts of what it was like, and it was devastating to read and look at. It stayed with her and haunted her thoughts.

Kai agonized for these innocent children and their families. They didn't *deserve* this, their small bodies cut open time after time, and these were the things her baby Fin would have to face by age two or three, without Kai finding ISOP. She would've listened to her doctors and done bracing, which would've failed, then Fin would have begun to be put under the knife before preschool. Had the Internet saved her baby's life, she asked herself? Or— could she already be too late?

And money was involved, too—*avarice*—she found out that the stink and rot of greed played a role in nearly altering her child's life for the worse. A child with a decade of bracing and surgeries could cost the insurance company *over a million dollars per child*. Mehta casting cost a fraction of that and was a painless, potential cure. Were these doctors and hospitals considering *their own pockets* when suggesting bracing and repeated spinal surgeries for Fin? Or were these obviously ineffective and invasive treatment recommendations due to complete ignorance? Were these doctors idiots, or was her child an *ATM machine* to them, was it all about *money*???

Anger, anger and rage began to boil inside her. *First, do no harm!*

A chill ran up her back and neck—she would give Fin her own spine, if only she could.

Heather had been in this quest, this battle, for nearly a decade to save other children, even though it was yet too late to cure her own child with casts. She had helped bring Dr. Mehta to Shriners Hospital to train Olivia's doctor, Dr. D'Astous, in her method, and as Heather had told her, he was one of the first U.S. physicians to practice Mehta casting in the States. D'Astous had previously been exposed to the Cotrel-Morel EDF technique when he was a fellow in France in 1978 and also in 1982, but after Miss Mehta came over to visit, he changed to using the appropriate table for the ideal technique. Without Heather's quest and purity of intentions, there would be *no* doctor properly trained to do this for Fin to go to, maybe no doctor in the U.S. would be doing it *at all*. If Fin were to be saved, she had this force-of-nature single mother to thank, a woman she had never even met in person. The weight of that boggled her mind.

An hour later, Kai's cell phone rang. It was Angie, the Care Coordinator from Shriners Hospital, who said, "Dr. D'Astous has looked at Fin's X-rays and Fin has been accepted for casting treatment!" Kai ran out into the hallway of the hotel and shouted with joy, jumping up and down.

There was only one problem. The earliest date they could get was March 30th, and Fin's second MRI was scheduled for *April 1st*. She would have to beg to get that MRI moved up, some way, somehow.

She thanked Angie profusely and said "We'll be there!" Then she asked, "Can Fin be put on a cancellation list for his first cast date, if anything opens up sooner?

We'll be there in a heartbeat, we'll be on a plane the next day. No, the *same* day!" She knew from her research he would likely be getting worse with every week that passed, that the train of his spine was not stopping.

Angie said, "Yes, I completely understand," and told Kai to expect an information sheet arriving in the mail. They said their goodbyes, Kai's nerves still buzzing with anxious excitement.

She pressed "end" on her cell phone, exhaled, and her whole body trembled with a strange mix of gratitude and residual anger. She thought about Heather—how do you thank someone for saving your child's life, for untying them from the tracks and letting them have a chance to live without pain and deformity, to laugh and play and easily *breathe*—to live a normal life and run free, as all children should be able to do?

There are no words. Heather was one brave, tough Mama, and she was simply an angel on Earth. What would motivate a single mother with her own child to raise, a child with serious health problems, to fight this battle for children she had never met, many who had not even been born, yet?

Passion, Kai thought, passion and tenacity for justice, mixed with *rage*—rage and anger that this was being allowed to happen to her own child—that *any* child had slipped through the cracks of our health care system, right here in America. When a cure was possible that was made of simple plaster, it was shameful, it was wrong, and it was borderline *criminal*.

Now Kai knew that there was a cure for what Fin had, but the clock was ticking, fast and mercilessly. She fell to her knees and prayed that the clock would not run out for her boy.

11
Fire and Ice

The poet Robert Frost knew that you could burn from ice, as well as from fire. As Kai prepared for the trip to the snow and ice of Salt Lake City in the winter, her world appeared to be going down in flames—one of the only positives was that her mother fire had been *lit*—and it was burning bright.

Within ten minutes of getting off the phone with Angie at Shriners, she was in the cab with Fadi behind the wheel, flying down the 10 freeway to downtown L.A., to Mercy Children's Hospital. She intended to talk to Dr. Becket. Fadi was a man on a mission, now that she had explained to him the facts about Fin's condition. He insisted she not pay for fares related to Fin's care, her money was no good with him—and said that he would be personally driving them to the airport, for the flight to Utah.

"Politely pushy." That was the advice she'd been given on the C.A.S.T. online support group—to be the best advocate for your child with medical professionals, being "politely pushy" to get them the care that they needed in time. She had long ago decided that when asking for a favor, it was best to do it in person—if at all possible. It was like a hostage situation, when hostages keep telling their captors their names and personal things, in order to humanize themselves to the prison guard—so the captors can't so easily *de*-humanize them.

116

Fadi weaved in and out of traffic, sweat beading on his brow. "Maybe I should come in with you, sometimes people listen more seriously to a man."

He was trying to help, not being intentionally sexist, she knew. Sadly, in some cases, he was probably right. "Hopefully not in this day and age, but I understand what you mean. But this doctor *will* listen to me today, believe me, or he's gonna need a flak jacket," she smiled. There is nothing more dangerous than a mama bear who will lay down her life for her child. *Nothing*.

Kai walked into Dr. Becket's office, Fin's neurologist, and approached the desk. She asked to speak to the doctor briefly, when he was between appointments if possible, explaining it was kind of an emergency. The office had several assistants at the desk, and the first woman she talked to said, "He has no spare time between appointments today, the Doctor is extremely busy."

She waited until that woman walked away from the desk for a moment, and found another assistant working there, a young Latina woman with dark, curly hair. "Hi, my name is Kai," she said, smiling, "are you a mother?"

"Yes," the young woman said, a little apprehensively, "I have two kids."

"So you understand. May I ask, what is your name?" Kai asked in a friendly manner.

"It's…Lorna," she replied tentatively, obviously wondering where this was going.

"Lorna, my eighteen month old baby, Fin, is scheduled for a second MRI here at Mercy, just to rule some things out, but he has an earlier appointment now at a Shriners charity hospital to treat his life threatening scoliosis. We may even get in on an earlier cancellation, if we're lucky. You understand, as a mother, that you would do *anything* to save your baby pain and suffering, and in this case, severe, lifelong deformity and lung problems. Could you please let me speak to Dr. Becket, just for a *moment* between patients, to explain the urgency of the situation? I would be forever grateful."

Lorna looked both taken aback and concerned, "If you have a seat in the waiting room, I'll get in the doctor's ear, honey," she said.

Kai sat down and waited anxiously near the fish tank, watching the fish go around the coral and a kitschy sunken plastic pirate ship. The other parents and kids, mostly Latino families, sat quietly in the chairs across from her as she fidgeted. In twenty minutes, Lorna came back up to the desk, "Kai?"

Kai jumped up, approaching the desk with light speed, "Yes, Lorna?"

"The doctor can see you for three minutes," Lorna smiled, leading Kai back to the doctor's office, where he sat behind his desk. Just like last time, the young Dr. Becket looked handsome, but tired.

Kai didn't even sit, she knew she had just a few minutes to plead her case. "Doctor, hi, thank you *so much* for squeezing me in. I know that you want my son Fin to get one more MRI of his brain and spine, but he is now set to be casted for his severely, dangerously progressing scoliosis one day before our MRI is scheduled. I also know that L.A. Mercy does the most anesthesia on children of any hospital in the city, so I assume your team is the most experienced with this. We even have a chance to get in to Shriners sooner, if there's a cancellation…Now *believe me*, I don't think any one child is more important than any other, but if you could keep an eye out for Fin, for a cancellation…he has a condition where weeks *matter*. Weeks and even *days* can matter in his future quality of life, and I just can't let him down on this—you know? I am not a perfect person by any stretch of the imagination, but this is something I just *cannot fail at*."

Her lower lip was quivering; she hadn't even taken a breath. She looked at him with pleading eyes, *please, please, please*…her bleeding heart palpitating in her chest.

Dr. Becket sighed, "Kai, I can't promise anything, as you know; our Radiology department is often booked for appointments two months out…"

Kai felt like a volcano was about to erupt inside of her, "*My son doesn't have two months*! I don't know how long he has, he could be having a growth spurt right now, for all I know, and his spine could be curving fast enough to crush his little heart and lungs! Do you want that on your *conscience*?!" Kai realized she was yelling at this perfectly nice doctor, this skilled surgeon who was tops in his field—someone who had done nothing wrong. She felt like maybe she had flipped her lid, he sure must think so.

He blinked, surprised by her outburst, but his eyes were compassionate and his voice was calm, "I promise you, I will do *everything in my power* to make sure the people in charge of the cancellation list know the serious nature of Fin's condition. You and your husband can rest assured that I'll do my best," he smiled, his tired young eyes crinkling at the edges.

"He's not my husband, he left us," Kai blurted out. Again, she thought to herself, *crazy lady*. Things were just popping out of her mouth before she could get her head on straight. She tried to pull herself together, attempting to muster a single shred of dignity. "Thank you so much for trying, and for listening to me," she said sincerely, "I really, *really* appreciate it, Doctor Becket."

"Please, it's Jack."

"Sorry, thank you Doctor, um…Jack," she awkwardly turned to go.

"And Kai," he said, stopping her a moment, "you are *not* failing at this. Your little boy is lucky to have you."

She shook her head, swallowing a sob. "No, *I'm* the lucky one," she said, and rushed out of his office. He watched her go, exhaling and rubbing his face in his hands.

Outside the hospital, Fadi was in his cab waiting, suddenly on guard as he saw her come out of the building looking upset. "Shall I beat him senseless?" he asked, as she climbed into the back.

"No, he's very nice...he's a good man...he'll do everything he can to help. It's just...scary."

Fadi nodded, giving Kai her privacy as she sunk down into the back seat, her hands over her face, her shoulders softly shaking the whole way home.

Back at the hotel, she sat down in the bar area at a small table. The bar was pretty empty at the moment, and she purposefully sat away from the few tables that had other people at them, finally calling her sister Janie from her cell phone and telling her about the casts, and Fin being accepted to Shriners.

Janie paused a long moment, then said, "Kai, I'm so, so sorry to hear about this happening to little Fin. You should've called me sooner, I could've had our whole congregation praying for him to be spontaneously healed of this scoliosis problem."

Kai bit her lower lip. "Um...it's not that I don't believe in miracles, Janie, but maybe it wouldn't have been cured just from prayer."

"Prayer is a *known entity*, Kai, prayer circles have made major differences in countless situations." Janie was beginning to sound annoyed.

"I believe that, but if I don't get this cast on him in time, his life will be forever altered for the worse. Please have the congregation pray that we get the cast on soon enough to avoid all of these multiple surgeries he'd have to face."

"I've never heard of a body cast for scoliosis, and I have to be honest, I'm not sure I like the idea of it on a little baby. It'll be heavy and rough on his skin, it could be itchy and hot...he might feel like he's *suffocating*.

What if he can't breathe well or eat in it, Kai? Can you take if off when he eats?"

"No, you can't take it off…it's about continuous correction, they can only remove it when he has a cast change, every two to three months," she explained.

"YOU CAN'T GIVE HIM A *BATH* FOR *THREE MONTHS*?!" Janie shrieked.

Kai cringed, she hated that part, too, but what choice did she have?

"He'll STINK, Kai!!! Oh my Heavens, that is *cruel*! He'll smell like a little *homeless* man!"

"I'm worried about that, but the other moms on the support group for this condition say it's not as bad as you think it'll be. I can wash his hair and give him sponge baths, and then full baths between the cast changes, make it a special thing."

"What about diaper leaks, what about *POOP*?!" Janie sounded horrified. It was as if Kai had told her she was inviting satan over to help BBQ her child over hot coals. "*Poop smells*!"

"I *KNOW* POOP SMELLS!" Kai suddenly noticed a few people had sat at nearby tables and were staring at her, now, overhearing her conversation. She got up and walked into the front lobby, anxiously pacing.

Janie continued on her diatribe, "Number two gets everywhere when you change a two year old's diaper…on your hands…they, have *blow-outs*, they try to stick their little hands down there. I don't care how many wipes you use, once in a while, there are accidents…What if he pees while you're changing his diaper? Won't that soak into the plaster? I mean, *yuck*, Kai…"

"I'll do my best—I don't really know—I don't even have the cast on him, yet!" Kai was getting exasperated.

"Well, what does Teddy think about all this?"

"He's…not crazy about the idea, to be honest."

"Well, he's the father, he has a say."

"Not really, Janie, he dumped us!" Kai snapped.

"He...*what*?" Janie gasped.

"He kicked me and Fin out of his house with no warning. Bags on the front lawn, cab waiting outside. He put us in a hotel." There, she said it.

There was a long silence. Janie exhaled, "*Oh.*" She paused again, finally murmuring, "Well, God doesn't give you more than you can handle."

"Well Janie, then He must think I'm *Superwoman*," Kai sighed.

"I always felt you should've gotten married before that baby was born. You should've gotten that wedding band on your finger."

"*I told you so*?" Kai rolled her eyes. "*Really*, Janie?"

"What is Teddy saying, about visitation rights and custody?"

"Nothing. I don't know if he'll even be in Fin's life. He acted like he may not be the father."

Another long silence. "*Is* he?" Janie couldn't help but ask.

Kai blinked, stunned, then angrily hung up on her. *UGH*! Was her sister implying she was both a liar and a slut? That she would try to trap a man in marriage with a child who wasn't even his?

That's why she didn't call her sister before this, that and the fact that she'd been in a whirlwind, downward life spiral. She didn't need this kind of bad energy right now, she really didn't, she had to self-protect.

She got in the elevator, rushed back to the hotel room, and hugged her precious boy. Doris was ironing a pair of jeans—Kai's jeans.

"Doris, um, you don't have to iron jeans," Kai said, trying not to snap.

"It looks neater," Doris replied.

"Please don't iron creases into my jeans, it looks weird…I'm a very casual person," she said, thinking how strange that suddenly sounded to her own ears. She wasn't barefoot Kai with bohemian rope sandals on her footloose and fancy free feet, anymore. She was a scared, worried young mom with the weight of the world on her shoulders. She felt a thousand years older than that "young Kai," even older than the Kai who had suddenly lost her Mom. She could never be that carefree young woman anymore, she had crossed over. She had crossed that great divide from non-parent to parent, and then the one that *no one* wishes to cross, the great divide between parents whose children had never had a serious health problem, parents like Janie, to the ones whose kids did.

What would she give to be able to go back? *Anything*, anything but Fin. She wouldn't give him back, no matter the price. The love was too huge, all encompassing, and she was truly grateful, so grateful to God that she got to experience that love. It shocked her to realize that she meant those words—*no matter the price*.

She closed her eyes to pray, praying out loud, right in front of Doris—this was no time to hold on to stupid pride.

"Please God, I know you think I'm resilient, but don't think I'm *too* resilient, don't think I could handle it if I lost him. And guess what? I am *angry* with you! First my Mom, and now *this* is happening, to my *baby*? IT'S NOT FAIR! HE DOESN'T DESERVE THIS!" Kai yelled at the hotel room ceiling, forcing herself to stop, so that she wouldn't scare Fin.

She checked on him, playing with a wooden train push toy. He didn't look upset. Maybe he would grow up used to having a crazy mother who freaked out and shouted at ceilings, Kai mused.

"I'm sorry to have yelled like that, in front of you and Fin," she mumbled to Doris, a little embarrassed, "please don't call Child Protective Services on me."

"It's OK to be angry with God," Doris replied, "God can take it."

Kai's cell phone rang and she just stared at it. "I can't answer it."

"Do you want me to answer it for you?" asked Doris.

"Sure."

Doris picked up the phone, saying "Hello?" in her Jamaican accent. "I did not hang up on you, Ma'am."

"Janie," Kai sighed, holding out her hand for the phone, "Yes?" she waited to see what Janie had to say for herself.

"Who was that woman with the accent on your phone?" Janie demanded.

"Doris."

"Doris? Who's Doris?"

"She's our temporary nanny."

"Oh. Well, I am calling because I assume Teddy is not going with you to this Salt Lake City charity hospital, so I'll go."

Kai realized that Janie was now playing "the good sister," the role she thought she should play. "I don't want you to come, you're against the treatment he's gonna be receiving."

"Just because I don't believe in it, doesn't mean you're not still family. You can't go alone."

"I won't be alone, I'll be with Fin."

"You know what I mean." Janie's tone was clipped.

"I can do it by myself."

"Oh, Kai, where are you right now? Where are you living? Not in that rickety beach shack, I hope."

"In a hotel, a very nice hotel. Teddy paid for it for two weeks."

"That's nice, I guess."

"Not really, Janie, he kicked out his only son and the mother of his child."

"I didn't call back to fight, I'm trying to help you. Where are you going to live after these two weeks?"

"We'll have to rent an apartment, I don't know where." Kai hadn't started looking for one, yet, it was another thing that was still on her increasingly heavy plate.

"Do you have money?"

"Yes, for now, I sold the engagement ring to a pawn shop."

Doris looked up, brows raised—she hadn't heard that part, yet.

"That's depressing," Janie said, stating the obvious.

"Yes, it *is* depressing." Kai could not believe her sister sometimes.

"Okay, it can take time to find a place to live, you better start looking. Didn't you sell your car?"

"Yeah, a nice cab driver has been driving us the last couple of days."

"You have to get a car. Those cab drivers in L.A. don't maintain the engines or brakes, it's not safe for Fin," Janie insisted.

"How do you know they don't maintain their engines?"

"I was in one once, coming from the airport, and the engine died on Pico Boulevard."

Kai rolled her eyes, "That was *one time*, Janie, you can't judge an entire profession based on one bad experience. That would be like me becoming a lesbian because Teddy's male and he's a *prick*!"

"I don't know how you threatening to go against God and nature in your sexuality has anything to do with this conversation!" Janie snapped.

"Oh, we are *not* having the homosexuality-is-against-the-Bible conversation, are we? What century are you living in?" Kai snapped back.

"*This* one, Kai, and I can't believe you're even thinking of dating at a time like this."

"I'm NOT thinking about dating! I just said I can't give up on the whole male population for life because Teddy's a PRICK!!!"

"I *hate* when you curse, Kai, you *know* I hate that. I'm hanging up."

"Thanks for the warning," Kai spat.

Janie said, "Blessings," not meaning it, and hung up.

Kai wanted to smash the phone, but she knew she needed it. She exhaled loudly, "Doris, I have to start looking for an apartment."

Fadi drove them around Santa Monica, where all of the apartments and houses were high in rent, and most of them didn't have air conditioning. At least the beach air was cooler than further inland or in the Valley, but Kai didn't know if the cast would be too hot during the Summer in the Valley, which was always around twenty degrees hotter than Santa Monica and ten degrees hotter than downtown L.A.

Apartment hunting sucked, because most of the places they looked at were inaccurately advertised and depressing, and Fin was getting crabby. Kai insisted they stop for a nice lunch at Urth Café, which had healthy food and great coffee and salads. It was her treat, she insisted, Fin also needed a bottle of milk and she had a spare with her, with a flexible ice pack wrapped around it to keep it cold. Fin liked to eat bread and butter at restaurants, so she knew he would enjoy the great bread, there.

As they walked out to sit at their patio table, Kai's face went white: Teddy was there with a gorgeous, skinny young actress/model type, a brunette in her early 20's with glossy straight hair and blue eyes. They were laughing over lattes, sitting close with his hand on her bare knee. Fadi heard Kai gasp and looked around protectively, asking, "Who is it? One of the asshole doctors?"

Doris recognized Teddy just as he looked up at them and Fin began to wail hysterically. Right on cue, Kai thought, and they were a motley crue—she, Fin, Doris and Fadi.

Teddy blanched; he threw two twenties on the table and stood up, whispering to the actress or model girl that they had to leave. She looked confused, and he tried to steer her away, to exit around them, but Kai wasn't having it.

Kai strode towards Teddy with their wailing baby in her arms and planted herself right in front of the startled brunette.

"So nice of you to visit your *son,*" Kai hissed at Teddy. Teddy started to sweat, tiny beads of perspiration popping out on his forehead. Doris and Fadi walked up to stand beside her, making his exit even more difficult.

"You—you have a *baby*?" the girl asked Teddy, stunned. Teddy opened his mouth to speak, but Kai cut him off.

"Yes, *sweetie,* he has a baby, and he is a *deadbeat father*—well, at the end of two weeks, he will be. And let's not even go into the fact that he threw his child with a life threatening health condition out of our—sorry, *his* house—three days ago."

Teddy struggled to think of what to say, "You...punched Lupe in the face. I had to pay her off, so she wouldn't sue."   That was all he could muster.

Doris looked amused, and Fadi looked like he was about to throw a punch at Teddy. Fadi clenched his jaw and his fists, "Kai, I will introduce his nuts to his stomach acid, if you so desire. This is your call."

Teddy glanced at Fadi, genuinely scared, "Who *is* this guy? Is he a terrorist, or what?" This drew attention from the other diners, who turned to stare.

Nice. Kai rolled her eyes—that was *so* Teddy, to consider anyone of Middle Eastern descent a terrorist. How could she not have seen the real him from the beginning? Was she still in a state of depression about losing her Mom?

"How did I ever get engaged to you? What was I thinking? Did you *drug* me?" Kai glared at him.

"She's violent, she *unstable*—probably mentally ill, I don't even know if the kid is mine!" Teddy sputtered to the brunette.

That was *it*. Kai handed Fin to Fadi with a look, and both she and Doris kicked Teddy in the nuts at the exact same time.

He crumpled, yelling *"AHHHH*!!!" as his terrified date bolted for the exit, alone.

"Sue me and Doris, you *weak loser*!" Kai yelled, taking Fin back from Fadi and turning on her heels to walk out. Fadi punched Teddy in the stomach just as he was trying to get back up, yelling, "Sue, *me*, too!" then followed after them.

As they drove away from Urth in the cab, Kai was silent, while she gave Fin his bottle in the car. Doris and Fadi stayed quiet, too, until Doris announced, in her very elegant accent and tone, "I don't *typically* condone violence."

This cracked them all up. Kai couldn't believe she was laughing, under the circumstances. "I'm glad he paid me in full at the beginning of the job!" Doris giggled, "I wonder if his balls are still up there inside his body cavity?"

Fadi grinned, "He may have to ask one of the waiters to help dig around and pull them out."

Kai was laughing, "I don't *ever* want to be on your bad side, Doris. You either, Fadi."

"Don't worry," Doris smiled, stroking little Fin's hair while he drank his milk.

"We are a team," Fadi said, "We are Team *Fin*."

128

Team Fin, Kai thought, smiling. She liked the sound of that.

12
Sandstorm

The next morning, Kai asked Fadi to drive her and
Fin out to the beach early, letting Doris relax in the hotel
room. She had physically assaulted two people in the last
week, something she had never done in her entire life—
outside of pulling Janie's hair in a kid's sister fight. Even
if these two particular people may have deserved it, she
wanted to reflect on her mental and emotional state, and
she needed sand between her toes to do so.

She had also yelled at a skilled surgeon in his own
office, a man who didn't deserve to be yelled at.
Hmmm…this was definitely a new, angrier version of
herself; one she hoped had not taken root in her soul.
Even righteous anger could be destructive to the vessel
holding it.

Fadi was sweet and took a walk down the beach so
that she and Fin could be alone. She went to her little
beach hut and opened the locks with her keys. This was a
place where she had gone into the deepest depths of
depression, and also a place where she had found peaceful
moments, happiness and hope. She looked around at her
things, the bikinis and sandals and necklaces she had
made by hand, with natural treasures from the sea. She
had a business that looked like it was full of potential,
before she met Teddy and took off on their supposed
"love tour" of the beaches of the world.

She had to ask herself, had he *snowed* her? Had he always been a total asshole, and she was blind to it, somehow? Had he *acted* like a great guy who loved her? *Fair weather friend*, that was one term…someone who pretends to care about you, to love you, when the chips are up. When they're down, they flee and let you fall. That sounded about right. Was there such a thing as a fair weather *father*? Sure, there was. Her own dad was, when he split.

She knew she wasn't stupid or crazy, Teddy *had* been loving and fun and kind to her, he had been warm and cuddled with her and made love to her, and promised her a future together. He had looked into her eyes under many a moonlit night and said *you* are the one for me, to be my wife, to share my life…you are *the one*.

Until we have a baby who's less than perfect. Then I run. That was *not* a deal she had signed on to, that was not a fair and just deal.

She looked down at her gorgeous boy with his wavy honey blonde hair, giggling with his toes in the sand. He could be wearing a halo and wings right now, and she'd believe it. He was an angel, he was *not* less than perfect, he just needed the right medical care.

And what was *perfect* anyway? None of us are perfect. We *manage* our imperfections, hopefully, we learn to grow from them and live with them. Beauty was not perfection; her own physical beauty hadn't saved her from pain. Beautiful people get cheated on, hurt and betrayed, they get cancer sometimes, and they age and die, just like everybody else. We're all in this human boat together, ducks trying to look like we're gliding smoothly across the surface, when under the water, we're paddling like hell. Everyone has their own "bag of hammers," their flaws to bear, their individual burdens to carry. There was yet to be a cure for every imperfection in human beings, both large and small, wouldn't it be boring if there were?

There were some human traits Kai would abolish immediately, if she were the Queen of the World, with a magical wand to wield over the universe. But she wasn't, she was a flawed, scared, fragile human who God loved anyway, she hoped. No, she knew He did—or She did, did God need a gender? Kai figured God was just *not* that petty. God didn't care if you called Him or Her God or Allah, or whatever else you chose, God was not insecure. She had read a quote once, something like "God loves you just the way you are, and He loves you far too much to let you stay that way."

She walked closer to the ocean with Fin, looking out at the horizon, the sun coming up blazing in the blue sky, a few surfers riding the waves in their wetsuits. Winter in Los Angeles, sunny and temperate, of course. She held Fin as he splashed his feet in the water and the froth rose and fell, chasing his little pork chop feet as he giggled with total, unabashed delight.

The ocean made most people feel small, in a good way, but it made Kai feel big, she expanded in the breadth and scope of nature. Fin wouldn't be able to be on a beach, in the sand or water, for as long as he was in casts…a year, maybe even two or longer. She couldn't believe she was looking forward to it, dying to get him to Salt Lake City and slap a cast on her little boy, but it was gonna make him better. That was all that mattered right now, not ambition, not money, not romantic love—she would gladly accept a simple, lonely life, if her boy could be saved from this. She would make that deal.

She looked up, seeing Fadi approaching them from down the beach, he had given them over an hour to play. She would force him to take some money for all of these lost fares, but having him drive them around somehow felt like a safety net, when her world was spinning out of control. She had started to think of him as a grandfather figure to Fin.

She waved to Fadi, just as her cell phone rang in her pocket.

It was Mercy hospital, telling her a cancellation appointment had opened up and that Fin could have his MRI done this Friday at 11am, a whole *three weeks* before their Shriners appointment. "Yes, we'll take it!" she exclaimed.

Dr. Becket had helped them, like he said he would try to do. She hung up, yelling "HALLELUJAH!" to the sky. It was a miracle, she thought, and hopefully not their last.

Fadi walked up closer and she yelled, "WE GOT THE MRI MOVED UP!" and he clapped his hands together, hugging her and shouting "HURRAY!"

They both looked down at Fin, who was eating a little bit of sand. "Oh, no!" Kai gasped, trying to get it out of his mouth with her fingers, "Toddlers put *everything* in their mouths."

"It's okay," Fadi shrugged, "It's roughage."

On the drive back to the hotel, Kai called the neurologist. "Dr. Becket...*Jack*, hi, this is Fin Verona's Mom, Kai, I just wanted to thank you *so much* for helping us get in on a cancellation, thank you a million times..."

"You don't have to thank me, it was nothing. I just explained the urgency of the matter," he said.

"No, you don't know, you may have already helped to alter his future for the better. At least he's getting a chance to be saved by these special casts they do in Salt Lake City."

"I'll be honest, that's not my field, but I wish you the best outcome for Fin, whatever you decide to do to treat his scoliosis. Let's first just make sure there are no new neurological findings in the second MRI."

She thanked Doctor Jack again, and they said their goodbyes. Back in the room, after Fadi left, she told Doris the news.

"So...you have over three weeks before this Shriners appointment?" Doris asked.

"Yeah, it still feels like a really long time to wait. To be honest, it's excruciating," Kai said.

"And you are only having this one doctor at Mercy Hospital look at Fin's MRI studies, only one opinion?" Doris raised her brow.

Kai hadn't thought about it like that, "Well, yeah, but he's supposed to be an excellent doctor, our neurosurgeon, Dr. Jack. I really like him—and we are getting two MRIs done, not just one...so don't you think the results will be pretty clear?"

Doris paused for a long moment, looking at her quite seriously, "If it were my child and I had this time, I would get at least one more opinion, from another neurosurgeon. It is his *spine* we are talking about."

Kai was surprised that Doris was taking such a personal interest in Fin's medical care, and she had a good point. "*Huh*...of course...I could research who's the best neurosurgeon in L.A. other than Dr. Becket, and just have him or her take a look at the two MRIs...I can't believe I didn't think of that myself."

Oddly enough, Kai found herself worrying that Dr. Jack would be offended, if he heard over the grapevine that she had gone to another neurologist. She didn't want to offend their specialist, one of the few doctors she had nothing bad to say about. What if she needed him to operate on Fin's syrinx cyst someday?

Doris spoke gently, "You have a lot to deal with Kai, but they did find this one cyst...yes? Well, what if the report was read wrong, and the spinal cord is actually tethered? If so, putting on this cast would not cure him, until the cord was released." Doris looked worried, glancing at Fin playing on the floor with his books— *Goodnight Moon, Goodnight Gorilla* and *The Little Engine That Could*, his three favorites.

Kai considered how silly it was to worry about offending a doctor, any doctor worth their salt should respect a person for seeking a second or third opinion on something this serious, especially when it came to their child.

"You're right, it's worth an appointment," Kai decided, looking at Doris suspiciously. "Doris, have you been going online and researching this stuff?"

Doris looked caught, glancing at the ceiling, "Yes."

"And?"

"And I may *perhaps* already have a short list of the top neurosurgeons in the Los Angeles area."

"You are *full* of surprises, Doris," Kai laughed.

"No, I'm just on Team Fin," Doris grinned.

It never rains in L.A., unless your toddler has an MRI that day. Friday morning it was overcast and pouring rain. Fadi drove Kai and Fin, dropping them off in front of the hospital. Fin was crabby and hungry, since she couldn't give him anything but clear liquids after midnight on Thursday, he wasn't a big apple juice drinker, and he refused Jell-O as if were made of boogers. He hadn't had calories all morning, for almost five hours since he'd woken up, and he was none too happy by the time they were ready for him in Radiology, at 11am.

Doris had wanted to come to support her, but Kai felt like this was part of the long hallway she had to learn to walk by herself. If she were going to make it as a single mom, she had to face the most difficult moments with some semblance of courage, and she needed to prove to herself that she could do it once Doris was gone. Well, that, and to be honest, she was afraid she wouldn't want anyone around, she might crumble to pieces the minute Fin left her sight.

She remembered being at Mercy Hospital for the first MRI, when Teddy had come with her. She remembered hoping she'd never have to walk those halls

again, and now she was walking them alone. She told
herself she had to be strong for Fin, though, she *had* to.

When they asked her to leave the MRI room, she
stumbled back out into the hallway, desperately wanting
to run back in and take her baby, to escape with him, even
though they had already begun to put him under. But what
if he did have a brain tumor that could drip into his spine,
what kind of a parent wouldn't cross all of their I's and
dot their T's before putting a child in a body cast?

Kai made it out to the hallway, as a nurse wheeled
a twelve year old boy in a wheelchair past her, both of
them wearing surgical masks. The boy looked at her
dully, his head lolling to the side. Suddenly, she was
shaking, her whole body trembling. She leaned her back
against the wall, feeling her heart pounding hard, and then
a sharp, sudden pain in her chest. Was she having a heart
attack? What if she died? Who would take care of Fin?
Would Teddy ever want him? Would her sister Janie win
custody? Would he get the health care he needed, before
it was too late?

"Kai?"

She looked up to where a man's voice was coming
from, realizing she was hyperventilating, the chest pain
was probably a panic attack.

"Kai, are you okay?" Dr. Becket was standing
over her, wearing his white coat. He was taller than she
remembered, at least six feet...Oh yeah, she thought
vaguely, he had been sitting behind his desk, the last time
they met...

"Oh...they just...he's in there, for the
MRI...and..." she muttered. She couldn't say anything
else, her throat felt dry and hot tears streamed down her
face. "I'm a mess, I'm sorry..."

"Can I get you a cup of coffee in the cafeteria?" he
asked gently. They had taken her cell phone number at the
Radiology check in desk, so she knew she would be

called as soon as Fin was done with the procedure and in the recovery area.

"You're w-working..." she stammered.

"It's sort of my lunch break, I took it early, I came down here to see if you needed any support," he said.

She nodded wordlessly, and he gently took her arm as they began walking together. It vaguely occurred to her that if he hadn't been holding her arm, she might fall down; her head was spinning with anxiety and fear.

In the hospital cafeteria, Dr. Jack sat her down at a booth and fetched two coffees, sitting across from her. She warmed her trembling hands on the paper cup, not looking up at him. "You are...so kind," she finally said. "I yelled at you, in your office..."

"This is a lot to go through, as a parent, and when you told me your husband..."

"Oh, we were engaged, not married—yet."

"Oh," he responded, surprised.

"And I think I said he left us. Well, he dumped us...me and Fin...on the lawn, with our stuff. He provided a cab, and a nanny for two weeks. She's terrific, actually...but...*yeah*."

Dr. Jack winced, "Wow. I don't know any nice way to put what I think about that guy."

"Shallow prick comes to mind," she murmured.

He smiled, "Yes, that's...eloquent. I am really; *really* sorry for everything you're going through. Like I said, I don't expect to find anything else on this MRI, but I can't make any promises."

"I know," she said, looking down at her hands. They had somehow stopped trembling.

"I can promise that I'll call you the second I get a chance to look at the films," he assured her.

"I greatly appreciate that. *Thank you.* And thank you for the coffee."

"It's nothing." The doctor flipped his light brown hair out of his face—he needed a cut, it was getting even

137

floppier in the front than it was when they first met. She looked into his kind, hazel eyes, brown and green, a darker shade than her own green eyes. His eyes were so kind. He wasn't Ken doll handsome, chiseled, like Teddy…he just had a face that made you want to know him.

"Do you have kids?" she asked, finally taking her first sip of coffee.

"Not yet," he replied, glancing away.

Why, she wondered? Was he pitying her? "Married?" she asked. She was just making conversation, she thought—well, okay, she *did* want to know more about him.

"Not yet. I'm in a relationship."

"How would she feel about you buying me coffee?" she blurted out, "Oh, I mean…I guess I shouldn't assume it's a woman…"

"Well, she is female, but she's a robot," he cracked, grinning, and Kai smiled, appreciating the moment of levity, "No, she's a human woman. She's the one who insisted I do it. She, Becky, that's her name…she was…concerned about you."

Kai looked up at him, surprised.

"Sorry, we're not like lawyers or therapists, we can talk about our practice over dinner. It does make an impression, when you get yelled at in your own office."

She felt relieved that she didn't have to be too grateful for his act of kindness. It wasn't even his idea to check on her and Fin, it was Becky's.

"Tell Becky thanks, if you hadn't found me in the hallway I may still be there, plastered against the wall, or huddled on the floor in a puddle of tears."

He took her in for a long moment. "I have a feeling you're a lot tougher than you give yourself credit for."

Dr. Jack had to go back to his next scheduled patient appointment, so Kai thanked him and paced the haunting hospital hallways alone for an hour, until her cell phone rang. They said Fin had come out of anesthesia just fine, and she could come and see him in recovery. She ran like lightning to find him groggy and smiling sweetly at the nurse, who was staying with him while he woke.

"Mama," he murmured sleepily, and she hugged and kissed him in his tiny hospital gown. After he had some apple juice and woke up more fully, she was allowed to get him dressed, call Fadi and take him home. Well, home to the hotel, anyway, where—just like after the first MRI—he was walking around and playing normally, almost as if nothing had happened. Boy, Kai mused, watching him, this kid was *resilient*.

She was resting on the bed, and bolted up when the phone rang at three o'clock. It was Dr. Jack, "*No new findings!*" he announced excitedly, "he still has the syrinx, the small cyst in his spine, but I still see no tethered cord, no Chiari malformation or tumors of any kind. It's good news, Kai."

Kai hooted with joy, shouting, "NO NEW FINDINGS! Those are the best three words, EVER!" Doris leapt to her feet, dancing and clapping, as Fin adorably copied her.

Dr. Becket continued, "So, I just need to have you do a follow up MRI in a year, to make sure the syrinx hasn't grown, but you are free to get the casting treatment, as far as I'm concerned."

"Thank you, Dr. Becket, Dr. Jack, thank you SO MUCH!" Kai could hardly believe how excited she was, considering her child still had a potentially crippling scoliosis. Still, it was a good step, a *much needed* step towards getting him well.

"Kai?" he asked.

"Yes, Doctor…Jack?"

"I just want to say…I'm so happy to be able to give you a small bit of good news. I wish you and Fin the very best."

"Thank you; you are a very kind man. I think you are one of the kindest people I've ever met. Please send good energy or pray that we get him in this cast in time."

"I will," he said, "take care, Kai."

"You, too," she hung up and hugged her little boy. "YAY, FIN!"

"YAY, MAMA!" he yelled back, giggling.

"Doris, we are making *progress*."

"Yes, Ma'am, we are!" Doris beamed.

"Am I cheating on Doctor Jack if I go see this other neurologist next week?" Kai cringed, she would hate to offend him, after he had been so good to her, to *them*, today.

"Are you having the S-E-X with this Doctor Jack, and planning to have the S-E-X also, with this new neurologist?" Doris arched a brow. The neurologist they were seeing was a woman. Doris knew that, she was being cute.

"Nope, not a lot of rolls in the hay happening, in my present or future."

"Then my answer is no, you are not cheating on Dr. Becket. But, if you want my opinion…I think you are crushing him."

"You think I'm *crushing* him?" Kai raised her eyebrows.

"Crushing *on* him, like the young kids say—you are developing a crush."

"What? Oh, *no, no, no*—he's in a relationship. Her name's Becky, she sounds nice."

"How do you know her name is Becky?" Doris was *all over* this topic, enjoying how she was getting under Kai's skin.

"Doris, I won't see the man again for a *year*, the only relationship I want to be in right now is the one with my child."

"Of course, I will zip it," Doris smiled, "but, *Becky* may have snapped him up by then."

Kai shot her a look and Doris abruptly stopped smiling, fluffing the pillows and folding Fin's blankets like the professional she is.

"There is no great rush. I'm simply saying…" Doris couldn't stop herself, "that one day, Fin will grow up, perhaps meet a young woman, and move out of his mother's home. You may want to open yourself up to the idea of male companionship. *Eventually*."

"Can we *not* talk about Fin dating women, right now? He's not even two, yet!" Man, Doris was really getting under her skin.

"I apologize," Doris looked chagrined.

"*Wait*," Kai suddenly turned to look at her, "*Say it again!*"

Doris was confused, "Say that Fin may move away, someday?"

"No…" the words caught in Kai's throat as unexpected tears sprung to her eyes, "the part about him *growing up*."

Doris ran to her and held her, exactly like she needed to be held.

Like a mother.

13
The Knowing

Kai knew they had to move out of the hotel in four days, but she had barely had the emotional energy to look for a place to live. She could stay at the hotel and pay for it herself, out of the money she'd made from selling her engagement ring from Douche Bag, but she'd be bleeding money—it was foolish to live like that.

Doris helped her scour Craig's List and she joined a rental website to find listings for apartments online, they were all really expensive. She decided they had to live in Santa Monica, not just to live near her beloved beach, but because the air was twenty degrees cooler there than in the Valley. The Valley could easily get up to 110 degrees on some days, and Fin wouldn't be able to go to the park and play comfortably wearing a plaster cast, which would make him slightly hotter than regular clothes. Fadi drove them around to look at a lot more depressing places. Kai even met with a few potential roommates, but nixed that idea as soon as she smelled pot coming out from under a bedroom door of some college age guys, and met one woman in her forties named Daphne, who had *Single White Female* stalker qualities and crazy eyes. Kai's life was complicated *enough*, right now; she couldn't deal with another person's mental problems in her own home.

She soon realized that it was crunch time, she had to decide on a place from the dregs of what was available right at that given moment.

She and Fin, Doris and Fadi walked into a small white house in the Ocean Park area of Santa Monica—not the chi chi part of town, but a nice, quiet, suburban looking neighborhood, a sweet house built in the 1950's with just a hint of beach air. It was on a little street called Ashland Avenue, about eleven blocks from the ocean. The owner's son, Jeff, a quiet accountant, was showing them the rental property for his father, a research scientist who'd taken a job on the East coast. Doris pushed Fin in his stroller through the house, so that Kai could quickly look around.

It was a small two bedroom, one and a half bath home, with some peeling paint and shabby tile. It was old and probably could use a lot of work, but it was charming and...*happy*. It just had a cheerful vibe—all hardwood floors, a little private fenced in yard in the back, with green grass for Fin to sink his little toes into and flowers and trees in the yard, one small lemon tree and big, bright pink bougainvillea plants. Doris and Fadi both clearly liked it, Doris' eyes lit up upon seeing the back yard. It was one of the only places they had seen where Fin didn't cry.

Kai gulped at the rent, it was more than two thousand dollars a month, but a decent two bedroom apartment in the area went for around the same price.

"My Dad likes to list under market value, because the place never goes vacant that way, and he likes young families with kids. They tend to...not have as many loud parties as the twenty something renters do," Jeff smiled at Kai and Fin.

"I'll have to think about it, thank you so much for showing it to us," Kai smiled back at him, shaking his hand.

Later that day at the hotel room, after Fin went down for his nap, Doris whispered to Kai, "You *must* take it. That is the house, my gut tells me things. It was meant to be."

"It's too expensive," Kai sighed, "there were livable one bedroom apartments for a third less."

"But they don't have a yard; Fin needs a place to safely play. He may have to learn to walk again, in this cast. He needs soft grass to fall in." Doris was insistent.

"I'll take him to the park. Honestly, it's being financially irresponsible, I don't have a job, right now, and I may have a lot of health care costs in front of me."

"*That* is the house—that is *our* house. I'll rent the smaller room from you," Doris said. Kai looked up at her, surprised, "I can't afford you in four days, Doris, Teddy only paid for two weeks..." This pained her; she hadn't wanted to think about losing her new friend.

"*Douche Bag*, we don't call that *thing* by his Christian name," Doris furrowed her brow.   "I'll rent the smaller room from you for a third of the rent, a third of that rent is what I pay, now, and my current rental lease is up at the end of the month. It's no additional cost to me, I'm well paid by the hour, you know I work for the best service in the city. I'll continue to work for the service as a freelancer, and I'll help take care of Fin in my hours off, for free—just until you get back on your feet. When you don't need me anymore, I will move out and we will remain friends, I hope," Doris offered.

Kai was floored by her generosity, asking "I...why would you do this? You need to think of your own family, your future...we'll be okay."

Doris locked eyes with her, "My daughter died when she was three years old. She had a hole in her heart; that is the non-medical term. The doctors didn't discover it, in time."

Kai's face was ashen, "Oh, Doris...oh my *God*..."

Doris set her jaw firmly, "I will not abandon you, in your time of need. I *will not* abandon that boy. I know what it's like, to have doctors tell you the wrong advice, to steer you down a dangerous path for your child's health. I have already lost one child, this way. *I will not lose two.*"

Doris gripped Kai's hands, she had a fierce look in her eyes that would make any enemy crumble. *This* was the woman Kai wanted watching Fin's back. This woman would lay down her life for Fin, just as she would—in that moment, Kai knew it, and it simply took her breath away.

Kai squeezed Doris' hands, "I can't tell you how sorry I am that you lost your daughter. There is nothing worse that can happen to you in life. The fact that you are still standing here, offering to help us...Doris, I'm in awe of you."

Doris looked overcome, fighting to stop her lip from trembling.

"I would be so honored, if you would share a home with me and Fin," said Kai.

Doris nodded, squeezing Kai's hands and releasing them. "I haven't spoken of that in sixteen years, and *we will not speak of it again,*" she said with finality.

Kai could see that Doris meant it. She nodded slowly, realizing she had just been let into a terrible, tragic secret that few people were allowed to know about her friend's life. She thought of all of the people you pass on the street, how you never know the depth of their stories. If she had passed Doris, and their paths had not crossed in this way, she would never guess the heartache, the heavy burden she had to carry, for the rest of her life.

Doris glanced lovingly at Fin sleeping in his crib, looking like a little cherub. "Let's call the man, and sign the lease on *our* new house," she stated definitively, and Kai threw her arms around her friend's neck.

They moved their stuff in over the next two days; neither Kai nor Doris had a lot of belongings. Kai was grateful to have Doris to accompany her, but she was still terrified of going to the second opinion neurosurgeon. She knew that going was the right thing to do as a parent, but

she didn't relish the thought of being in yet another
doctor's office with her little boy.

This second neurologist, Dr. Zelia Andreas, had an
office in Beverly Hills that was far and above the most chi
chi of any of the offices Kai had been to. Dr. Andreas
practiced at St. Mark's Hospital, where Kai actually gave
birth to Fin, and she had a great birth experience. It was
the L.A. hospital where most celebrities gave birth,
because of its reputation for having an excellent neonatal
program. St. Mark's was a highly respected, major
medical center, and if Dr. Andreas was the top pediatric
neurosurgeon there, she had to be one of the best in the
country.

Doris and Kai's online research had confirmed as
much, so they checked in at the front desk with Fin in his
stroller, then took seats in the vast, upscale waiting room,
which was filled with patients waiting for appointments—
more worried looking parents and their children. Kai
filled out the usual paperwork for a first appointment,
while Doris let Fin play with big Lego blocks and watch
the giant flat screen TV on the wall, which was showing
an amazing educational program about undersea life.

Fin was mesmerized by the ocean scenes on the
TV screen, as well as an exotic fish tank, which was at
least seven feet wide and filled with brightly colored,
expensive looking fish. Kai felt a knot forming in her
stomach as she overheard two pretty mothers in their
early thirties, an African American mom and a Hispanic
mom, who had run into each other for the first time since
going to high school together. Kai didn't mean to be rude,
but the women were saying that both of their children,
who looked about eight or nine years old, had Chiari
malformations at birth.

Her ears perked up; because that was something
they had been looking for in Fin's two MRIs, as it
sometimes occurred in kids with scoliosis. The two moms
were talking animatedly, and Kai gleaned that one child, a

cute black girl wearing pigtails and thick Coke bottle glasses, had needed surgery for her Chiari, something they called decompression surgery, and the other, the Latino boy, had not needed surgery, yet. His Chiari wasn't as severe, but they had to keep watching it by doing regular MRIs. The kids looked bored and quiet, the little girl sitting on the floor and leaning her head on her mother's knee, while the boy sunk down glumly in his waiting room chair, *not* happy about being stuck in the doctor's office.

The little girl's mom was dressed to the nines in an elegant, lavender and white polka dot silk blouse, slim gray skirt and heels. Kai wondered if she had come from her office job or if she dressed up for doctor appointments, as Kai had for Fin's first appointment with Dr. Becket. When the mother of the girl mentioned that her daughter had just been diagnosed with scoliosis, Kai couldn't help herself; she stood up and walked over to them, smiling at the quiet little girl on the floor.

"Hi, I'm so sorry, I don't mean to be rude…but I um, overheard you mention that your daughter has scoliosis, and my son, Fin…he's not even two yet, but he's recently been diagnosed with a very rare, severe form of it…" Kai wanted to tell this mom about the casting option in Salt Lake City, or see if she had any advice to share.

The two pretty mothers looked up at her, politely irritated, and she suddenly felt self-conscious. The little girl's mother took her in and spoke evenly, "Hello, my name is Claudia, my daughter Leigh only has a slight scoliosis, seven degrees right now, but she's already been through brain surgery and she was born with a tumor behind her right eye." The woman was beautiful and poised, but the tone of her voice made it clear that she felt Kai had butted into their conversation.

Kai looked at Leigh, who was looking up at her. She suddenly noticed the little girl had a glass eye behind her thick glasses. Kai warmly smiled at the girl, "Well, you are a *very brave* girl!" she blurted out.

Her mother looked at Kai with eyes of steel, replying coolly, "She's a *lion*."

Kai smiled again and shrunk back to her seat. This was still a new world she was in, a world where mothers have to bring their children back to doctor and hospital visits many times over the years, for conditions far above the normal colds and flu viruses. She deeply admired those mothers for their strength, and for both their bravery and their children's.

She looked at Fin, having a blast with the toys in a big bin in the corner, having no idea why they were in this place with the impressive exotic fish tank. The older kids knew.

They finally called Fin's name and Kai carried him in her arms down the hall and into the room to meet the doctor. Dr. Zeila Andreas entered five minutes later, wearing a tailored ivory skirt, red blouse and a white coat. She was petite and attractive, with dark brown, glossy hair swept back off of her face, olive skin, and no makeup. "Hello, I'm Dr. Andreas," she smiled with an exceedingly confident manner, shaking both Kai and Doris' hands.

"I'm Kai, this is my friend Doris, and this is my son Fin." The doctor nodded, looking at a file. Kai noticed she didn't even look at Fin. He was bouncing around the room, so Doris got up to chase him so that Kai could focus on the conversation.

"So, I see you've had two MRIs. I just took a look at them," the doctor said.

"Yes, we've had two done at Mercy Children's, but we wanted a second opinion before going for Mehta Method casting for Fin's Progressive Infantile Scoliosis. He was at 34 degrees at the end of December, but he looks worse, now. He was accepted to Shriners Hospital in Salt Lake City for these casts, to hopefully cure him, but we wanted to make sure his spinal cord isn't tethered before going forward with it."

The doctor nodded, "May I ask what type of insurance you have?"

Kai was a little surprised; doctors didn't often ask that during appointments, that was usually dealt with by the front desk. "Oh, we have excellent insurance, right now, a PPO," she replied. They were both still covered under polices paid for by Teddy through the end of the year.

"The reason I ask is that some people can't go to any hospital they choose to, because..." the doctor glanced away.

"Oh," Kai realized what she was implying— Shriners was a charity hospital, and Mercy Children's took a lot of patients without any insurance coverage at all. She was asking if they were covered. "No, no, we can go *anywhere* we choose to, right now," Kai explained, "I just want the *best* treatment for my son."

Dr. Andreas smiled at Kai, looking directly in her eyes. "I see. Good. Well, I have to be honest; I think these films are fuzzy, almost unreadable."

Doris looked up. Kai was stunned, "What do you mean?" she asked, "Isn't Mercy Children's good? We had two done...surely one of them is readable..." Fin had already endured full anesthesia twice for these MRIs.

The doctor cleared her throat, "I do not feel confident diagnosing Fin without another MRI. The two best places for those, for children in Los Angeles, are here at this hospital and UCLA Medical Center. I don't care which one you go to, but I can't say for sure, based on these films, that Fin does not have a tethered cord or even a potential spinal tumor. He doesn't have Chiari," she announced flatly.

The doctor then stood up, feeling the back of Fin's head and neck, then lifted his shirt to look at his back.

"This type of scoliosis often comes with other syndromes."

"Really?" Kai asked, her heart pounding.

"Almost always," Dr. Andreas replied coolly.

"But…we have this appointment at Shriners on March 30th, doesn't it take up to two months to get an MRI appointment in L.A.?"

"I can get you in here within two weeks, we have a wonderful team. It's up to you, here or UCLA. I don't care which you choose." Dr. Andreas finished examining Fin and walked back over to shake Kai's hand, saying, "It's been a pleasure to meet you."

"Thank you, Doctor Ah-Andreas," Kai stammered, as the doctor left the room. She and Doris looked at each other wide-eyed; they certainly hadn't been expecting this.

Back at the new rental house, Kai paced the living room, "*Another* MRI? It would mean full anesthesia on Fin, *again*…for the third time in less than two months…what if she's wrong? Then I would put him through it for *nothing*!"

"You don't have to take her advice. Maybe doctors always want their hospital team to take their own X-rays and MRIs, maybe it's an 'our team is better than theirs' thing?" Doris suggested.

Kai nodded, beginning to feel overwhelmed again, "Plus, it makes money for the hospital, and the doctor gets another follow-up appointment fee…maybe she's *hoping* to find something, so she can perform surgery? Surgeons want to do surgery, right? It's what they're trained to do…they're like race car drivers, of *course* they want to get behind the wheel…"

"I'm sorry I suggested we go, today," Doris frowned.

"No, no, you will have saved the day if she's right…if Fin could still have a tethered cord, or a *tumor*…" Kai shuddered. "There's only one answer. We have the time to do the MRI. Now that doubt has been raised, how could I *not* do it? I have to do it."

She didn't like it one bit, but it looked like she was going to have to put Fin through another one. Anesthesia was scary each time, especially on your baby. There were *always* risks, but if Fin had a tumor and she didn't catch it, how could she ever live with herself? She couldn't. It was as simple as that.

Kai called UCLA and they were booked far in advance, but St. Marks could get them in within two weeks, just like Dr. Andreas promised. Kai thought about the fact that the doctor probably knew UCLA would be booked two months out. She cringed and made the appointment.

"We'll just get through this, and then get the cast on at the end of March," she told Doris. "We have the time, and insurance will cover most of the cost, not that money even matters at this point."

She had made her decision, and she was glad she didn't have to ask for Teddy's permission to make it. A strange silver lining, in being left out on the lawn.

The next day, Kai was feeding Fin a bowl of organic blueberry applesauce with yogurt, when her cell phone rang. Doris answered it for her, "Hello, this is Kai's phone."

Doris looked at her, holding out the phone. "It's Angie Livingston, from Shriners."

Kai gave Fin the last spoonful of blueberry, handing him to Doris and taking the phone. "I'm happy to tell you that we have a cancellation slot for you," Angie said.

Kai blinked, "When?"

"On February 15th," Angie replied.

That was in just five days, three days *before* the 3rd MRI appointment. Holy...

Kai couldn't think of what to say,

"Oh....wow...um, thank you so much, it's just that...I

have to think about it…can you hold it, for an hour or so? It's…well, we have an additional MRI scheduled for Fin, and it's next Friday…"

"Sure, I completely understand, just call me back or email me today, and let me know," Angie said.

Angie was an angel for staying on top of this, and finding them an earlier casting day appointment, but now Kai didn't know what to do. This casting date was a whole six weeks earlier than the original date. Kai knew Fin's condition was *progressive*; time was of the essence, time was *vital*. This was an *oncoming train*. At the same time, what if the first two MRIs were really "fuzzy"? Was that even *possible*?

She filled Doris in, and her face fell, "I'm so sorry that I put you in this position, honey," she said.

Kai needed some time alone to think. Doris took over watching Fin and she drove to the beach by herself, gripped with panic and fear. Her heart was thumping so hard, she felt like it might explode. She was at a fork in the road of her child's life, she *couldn't* make the wrong decision on this one.

There was something that Kai had noticed in just the last two weeks—Fin loved to run, fast, and now every time he did, he coughed a little. He wasn't sick, though, he never coughed except for when he ran. Could his lungs already be becoming compromised, from the pressure of his spinal curvature?

He also would stop after running and do kind of a yoga move, sort of what they call in yoga the *downward facing dog* position, putting his arms down and bending his head down to the ground in a "V" pose. It looked like he needed to stretch—could he be doing that as a natural reaction to what was going on with his spine? Did he feel pulled to his right side? Kai didn't know. She did know she was in a race against time.

Robert Frost wrote about two roads diverging in the yellow woods. Which path was the right one to take?

The Mehta casting path was certainly the one "less
travelled by," it was not the current norm in the medical
community at all. Was it crazy? What if she went down
the wrong wooded path, and her child's future was
forever altered for the worse by her incorrect choice?
What if she made a choice that caused him deformity,
physical pain and suffering, what if she made a choice
that *killed her child*??

It was too cruel to comprehend; it was too mean of
the universe, too *mean* of God to allow that to happen.
He's just an innocent *baby*! How can anything horrible
ever happen to precious *children*?

She felt as if she had a sword going down her
throat, through her esophagus, piercing her stomach.
Looking out at the vastness of the horizon, she fell to her
knees in the sand and begged and prayed for the right
answer to come, "God, just *tell me what to do*. Guide me
to the right choice, *please*. I'll never ask anything of you
again, just *please, please*, don't let me make the wrong
choice for my child's future."

She said "Amen" aloud, then called Angie
Livingston from her cell phone, explaining what was
stopping her from saying "Yes." Angie said she
understood, and explained that her Shriners hospital
didn't do MRIs, but they did have radiologists who could
take another look at Fin's films. They could weigh in on
whether or not his spinal cord was tethered, and if the
films could be considered "good studies."

Kai suddenly felt something she couldn't explain,
a mother's gut instinct, the voice of God—she didn't
know for sure, but it was *loud and clear*. It was
practically shouting.

The voice just said these seven words: "*THE
DOOR IS OPEN. WALK THROUGH IT.*"

Kai gasped, tears springing to her eyes, burning
hot as they streamed down her face. In that moment, she

knew the message—call it gut instinct, call it God—she knew it was the *truth*.

"Angie, please do have your radiologist look at the first two MRI's and get back to me as soon as possible, but we WILL take the cancellation appointment on Tuesday, *we'll be there!*"

She would cancel the 3rd MRI, and they would go to Utah. She gratefully thanked Angie, said goodbye, and looked to the sky. Maybe her luck was never just good luck or bad luck, maybe God loved her and God loved Fin, and they had a purpose to fulfill in their lives, one that had yet to be shown.

She was still scared to death. But she had never felt surer of *anything*.

14
Snow

Kai cancelled Fin's third MRI appointment and booked three tickets on a flight to Salt Lake City. Doris would be coming, of course—and she bought Fin his own plane seat to sit in, strapped in his travel car seat, for safety in the event of turbulence. It would be cold in Utah, possibly snowing, so she and Doris shopped for warm clothes for Fin in a size up from what he currently wore, getting him a puffy navy blue winter coat with a bright green lining and soft, stretchy pants with elastic waists to go over or under the bottom of the cast.

She had been online with the support group, and the other moms, and even a couple of dads were giving her great advice. Everyone said they went up at least one size up in shirts after the first cast was applied, because it added about three pounds of bulk on the baby's frame. They all said that the first casting day is long and tough, but that across the boards, the children bounce back and are amazingly resilient.

The upside to buying children's winter clothes in February in L.A. was that they were mostly on the sale racks, and they got great deals. Doris found some really cute cotton long sleeved t-shirts with race cars and trucks on them; they had snaps at the neck that would be easy to get over the cast, and were a score at originally twenty five bucks, down to five dollars apiece. While they were at the mall, Angie Livingston called on Kai's cell phone, to tell her what the Shriners' radiologist had said about Fin's first two MRIs.

Kai held her breath, steeling herself for the news.

Angie relayed that their radiologist had confirmed that they were "good studies," in her opinion, and said the same things that Dr. Becket had said: that there was no tethered cord, no Chiari malformation of the brain, and no tumors. She noted that the small syrinx cyst was there in Fin's spine, but the doctor had said that would not prevent them from doing the casting. Kai told Doris and they hugged, relieved, it was another sign she was doing the right thing. There was still room for human error, which scared her, but she had to trust in God and her gut instinct.

Today was Friday; they were still scheduled for check in at the hospital on Monday afternoon, and for the casting to be done on Tuesday morning. They spent Saturday packing and worrying, Kai could barely speak, she was so nervous. Doris cleaned the house like the Queen herself was coming to visit, to keep herself busy— she kept saying they would want a spotless, germ free house to bring Fin home to, after being in the hospital.

Kai had learned from the other I.S. parents that hospitals won't cast a child if they're sick, they won't put them under anesthesia if their lungs aren't clear, so both she and Doris obsessively washed their hands and used antibacterial wipes everywhere. Kai practically bought out the drugstore of their hand sanitizer and wipes, and stocked up on the other things the moms had suggested she bring: Fin's favorite snacks, blankets, toys and books and a portable DVD player for children's videos. Everyone said that when the child first wakes up in the cast is the hardest point, so any distractions are a positive to have on hand. The experienced moms recommended water resistant bibs, to keep the cast dry from milk and juice splashes or spills, and duct tape, of all things, to apply to the bottom of the plaster cast. One more use for duct tape! This trick was to avoid any diaper leaks from soaking or "wicking up" into the bottom edge of the cast, which can obviously start to smell rank if pee is soaked in there for two to three months, before the next cast change. The hygiene issues were scary, but not as scary as crushed lungs.

Then there was the complex diapering advice: many moms put a Poise pad, or a pad for adult women with bladder leakage, into a diaper, sticking the sticky part right into it, like a feminine pad. Kai had to laugh at the thought of buying loads of those at her local drugstore, so that the cashier and the other customers could think she had bladder control problems, and peed on herself all the time. Oh, the glamorous life! Maybe she would ask Doris to buy them, she mused.

After step one, when the pad was in the diaper, some mothers also put a toddler pull-up over the diaper, as a back-up plan. It seemed it was a *very* big deal to try to avoid soiling the cast with pee or poop, and Kai worried Fin would reek of stale urine like a very small homeless man. Well, it was better to be *ripe* for a little while and to have a straight spine, than...*yeah*—she would take a little stink any day, if those were her options.

There was nighttime diapering advice too: some moms put a water-resistant, washable training pant over the diaper with the pad in it, because it had an elastic band at the waist and legs, which "sealed" better overnight to avoid leaks than the pull-ups did. And then to take it even one step further, some moms put two feminine panty liners with the sticky sides stuck back to back, and pushed that under the front of the cast at night, as a final barrier to leakage. *WHEW*! Let's not even talk about diarrhea or vomit getting inside the cast. It was all making Kai feel a bit overwhelmed; thank heaven she would have Doris to help her fumble through it.

She had booked a rental car in Salt Lake, but if it snowed, she knew she would be very nervous driving in a strange city—especially since she had never driven in snow in her life, and her precious baby would be in the back seat. Kai was good at a lot of things, but her sense of direction in a place she had never been to before was fairly poor. She could follow directions, but still…she hated to get lost, it frazzled her and kept her from thinking straight.

After she put Fin to bed, she could barely sleep on Saturday night, the night before their flight. They had decided to fly Sunday instead of Monday, she didn't want to take any chances that they would miss the flight somehow, or that the plane would be delayed. She couldn't miss this precious appointment, not under *any* circumstances.

Sunday morning, Doris stumbled into the doorway of Kai's bedroom, looking awful. "I'm afraid to tell you…." Doris cringed, gripping the door frame.

"You're sick," Kai bolted upright in her bed, "Oh, *no!*"

"I'm so sorry; it came on in the middle of the night…fever, chills…" Doris coughed, blowing her nose into a tissue, "I can't get Fin sick…this trip is his future. I'll ask for a different seat on the plane, I'll sanitize everything…"

Kai shook her head, "No, no, just go back to bed. I'll take the trip alone, I mean, alone with Fin."

"You can't…" Doris wheezed and coughed again, a horrible wet, hacking sound.

Kai winced as she covered her mouth. "I have to, planes are the worst incubators—he'll catch it for sure, if you come. They won't put him under anesthesia if he's sick, we don't know when he can get another appointment…it could be weeks…"

"I can't abandon you right now; this is too much for you to take on, by yourself." Doris looked devastated.

"You're *not* abandoning me; it's not your fault."

158

"Allow me to call someone for you, maybe Fadi? If he got his own hotel room? Or, I'll pay someone from the service, someone to take my place," Doris offered.

"No, *I can do this*." Kai said decisively. "I'm his mother, and it looks like I'm going to be a single mother, so I may as well get used to the heavy lifting." She stood up, taking a deep breath. "Doris, please, right now, just go back to bed so I can get him ready. I promise I'll call you every step of the way."

Doris finally sighed, defeated. "Kai?"

"Yes?"

Doris looked her in the eyes. "Your Mother would be *very proud* of you."

Kai felt a lump forming in her throat.

"She is watching over you and Fin, and she will hold you in her arms and protect you the whole way. I feel it."

Kai put her hand on her heart, and softly replied "*Thank you*," as Doris smiled and reluctantly left the doorway to go back to bed.

After a lot of frenzied packing, feeding Fin and herself a fast breakfast and getting them both dressed, with Fin wriggling like he was in the World Wrestling Federation, Fadi drove them to the airport. "I should come with you, you can't do this alone," he said.

"I'll be fine. I'm not worried," she lied. She *was* worried, but she didn't want to worry him.

"I'll get a separate hotel room, of course, I'll just drive you to and from the hospital and I'll be on call, if you need me for anything, absolutely anything," he said.

Kai knew he meant it, he treated her like a loving uncle, even sometimes like the father she never had. "No, that's crazy—you need to work, you've done too much for us, already. I'm a *grown-up*, remember?" She was sitting next to Fin's car seat in the back of Fadi's cab, as usual, so she attempted to smile brightly at him in the rearview mirror. He still looked worried.

The truth was, she didn't really *feel* like a grown-up. Maybe all of life was just pretend, she thought vaguely, as she stared out of the window. As they pulled into LAX, her jaw dropped open. *"Holy…"*

A line of about five hundred people filled the Southwest terminal for baggage check-in, snaking out of the door and all the way down the sidewalk outside. It was a mass of humanity, and nobody looked very happy about being there. The first thing Kai thought was, *Crap, we're gonna miss the flight*! Her second thought was, *Even if we don't miss the flight from standing in this line for hours, Fin is gonna be screaming and crying the whole time, and look at all of the potential for GERMS*!

With five hundred people randomly gathered, there had to be some sick ones in the middle of winter cold and flu season. She couldn't anti-bacterial wipe the entire airport, plane and *world*.

"Damn it!" Fadi cursed, pulling the cab over to the curb. He got her bags out from the trunk of his cab, and opened the door for them; setting up Fin's stroller and helping Kai unlatch the travel car seat from the back. As Kai put Fin into his stroller, a tall man with white hair walked by them hurriedly, suddenly stopping to check his watch and coughing almost *directly over Fin.* A MORTAL *SIN*! Sometimes Kai just couldn't *believe* people.

Fadi gave the man a dirty look, "Cough on that child again, and I will *end* you!" he barked. The man looked scared, rushing away through the crowd. "I'll park the cab, I should stay with you until you go through security," Fadi muttered, furrowing his brow.

"No, we'll be okay…you have to go back to work. I *insist*." Kai forced a smile, hugging him. "I'll call and keep you updated, I promise."

Fadi pulled back from the hug, holding her firmly by the shoulders. "Safe travels, come home safe and sound, strong young lady and brave little man. My heart flies with you." Fadi was choking up, Kai had never seen him get so emotional.

Kai kissed him on both cheeks. "Team Fin," she said softly, turning to go.

"*Team Fin*," Fadi echoed.

Kai told herself that she had to hold it together, so she ventured into the terminal, through the irritable mass of humanity, and saw how far the line went back. Steeling herself, she followed the line all the way through the terminal, outside the airport doors, and seemingly a mile down the sidewalk. When she got to the very end, Fin was already starting to fuss in his stroller, a combustible situation about to explode. Her mind raced as she stood there a minute, noticing a male Southwest Airlines employee standing nearby. What did she have to lose?

She approached him, struggling to push and pull her stroller and roller bag at the same time. "Hi, I'm travelling with my baby to a major medical appointment; he has a rare form of severe scoliosis that can damage his vital organs if he doesn't get proper treatment in time." She took Fin out of his stroller, lifting up the back of his long sleeved t-shirt and showing the man the curve in his spine. The man blinked, taken aback by the visual evidence of this crooked little child. "We're flying to get to a Shriners Hospital," Kai explained.

The man paused for a moment, nodded, and simply said, "Come with me." He led them directly to the very front of the line and checked them in himself, without saying another word about it.

Kai was stunned and filled with gratitude as he handed her their tickets, "I can't thank you enough," she said.

"No problem, have a safe flight," the man smiled.

Kai walked away, goose bumps rising on her arms, the good kind. *Angels were everywhere.*

Blessedly, the flight was uneventful. Everyone was nice to them, Fin actually napped most of the way,

and an older woman even helped Kai carry the travel car
seat off of the plane. It was icy and cold in Utah, but it
hadn't snowed recently, the online weather report said
that it would snow that night. She got the rental car, a big
SUV because it had four wheel drive for the snow, and
nervously drove to the hotel near downtown Salt Lake
City, a place called The Snowflake Inn.

It was, perhaps, not the most glamorous hotel she
had ever seen. She figured they got a lot of skiers, there,
and they also had a discounted rate for the Shriners
Hospital patients and their families. It was fine, not
exactly The Four Seasons, but they checked into a large
room with two queen beds, a TV, a desk, a coffee maker
and a small fridge. Plus, it came with a free breakfast
buffet, and they even had a small "convenience store"
near the front desk, for snacks and microwaveable food
that was open 24 hours. Cheddar flavor Pringles, *perfect
for emotional binge eating*, Kai mused.

She had asked in advance for a portable crib,
which was already set up in the room between the two
beds—a Pack n' Play that she had brought her own sheets
and Fin's favorite blankets for. Fin ran around the large
space, having a blast, while Kai called the hospital,
getting directions for their initial check in that afternoon.

They would stay the night in the hospital on the
actual casting day tomorrow, but after they checked in,
she had been told that they could come back to their hotel
to sleep tonight.

She was nervous on the drive to the hospital,
which, thankfully, was less than fifteen minutes. As she
came up the hill and saw Shriners Intermountain Hospital
for the first time, she was awestruck. Kai had seen many
beautiful sights in her life, but it was a truly striking
building, surrounded by mountain views and snowcapped,
majestic peaks. The hospital's architecture was stunning
and modern, with a circular center with a dome on the
top; it looked wildly different than any hospital she'd ever

seen. It was immediately clear to her that someone, or
many someones, put a lot of love into this building.

She parked in the large parking lot and carried Fin
in her arms to the front door, which was an automatic
turnstile with stuffed animals and toys displayed behind
the glass, for the kids to enjoy on the way in.

Everything about this hospital felt welcoming and
special. The middle aged man at the front desk warmly
greeted them, directing them to the check-in desk behind
him. The older white haired woman at the check-in desk
was kind, and gave Kai a visitor's pass to wear on her
clothes while they were there. She directed them to check
in on the inpatient floor, so Kai and Fin took the nearby
elevator up to the 2nd floor, exiting the elevator into a
giant, round, open playroom. The expansive room had
tables and chairs for families to gather, a basketball hoop,
a pool table, soft chairs and couches facing a big screen
TV, and rocking horses and toy cars for kids to ride on.
The snowy mountain views could be seen from large
windows.

Kai stopped in her tracks for a moment,
considering the thought that had gone into this room, all
for the sick children they treat, here, to give them a
chance to be normal kids in the eye of their storms.

Kai had read that the Shriners began their
hospitals all the way back in *1922*, they're a fraternal
organization who took a vote and decided to start these
charitable hospitals that do state-of-the art, cutting edge
treatments for countless children, both saving and
transforming their lives. If they hadn't taken that vote pre-
1922, Kai didn't know where she and Fin would be right
now. They would be lost.

She had read that two of their first patients were a
girl with club foot and a boy with polio. The first hospital
opened in Shreveport, Louisiana, and after polio was
mostly wiped out due to vaccines, they also began treating
children who were burn victims. Much of their practice is

still orthopedic conditions, as well as burn treatment, and they do not turn away a child who they can help, regardless of insurance or ability to pay. Kai was amazed, reading about these hospitals, it almost seemed too good to be true. It was a dream of what medicine *should* be.

She carried Fin down the hallway to the check-in desk on the inpatient floor, being warmly greeted by the woman there. Fin just wanted to be loose to run around, so he wriggled and kicked in her arms, and she put him down a few times, letting him run up and down the hallways with unabashed delight as she chased alongside him.

Moments later, Dr. Jacques D'Astous approached the desk; the man who would be Fin's casting doctor. Kai knew that he was one of the first doctors to do this Mehta Method casting in the U.S., which in her eyes, made him a pioneer. Heather Hyatt-Montoya had told her that he was the first doctor in the States who was even willing to listen, to take interest in this method, and to be trained by Dr. Mehta herself. He was the most experienced doctor in the entire country for this treatment, so Kai knew that if this had a chance of working for her boy, they were in the very best of hands.

Dr. D'Astous was a fit, trim, handsome man in his fifties, with dark hair and very kind eyes, and an intelligent, modest demeanor. He was obviously busy, on his way between patients.

"Hello, I'm Dr. D'Astous," he smiled, shaking Kai's hand, as she struggled to hold her wriggly toddler in her arms.

"Hi, I'm Kai, and this is Fin...Dr. D'Astous, we've heard the most wonderful things about you and we are *so* grateful to be here." Kai was breathless; she just wanted to say the *right thing* to this important man who could help them. She lifted Fin's t-shirt in the back, to show the doctor his curve.

"Yes, I see. I remember Fin's films, he has a syrinx," Dr. D'Astous said, checking his spine.

"Yes," she breathed.

"I have another patient, a little boy named Noah in Wyoming, who reminds me a lot of your son, in his structure and physiology. He also has a syrinx, and he's doing wonderfully, now."

"Oh, wow…" Kai was overwhelmed.

"We can't make promises, as every child is unique…" he explained honestly.

"Of course."

"But, we've had a lot of success with this method. So, we'll see you in the morning," he said, smiling. Kai wanted to hug him, but Fin was already wriggling out of her arms and running down the hallway again, so she chased after her active boy.

"He's high spirited, that's a *good* thing!" the doctor called out cheerfully, as he walked away in the other direction, towards the inpatient rooms.

A young nurse arrived a few minutes later, and took them back to an exam room to get Fin's height and weight. The nurse gave him a new toy, a cute little stuffed animal tiger that he loved. Free medical care *and* free toys, wow, Kai thought. She answered a list of general questions and signed some papers, and they were told to be back at 6am the next morning.

It was all as lovely as possible, but her nerves were on edge, nonetheless. She was still alone with her child in a strange city, and when she walked back outside, it was already dark outside and had begun snowing.

The rental car she had been given was a white SUV that looked like a giant marshmallow, it was bigger than any vehicle she had driven before in her entire life. She had some weird notion at the rental counter that the larger vehicle would keep them safer in snow, but now she was scared to maneuver such a big thing on dark, wet, icy streets.

Okay, *calm down*, she thought, her mind freezing up from her nerves on the details of how to get back to the hotel. It was just two turns, that part, she remembered. *Easy, easy peasy*, she tried to silently pep talk herself. Just go down the hill, at the bottom, make a right on Temple, a left on 500 Street, then follow that all the way to the hotel.

She strapped Fin into his car seat in the back and drove, terrified, in the unfamiliar snow, in this unfamiliar city, thinking *Please don't let me kill my baby before he gets medical help for his spine, please*. Her heart was racing. She squinted and counted the street numbers to 500- *YES!* She found it and made a left turn, and kept driving, and driving…and *driving*. Fin was starting to get restless, whining and fussing from the backseat.

Oh, crap—this couldn't be right. Nothing looked remotely familiar. Where was the hotel? She knew there was a McDonald's near her hotel, she thought she'd see the yellow and red lighted sign, but it was nowhere to be found. Finally, she saw a well-lit 7-11 on a street corner. Now, Fin was really crying, as if he sensed her frayed energy. She pulled into the parking lot, shakily dialing the hospital phone number and getting directions.

The man on the phone at Shriners kindly informed her that there was not one, there were *two 500 streets in Salt Lake City,* an East and a West. She had turned down the one that came first on Temple, the wrong one. She thanked the man at the hospital and put the rental car in reverse. Fin kept crying, wanting out of the car seat. "It's okay, Fin, don't cry, Mommy's got it," she cooed, trying to soothe him. She felt guilty, she knew he was probably getting hungry and so was she, but she needed to buy some milk on the way back to the hotel. She just wanted to get them *un-lost*, first.

As she backed the big rental SUV up a few feet in the 7-11 parking lot, she heard an excruciating *CRUNCH.* She looked to her right, realizing she had just smashed into the side of a parked, low riding old black Chevy Camaro. *CRAP!*

Fully rattled, Kai pulled the rental car back up and turned off the engine, as a young Hispanic man with a moustache, in his late 20's, approached her SUV. She buried her face in her hands.

Pull it together, you just hit somebody, her addled mind reminded her, as Fin wailed and she forced herself to get out of the car. A young Hispanic girl, 18, with acne and a lit cig dangling from her lips, approached Kai behind the moustache guy, who appeared to be her boyfriend.

"I am *so, so* sorry…" Kai began, seeing a dent in the guy's car that was about the size of a gallon of milk. "It was all my fault. My baby has to get treated at the Shriners hospital, here…" Kai felt her face crumbling. Fin continued wailing from the back seat of the car.

Suddenly, both the young man and woman's faces softened. The teenage girl with the acne and the lit cig dangling from her mouth opened up her arms wide, as if to say *Come're*, and bizarrely, Kai took the invitation and hugged her. Snow lightly fell on them as the teenage girl's cigarette smoke swirled around Kai's head, and she couldn't believe the moment she was living in. It was so strange, and at the same time, it was oddly human and beautiful.

"Don't worry about it. I'll fix it myself," the young man suddenly offered.

"What? Oh, no…are you serious?" It sounded too good to be true, but the thought of not having to wait for the police while Fin screamed was tempting.

"Yeah," the moustache guy muttered, thinking. "But…do you have a hundred dollars?"

In that moment, her brain was so overloaded that she couldn't remember. "Maybe. Let me check…" Kai got in the car and dug in her purse—yes, she had cash for travelling—she took out five twenties, handing them to him.

"Thanks," he said, pleased.

"No, thank *you* so much, I'm *so sorry!*" she apologized again, and the young man and woman got into their car and drove off from the 7-11, as Kai nervously got back behind the wheel of the SUV and pulled out from the parking lot.

The next ten minutes felt like forever. Fin kept crying, and she was still shaken to her core from the car accident, wondering if that guy was not a U.S. citizen, or if he didn't have car insurance. Could he have just have let her go to be nice? Did he feel that sorry for her, because her child has a health problem, or could he really easily fix the dent himself, and the hundred dollars was a bonus? Either way, she was desperate to get Fin's milk and something to eat, and get back safely to the hotel.

Beyond rattled, she overshot the street the hotel was on, and almost went the wrong way down a major, four lane one way street. *UGH!* She really thought she was gonna have a heart attack. She didn't even feel safe to be on the road, in her frazzled state. She *finally* saw the golden arches of the McDonald's near the hotel, and pulled into the drive-through, to order Fin's milk and some comfort food. French fries, chicken nuggets, a big salad *and* a hot fudge sundae, *please*.

Luckily, Fin had stopped crying; maybe he was too scared by his Mommy's driving to cry. The woman working at the drive through window had white hair and looked to be very much a senior, in her 70's or 80's. She appeared to be new on the job, and was currently being trained by a younger male employee at the window. The older woman was super friendly when Kai mumbled that she was a little discombobulated, she'd just gotten lost in the city—she was from out of town. It was all she could do to not blurt out that her child had a potentially fatal condition and was to be put in a body cast the next day. *Don't bleed all over everybody*, Kai reminded herself...

"Oh, I hope you're enjoying your visit to Salt Lake City!" the grandmotherly woman exclaimed, as if assuming they were there on vacation.

"Oh...I'm...well...it's *not* a good visit." That was all Kai could manage, with her hands still trembling and her heart thumping wildly in her chest.

The older lady looked uncomfortable, handing her the bag of food through the window, and Kai reminded herself: *Have some grace*. This woman didn't know what she was going through, and vice versa. Maybe this woman had retired, and then the economy had gotten bad and she had to go back to work, at age 80? Maybe her husband died, and she lost their retirement money in the down stock market? Kai remembered a great quote she had once heard, from the philosopher Plato: *"Be kind, for everyone you meet is fighting a hard battle!"* Be kind. Just try to be kind, Kai reminded herself.

"I'm sorry, it's beautiful here, we're so lucky to get to see the snow," Kai said, forcing a smile.

The woman lit up, "Oh *yes*, it's just gorgeous on the mountain tops, isn't it?"

Driving back to the hotel, finally, Kai gripped the wheel and prayed tomorrow would go well. She parked the car in the slushy parking lot of the Snowflake Inn, glancing at Fin in the back seat. She was with the person she loved most in the world, but she had never felt more alone in her life.

As she got out of the car and unstrapped him from the back, it was snowing a little more heavily. Fin wrinkled his cute little nose as the icy flakes fell on his face. As Kai carried him into the front lobby of the hotel, clutching her small child and her McDonald's bag that smelled like French fries, she stopped in her tracks and her jaw fell open.

She would *never* have expected to see this person standing before her, here in Utah, never in a *million years*.

"Kai, I didn't call, because I knew you'd tell me not to come." Janie was standing in the lobby, pulling a small forest green travel suitcase on wheels.

"Why...oh my God, Janie...let's talk in the room." Kai hustled with Fin in her arms to the elevator, a wave of emotions running through her, most of them unpleasant. Janie followed her into the elevator as it opened, and Kai pressed the third floor.

"I left my husband and three children to be here with you, in your time of need. You don't desert *family* when a child goes into the *hospital*," Janie announced, enunciating a little too loudly, since they were standing right next to each other.

Kai sighed, as the doors opened and she walked to her room, opening it with the key card and letting Janie in. The door closed behind them, and Kai set Fin down to play with his books and toys, while she quickly fixed him his bottle of milk.

"I know you think coming here was the right thing to do, Janie, but it's actually intrusive to not ask if I *wanted* you to come," Kai was trying to remain calm. "How did you know I didn't have someone else with me?"

"I called Doris, and she said she was too ill to travel. I was planning to come anyway, but that sealed it for me. You can't go through this alone, you need someone to pray with and help God carry you through."

"I pray just fine." Kai exhaled.

"I'm sure you try." Janie replied tightly.

"Because I had a child out of wedlock, and I'm not married to a preacher, God doesn't hear my prayers?" Kai worked to keep her tone even; she didn't want to upset Fin.

"No, of *course* God hears your prayers, Kai, and I am not here to judge you for any predicament your bad

170

choices may have gotten you into. I just couldn't let you go through it alone, since Mom's not here." There was a long pause as the sisters looked at each other, the subject of their mother's death still highly charged for both of them.

"She's here," Kai said softly. She really didn't want to fight, not the night before Fin's cast day. It was typical of Janie to make this *all about Janie*, her doing the "right thing," not about what Kai wanted, or what she and Fin were going through.

"I mean...*physically*, Mom's not physically here to help you." Janie added awkwardly, "Well, this is great; you have two beds, should we just share this room?"

"I...guess." Kai finished giving Fin his milk and let him off of her lap to run around the room and play. She finally opened her bag of food, taking out the French fries and eating some, almost in a daze. Janie grabbed a few, munching on them.

"I'm *starving*, thanks. I'll pay for half the room, of course," Janie said, her mouth full.

"You don't have to; it's a discounted rate for the hospital." Kai grabbed the diaper bag to change Fin, and started laying out his pajamas for bed. She turned to face Janie, "Listen, you can come tomorrow, but you can't talk to the doctor or nurses, or tell me I'm making a bad decision. I am the mother here, I am an *adult*, and any decisions about Fin's medical care will be mine. Are we clear on that?"

Janie nodded, "Of course, I'm only here for support."

"Good." Kai opened her grilled chicken salad and started picking at it with a fork. She had hoped to eat one healthy thing on this trip, but gave up and put it down, stuffing chicken nuggets in her mouth, then digging a spoon into her melting sundae.

Janie walked over to Fin, "Do you want Aunt Janie to read you a book?" she trilled. Fin smiled and nodded, he loved to be read to. Fin handed her *The Little Engine That Could*, ready to be pulled on to her lap. Kai softened at the sweet sight.

"Thank you…for thinking of us, for thinking of my boy," Kai smiled, *You're under stress*, she reminded herself, *Be kind*. "I know it's hard to get away with three small children."

"Blood is blood, and family is family. You would do the same for me," Janie replied.

"Yeah, I would," she said sincerely. Janie began to read the book as Kai sat on the bed, looking on. It was a sweet sight. *"I think I can, I think I can…"*

Maybe it would be okay to have Janie there, tomorrow. At least she wouldn't have to wait for him to come out of the surgical room alone. He had to be fully intubated and under anesthesia, even though they wouldn't be cutting into him, it was necessary; otherwise a child of that age would wriggle too much for the cast to be applied effectively. The whole thing was scary, but here they were. It wasn't that there was no going back, but what was there to go back to? Watching Fin's spine curve more dangerously, every minute of every day? She had no choice; she had to take this leap with no net. *It is what it is*, Kai told herself.

She set the alarm clock for 4:30am and laid out some clothes for both her and for Fin, so she wouldn't have to think about it in the morning. Even with all of the advice the other parents on the support group had given her, it was still *her child* going through this procedure for the first time—it was still the terrifying unknown. She lay back on the bed and watched the snow flurries fall outside the hotel window. Each icy flake was as light as the feathers she was resting her hope on, shimmering silvery white, as they drifted to the Earth.

After Kai and Janie had both read Fin some more books and he had fallen to sleep in the crib between the

beds, the sisters each got into the separate beds, to at least
try to sleep.

"Kai? You awake?" Janie whispered a few
minutes later.

"Yeah," Kai whispered back.

"I read something in a magazine on the plane, that
only one out of every hundred turtle hatchlings live. They
hatch from those eggs buried in the sand, and run like
mad to the ocean, but I guess most of them just don't
make it. 99 out of a hundred die, before they've even had
a chance to live. That's so sad." Janie murmured.

"*Why*, exactly, did you feel the need to bring this
up, now?" Kai asked, feeling a lump forming in her
throat. "Fin is gonna make it to the ocean, Janie, because *I
will carry him there.*"

"I wasn't talking about Fin, I was talking about
turtles. *Sorry.*" Janie rolled over, pulling up the covers as
Kai lay in bed, staring at the ceiling. It would be a long
night.

15
The Kindness of Strangers

Kai woke up at 4:30am, she had only gotten about four hours of restless sleep. She looked at her precious baby boy, cozily curled up in his favorite soft blankets in the portable crib, thinking about the fact that he had no idea that he'd be in a body cast by the afternoon. The thought just killed her; it made her stomach twist into sickening knots. The fear of the unknown, the panic was so strong that morning, it almost made her want to die, to cease to exist at moments, so she didn't have to watch him go through it—what was to come. She didn't even want to take him to the hospital, but she knew she had to. Dying was quitting, and she wouldn't *ever* quit on Fin.

Just as with the MRIs, she couldn't give him any milk or anything to eat after midnight, because of the anesthesia, so she was grateful he hadn't woken in the middle of the night, wanting his bottle. She forced herself to get up and brew some coffee in the little coffee maker that was provided in the room, then she woke Janie, who looked bleary eyed.

"Janie, we have to go in about an hour." Janie groaned and got up. Kai nodded towards Fin, "Let's let him sleep until the last ten minutes, then we'll just quickly get him dressed and go."

Both sisters got ready in front of the mirror with double sinks in front of it that was part of the wide room, drinking the coffee Kai had brewed and quietly putting their clothes on. Kai felt like the day was already moving in surreal, slow motion. She woke sleepy little Fin and put on his clothes, hugging his still soft, warm, pliant body and trying to give him some apple juice. Clear liquids were allowed before 6am, but Fin refused it, which made Kai's heart hurt, because she knew he'd be starving later.

They put on their winter coats and brought a big bag packed with Fin's favorite toys and a DVD player, taking the elevator down and walking through the lobby, nodding silently at the young, bespectacled male check-in clerk behind the counter. Walking out into the pitch dark morning, with the parking lot now blanketed in thick snow, was like being in a *completely* different world from Kai's old footloose and fancy free, beachy California life.

Janie drove, so that Kai could sit in the back seat with Fin in his car seat, holding his tiny hand. Kai was finally happy to have Janie there, even though they barely spoke on the way—after the car accident she got into the night before, at least she didn't have to face driving again that morning.

Parking and walking into the beautiful hospital was calm and quiet, the nurse had told Kai that Fin would be the first "surgery" appointment of the day, and the place felt pretty empty and serene that early. The snowcapped mountain peaks surrounding the hospital were majestic in the early morning dawn.

Janie looked around in awe, "*This* is the charity hospital? Wow."

"I know. Isn't it something? Although, I think the work they do here is even more beautiful," Kai said softly, as she carried her sleepy little boy inside.

Everything went smoothly that morning. They checked in at the registration desk and got Janie a visitor's pass to wear, then went up the elevator to the second floor, past the large circular playroom to the inpatient rooms. Everyone was warm and welcoming, giving them a room with a stuffed spotted seal toy waiting in the crib-style hospital bed for Fin, along with an Elmo book that he loved. There was a big, super soft blue blanket in the bed, with brightly colored sea horses, fish and octopus, an underwater sea scene that was a gift for them to take home. Every child got one; an orderly told them that they all came from the same generous donor.

Their more senior nurse for the day, Claire, came in and introduced herself, telling them to press the call button if they needed anything. She had blunt cut, short blonde hair and was clearly experienced, intelligent and warm. Claire said the kids who were casted were usually very crabby when they woke up from the anesthesia, and that was normal, but he'd be doing much better as the day progressed. She said, just as the parents on the C.A.S.T. group had assured Kai, that the kids were incredibly resilient, and it may not look like it at first, but they *do* bounce back.

Fin was given a small flannel hospital gown, and they took his blood pressure and listened to his lungs and checked his temperature. The anesthesiologist, a kind man from Pakistan asked a number of thorough questions, making sure he was healthy enough for the procedure.

Claire instructed Kai and Janie to take Fin down to a lower floor for a pre-cast X-ray. This hospital took a standing image versus a lying down or "supine" one, and Kai had heard standing was more accurate in getting the true measure of his curve with gravity. They also took a second X-ray of him lying down, stretching his spine as straight as they could for the image. Fin hated it and cried, but the female X-ray technicians were lovely and warm to them, and gave him a Cookie Monster sticker as a reward.

Back on the second floor in their room, Dr. D'Astous came in and said hello, he was on his rounds for the morning. He gently informed Kai that, "Fin's spine is now curved at 63 degrees."

63 DEGREES! Her jaw dropped. He had been at 34 degrees only *six weeks earlier*! If she hadn't gotten

176

him in on cancellation slots for *both* MRIs *and* for this casting date, he could've easily been at 80 or 90 degrees before being put in the first cast—Kai knew from the support group that those numbers can mean *permanent organ damage*, particularly to his lungs. Kai thanked the doctor, barely able to process that number change. Fin's first two orthopedic surgeons in L.A. had done her baby a terrible disservice, to say the least. They had almost ruined her baby's life.

It was now crystal clear to Kai that she had almost missed the window to save her child.

Janie's face was white; she looked like she didn't know what to say. Kai told herself not to freak out, to stay in the moment. The Physician's Assistant Matt, a good looking man with a friendly, upbeat vibe, stopped by their room to introduce himself and to see if Kai had any questions. Matt gave Kai all of the time she needed as she peppered him with a few last minute worries, then he explained, "It used to take us up to four hours to do a cast, when we first started doing this, but now we have it down to about an hour. They'll page you in maybe an hour and a half or so, after he's begun to wake up."

When Matt had left and they were waiting to be called for Fin's procedure, Janie turned to Kai, pursing her lips.

"You don't have to go through with this, you know." Janie's face was pinched.

Kai looked at her in disbelief. "He's at *63 degrees*, Janie…you said you were here for *support*."

"I am, and I will support you if you decide to spare Fin this pain. You can just do bracing and get the surgery, later."

Kai set her jaw. "Janie, I have researched this *extensively*, and I *promise* you, these casts are not supposed to be painful, *at all*. We've almost missed the window to save him without multiple spinal surgeries. Fin would have pain later, a *lot* of pain, if I don't get him in

177

this cast *today*. If you don't like it, you can go back to Kansas. I told you not to question my choices as a parent, not today. Or *ever*."

Janie closed her mouth, looking out of the room's window at the snow, as Fin played happily with toys and his new book. He was such a trooper; Kai knew he had to be hungry without his morning milk. She thought about other mothers in third world countries, who had to endure watching their children go hungry, every single day. There were far worse things than this.

She was still one of the lucky ones, Teddy or no Teddy. She couldn't forget that.

A different, heavyset brunette nurse came for them, and Kai carried Fin in her arms to the prep room, with Janie following silently, judgmentally behind them. In the prep room, they gave Fin a dose of Versed, a drug that made him giggle and act silly and sleepy. *Baby Valium*, Kai figured. Too bad they couldn't give it to the parents.

The nurse asked if Kai wanted to choose a color for the fiberglass part of the cast that went over the plaster. She chose "blue for boy," deciding to keep it simple. They gave Fin an I.V. in his foot and Matt came in and put two thin, stretchy tubes of beige fabric over Fin's body. Matt decided he needed the smallest size for the stretchy gray, short sleeved anti-microbial medical t-shirt they put under the cast. It was a mock turtleneck style T, Kai had heard that it helped keep things like crumbs from falling down inside the cast, as well as helping to protect their skin. The t-shirt was "impregnated" with silver thread; she had heard, to prevent bacterial growth—pretty high tech, for something as low tech as plaster.

A few minutes after Matt had sized the t-shirt, they told Kai it was time to take Fin back for the procedure. Janie was quiet as a mouse the whole time Matt was there, but she glared at Kai, saying everything with her eyes: *Don't do this. It's not too late to change your mind!*

Kai kissed and squeezed her soft baby boy one last time, ignoring Janie, and let the medical professionals wheel him away in the hospital crib, feeling her heart rip a new jagged tear down its middle. It was painful, but not nearly as hard as she would have thought—because she knew they were going to help him and possibly save his life. She clutched the beeper she had been given, for when he was to be brought back to their room.

The next hour and a half dragged on slowly. Kai wondered how she could be so tired and so scared at the same time. She and Janie went down to the cafeteria, where all of the food for the patients was free, and it cost very little for the visiting families. They ate in silence, and Kai even managed to choke down some biscuits and gravy—heavy, creamy comfort food. Sometimes under intense stress she couldn't eat anything, and other times no greasy food was safe within miles of her mouth.

When her beeper went off, Kai literally ran to the elevator and back towards their room, practically knocking Matt over as he entered the hallway in light blue surgical scrubs.

"Fin did great! He's still very sleepy," Matt said.

"Oh, thank God!" Kai exclaimed. "Is it okay if I hug you?" she nearly squeaked.

"Sure," he grinned.

Kai embraced Matt, "Thank you, thank you *so* much. I'm just *so grateful.*"

"Of course, we love what we do. Listen, when they wake up, they can be upset and cranky, that's normal."

"Okay, I'm prepared for that." She was dying to see her boy.

"They'll bring him back to the room when he's woken up a little more." Matt smiled again, waving and

walking off down the hall, as Kai and Janie walked back
to their room.

No Fin, yet—his hospital bed had not been
wheeled back in. They sank down in the two chairs, they
were lucky to have a private room, because there was a
second child's hospital bed that was still empty.

Fifteen minutes later, Kai leapt to her feet as the
nurses wheeled Fin in, lying on his back in his new blue
cast in the metal hospital crib. He was moving his head a
little, but he was still half asleep.

The cast looked good, but he looked like a turtle
stuck on his back, unable to get up by himself. Kai's heart
sank as he started to wake up more, beginning to cry.

"Oh, Fin, baby, Mommy's right here…" she
soothed. He suddenly looked down at the foreign object,
the cast, which must've felt restrictive and heavy on his
small body. Her baby then looked back up at his Mommy,
Janie and the nurses with fear and accusation in his eyes,
like he was thinking "*What did you DO to me?*"

Kai winced; it broke her heart to see the fear in his
big green eyes, when she couldn't truly use language to
explain it to him, not in a way that he could totally
understand. "Oh, my baby, I know, I'm sorry…this is
gonna make your curvy back better…"

The nurse, Claire, helped Kai prop him up with
pillows. He still had the I.V. in his foot, and he began to
struggle to try to sit up, confused.

"They almost always wake up really irritable, in
the first cast. It is much harder on the parents; your son
will amaze you. I know it's difficult to believe, but within
a few hours he'll be doing so much better," Claire said to
Kai comfortingly.

It didn't really register for Kai, all she could think
about was that *Fin was scared, her baby may be in pain,*
and he was too young to have the language skills for her
to be able to soothe him and explain what was happening.
It was, bar none, the worst moment of her entire life.

"SAW IT OFF HIM! THIS IS *BARBARIC*! *How could you do this to your baby*?!" Janie shrieked. Fin cried even harder, he began screaming, and tears sprung from his eyes and started streaming down his pink cheeks.

That did it. "JANIE, GET OUT OF THIS ROOM *RIGHT NOW*!" Kai yelled, furious. Claire looked startled by their outbursts, as Kai shouted, "Go back to the hotel and get your things and *GO BACK TO KANSAS*!"

Janie jumped back at Kai's fury.

Claire firmly and politely said to Janie, "Ma'am, I'm going to have to ask you to leave the room."

"I...I will." Janie backed out of the room, shaken, "God bless you, Fin," she mumbled, leaving, as Kai hugged her crying child.

Claire turned to Kai, "I promise you, he *will* bounce back, I've seen it time and again. Let's try to keep things calm in here. I'll get him some infant Tylenol for muscle aches." She patted Kai's shoulders. Kai willed herself not to fall apart.

The next few hours were rough. Fin was extremely upset that he couldn't sit up by himself in the bed, without being propped up with pillows. The infant Tylenol really helped, though, his muscles must've been sore from the three dimensional traction table they use for the casting. The cast had rough edges, and the other nurse had already "petaled" some of them while he was still sleeping, covering them with moleskin, which is a white medical tape that has a sticky side and a side that was like soft felt. Claire said they would cover all of the rough edges of Fin's cast before the end of the day, and that Kai could take some extra tape home.

Fin wanted badly to get out of the crib bed, so Kai put him in her lap in a chair and read him books and gave him an orange Popsicle, which dripped everywhere. He was able to be distracted from the cast for short periods of time, with toys and books and the DVD player, but then he would want to stand up, and he would just sink to his knees from the weight of the cast and cry again. It weighed about three pounds, more than one fifth of his entire body weight. Kai figured it would be like someone put a 25 pound weight vest on her body, without warning. Like one day she just woke up and it was on—and she couldn't take it off—*not* a very fun surprise.

I'm doing the best thing for him; she repeated in her head like a mantra, *I'm doing the best thing for him…*

Claire gave Fin some infant Motrin a few hours later, and within thirty minutes of that, he was standing up and wanting to try to walk. Claire then removed the I.V. from his foot, which was a big relief, because he frickin' *hated* it, and Matt stopped by the room to check on them as Kai was feeding him some vanilla pudding as a treat.

At Fin's tailbone, the back of the cast was pretty snug; it seemed almost too tight to be comfortable. While it was important for the cast to be snugly anchored at the hips to work, Claire was concerned that a diaper couldn't be tucked under it, so Kai mentioned it to Matt.

Matt checked it, nodded and said to come with him. Kai carried Fin behind him to a room on the lower floor, where he used a big pair of duck billed, rounded medical pliers to bend or "flare" the edge of the back of the cast out a little bit. Fin wasn't too crazy about being poked and prodded again, but ten minutes later, he began walking on his own in the cast!

Kai was astonished; it had been less than five hours since he'd been under anesthesia. He was smiling and holding on to chairs as he navigated the big lobby area on the first floor of the hospital, getting his sea legs under him.

Kai felt her tears well up as she let out a loud *whoop*, shouting "He's already WALKING! YAY, FIN! GREAT JOB!"

Heads turned in the lobby to watch him, and her heart soared with pride. He was *already* bouncing back!

Fin had a blast playing in the huge circular play room upstairs, darting into sunbeams on the floor like he was playing hopscotch, and throwing basketballs to the ground. He couldn't bend down to pick them up yet, but when she handed them to him, he was good to go. Pretty soon, he was *running* like the wind! Kai had to chase him around, within a hugs reach, to catch him from falling. He started to nearly wipe out a bunch of times, as he was top heavy with the weight, and he still had to relearn his balance point.

If Janie could only see him *now*! All of the parents on the support group were right, the kids were incredibly resilient. She called Doris and Fadi from her cell phone in the playroom, and they were both over the moon to hear the good news. She didn't tell them he had been at 63 degrees this morning; she didn't want to worry them more. There would be a second X-ray soon today, taken in the cast, that's when she would know how much correction they got.

Something suddenly struck her as Fin ran around and played. *His cough was gone*, the one he always had lately, when he ran fast. Maybe the cast correction had taken the pressure off his lungs, already? Going on maternal instinct, Kai couldn't help but think it had.

Twenty minutes later, Claire came out to tell her that they were ready for Fin's "in cast" X-ray. Kai took him downstairs to the lovely, positive and spirited ladies who were the technicians, and he cried through it, but they got it with him standing up, as Kai sang songs to distract him—Bob Marley, of course.

One of the technicians then pulled up his two X-rays next to each other on the computer screen, allowing Kai to take a look. The first one, the 63 degree one from that morning, made Kai gasp. Fin's spine had been curved in a very severe "C" shape to the naked eye, and on the X-ray, she could see that it was beginning to corkscrew and wind into an even more frightening "S". The X-ray in the cast was much, much better, but still obviously curved.

Kai took Fin back to their room and Claire helped her do the petaling with the white moleskin tape, covering all of the rough edges on the cast. Fin was pretty tired of nurses and doctors by this point, and got crabby again, beginning to cry. Kai felt her stress levels rise; she hated to see him go through even more today.

They finished the job, and as Claire was leaving the room, she turned to Kai. "I'm sorry, about what happened with your sister, this morning. You are a beautiful family, and I think you're *amazing*," she said.

Kai smiled warmly back at her, "You're amazing, thank you, for everything, today." Yes, she and Fin *were* a family, Kai thought proudly, even just the two of them.

Dr. D'Astous came by the room next, with Matt, both looking pleased. "So, I am very optimistic," the doctor began, as Kai felt herself holding her breath. Luckily, Fin was occupied with his books and toys in the hospital crib.

"How did he do?" she asked nervously.

"We got him down from 63 degrees to 34 in this first cast," the doctor replied.

Kai exhaled. "That's good, right?" She knew from the support group that the first cast was usually the most correction you would get, more than any of the following casts.

Dr. D'Astous nodded, "It's good; I'm pleased. Like I mentioned, Fin reminds me of another patient named Noah, they both have a syrinx cyst and had similar curves. We've had great success with Noah, he's now out of casts and wearing a brace, and he started with an even bigger curve than Fin."

Kai's face lit up, "So, do you think we'll be able to avoid surgery?"

"I can't say for sure, but I'm hopeful. I think so," the doctor said.

"How long do you think he'll have to wear the casts?"

"Well, each child is different, but an educated guess for Fin would be around two years, changing them every 2-3 months. Fin started at a high number, at 63, he may never get back to zero, but if we avoid the surgeries, that would be a big success."

"Well, if we avoid surgeries for this, I will consider it a *complete* success. I don't need a zero," she grinned.

Dr. D'Astous smiled. "I will tell you, I do the surgeries, as well, for this condition, and my colleagues and I are becoming less and less...*enchanted* with the outcomes."

"The surgeries have a very high complication rate," Matt agreed.

"And many of the kids have more than one complication," Dr. D'Astous explained, holding out his hand to shake Kai's.

"Can I hug you?" Kai asked.

"Sure," he replied, and she hugged Fin's doctor, this kind, humble man who was *already* saving his life.

"I'll check on him first thing in the morning," the doctor said, smiling as he left the room. Matt stayed behind to answer any other questions she had.

"Are the complications really bad, from the surgeries?" Kai was almost afraid to ask.

Matt nodded, "It seems like we're doing another surgery to try to fix one of the 'complications' all of the time. We see it all. The VEPTR rods can begin protruding through the child's skin on their shoulders, and the bone can form around the metal hooks that are placed in the hipbones. We've had to make a decision to crack an eleven year old girl's pelvis or to leave the hooks in, potentially permanently."

Kai's face went pale. "Those aren't the spinal growing rods, right? That's what we were told Fin would need before age 3, without the casts."

"Oh, once you start surgery on the spine, unfortunately, there is no going back. Surgical expansion of the rods has to be done every six months and complications can vary from broken rods inside the child's body, metal eroding through their pelvis permanently, broken ribs, metal protruding through the skin, infections, rod dislodgement, and the risks associated with repeated anesthesia and psychological distress... You can imagine it affects their normal growth, and the rest of their life. It's horrible stuff, but if they miss the opportunity for casting young with this early treatment, those are the best options we and the parents have, at this point."

Kai looked at Fin, happily playing in his new cast. He was frustrated by the newness of it, but he was clearly in no pain.

Matt continued, "There's halo traction, that can buy some growing time for some kids, but we have to put metal pins in their skull and add weight to it gradually. They have to stay in the hospital the whole time, in some cases months. Some kids have to have it done 2, 3 times...*then* get the growth rods or fusion. You'll see some of them, on your visits here, there's a girl here with a halo, right now. Ella."

"We like to say they are angels with an *actual* halo," Claire said as she walked in.

Kai was trembling, for those beautiful children and for their families. "I know those are things Fin would've had to endure, without finding you guys and ISOP. There just aren't enough thanks yous."

Matt smiled, squeezing her shoulder gently and walking towards the door, "We appreciate it. A hospital like this...it's what medicine *should* be, but usually *isn't*."

186

As Matt left, Claire asked Kai if she had any more questions, and reminded her what time the cafeteria closed, adding that she could also order pizza delivery to her room, if she preferred to. They did the diapering technique together, and Claire showed Kai how to tuck the edges of the diaper under the cast, adding that different parents often had their own techniques that worked the best for their child.

It was twilight, and Kai suddenly felt inspired to put on Fin's coat and take him out to see the snow outside the hospital. He had never really played in snow before, so she took him down and out of the front lobby and chased him while he toddled to a small snowdrift. He was so excited and happy, reaching out to touch the cold white, fluffy substance, fascinated; it was like he hadn't gone through anything that day, at all.

Their anesthesiologist walked past them on his way to the parking lot, saying "We ordered that snow storm last night, just for our California visitors!"

Kai laughed as Fin giggled, just a normal little boy, now one of the luckiest children in the entire world with his condition. She knew she had done the right thing. Not the *easy* thing, but the right thing, she knew it in her bones.

Back in the hospital hallway, she passed a stunningly beautiful little blonde girl with halo traction applied to her head, walking while pulling the medieval looking contraption behind her. It must've been Ella, the child Matt mentioned. She had a serene smile on her face, and she *did* look like an angel who had alighted on Earth. Kai didn't know if it was the tears welling in her own eyes, but the girl literally appeared to glow.

As Ella passed them, she looked at Fin, smiling at the sight of him joyfully running down the hall in his cast, then up at Kai, gazing directly in her eyes. There was something in this child's eyes that was *beyond* special...it made Kai feel like the Holy Ghost was passing through her.

Could certain special children be chosen by God to endure things like this, and if so, why? She didn't know the answer, and she wasn't sure if she'd ever know, until she passed from this Earth someday, herself.

Kai took Fin back to the playroom. A dark haired, very pregnant woman, around 30, was there, watching her child, a little boy about 3, dragging himself around on the floor with his arms. He looked incredibly happy, not self-conscious at all. "Hi," his mother said to Kai, "I'm April, and that's Joey."

"Hi, I'm Kai and this is Fin," Kai said, "He just got a cast put on for Progressive Scoliosis." Kai noticed the woman's little boy also had something wrong with his eyes, they looked in two different directions—Gaze Palsy? Was that the right term for it?

"Ah, I just found out my second baby, the one in here," the woman touched her swollen belly, "He has it, too, the same thing Joey has…severe club foot. He's getting his second surgery for it, tomorrow. It came back, after the first surgery."

"I'm so sorry." Kai's jaw dropped, to have *two* kids with the same condition? This poor woman…and being pregnant, knowing her new baby, still in her belly, would also have to endure surgery at a young age. It didn't seem fair.

"Yeah…the surgery is pretty horrible, they have to cut through his Achilles tendons," April said.

Kai shuddered. "Oh, my God."

The young mother nodded sadly.

"Do you mind if I ask, is it genetic?" Kai looked at the joyful little boy on the floor, picking up a ball, throwing and chasing it by dragging his legs and scuffling along.

"Yes, one of my husband's great uncles had it, and it's on my side, too, a cousin. But when people feel sorry for me, I just tell them that at least my child has something that is *fixable*." April said, "My husband is coming to visit and bring dinner, so we better head back to the room." She picked up her little boy and carried him off, as he smiled and waved at Kai.

"Bye, Joey, maybe we'll see you tomorrow!" She winced after they turned down the hall, not wanting to think about what he'd have to endure.

Kai would see many more kids around the hallways and the playroom, one pre-teen boy with titanium, state-of the art prosthetic legs, casually playing pool by himself, and several families from Mexico watching TV on the soft couches, a program in Spanish. She saw kids who had casts on their foot and lower leg, being treated for clubfoot. Clubfoot—it was one of those things you heard about, but it seemed like it existed in the past—she had never known anyone with it in modern day.

Matt came by and said hello and Kai quietly asked him about the kids with leg casts. "Yeah, it's very similar to the Mehta casting treatment in that Dr. Ponseti, Ignacio Ponseti from Spain applied these specialized casts to his young patients with clubfoot for years with great success, while everyone else in the orthopedic community was doing surgeries that didn't work as well. His colleagues scoffed at him for over twenty years, just like with Mehta and what we're doing now, and finally parents of the children Dr. Ponsetti had cured demanded that he get recognized, and that casting for Clubfoot become common practice, because it works better than the surgery. Unfortunately, things can take *a long time* to change in the medical community," Matt smiled sadly.

"Wow, that's amazing. I hope it doesn't take that long for Mehta casting to be common practice." Kai frowned.

"Me, too," Matt nodded, "I better get back to the clinic."

Fin fell asleep in the stroller as she pushed him around the playroom a bit more. Kai couldn't stop thinking about all of the children who wouldn't get the right treatment if this casting took decades more to become common practice by doctors- it was so wrong and so heartbreaking. She put a blanket over Fin and went down to the hospital cafeteria for a quick bite, sitting alone with her boy at a table for four. It was then that she noticed an old man, maybe anywhere from 80 to 85, sitting by himself near the window. He had on a red Shiners jacket and baseball hat, with white hair, pale mottled skin and kind eyes. He waved at Kai and pulled himself up to walk over.

"Hello," he smiled, extending his hand with a small lollipop in it, "This is for your little boy when he wakes up." His voice was faint, hoarse, but his eyes were lively. Kai wondered if he had served in the war as a young man. He was still serving their country, she realized, even at this advanced age, he was a proud Shriner who was probably volunteering at the hospital, maybe he was driving families to and from their hotel rooms or to the Ronald McDonald House and the airport. Kai was weary from the long day, but she beamed at this kind man, extending her hand and shaking his, "I am—we are—so *grateful* to be here. *Thank you.*" The man smiled and nodded, modestly tipping his hat before walking away.

Kai was in awe, seeing what the Shriners Hospitals do, close up. It was full of grace, the kindest thing she'd ever witnessed. It was both the worst day of her life, and the best, if that made any sense. She had been dropped into another world, another life, and there was much sadness here—and much light, as well.

It was another long night. Clarie gave Fin one more dose of infant Motrin around 7pm, and he fell asleep on his back by 7:30. Kai tried to sleep in the fold-out easy chair that converted into a slim bed for one, but her mind was racing, despite her exhaustion, she had such a mix of emotions. A different nurse took over for the night shift, and had to keep checking on Fin throughout the night. Between that and Fin waking up every half hour or so, fussy because he couldn't turn over in the cast, Kai got maybe twenty minutes of sleep at a time.

The next morning around 6:30, they had visitors, well actually, neighbors to share their room: another young mother who had light brown hair to her shoulders, a thin woman in her forties with red, curly hair, who looked to be the child's grandmother, and a 2 year old boy, with reddish brown hair. The little boy was adorable and the family was very quiet. Kai was busy taking care of Fin when he woke up, so they didn't talk much, they just waved hello, quickly introduced themselves and smiled.

The morning was pretty uneventful. Fin was in much better spirits, he just wanted to have his milk, and then run through the hallways to the playroom and play. The nurses all commented on how fast he was. Janie called on Kai's cell when they were in the playroom and Fin was occupied with some toys. "Hello?" Kai answered warily.

Janie blurted, "I'm sorry, I was out of line. He just looked so scared to death in that body cast!"

As Kai updated Janie on how Fin was doing, she saw April, the pregnant mother, walking with her child, Joey, to go into surgery. April's husband, who looked like a biker dude with a beard and a blonde ponytail, lovingly carried his boy in his strong arms, as a nurse rolled his hospital bed and April waved sadly at Kai from across the playroom.

Kai waved back to April as her family disappeared down into a hallway. The happy little boy was still smiling, on the way to have his Achilles tendons severed. Kai's eyes misted over, and she tried to shake off her sadness for him, turning her attention back to Janie on the phone. "Fin's doing great, he's running around and playing, and they got him down from 63 to 34 degrees in this first cast. We'll get another one in ten weeks."

"Well!" Janie exclaimed, "That is a *MIRACLE*!"

"Yes, it really is. Listen, I have to go, I have to stay close in case he loses his balance, he's top heavy in the cast." Kai began to chase after her fast little guy as he ran for a rolling soccer ball.

"I love you, sister." Janie said softly. "Mom's watching over him."

How could Janie be so horrible, and then suddenly say the right thing? "Thanks for saying that. Bye." Kai sighed, hanging up.

As she carried Fin back to their room, a nurse she hadn't met before stopped her in the hallway, "Hi, I'm Mary, I'm good friends with your nurse, Claire."

"Hi, Mary, I'm Kai and this is Fin."

Mary stood near her, her hands firmly on her hips, looking directly in her eyes. "*No pity,*" she said simply.

Kai took that in, not quite sure what to say. "Oh, okay…no pity…for my son, or for myself…or for both of us?"

"It's what I tell all of the parents here, we see so many different conditions…these kids shouldn't be treated like you feel sorry for them, they should be allowed to be normal kids. Just treat him as normally as possible," Mary replied.

"Thank you, I'll remember that." Kai was a little taken aback by the pointed nature of the woman's words, but she nodded and smiled. Everyone here genuinely seemed to care about kids and want to help.

Back in their room, Dr. D'Astous and Matt checked on Fin, before they were discharged by Claire.

"He's doing great. This will be…a *project*. A lot of the parents say *'Slow and steady wins the race,'* with casting," the doctor said.

"Sometimes you get one, two or even three casts with no correction, and then boom, the child hits a growth spurt and you suddenly get a big leap. So we all have to be patient," Matt explained.

"Oh, wow…but even if we get zero correction in a cast, it's still keeping him from getting worse, right?" Kai asked.

"Oh, if he didn't have the cast on, I guarantee you, he would be getting *much* worse," Dr. D'Astous replied.

"So it's still a success, either way," said Kai.

"Yes, and…we'll see you in ten weeks," the doctor said.

"Thank you both *so much*, everyone here has been incredible…" Kai barely had the words to express her gratitude, as the doctor smiled, shook her hand and moved on to his next patient. He approached the other family sharing the room, the young mom, young grandma and the brownish red haired boy, who was playing on the floor in a new cast that had just been put on first thing that morning. He had arrived in a cast, so it was at least his second one. It was blue, just like Fin's, Kai thought, they matched.

As she began to pack their things, she overheard the doctor tell the family that they had been able to get their boy down to 80 degrees in this cast; they had started casting him at *105* degrees. Kai almost could not believe her ears. *One hundred and five*. The doctor kindly explained that this blue cast could be the boy's last one; surgery would probably be needed in the near future.

This boy had missed the window to get a Mehta Method cast for a potential cure, before his curve got too severe. He would face the multiple surgeries that Fin would hopefully avoid. He was two years old and four months, she had overheard his mother say earlier. Just a baby, with no idea what was ahead of him—he may already have permanent lung damage—he would certainly have to endure the pain of surgeries and possible deformity. This young mother's doctors had not given her the right medical advice, and now it was too late for these casts to cure him, or even to prevent inevitable surgery, very young.

Kai clutched Fin's blankets, glancing up at the young mother and grandmother, who looked to be in shock. She could almost feel like she was inside their heads, imaging the rush of terrible adrenaline clouding their senses, as they tried to comprehend what the doctor was really saying. She didn't feel separate from these people, this family, she felt like they were exactly the same.

When the doctor and Matt left, she approached the family, "Hi, my name is Kai, and this is Fin, he has the same condition."

They softly said "Hello" back, introducing themselves as mom Sandy, grandma Sylvia and baby Miles.

"Did your original doctors tell you about this casting, that it had to be started early?" Kai asked.

They both shook their heads, the young mom answering, "No. Our doctors didn't tell us about this, at all."

The little boy's grandmother nodded, "Only after we had been to our third specialist did they direct us here to Shriners."

"Doesn't that make you *mad*?" Kai blurted out.

"Yes," the young mom softly replied, as her mother nodded silently.

Kai told them about the C.A.S.T. support group and ISOP, and they said goodbye. A chill accompanied by a mental numbness ran through her nerves and brain as she left the room, pushing Fin in his new cast and stroller.

She had just seen two roads diverge, and her child had gotten the better one. It wasn't fair to that family, to that boy, and it was simply *unacceptable*.

She felt an urgency to do something to help change that, at least by spreading the word about this treatment, and guiding as many other parents as she could reach. But first, she had to get her little turtle man safely home to the ocean.

16
Baby Steps

Fadi triumphantly picked them up at LAX airport with Doris in his cab; they were both thrilled to see them. Doris' mean virus had passed—it had thankfully only lasted forty eight hours. The return flight had been blessedly uneventful. As Kai had lovingly carried Fin off of the plane, with him facing her, his arms around her neck in a hug, the female airline attendant had joked, "I wish someone would carry *me* that way."

Don't we all, Kai mused.

The only small glitch had been in the Salt Lake City Airport, going through the security check. They had to examine Fin's cast to make sure it didn't contain explosives. Kai didn't mind, they were very nice about it, but they had to go off to an area for his cast to be swabbed and his hands to be checked with some kind of wipe. Kai couldn't imagine somebody strapping a bomb to their baby, but crazy things happened in this world, and she realized that these people were just doing their job to try to protect the passengers. They were cleared to go through security after just a few minutes.

Back at their little house in Santa Monica, she and Doris took some photos of Fin walking around in his cast and some soft navy blue pants, smiling from ear to ear. He was in no pain and he was as happy as ever, but Kai's initial elation at getting him safely there and back soon turned into a mixture of raw emotions: sadness, anger, fear. In particular, the *anger* rose up in her with a fury, at the thought of how close she came to missing this opportunity. She was blown away by the thoughts of what could've happened, certainly *would've* happened, had she taken the two orthopedist's advice, and not found ISOP by *Googling*! Finding it on the *Internet*!

Had she had her baby less than ten years earlier, she wouldn't have even done an Internet search; it was a different world, now. A retired Indian female doctor, a single mother from Colorado and her daughter, a French Canadian doctor, two French doctors who invented this three dimensional table in the '40s, and a group of men who wear tall, red hats—it took *all of these people and more* to save her child's spine and life.

It took a *village* to save Fin; that was for sure. That village also included Dr. Becket, the young neurologist, who had helped her get Fin's MRI appointment moved up before the casting date, and Angie, the wonderful Care Coordinator at Shriners, who had given her the cancellation slot; that surely was the final stroke of luck for Fin to be treated in time.

She maybe thought of Dr. Becket, a little bit....sometimes, for a moment or two. But he was engaged, and she was in no good place to even *think* about dating. It was *ridiculous* to have a crush right now, she told herself.

But *still*...his thick tuft of light brown hair that hung over his forehead, that part that looked like it needed to be cut, for him to look completely professional...it was, perhaps...memorable. It looked touchable. *No no no no no no*...she realized, she was just a little lonely. Maybe a lot.

But she wasn't alone. She had Doris and Fadi, who very recently had been two total strangers, and were both now dear friends—practically family, to her. Kai was overwhelmed by gratitude for all of these new people in her life, and the gifts they had given her—and she certainly wasn't forgetting about God answering her prayers, and the gut instinct that had been the answer to the most difficult decision of her life.

At the same time that she felt this immense, life altering gratitude, she was so deeply angry at the doctors and the medical system that had almost allowed her child to fall through the cracks. A medical system that was still allowing children like Fin to be led to early and multiple spinal surgeries—it made her sick with fury. This anger was intense and like nothing she had ever felt before. Sure, she had felt anger in her life, most recently at Teddy—but this was something bigger, the sheer *wrongness* of what almost happened to Fin's future, what still *might* happen if the casts didn't work for him, it nearly made her heart and head explode.

She knew she had to contain these feelings and focus on Fin's joy for life. There were practical matters; she had to be his mother 24/7. Anger could eat you up inside, and she couldn't afford to be eaten alive by these feelings.

There were obviously going to be some growing pains in the cast. Fin was still top heavy from the weight of it, and he would fall fairly often, so there were more small bumps or "eggs" on his forehead. He also had a lot of trouble getting down to the floor or ground to pick something up.

He really was her little turtle man, because many times a day, he would try to get down on his knees to pick up a toy or something from the floor, and he couldn't easily get back up by himself. Sometimes, in trying to get back up, he'd get stuck on his back or his belly, in his hard little turtle shell. The surprising and precious thing is that he didn't really complain about it. He would sometimes even "hang out" down there on the floor and play with the toy he had been reaching for.

After a few minutes, Kai would hear him sort of quietly moan, "*Ahhh...*" and she would run and put him back on his feet. At first, this happened so many times a day, just seeing him lying there again each time broke her heart. "It's harder on the parents," everyone had told her. She wanted to believe that, and it did seem to be true.

Those first few weeks were emotionally painful; there was no way around it. Even though she had Doris, the absence of her own mother and a father for Fin was palpable to her, when her little boy was going through something so huge. The cast weighed only around three pounds, but it felt heavier to lift than that. Doris called it "dead weight," meaning it didn't *move* with you like a child's body did, which made it seem heavier and awkward to carry him, cumbersome, at first.

He also loved to pick up leaves and sticks at the local park, and it was so hard to get back up, at first he wouldn't even attempt it. That made Kai sad, before the cast, he had just *loved* collecting leaves, he would compare them side by side, studying them like a little botanist. He would walk around the park most days with at least one or two choice leaves in his little hands, along with a handful of select sticks. Boys will be boys, and it broke her heart to see him look down at the leaves and sticks he loved so and decide not to gather them, it was too difficult to get back up—his expression said *It just isn't worth it.*

Kai had once thought to herself that it never rains in L.A., unless your child has to get an MRI that day. Correction: It never rains in L.A., unless you have a child in a *body cast*. She found herself caught at the park in a sudden downpour, without an umbrella for Fin—which was a heart attack. She found shelter under an awning until it stopped raining, and never forgot her umbrella again. On another day when it began to lightly rain, a father walked by with his son and saw her covering Fin with the umbrella. The man joked to Kai, "He won't *melt!*"

She replied, "Actually, he *will*, he's in a body cast."

Score: Fin's Mommy: 1, rude dude: 0.

Fin also fell at the park many, many times in the first few weeks—that balance issue again, twice falling forward like he was being catapulted, hitting his forehead on the hard concrete sidewalk that wound around the softball field. Kai always rushed alongside him, trying her hardest to stay within a "hugs reach" of him, but he would still try to run ahead, and she didn't want to take away his zest for life. She would cringe when he fell, lift him and soothe him, kissing his forehead to make it better and drying his tears. It was the same as with any child, but the cast made everything harder at first, a reality which came with a large side helping of maternal guilt. Fin also stopped climbing stairs at first, and still couldn't roll over in his crib. Kai put him to sleep on his back for naps and bedtime, and propped him up with some small pillows under his fitted crib sheet; he did seem more comfortable that way.

She felt herself getting down and even depressed at moments the month after the first cast, and she tried not to let him see her cry. She would go online and get support from the C.A.S.T. group, and everyone promised her she was doing a great job, writing that "It *will* get better!" She clung to this group of strangers she had never met in person, but who had now become some of her most valued friends, via the Internet.

Within the first two weeks, Fin turned over in his crib, Kai entered his nursery one morning and there he was, rolling over and beaming at her with pride. In less time than that, he had figured out how to pull himself up from a kneeling position, by holding on to the coffee table, Kai's legs, or a tree, and he was *back in business* with his stick and leaf collecting.

What everyone had said was right, he *amazed* her, every day re-learning another skill. Soon, he was climbing stairs and going down slides at the park, doing everything he had ever been able to do before. His resilience simply floored her. He was *so* much more resilient than she felt, but his joy lifted her back from her moments of darkness—the nightmares that still sometimes came. She knew it; it was time for her to try to lift somebody else.

Kai went on the support group every single day, finding that at least two new families were joining every week, mostly the moms, and they were all just as lost and terrified as she had been. They wrote in from all over the U.S., the U.K., Australia, India, and Ireland. She, little damaged, almost broken Kai, could help, she could tell them what she'd been told, the advice she'd been given, and what her experience was so far. She almost couldn't believe that she actually had something to *give back*—something positive arising from this dark, frightening pit she and her child had suddenly been plunged into. It was a true gift, and she didn't take it for granted.

It was heartbreaking, though, to read of cases where the child had missed the window for early treatment, and situations when the family lived in an area or country where no doctors did proper Mehta Method casting, period. They couldn't always afford to travel, certainly not from India to the U.S. every two to three months, and ISOP was struggling, grass roots, non-profit charity that had little money, ISOP couldn't pay for all of the families around the world.

Many families in the U.S. travelled out of state to get the treatment for their child, like Kai was doing, and while some received travel assistance from the Shriners, a lot of them were going into debt or barely making ends meet as a result.

The other knowledge that hit her with the palpable force of a boulder was what Heather Hyatt-Montoya had really done for Fin, and for countless other children, by nearly *single handedly* bringing Mehta's Method to the U.S., even though it was yet too late for her own child,

Olivia or "Liv," to be saved by the treatment. What kind of a person *does* something like this, when their own child's serious health problems are ongoing? She had devoted a decade of her life to this cause, and she was living at the poverty level by choice, in order to run the not for profit charity. Who has that kind of energy and devotion, that kind of love for the children of strangers? How do you thank someone for saving your child's life? You simply can't. There are no words. Kai donated what she could afford to ISOP, she sent emails and letters to all of the websites she could find, telling Heather's story, she wrote to the President. Any time she saw a contest for an extraordinary person or even an "every day hero," she wrote in about Heather and what she was doing for countless children who would never meet her.

In those first few weeks, Kai wrote letters to each and every doctor who had seen Fin, sending photos of his back before the cast and one of him smiling ear to ear wearing it. Each letter explained his story so far and included brochures and information sheets on Early Treatment casting, and she made sure they were mailed with signature required, to ensure they'd be received. She figured these doctors may still not believe in casting being the best course of treatment, but they *damn well* couldn't pretend they'd never heard of it. They could *not* claim ignorance in the future.

To her surprise, just two days after she mailed the letters, Dr. Becket called her. "Hello, Kai, this is Jack Becket, I just wanted to see how Fin is doing, and to thank you for your letter."

She blinked, suddenly nervous; she didn't think any of the doctors would respond at all, and definitely not so quickly. "Oh! Hi, Dr. Becket…Fin is doing just *great*, he's thriving, thank you for calling. He's back to doing everything he did before, he doesn't even realize that every kid doesn't have a cast under their t-shirt!"

"That's good to hear," he said, it sounded like he was smiling. "I also…have a strange request."

"Okay, what is it?"

"I'd really like to see the cast in person. I've never seen one of these Mehta Method, or EDF casts before…I think it would be useful knowledge for me to have, for my future patients with Infantile Scoliosis. It's interesting to me that a number of I.S. patients have underlying neurological conditions, like Fin's syrinx cyst."

"Oh, of course," she replied, it was an opportunity to possibly help another family. "*Great*! Would you like us to come to your office one day?" Why was her voice going up so many octaves, she wondered? She sounded a little girly-giddy, even to her own nervous ears.

"You absolutely can, anytime, or…we could meet somewhere, or I could come to you. I don't want to inconvenience you." He also sounded a little nervous.

Huh, she thought, why do I feel like I'm in junior high? He's *engaged*. And I'm not dating, anyway, right now. *It's stupid, Kai, don't get your panties in a twist.*

"It's no inconvenience at all; I'm thrilled that you're interested. Not in me, in Fin. No, in the cast, the Mehta Method…*obviously*…" *Ouch*. She winced, why was she was acting thirteen? "What I mean is, we can meet anywhere in L.A., we're in Santa Monica."

"What about Tickles n' Luv in Brentwood, this Saturday afternoon?" he asked.

"Tickles n' Luv?"

"Oh, you don't know of it…silly name, sounds very macho, right? It's a kid's playroom place with a restaurant area; I took my niece there when she was visiting."

"Oh, sure…perfect. How about four o'clock? That's after Fin's nap," Kai said.

"Done."

"Please feel free to bring your fiancée—it's the weekend, after all, you're not working." She winced, she sounded like a social spaz.

"Ah. *Rebecca*. Well…we're not exactly…together, anymore," he replied awkwardly.

Butterflies in her stomach, *really*? Was she seriously attracted to her child's neurologist? "I'm so sorry," she said weakly. That was obviously a lie.

"Thank you," he replied. "So! I really look forward to seeing you and Fin."

"Me, too. I mean, so do *we*. I mean, Fin doesn't really know, but if he did, I'm sure he'd be happy, as long as they sell milk." As long as they sell milk? Now she had *completely* humiliated herself.

"The milk's on me," he laughed. "Bye, Kai."

"Bye, Jack—*Dr. Becket*."

He mercifully hung up. Doris walked in the room, chasing Fin, and seeing Kai spontaneously jump up in excitement. "WHOO HOO! I think I have a date," she grinned, despite her spazzy phone performance.

"A date?!" Doris smiled from ear to ear, "Thank you, *Jesus*!"

The next few days, Kai tried on numerous outfits for her Tickles n' Luv experience. It wasn't a real date, but she had to admit, she may just be feeling a *little* desperate for some adult conversation outside of the home. Like, maybe with a man who didn't have one long, connected brow and wasn't Burt from Sesame Street or Fadi. That was all, because in reality, she knew that a young doctor freshly out of a broken engagement would not be looking to begin a relationship with the mother of a boy in a body cast. This journey ahead of them was gonna be at least two or three years long—it was going to be an emotional, long term "project," as Fin's medical team told her.

Who was she kidding, she had *major* baggage at this moment in her life, not the least being what happened with Teddy, and the serious chip on her shoulder against a large portion of the medical establishment. She wasn't exactly the easy-breezy girl on the top of every single guy's *want to date* list.

It would just be nice to see Dr. Becket—*Jack*— again, he had been so kind to her during an unbelievably stressful time. She had felt like a complete mess the last two times he saw her in person—now she was still a mess, but a slightly more *together* mess. That was something, right? You have to take your little wins, in life.

A little embarrassed to ask Fadi to drive her to her *not-a-date*, she finally bought a three year old, used white Honda Civic; she needed a reliable car that wouldn't break the bank. Fadi insisted that he would still *always* drive her to and from the airport for Fin's casting trips, and she promised she would call him every time.

On Saturday, she pulled up into the parking lot for Tickles n' Luv, dressed in jeans and a cute, bohemian scarf top and flat cognac brown leather boots. She felt a little like the old Kai in her clothing choices today, unlike the black executioner outfit with heels she had once worn, so the doctor would take her more seriously. It was March in L.A., still sunny and cool; she carried a jean jacket instead of a sweater.

Butterflies in her stomach, again, *hmmm*. She was here to spread the word to a medical professional about this life saving treatment, she reminded herself—not to be spun around Tickles n' Luv like she was in an Audrey Hepburn movie. She imagined Jack swinging her around and around in his arms, barely missing small children at play—*ridiculous*!

When she walked in, pushing Fin in his stroller, she realized how surprised she was to see Jack standing there, just inside the doorway, not wearing his white doctor's coat. He was in jeans and a relaxed, wheat colored summer sweater with a crew neck, maybe a light

cashmere, but masculine and unpretentious. He hadn't
shaved that morning, so he had a hint of rugged stubble
on his handsome jaw. His hair was a little floppy on top
and messier than usual. Out of the hospital setting, in his
weekend clothes, he looked less formal and doctorly…he
just looked like a cute, casual guy. Kai's heart fluttered a
tiny bit.

"Hey," he said, smiling at both she and Fin, "So
glad you guys could make it. Hey Fin, little man, how ya
doin'?" Fin grinned at Jack; he had always seemed
comfortable around him.

"This place is great…" she looked around. There
was a counter where you could order healthy and kid
friendly food, table and chairs for dining, and a large play
area with tons of toys and things for kids to climb on.
Bright, colorful murals were painted on the walls, to make
it even more fun for the kiddos.

"Yeah, my niece, Abby, loved it—she's three and
usually wears a Princess costume, if she can get away
with it," he laughed. "Do you want to order, are you
hungry? Or we could just let Fin play?"

"He's dying to run around," she said. "You can
see him in action!"

"Perfect."

They had moved up in the line to the counter,
where a young employee smiled at them, "Hi, welcome to
Tickles n' Luv!"

Both Kai and Jack couldn't help but laugh at the
name; it was cute, but so silly. Fin was kicking to get out
of his stroller and run around. That decided it. "Hi, I think
we're gonna eat later, but can we just buy a pass for my
little boy to play for now?"

"Sure!" The young woman rang up the pass, and
Jack paid for it before Kai could open her purse. "I invited
you," he insisted.

They took off their shoes and put them in the
cubby holes that were provided, all three of them entering

the playroom gate in their sock feet. Fin was off like lightning—as usual, he was so excited to play with all of the stuff. While he played with a dragon's castle, Kai lifted up his shirt and showed Jack the blue cast.

"Amazing. It doesn't slow him down one bit, does it?" Jack shook his head, impressed.

"Nope. As you can see, he's in no pain, and he's gotten all of his skills back in a few weeks."

They watched Fin as he climbed the stairs to a child sized slide, sliding down with glee and landing on a big dinosaur stuffed toy. He snuggled into the dinosaur, giggling and looking adorable.

"Do you mind if I pick him up?" Jack asked.

"No, please do—I normally use my hand to support him under his leg when I carry him, or just pop him on my hip," Kai said.

Jack walked up to Fin, still snuggling on the dinosaur, as other adorable kids ran around them. "Hey, little guy." Jack picked Fin up gently, and Fin did a silly baby raspberry in his face, both of them laughing as the spittle flew.

Jack popped Fin carefully behind the wheel of a small toy car. "Is this okay?" he asked, checking with Kai, first.

"Sure."

Jack pressed the pedal for Fin, and the car was actually battery powered and *vroomed* a bit forward through the room. "*Wheee!*" Fin cried happily.

It made Kai's heart hurt, just a little, to see Jack acting like a fun Daddy, which Fin so *deserved*. She shook it off; she couldn't put her heart on the line again, not this soon. The wounds were too fresh.

They played for a half hour, and then ordered some food. Kai got a big chopped vegetable and chicken salad and Jack got a chicken Panini sandwich. Fin sat in a high chair at the table as they ate, all he wanted were a few French fries from Jack's plate, with lots of ketchup, and his bottle of milk. Kai told Jack everything she knew about the Mehta Method of casting. He was fascinated, soaking it all in, especially the human element of the story. What Heather had done simply blew him away.

"*Wow*. I can't imagine what a whirlwind and an emotional upheaval you've been through as a mother; in the last two months...I think you're brave."

"I'm *not*," she said, "I just did what any parent would do, under the circumstances."

"No, you did what an exceptional parent would do. You fought for your child, when others would've taken what appeared to be the easier path."

"Thank you, for saying that. I'm just trying my best. I—we, Fin and I, go*t so lucky*."

"It's a lot more than luck. It's love in action, if you ask me," he said.

She looked into his eyes, speechless, as he gazed at her.

"I *really* appreciate this, Kai, you taking the time to see me today. You may allow me to better help future children who cross my path with this condition, even to educate more of my colleagues about it."

"Thank you, for caring enough to listen. I'm sorry about your own recent loss, your break-up..." she didn't want to be insensitive and only talk about her own problems.

"Oh..." he ran his hand through the floppy top of his light brown hair, "I actually ended it. We had only been together a couple of months. I found myself becoming attracted to other people, and it wasn't fair to her."

He noticed Kai's slight cringe. Men cheating was not a savory subject, especially not in a kid's restaurant.

"I didn't act on it, believe me...but I found myself becoming attracted to..." he looked nervous, glancing away. "No, that's not true, exactly...I didn't find myself attracted to other *people*, just to *one* other person. One who I found myself thinking about, a lot."

Her heart sunk. He was already taken, again. "Are you dating her, now?" she asked, not really wanting the answer.

"No. Not unless you consider this a date," he blurted out, his face suddenly flushing.

Whoa. Her knee jerk reaction was sudden. "It can't be. I have to focus on Fin's health. I'm probably…not in a good place…" Oh *why oh why* didn't they serve wine in places like this?! "And this casting thing is gonna be a lot, a long journey…it's not the time for me to be starting something new. It's like the sands are constantly shifting under my feet, and I'd, I'd—I'm kind of still a mess.…*Nobody* wants to be around me, right now." It all came out in a rush, and it surprised even her. Maybe she had some good sense, despite the fluttery butterflies still trapped in her abdomen.

"I completely understand, and I respect that, one hundred percent," he replied sincerely.   God, he was so cute. "Thank you," she mumbled, feeling like she could melt all over the floor into a puddle. "I should go." Kai stood up, taking Fin out of the high chair with a French fry from Jack's plate still clutched in his small hand. Ketchup was smeared on his hands and around his mouth.

Jack faced her, speaking softly, "Kai…please know that if you change your mind…*I do. I* want to be around you. You can be a mess around me, any time you want."

She nodded nervously and shook his hand in an oddly perfunctory manner. "Noted," she said. *Noted? Ugh!*

"Good, noted…" Jack graciously helped her get Fin into his stroller, as she raced nervously out the door to the parking lot, feeling like an utter fool.

17
Wrench

Kai drove home from the kid's restaurant cringing and sighing, pulling her car up into the driveway on Ashland, and getting out to un-strap Fin from the car seat in the back. Her back was to the open door as she gently lifted him out, turning and suddenly screaming at the top of her lungs.

A dark male figure was standing over her, right in front of her, as her vision was momentarily blinded by the sun. She could only make out the silhouette of the hulking figure.

Fin started to cry, startled, as Teddy stepped forward, reaching out to feel the cast on his body.

"DON'T YOU TOUCH HIM!" Kai yelled, as Doris came running outside.

"He's my son," Teddy said, taking a step back from her.

"How do you know that, you said you wanted a paternity test?"

"If you say he's my son, I believe you. I'm also happy to take the blood test to prove it."

Doris' eyes blazed, "What are you doing here?" she demanded.

Teddy turned to her, squinting, annoyed. "Didn't I only hire you for two weeks? What are *you* doing here?"

"She's my friend. We're roommates," Kai answered defensively.

"You're scaring the child," Doris abruptly walked over and took Fin, who was still crying, into her arms and up to the front door. "I'm taking him inside."

Kai nodded as Doris shut the door behind them, locking it. Kai closed the car door, facing Teddy. "*Why?*"

"I want to file for shared custody," he said.

Her throat went dry, "Why??!! Why *now*???"

"My Dad..." he began, shifting his stance, "he had a heart attack. He's alive, but it was a close call. I went up to see him in the hospital, and he reminded me that Fin is his grandson, he's my male heir, and the eventual heir to carry on our lineage...our family name."

Kai could not believe her ears. She felt sick. "I'll fight this. You left us on the *lawn*."

"My parents want me to be able to bring Fin up to the vineyard alone, obviously it would be awkward to have you there, after...and you and my mother never really got along."

"You can't take my baby *anywhere* alone, he's in a body cast; you don't know how to care for it. If he got wet, like your mother spilling a glass of red wine on the cast, it would stain and soak into the plaster and smell for *months*. If God forbid, he got really wet...someone was careless and he pulled over a vase full of water, or got in a sprinkler, or a fountain, or a rainstorm...the cast would melt. The continuous correction would be broken. The cast has to stay intact, or Fin could regress all the way back. He could need the invasive surgeries, starting at two or three years old."

"I'll be careful with him, Kai," Teddy insisted.

"Surgeries where they slice open his little back and insert metal rods, wires and staples into his spine, metal parts that can get lost in kid's bodies...and worse..." she fought back tears.

"Kai, don't be dramatic, my parents aren't kooks."

"Your mother is clumsy."

"Who isn't, sometimes?" Teddy spat.

"She spilled an entire bottle of pinot in my lap, once."

"Okay, *fine*...I hear you..." Teddy exhaled, frustrated by her vigilance.

"I'm a mother. It's my *job* to worry." Kai knew she couldn't trust Teddy and his parents to take care of Fin properly. She would *never* let Teddy take him out of her sight.

"I wouldn't let him get wet, but tell me this...how do you bathe him?" Teddy looked confused.

"We do a sponge bath, Doris and I, on a towel on my bed, then we lay him on towels on the kitchen counter with a rolled up towel to support his neck and wash his hair in the sink. It's Fin's Spa Day."

"That's cute." Teddy smiled thinly.

"And diapering is harder, there's a whole trick to it...you can't get food or milk down the cast, or poop up it when changing him. A few things are harder, and by the way, it's freakin' hard with a twenty month old *without* a cast!"

Teddy looked borderline embarrassed, as she continued, on a rant.

"If he has a pee leak on the medical t-shirt—it's this thin sweater that protects his skin under the cast—it really takes two people to wash and dry it with a blow dryer, without getting the cast wet. He wriggles like a baby alligator."

"My Mom could help me...but that brings up another issue. My parents aren't thrilled about this cast on Fin, and neither am I. You never got my permission, as a parent, to go through with it." Teddy looked a little uncomfortable saying this, but not too uncomfortable to stand his ground, not breaking his gaze from her face.

Kai was stunned. "You were *A.O.L.,* you selfish prick! I had to do *everything* on my own! The *lawn*, do you remember the *lawn*?!"

"I was in a bad place. My son developed a rare health problem, and I panicked. It was fight or flight syndrome, Kai."

Oh, poor *Teddy* was the victim. Was that how he really saw it?

"I got him into this life saving cast, with the help of a lot of incredible people—people who showed more care and concern than the child's own *father*—who would've let him curve until his *lungs crushed*!" Kai was about to go ballistic.

"No, I would not have let that happen. I've talked to more doctors, and researched the spinal surgeries, and it is not too late to make a different choice. It's called a cast saw; you can buy one that doesn't cut skin."

"*What are you saying to me, right now?*" Kai couldn't breathe.

"I think I have some legal rights, and I'm going to look into them. My parents have asked me to," he replied coolly. "Why does that *nanny* in there have more of a right to spend time with my own son than *I* do?"

Well, she could really pick 'em. This guy probably needed to be *killed*, Kai couldn't help but think, and she had wild thoughts flying through her head about ways to do it—but that would leave her little boy in the custody of either his parents, or Janie. Not that she believed violence was *ever* the answer, but if anyone deserved to be hit over the head with a heavy, blunt object, she had her man, right here.

Kai suddenly felt a strange sense of calm come over her. She took a slow, deep breath.

"Let me lay this out for you in terms that you can understand. You are a *bad person* and a *horrible father*. You are the most selfish bastard I have ever met, or even heard of in my entire life. I think you are lower than scum, and that little boy in there is the most precious thing in the world to me. I would sooner lay down my life than let you cut him out of that cast, or even take him out of my sight for a *moment*."

That took Teddy aback. He stood there, squinting at her, weighing his options. "Well, I can see you're still angry."

"You have never really *seen* me angry," she hissed.

"I'm ordering the paternity test."

"I'll say you're not the father."

"My name is on his birth certificate."

"I'll say I lied on the birth certificate, pregnancy brain, I was *confused*," she spat angrily.

"That won't hold up once I have to blood test," he smirked.

"Do whatever you want, Teddy, you can't have him."

"I don't want full custody, just shared."

"You won't get it. I'll tell them you are trying to cripple and kill him, which you *will* be, if you remove the cast that is saving his life."

"Not if he has the surgery! The doctors tell me these types of casts are too new, they're practically *experimental*!" Teddy was shouting, now.

"If he has the surgery, he will likely suffer far more pain in his lifetime, and possibly experience severe deformity. His pulmonary function will be affected for life, that's his ability to BREATHE- not to mention his mental state and psychological distress. Did I leave anything out?" She squared her hips— this was *not* something she was gonna back down on.

"You don't know that would happen, these casts aren't guaranteed to work, either."

"Nothing is guaranteed, scoliosis is not a one size fits all monster, but his chances are very good of avoiding surgery altogether, if we *stay the course*."

"How long is 'the course'? Did they give you an estimate?"

"Maybe one and a half to two years in casts, then a year or so of bracing, maybe longer…as long as it takes…"

"*Two years*? My Dad could be *dead* by then, and never get to hold his grandson without a hard cast between them?"

"If he loves his grandson, he'll love what the cast is doing for him," she said.

"You have to do bracing, anyway?" he asked.

"Yes, but with no cutting into his body or *spine*! Can you imagine how painful that would be? Do you want to be in the hospital room when he's screaming in pain? When he's old enough to know what's going to happen, as he has to go back there every six months of his childhood, probably more often, facing that pain again and again? Do *you* want to be in the recovery room when he's screaming what other mother's kids have told me their child said, "*Mommy I hate you! You don't love me!*" Kai's face was burning crimson with anger. She had heard these stories and they were not out of the woods, yet, in avoiding it for Fin.

Teddy finally sighed. "You'll be hearing from my lawyer."

"The words of a *wuss*," Kai spat, "Or should I call you by your Christian name, "Douche Bag?""

"You're nuts," he muttered angrily, walking to his car with his tail between his legs.

She wasn't gonna dignify that. Kai turned and walked into the house, locking the door behind her and sinking to the floor, trembling.

Doris walked into the living room, holding Fin and looking out of the window as Teddy climbed into his BMW and sped off.

"The Devil has returned," Doris said, shaking her head gravely.

"Yes," Kai whispered, standing up and taking Fin into her arms.

"I heard he wants shared custody," Doris murmured.

"He said that." Kai nuzzled and kissed Fin's cheek.

"I know a little bit about this. Abandoning the mother is between the father and the mother. Abandoning the child, not great, but he can plead emotional panic, in the stress of the health crisis. His chances of getting sole custody—low to impossible. He would have to prove that you as a Mother are "unfit." There are mothers with needles stuck in their arms who don't lose their kids. Won't happen."

Kai looked up at Doris—as usual, she knew more than Kai thought.

"The chances of the biological father getting *shared* custody are not bad. Not if he can prove he is currently a stable person, who is not a violent criminal. Douche bags still get to see their kids," Doris sighed.

"That frickin' *BLOWS*!" Kai exclaimed, not wanting to curse around Fin.

There was a lot to think about. She had no idea what California Law stated about a father who temporarily abandoned his child, and then requested partial custody. She knew the blood test would come back as a match, she knew he was the father. That would be no more than a stalling technique. If he won the right to get the cast removed, Fin could begin to get worse again, his back rapidly curving, and he would surely need the surgeries very young—the casting window for a possible cure would be lost.

Could she flee to another country? Probably not, it was illegal, she was pretty sure, but also Dr. Mehta was retired and teaching, now. There was a mandatory retirement age for doctors in the U.K., Mehta now couldn't even legally walk into a hospital there and practice. Kai didn't know for sure where she would go elsewhere for the treatment—outside of Dr. Mehta, Fin already had the most experienced doctor in the world doing his casts. Most of the Mehta trained doctors were currently working in the U.S., she knew that from the online support group. What would she do, assume other identities and change their names? What about accessing their medical insurance, without being caught?

It wasn't until she had put him to bed that night and finally let herself have a glass of wine that she remembered Jack saying he wanted to be around her. She truly doubted *anyone* would want to be around her, now.

And she didn't really need a doctor, right now— she needed a lawyer, and a very good one. Teddy Verona would have a top attorney. This was going to be expensive, if not impossible.

She woke up the next morning, feeling like a heavy cement block was pressing down on the middle of her chest. *Fear.* Kai felt a sense of impending doom. Her heart was beating irregularly, rapidly—she wondered if she had a ticking time bomb in her chest.

No, the time bomb was not inside her chest, the time bomb was her *Ex.* Was this ever gonna get easier? Was life ever going to return to normal? Or was this *it* for her, the constant peril and drama surrounding their lives, the way it was, now?

She had to drag herself out of bed. Fin's delight in awaking to another day was the only bright spot that kept her going. Fadi dropped by for breakfast, and he, Kai and Doris sat grimly around the table, while Fin happily jumped around the room, oblivious to the drama.

"What if somebody threatens this Douche?" Fadi asked, eating the organic scrambled cheese eggs with whole grain toast and sliced avocado Doris had made.

Kai sighed, "You mean, you?"

"*Someone,* I'm not saying *me,*" Fadi muttered.

"That's not really a good option, Fadi," Kai sighed.

"What if someone breaks his legs?" Doris asked innocently, adding, "I'm not saying *me*."

Kai took a sip of her coffee, "I honestly don't know what to do…would somebody take a case pro bono, with a condition and a treatment that's so rare? I can just imagine cold calling lawyer's offices and trying to explain why I chose to put my child in a body cast, when there are more "popular" options. If most *doctors* have never heard of it before, most *lawyers* certainly haven't. I'll probably sound like a kook with a screw loose."

Fadi nodded gravely. "I can see how the Douche Bag could look like the rational parent, if he brings these so-called "top L.A. doctors" to the stand…"

"Maybe Dr. Jack knows a good lawyer you can at least consult with," Doris suggested.

"Dr. Jack?" Fadi's interest was piqued, "Who is Dr. Jack?"

"Kai had a *date*," Doris smiled.

"A date?! A *date*?!" Fadi was beside himself, "And you didn't tell me?? Why am I being shut out of your lives?!"

Kai rolled her eyes, "It was *not* a date, Doris knows that, she's being cheeky."

"Which doctor is this? I must know," Fadi insisted.

"Dr. Becket, at Mercy, he just wanted to see what Fin's cast looked like in person."

"The one who I drove you to meet with, and then you cried the whole way home? With your face cupped in your hands?" he asked.

"*He* didn't make me cry, it was the whole situation with Fin—he's nice. He's a very nice man," Kai said.

"Handsome?" Fadi raised a brow, taking a large bite of scrambled eggs and avocado.

Doris giggled, as Kai shifted uncomfortably, looking away. "Yes, he's handsome, but we are *not dating*."

"He makes a *fine* living," Doris smiled slyly, sipping her orange juice, "and he is *into you*, girl!"

"Doris, I may have to advertise for a new roommate," Kai said flatly, standing up and slapping her thighs. "Fadi, don't you have to do some driving today? Don't you have some fares to pick up?"

Doris and Fadi exchanged a glance, "Now, she thinks we're her servants," Fadi said teasingly, rolling his eyes heavenwards.

"How *quickly they forget*," quipped Doris, as Kai poured them more juice and refilled their coffee mugs.

"Like I said, Miss *Ma'am*, Dr. Jack is into you, but even more importantly, he is *interested in Fin*, and *you* are into *him*." Doris was not letting up.

"I never said that!" Kai protested.

"You didn't have to," said Fadi, "It's all over your face. You're blushing like a Catholic schoolgirl."

Kai put the coffee pot back on the stove. "You really expect me to start *dating* while this family is in a major crisis?"

"In my *arrogant opinion*," Doris stated, "I think you have to keep living your life, because life can sometimes be a series of crises, and meanwhile, you don't want to miss out on the good stuff."

Fadi raised his heavy eyebrows, as if to say; *the woman has a point*.

Kai looked at them with a tired expression. "You people are giving me a heart attack. I've probably had high blood pressure for months. You're literally putting me over the edge."

"You're young; your heart can take it," Doris smiled. "Not like us old people. Besides, I just fed you avocado, those are heart protective, good fats."

"*Fine*," Kai exhaled. "I'll call him!"

She went outside with the portable phone and dialed the private number Jack had given her when they had lunch. She was super nervous, despite her protests in the kitchen.

"Hello?" he answered.

"Dr. Becket...*Jack*, it's—"

"Kai?" he recognized her voice. "Hey, it's great to hear from you."

She started pacing the lawn to try to shake off her nervous energy. "Thanks, I apologize if I was a little weird, at that kid's restaurant..."

"You weren't weird at all. How are you?" he asked.

"Not...great..." she admitted. "I have a problem. I could use some advice."

"Is it Fin? Is he okay?" he sounded worried.

"No, well, yes...it is about Fin...but he's okay, for now," she said.

"I'm at the hospital today—it's crazy busy, but I can meet you for dinner around eight, if you're free."

She considered that, what should she do? Just ask him for the name of a lawyer on the phone, or meet him in person? She knew Doris would be home tonight, she could watch Fin. He would think it was a date, though, since food was involved.

A date? She couldn't handle a date, right now— *crap*.

"Do you know any child custody lawyers?" she blurted.

"I have a good buddy who's an entertainment lawyer...but I bet he can give you some basic legal advice. Listen, Kai, I have to run. If you don't want to have dinner, I can just call you back tonight and we can talk then."

"No, dinner would be nice..." she was asking him a favor, she thought, why not do it in person? She had never been a fan of heavy conversations on the phone.

Oh, who was she kidding? She didn't have a lot of friends with *any* connections, right now. Doris and Fadi didn't personally know any lawyers, and neither did she. She could use as many friends as she could get, at the moment.

And…Dr. Jack was cute. There *was* that. Just the simple pleasure of being in his presence, again. Maybe this time, she wouldn't rush out of the restaurant, like her hair was on fire. *Ugh*, she felt like such a mess.

"Great, dinner it is!" he sounded like he was smiling. "Can I pick you up at eight?"

"Sure, why…the heck…not?" Those damn butterflies were going nuts in her stomach. "I, um, I don't think you have my address…"

"It's in my computer files, Fin is my patient," he said.

"*Right,* of course, Dr. Stalker," she joked.

He laughed. "See you at eight, Kai, looking forward to it."

"Me, too. Bye, Jack." They both hung up, with Kai instantly worrying she had made a huge mistake. Was she leading him on? *Oy*, Doris and Fadi were gonna have a field day with this one.

Kai slowly walked back into the house, seeing them both still sitting at the kitchen table, while Fin happily stacked colorful blocks on the floor and played with an Elmo doll. She tried to look nonchalant, setting the phone down on the kitchen counter.

"She has a *second date*!" Fadi exclaimed, grinning at Doris. "Look at the flush in her cheeks!"

"There's *no flush* and *no date*." Kai looked away, embarrassed. "He's just gonna give me the name of some lawyers he knows, tonight after work."

"Oh, good, I'm glad you didn't plan on meeting him anywhere, because *I'm* going out, tonight," Doris said, with pursed lips.

"You can't, I need you to watch Fin; he's picking me up at eight!" Kai exclaimed.

Doris shot Fadi a knowing glance. She was a little stinker, sometimes.

"Of course, it's a *legal* briefing," Fadi nodded, teasing her.

"You two think you're a couple of pimps." Kai sighed, shaking her head. "May God strike me down with a thunder bolt, if I so much as kiss him on the cheek!"

"Thank you for a delicious breakfast." Fadi smiled, standing up and clearing his plate. "I have some driving to do, ladies and *gent*," he ruffled Fin's hair, bemused. "The only question left for the young lass is, *which cheek?*"

Kai went to smack him, as he playfully winked and Doris giggled, and Fadi swept out of the door before she could reach him.

Seven wardrobe changes later, she decided wearing red would look like she thinks they're on a hot date. Even *sporty red outfit* was a little too romantic. She decided to go with *cheerful yellow blouse*, with a navy cardigan and jeans. That was kind of an acceptable "mom" outfit, still cute, but not too vixen-y.

Jack arrived right on time, wearing a slightly crinkled white button down shirt, jeans and a navy blazer. He looked a little nervous and kind of gorgeous.

"Hey, you ready?" he smiled, shoving his hands in his pockets as his hair flopped over his right eye.

Doris came to the door, holding Fin and grinning, "Hi, I'm Doris, the roommate!"

Kai cringed, saying, "I'll get my purse!" She rushed to grab it, before Doris could embarrass her.

"Hey, tough little guy," Jack smiled at Fin, who grinned back and shyly rubbed his face into Doris' neck. "Doris, it's a pleasure to meet you, I've heard a lot of great things about you."

"All true," Doris replied, "and if you hurt her, I'll lock you in the trunk of my car."

Kai ran back to the door, "HEY, this is *not* a date, you know that!" she blurted—thinking *thanks a lot, Doris*.

Jack laughed, "Of course not, we're meeting my friend Toby, he's a lawyer with some advice for Kai…I'm just here to help."

Toby? Kai suddenly felt a little disappointed that it wasn't just the two of them for dinner, but she kissed Fin on his chubby cheek and raced out the door, before Doris could say anything else. "Home by 10! Love you, *BYE!*" she called from the porch.

The drive to the romantic, old school Italian restaurant was less than ten minutes. Kai made small talk until they got there, where the hostess took them to a table where there *was* already a guy named Toby sitting. He got up to greet them in his serious charcoal gray lawyer's suit, standing about five foot seven inches tall, with brown curly hair and a glint in his eye.

"You must be Kai," Toby smiled, looking thrilled by the sight of her. "*Stunning.* Why would any man let you slip through his fingers?"

"Toby. *Down*, boy." Jack shot his friend an annoyed look, shaking his hand, pulling out the chair for Kai and taking a seat at the table. He turned to her apologetically, "Sorry, my old roommate is a little effusive, at times."

"You don't think she's stunning?" Toby arched a brow.

"Of course I do. We're here to talk about her legal options," Jack replied stiffly.

Did Jack mean it, that he thought she was pretty, Kai wondered? Or was he just being polite? She was feeling insecure, lately; she honestly didn't know how anyone could find her attractive at the moment.

"This is not my field," Jack said to Toby, "I'll let you cover it."

Toby settled into his plush leather chair, "I've taken the liberty of ordering a bottle of wine…" as if on cue, the young male waiter brought the bottle of vintage Chianti to their table, showing the label to Toby, who nodded. "Excellent, so I'll just begin. I understand that you need to know about paternity and custody law."

"Yes," Kai replied, as the waiter tried not to look interested. He eased out the cork from the bottle and began to pour a taste into Toby's glass. Toby swirled, examined the wine's "legs" and sipped, nodding to their waiter and beginning to pour a glass for Kai.

"I'm sure Jack has told you that this isn't my specialty, but I can give you the basic things you need to know, and a referral, if you'd like one," he said.

"I'd appreciate it," Kai took a small sip of her wine. It was full of heat and complexity, a welcome fire down her dry, anxious throat.

"Jack filled me in on the basics, and I'm sorry to hear that you're going through this," he politely offered.

"Thank you," she replied.

"The potential father wants to file a paternity case?" he asked.

"He's the actual father, but yes. He said so," Kai murmured.

"Child custody cases can be tricky. Paternity can legally be established in three ways: presumption, as in a marriage, acknowledgement, when the man signs a form that admits paternity, or by court order, which is based on DNA evidence and possibly a hearing," Toby explained.

"I know he's my son's father, but he denied it, or questioned it, after Fin got a serious health condition."

"DNA tests are not covered by insurance. They can cost around four hundred to two thousand dollars," he said.

"Oh," Kai gulped.

"It would be easier on both of you to agree to sign a document, if he's not contesting paternity."

"I'm concerned if he legally proves paternity, he'll win unsupervised visitation rights, and he may put my son's health—his life, even—in danger."

Jack, who had been leaning back and listening, sat forward, concerned, "Did he threaten you?"

"He's against the casting process, and so are his parents. They have a lot of money for a court battle. He mentioned buying a buzz saw to remove the cast that's saving Fin's spine. The whole point is that it's providing *continuous correction*—it can reverse and everything we've gained can be lost, if he does that." Kai shuddered involuntarily.

"Somebody needs to threaten this creep." Jack shook his head, disgusted.

"Let's stick to the facts," Toby said. "It's unusual for the potential father to ask the courts for a paternity test, but it happens. Once he gets the court order and they run the test, it won't take long for the results to come back. That is, if this is a stalling technique."

"It is," Kai admitted.

"How long does your son need to stay in these casts?" Toby asked.

"Maybe two years, to hopefully avoid future spinal surgery. At least a year, but probably longer," she said.

"Ah, that's tough," Toby replied. "So, if he wins unsupervised custody in under two years…"

"My child's future could be altered forever, yes. Because this treatment is still not the norm in the current medical community, I'm afraid he could win—even win a court order to stop the treatment before it can save Fin," Kai explained gravely.

Jack was becoming more and more angry for her, "That is so wrong, it's sick."

Toby nodded, "Kai, you can't do this without a lawyer, and again, it's just not my field. It could get expensive."

Kai's eyes lit up, her anger at Teddy rising, "What price would *you* pay, to save your child's spine? Seriously, how much would you pay?"

Both men just looked at her, speechless.

"There *is* no number, no price too great..." she was near tears again, silently vowing to herself that she *wasn't* gonna sob in this public restaurant..."I'm sorry, I really appreciate your help. I'm just...it's emotional...I don't think I can eat, right now."

Jack stood up just as she did, gently taking her by the arm. "I'll drive you home. Thanks, Toby."

"Anytime," Toby waved goodbye, draining his glass of wine in one gulp and watching them go.

Kai was silent the whole drive home, she kept the tears at bay. As they reached her house, Jack pulled up to the curb to park.

"I'm sorry that I took you to...hear news you didn't want to hear..." Jack awkwardly began.

"It's not your fault. You're helping us, thank you," she said sincerely.

"Toby can be...a jerk...he's too blunt, arrogant..." Jack shook his head.

"He's a lawyer; I wanted him to be straight with me. I don't need more friends right now, I needed a legal opinion..." she looked down at her lap, realizing as it came out that she didn't mean it, not in the way it sounded. "I take that back, I need *all* of the friends I can get right now. That was a defense mechanism. I just blurt so many random things out, lately, I—"

She impulsively reached for his warm, rugged face...touching the dark stubble that had just come in that day, rough again her hand...

The rich Chianti still mingled on their breath, silky and smoky, as they kissed, melting into each other. His hands were tangling in her long, wavy hair...hers trailing down his chest...their tongues finding each other in a breathless, urgent pattern. He smelled like firewood and musk and kindness, sea air, protective anger and *welcome danger*. The kindness of a near stranger and still—*danger*.

Her taste in men had led her down the path she was on now, where malevolent forces threatened to hurt the innocent soul she most loved. She was drawn to Jack like gravity was pulling her to Earth, but she pulled back, gasping for breath, her damaged heart pounding.

"I...*can't*..." she whispered.

He pressed himself back against his car seat, moaning and nodding, knowing he couldn't reach for her, despite his own chest heaving from wanting her lips on his mouth again.

"Goodnight, Jack..." she breathed, awkwardly climbing out of the car and rushing to the door, before he could say another word.

Jack opened the car door, jumping out to say something, but she had already slipped inside the house. He rubbed his face in his hands, leaning against his vehicle in the moonlight, the night air thick with her warmth and presence, as if she were still in his arms.

Fin was sleeping soundly, the house was quiet. Doris mercifully stayed in her room. She seemed to have a sixth sense about when to let Kai have some breathing room, which she needed so desperately, right now. Kai shakily double locked the front door behind her, pressing her back against it, as if to keep the monsters out. Not that Jack was a monster—she just didn't know who she was, right now.

Her head was spinning with a swirl of desire and regret and fear. Part of her wanted to run back out to Jack's car, and part of her just wanted to grab Fin from his crib and get on a plane to anywhere—*anywhere* but here.

She nearly jumped ten feet in the air when she felt a knock behind her back. Someone was on the porch. She spun around and opened the door very slowly, thinking— *Why didn't I look through the keyhole?*— just as she was doing it. What if a murderer were standing on her porch, she asked herself? Or Teddy? What kind of crazy was she?

It was Jack standing there, inches from her, looking red faced and chagrined. Just her kind, sweet Jack—not a monster, at all. She softened as he shifted his stance, self-consciously shoving his hands in his pockets, his sexy hair flopping forward again. "I'm so sorry," he said, "I was…that was…*completely* out of line."

Kai swung the door open, and in one swift motion, she reached for him and pulled him to her body on the porch. *Mouth…open…now.* She had to taste him again, she *had* to. She felt fire sear through her entire being, kissing him long and hard on his beautiful, succulent mouth; her hand cupping his strong, rough jaw. He reached around her with his protective, masculine hands, and they melted into each other again, fitting like two perfect pieces of a puzzle. It felt so good, she wanted to cry out, or just cry, but she didn't want Fin to hear them. Or the neighbors…oh, God…or Doris…

They both slowly fell to their knees, and then her body was on top of his, kissing this man out on the porch with a hunger she didn't know she possessed. *Alive, mouth…mine…*

She had felt so lonely, so deeply lonely, these past few months—even with wonderful friends, no one could go through this *for* her. There were moments she'd wondered if she'd even get through this *alive*, let alone feel like her body belonged to a woman, again.

Coming to her senses, she untangled her body from him, drawing back, breathless, her fingers still wound in his hair. "*I* kissed *you*," she whispered, "don't apologize."

She pulled herself up and crept back inside the front door, slowly closing it and locking it behind her, leaving him outside. Her heart almost stopped when she saw a dark figure in the hallway, in the moonlight—

Doris, padding towards her through the darkened living room in her pajamas.

"Fin's in his crib," Doris said plainly. "Don't get your panties in a bunch, if you're wearing any—I just got up for a glass of milk."

Kai nodded wordlessly, a little ashamed of her disheveled appearance, her *not-too-vixeny* navy cardigan and yellow blouse askew. Doris walked into the kitchen, poured herself a tall glass of the aforementioned milk, and walked back to glance at Kai, whose back was still to the door. Kai's breathing remained heavy, and matched the labored breathing of the man on the other side.

"Go on, go back out there," Doris said, "He's waiting." She silently turned and walked back to bed with her milk.

Kai thought of going back outside, she did. She thought of putting her hands back in Jack's thick, light brown hair…becoming entangled with him, losing herself in his warm mouth, his broad chest, his strong hands. Letting the world end in fire, not ice…she could hear him, still on the porch, standing up and getting his bearings. She could spend the night wrapped safely in his arms, against his muscular thighs, warm, protected, and *not alone*. All she had to do was open the door.

It physically hurt, not to open the door again, but she didn't. She got into her pajama pants and large t-shirt and climbed into bed alone, pulling up the covers to her neck. This wasn't a fairytale, or even a guaranteed happy ending. Her boy was in danger.

Jack may be a good man. He may have been standing sentry outside her door, caring deeply for her. He may even make her forget for a night.

But the monsters in her closet were still real.

18
Twisting

Kai barely slept, that night. She finally got up at 5:30 in the morning and sat on the couch in the living room in the wee, still dark hours before sunrise, looking out through the filmy linen curtains and seeing an eerie apparition in the yard.

Ghosts. She blinked; her eyes still bleary from lack of sleep. It looked like her mother, as a younger woman, walking towards her front door with herself and Janie as little girls. There was a third child with her ghost Mom—tiny, with short blonde hair. Kai began to panic, *was she really going mad? Was it Fin?* Had her mother come to take him to Heaven—and if so, why were she and Janie with her, as children, too?

Kai screamed—and then, so did the ghost of her Mom and the three pale ghost children.

"*KAI*?! It's *US*! Janie and the girls!"

Kai leapt from the couch, gasping—it was *Janie*, what was Janie doing here? She unlocked the dead bolt and opened the front door, seeing her sister and her three little girls, Micah, Sarah and Ruth standing on the porch.

"Come in, you scared the life out of me!" Kai exclaimed.

Doris woke up and stumbled into the living room, carrying Fin, who was crying from being startled awake.

"Why didn't you call?!" Kai asked her sister.

"You would've said not to come. You're mad at me, I know it. We took a red-eye," Janie blurted, her words coming out in a rush, "I haven't been able to stop thinking of you and Fin, since Salt Lake City. I just had to see you and hug the poor little guy. I thought he could use a visit from his cousins, to cheer him up, after all he's been through."

Well, she had that part right; Fin deserved all the love he could get. Doris set the now-wriggling little boy down on the floor in his cast and PJs, and all four kids recovered instantly from the yelling, as resilient little ones do. They were running around and playing with Fin's books and toys before you could say "Ready, set, *go*."

"FIN, FIN, LITTLE FISHIE FIN!" the adorable girls chimed, dancing around him, as he bounced like Tigger and giggled with delight, exclaiming "HI, YAY!" and "YAY, WE DID IT!"

"That porch has gotten a *lot* of action in the last ten hours," Doris mumbled, still managing to be cheeky while half asleep. "Hi, Janie; I'm Doris, Kai's roommate…"

"She's Fin's best friend. And mine." Kai chimed in.

"Well, hello Doris, I'm so sorry to intrude in your home, at such an early hour." Janie had suddenly put on her manners hat, but Doris wasn't buying it.

"No, you're not. I'll put on some coffee and get the kids a snack," Doris yawned, disappearing into the kitchen.

"What does she mean, 'that porch has gotten lot of action?'" Janie asked, bewildered.

Kai winced, "There was a small, scattered thunderstorm. Lightning struck the old metal rake that's leaning behind the bench," she muttered. Like she was *really* gonna talk about making out with her kid's neurosurgeon on the welcome mat.

Janie furrowed her brow. "Oh, that's crazy, I checked the weather report and I didn't even hear about that," she fretted.

Kai glanced away, "The storm already passed—freak occurrence—don't worry."

"Thank God Fin wasn't out there," Janie said, exhaling.

"Yeah, thank God." Kai smiled, despite herself.

"Wow, I am just...*speechless*."

Kai followed Janie's wide gaze to where Fin was playing with the girls, running, jumping, climbing and dancing.

"He's doing all of that in a *body cast*?" Janie marveled.

"Yes, I told you, his legs and arms are totally free, he's not in any pain. He doesn't even know that every twenty month old kid isn't wearing one under their t-shirt."

"Well, he's just...*thriving*!" Janie shook her head in astonishment.

"Yeah," Kai grinned, despite the hunger gnawing at her belly from the lack of shut-eye, "he really is."

After strong coffee and a leisurely, healthy breakfast for the kids, Doris offered to take the little ones to the local park to play, so that the two sisters could spend some time talking privately. Clover Park near their house had a play area for younger kids which had those slightly rubberized cement floors, instead of a giant sand box under the slides—perfect for a casted kid. The girls were thrilled to go, too—Janie, not so much. She pretended to be happy about the *sister alone time* idea, but she knew Kai was still pissed at her.

Kai drove them out to the beach, bringing along some light Mediterranean snacks for their lunch, hummus and pita chips with feta cheese and tabouli salad that they picked up from the health food store. It was a mildly chilly day for L.A., but still sunny and breezy and beautiful—it was a guilty luxury for Kai to be able to go to the beach, now that Fin couldn't run around and play there. The thought of him throwing up handfuls of sand in the air and getting it stuck inside the cast for weeks or months made Kai's skin itch, just thinking about it. And then there was the ocean…he'd *so* want to chase the pretty, frothy waves. It felt mean to show him something he couldn't experience—not for a long time, anyway.

They parked and quietly began walking on the beach together. Janie asked about Teddy, and Kai explained the latest threat Fin was facing. Janie's face went white. "I owe you a *big* apology, a face to face apology, not on the phone," she finally said. "That's why I'm here."

"Okay." Kai looked out at the ocean, her favorite thing, next to looking at Fin's beautiful little face.

"I've always judged you, I've always thought your choices were wrong, or flighty or dumb…but you're not dumb, Kai, we both know that. You're the golden child, the smart one, the kind one…the beautiful one…"

"I'm not anyone's golden child."

"You were Mom's," Janie said plainly.

Kai blanched, "That's not true, and you know it, she loved us equally and *uniquely*, for who we were."

"I guess it's my personality, Kai, to feel self-pity…'Woe is me,' like I got the bad hand of the genetic 'cards,' or whatever."

Kai looked at her sister; Janie looked like she had been holding this in for a long time.

"Kai, you know the way I was treated our entire childhood, by the other kids in school, the boys and the girls, the teachers…*society*. You may as well have come out of the womb with *jazz hands* and a sequined gown, all dressed up for the Oscars, the way they treated you. It's just people, it's not your fault—even babies too young to speak smile more often at so-called mathematically 'beautiful' faces, ones that are more *symmetrical*—big eyes, wide forehead, long legs—you think people are nice to Angelina Jolie and Brad Pitt just because they do a lot of charity work?!"

"You're smart and beautiful yourself, Janie, you have three gorgeous girls and a husband who worships you. Your kids are *healthy*! Be *grateful*!"

Janie pursed her lips, "I *am* grateful, I am grateful to God that my girl's don't have Fin's…*affliction*…"

Kai shuddered at that word. *Affliction*. It sounded like a curse, which it wasn't meant as, but she wanted to let her sister say her peace.

"But I tried to shield myself in a different state, in a small town, where people judged each other based on their *character*…and came to find out that my devoted preacher husband is banging the whole goddamn *CHOIR*!" Janie gasped, her hand flying to her mouth, as if she couldn't believe she had said it out loud.

"Oh, my *Gah*—all—*female*?" As soon as Kai said it, she wished she could take it back.

"I exaggerated, it's not the *whole* choir; it's four women, that I know of. I found evidence and he confessed." Janie began to sob, as Kai took her sister into her arms.

"That has nothing to do with you not being beautiful or special. I am so, *so* sorry that you're going through this. That behavior is entirely on him, he betrayed you, and I hate him for it!"

"I moved away from California to get *away* from the dicks!" Janie sobbed.

"Oh, honey," Kai couldn't help but laugh, "this world is full of 'Dicks Without Borders,' Take my Douche Bag Ex, for example…"

"Yes," Janie sniffled, trying to stop crying, "But this is my *husband* and the father of my *children*!

Kai just looked at her.

"Oh, right, Fin's father put you on the lawn," Janie said, "Sorry, I'm not at my best, right now…"

"Who is?" Kai sighed, looking out at her beloved ocean.

"The sex part, Kai," Janie shuddered, "In their *vaginas*, and in *mine*. I had to get tested for a whole salad bar of VDs!"

Kai raised a gentle, questioning brow.

"Clear, no diseases, thank God. But, it's *humiliating*…and it's just…*gross!*" Janie yelled.

Kai nodded gravely, putting her arm around her shoulders. "It's time for a lot of fried food and wine."

Kai drove them to Neptune's Net, a casual seafood restaurant on the Pacific Coast Highway in Malibu that always had lots of friendly biker dudes eating there. It was the kind of place where you had to stand in line to order your food, and maybe the wine wasn't a very, let's say, *fine vintage*…perhaps you may have to use a port-o-potty for a loo…but you could relax, and talk about your husband cheating on you with four choir girls.

"Maybe I'll run away with one of these bikers," Janie mused sadly, taking a sip of wine in a plastic cup, a chardonnay that came with a screw off top. "I've always liked beards with kind eyes. Beard porn…it must give you a soft place to sit."

"Janie!" Kai giggled. "No, you have children to raise, remember them?" she joked. She took a small sip of her own glass; she planned to stay here over an hour to make sure it was out of her system before driving.

"Oh, right—the *children*," Janie joked, taking a bite of fried clams with cocktail sauce. They had ordered a feast—boiled shrimp, crab legs, fish n' chips, fried oysters and clams, with French fries and some cole slaw on the side—vegetables, you know, to keep it healthy, ha.

"We never talk about Dad." Janie was into full confession mode.

What was gonna come out of her mouth next, Kai wondered? *I'm becoming a Hari Krishna?* "What's there to talk about? He left us." Kai hated to think of him, especially now. He had not been there when they needed him and he was not here now. *Who cares,* she thought to herself. She was *so done* being hurt by him.

"Dad's...dead." Janie stated simply.

"*What?*" Kai dropped her fork into her cocktail sauce, stunned. "How do you know?"

"Right before we came here, after I found out about Joe...I was in panic mode, and I was doing all of these Internet searches. I was thinking about you, and Mom, and then Dad...so I found one of those websites that searches for people, and they located a tiny obituary."

"It could be someone with the same name," Kai sputtered quickly, wondering why she cared, she didn't think she cared just a second ago.

"No, it was him. He overdosed on drugs," Janie said.

Kai absorbed that. Part of her had always known she would someday get news like this about her father. Still, it was a shock. She could feel herself going numb.

"He must've had somebody who cared about him...a girlfriend, maybe, because somebody paid to have a small picture of him printed in the paper. He looked a lot older than we remember, but I recognized his face, it was Dad." Janie finished her wine and set down her glass. Kai knew her sister almost never drank; she didn't like to feel out of control. No wonder she got a buzz today.

"Where...where was he, when he—?" Kai began to ask.

"In a cheap motel, in Atlantic City. Gambling again, of course. I'm sorry; I didn't want to tell you on the phone." Janie's voice was getting very quiet, now. "After...you know, losing Mom so fast, like we did."

Kai reached out and took her sister's hands across the table. She had lost her appetite. "Janie, we're the only family we have left. I don't want to lose you, again. When you walked up across the lawn this morning, with the girls...for a second, I thought you were Mom."

Janie choked back a sob. "I don't look like Mom. *You* do."

"No, together we are each a half of her, and our kids are part of her, too. I want to be in my niece's lives…I want you in Fin's life," Kai said sincerely.

"Me, too," Janie replied, overcome.

"What are you gonna do, about your marriage? Do you know?" Kai asked.

"I'm movin' to *Cali, Cali, Cali…*" Janie said in a sing-song voice, smiling, "…to take care of my four girls, and get to know one brave little boy."

Kai was the one choking back her tears, now. "To take care of one brave little boy and *five* brave girls, include yourself in that number, big sister."

"I may just start doing that, little sister," Janie smiled.

Hours later, after they went back to the house, played with the kids in the yard (blowing bubbles), and Fin went down for his nap, Kai shut herself alone in her bedroom. She finally allowed herself a chance to really cry, but strangely, the tears didn't come.

Her Dad was dead. Her only father, her Daddy, and she could not cry for him. Yes, he had left when she was so young, just a little girl. Yes, he was pretty much a total failure in the father department, but he was the only one she'd ever have. Both of her parents were gone from this green earth, now, their souls passed on from this troubled, beautiful planet. Would she meet them again, she wondered? She hoped she'd meet her Mama, of course, her Dad—she didn't know. In some ideal situation, maybe, where he said all of the right things, apologizing for everything they had lost when he left.

Or, maybe they didn't lose much. Maybe their lives would've been worse if he had stayed. Would it have been a completely unstable home, with constant fighting and domestic violence? He was an unstable man,

he couldn't be counted on—maybe he did them all a favor
by leaving.

Kai heard the word "Daddy" choking from her dry
lips, as her whole body shook with grief, but she still
could not find a single tear. She hadn't imagined she'd
feel this way about him dying, her Mom always said he
was handsome and charming, but a bastard. Could you
grieve someone as a Dad who had been such a terrible,
disappointing one?

Yes, she knew now, from the hollow, lost feeling
in her gut. You not only grieve whatever good memories
you can conjure up about that person, especially with a
parent, you grieve the relationship you will now never
have with them. Gone, baby *gone*—her Daddy was a dead
man. She wasn't making light of it, she just reeled over
the fact that Fin may never really know his own father in
the first few years of his life, if she had to prevent him
from having shared custody. If she couldn't trust him not
to harm her child's health and future, by recklessly
removing the cast too soon.

The memories flooded in, she couldn't stop them.
Her Dad, with his curly honey blonde hair and hazy, lazy
green eyes, his goofy grin and his beach papa beard. He
was naturally thin and tan, with lean muscles he didn't
really have to work for—which was good, because he
didn't work for much.

He played the guitar for Janie and her when they
were little girls, by a beach bonfire, and made up
goofball, sweet songs about grains of sand and the rain,
and the stars he stole from the night sky and put in their
eyes. One of his front teeth was broken in a bar fight, a
snaggle tooth which he never got fixed, and it somehow
made his smile even more endearing. He told the girls he
gave a chip of his front tooth to the tooth fairy, and they
were so young and innocent—and gullible—they believed
him. All the ladies were putty in his hands, unless they

had top shelf liar radar. The ladies he picked up in the strip clubs and bars he frequented never did.

He was the most handsome man in the whole wide world to Kai when she was little, and he made her feel like the most special girl alive. That was, when he was around—which wasn't often. If absent Daddies only knew the impact they have on their girls, and their boys, if they only had a *clue*. They didn't deserve to be called Daddies, or Dad, not if they left and abandoned their kids, both physically and emotionally, and never returned. But *Daddy* is what she whispered, muffled under the covers, so that Fin or Janie's girls wouldn't hear. "Daddy, I'm *so sorry*…"

She hated herself, at moments, she felt not good enough, because he hadn't loved her more, enough to stay.

To overdose, alone, in a motel room. He must've been so sad, so lonely. He would never get to meet his gorgeous grandson or three beautiful granddaughters. She was truly so sorry for her father, for Fin, for herself, for everybody involved.

"May he rest in peace," Kai prayed softly aloud, "May he no longer be in pain. Dear Jesus, God, please take him into your arms, and forgive him. *Amen*."

If there was such a thing as an easy journey, a pain free path, Kai was not going to get it in this lifetime. As she felt the trembling stop, she heard a gentle knock on the door. She looked out from under the covers as Doris peeked her head in the room. "Come in," Kai said, "I can't even cry for the bastard."

Doris smiled softly, "Honey, a lot of bastards in this world. Don't let the bastards get you down."

"Yeah, this one was just my father," Kai murmured.

"I know. But, do you think *you're* so special, to have the only father who was a lying, cheating, gambling, drug addicted bastard?" Doris arched a brow.

Kai laughed. If you don't laugh, you cry, and she was so *over* crying. If crying made you look old, she would look a hundred, by now.

"Doris, my Mom died suddenly, Teddy is *Teddy*, my child is in a major health crisis, Janie's husband is cheating on her with four women…and now I find out my father overdosed alone in a hotel room? Really? *Seriously*? Am I *cursed*?"

Doris sat down on the bed beside her, sighing. "No, not cursed, just human. They don't hand out the bags of hammers fairly or evenly."

Kai winced, feeling guilty that she was focusing on herself. "Doris, you *lost a child*…that's the worst thing *possible*…I'm so sorry to rant on."

"You rant, my girl, you *deserve* a rant. And you deserve to get out—*call him*."

"Who, Jack? Who would want to be with me when I'm like this?" Kai whimpered, knowing she sounded pathetic.

Doris touched Kai's dry cheek. "I'm here with Fin tonight. Janie is here. That man can't fix this, or save you from what you're going through, but he *can* hold you."

Kai ran her hands through her hair, shaking her head. "Doris, are you my Fairy Godmother?"

"I wish. I truly wish I could just cast a spell or wave a wand for you, for Fin," Doris replied, looking at Kai with the saddest, kindest eyes in the world.

Doris gently patted Kai's leg, leaving the room to allow her to think.

To call or not to call Jack? Kai lay back on the bed, ruminating. Could she drag herself from the bed, when she felt so deeply low and *unpretty,* in every way? Could she politely smile and laugh at his jokes, charmed by his wit, offering hers back—the way normal women acted on a first date? This was no romantic comedy set-up by the late great Nora Ephron.

The truth was, they hadn't even *had* a date, yet. Not an official one. If she was cursed, would she be bringing Jack into her cursed little *fffed* up world of sad fates and strange terrors, the kind that can only be felt when you fear for your child's life?

She didn't know what a panic attack felt like, but she felt like she was having one. Instead of wanting to run, she felt paralyzed, trapped inside her own body in this bed. Her twisted family, her twisted life, her boy's still twisted spine…and yet: the way Fin smelled, the way he smiled, the sound of his laughter as he chased the bubbles in the yard with his cousins today, his eyes bright in the sunlight…he was perfect. He was the one perfect thing, in what seemed to be a darker and darker world. The thought of her little angel Fin lifted her up, up, *up*.

She rose, forcing herself to think lighter thoughts, to cling to hope, the thing with feathers, the thing that could still fly in the face of fear. For Fin, she would get up off the mat every time, like a fighter in the ring. That was the only thing she could be sure of.

If she lost him, she would gladly drown, pulled down by the Undertoad, into the waters, cold and dark and deep.

19
The Land of the Living

Even as she was dialing his number, hearing her own breath unsteady into the phone, she couldn't believe she was doing this. When he asked her to come to his place, she had a crazy thought, that meeting in a public place would be safer, after their last, breathless encounter on her porch. He suggested the lobby of a hotel called Shutters on the Beach, which was only a short drive from her house, where they could sit on the patio and look out at the ocean.

It sounded innocent enough, until they were opening the room with the key, fumbling to close the door behind them, and tumbling on to the plush bed, in a room that looked like the most elegant beach villa imaginable. She wanted him, on her, inside of her, to both bring her back to life and to make her disappear. She wanted to dwell in the land of the living for a few hours, to pretend she was somebody else, somebody worthy of love.

She kissed him roughly, hungrily clutching and digging her hands into his thick hair. She wrapped her thighs around his waist, arching her back and vanishing, losing herself in his scent, the feel of his skin, the heat that melded their bodies into a perfect fit. Safe, warm, wrong, *now*.

"Kai," he whispered into her lips, pulling away. His lips were succulent; his probing, worried eyes drew her into his mind. "Kai, *no*...not like this..."

She couldn't believe what he was saying, and then his mouth was back on hers, needing her; then pulling back again. "You're not ready for this, you need time. I...*can't*..." he pulled away from her, holding her face gently in his hands. "I can't believe I'm saying this, but I just want to talk. Will you let me in?"

The shock of the rejection, here—in a rented, romantic hotel room, of all places—took her aback for a moment. She had never been rejected sexually by a man in her life. She sputtered, "My father, my Daddy...he's dead. I just found out today."

Jack's face drew into an even more concerned, now pained expression, and he pulled her tightly into his arms. *"Come here."*

There, as the ocean waves crashed and the salty breeze blew in through the curtains, Kai finally cried for her father. Jack just held her, enveloped her in his strong, muscular arms, and looked at her as if he were trying to take every ounce of her hurt away. As if he wanted to protect her and keep her safe from harm, from the acute, searing pain of this whole crazy life, forever.

"Give your pain to me; give me your grief, at least for now. I'll protect you. *I'll carry you*," he whispered into her ear.

They stayed like that for hours, as the sun went down and the room darkened, lit only by the moon and the stars her father had once promised her; and the spinning, multicolored lights from the Santa Monica Pier. It was the most safe that Kai had felt, since Fin was diagnosed. Actually, it was the most safe she had *ever* felt.

"Can I ask you something?" Jack finally said when he spoke again, gently stroking her hair off of her forehead.

"Yes," Kai breathed; her cheek and hand resting against his strong chest.

"What did you dream about, before all of this happened?" he whispered.

Before. She had to think, there was such a clear line of delineation, between *then* and *now*. Before she saw the train coming. What did she dream about? Was there ever a time she didn't just dream about saving her boy?

"I, uh...made things, I have a little beach hut, a tiny shack. I bought it when my Mom died. I made sandals and sarongs and scarves and some bathing suits, natural looking stuff...I used shells and beads and sea glass to make it unique," she said.

Yes, there *had* been a before. She had almost forgotten.

"Do you have any of it left?" Jack asked softly.

"Some...some old things..." she murmured.

"Would you show me?" he asked, smiling.

She had the key to her hut in her purse; she always carried it with her. They drove in her car, walking silently along the beach to her old, rickety little dream spot. There was a full moon over the water, reflecting on the dark waves. She unlocked the padlock, opening the creaky door to her hut and letting him in.

The only light was from the moon, but they could see around, as Jack took in all of Kai's old dusty, handmade treasures.

"Wow," he finally said, "You made all of this stuff?"

"Yeah, a long time ago," she said, taking in the sand and dust that had covered everything, it was almost like a mausoleum.

"It's...beautiful," he said.

"Thanks. I was...sort of...in a magazine, once." Boy; she thought, did that glamorous time seem like several lifetimes ago. It wasn't. It was less than three years.

"You're a designer." He lightly ran his fingers over a delicate, hand painted shell necklace.

"It's just little things," she replied, kind of embarrassed.

"Little things made with great love and care. You're very talented." He held up one of the rope sandals, examining the design of the colored sea glass woven through the top. "It took time for the ocean to polish this glass, to burnish it. That's what's happening to you right now, I think." He looked in her eyes, "The universe is making you even more beautiful, your life, your pain…it's not dulling you. It's burnishing you."

"If I live through it," Kai smiled sadly. "Yeah, I'll really *shine*." She choked back a muffled sob, looking heavenward.

Jack winced, taking her into his arms and pulling her close. He looked like he wanted to physically absorb the pain she was going through.

He whispered in her ear, "Oh, baby…sweet Kai…don't you see you already *do*?"

Afterwards, they walked together along the ocean, saying very little. Kai wanted to tell him her memories of her Dad, but it was too painful, the wound was too fresh.

It felt odd to be the only couple to probably ever check into a gorgeous hotel room with an ocean view, and check out the same night— *without* having sex—but Kai wanted to sleep at home, in case Fin needed her in the night. Sometimes he woke up screaming, probably from a nightmare, but Kai couldn't help but worry that he felt trapped or scared in the cast. The reality was that it was like a second skin to him during the day, it was just normal, and he had nightmares just like any other toddler might experience during sleep. There are so many scary things in the world that are hard for an adult to process, let alone an almost two year old mind with a growing imagination.

They kissed one last goodbye, as they waited for their cars at the valet in front of the hotel. Jack had paid for the room, and for her parking. He insisted on it, despite her protests.

Her modest little car pulled up and she turned to him as he opened the door for her. "Was this a date?" she asked.

"Yeah, I hope so. It was for me," Jack replied, kissing her forehead.

"Good. It was for me, too," she said, smiling and putting her seatbelt securely on, bracing for the drive back home to her rocky life.

The next day, she and Janie decided they wanted to do something to say goodbye to their wayward father. A little ceremony, a small way to mark his life. It was more for themselves than for him, they agreed; it was just a ritual that they needed to do, an attempt at something resembling closure.

They dressed up the kids, the girls in their prettiest dresses, with fresh flowers in their hair, and they dressed Fin in a button down shirt and khaki pants, a little boy's church outfit. Kai spit combed his hair to make him look presentable—a mom's bargain version of styling gel.

Since their father had been a beach bum type, they wanted to do a bonfire on the sand, but sand was too dangerous for Fin, and open fire was too dangerous for little kids, period. Instead, they rented a small sailboat in the Marina. It was a splurge, but Janie chipped in half. The kids all had life preservers on, and the "captain" came with the two hour fee, so they didn't have to be experts in sailing. Their Dad had loved the ocean, and he also loved boats. He had a fantasy, like a lot of dreamers, about sailing off into the sunset, after he had struck it rich gambling, and living like Jimmy Buffett on an island somewhere. Barefoot margaritas and beautiful women. He had been far too lazy to be a good pirate, so a beach bum it was.

They skipped the margaritas, but they brought Kai's iPod player and played Kenny Chesney songs and

Jimmy Buffett's greatest hits, and the two sisters told the kids and Doris their small, happy memories of their Dad. Kai held Fin and they sang along with the songs, cuddling up in blankets until the sun set, all pink and red and stunning swaths of gold light. They said a prayer, just as the sun went down, and it was probably more beautiful than their old crazy Dad deserved.

The next three days were near bliss of cousin playing and sister bonding. They baked cookies and ate red velvet cupcakes with cream cheese frosting, they took the kids to the park every day, and to Tickles n' Luv, to play in the play area with all of the toys. They went out to all of the lively outdoor walking malls and toy stores they could find. The kids drew with large pieces of colored chalk on the sidewalk, and played with classic toys that reminded Janie and Kai of their own childhoods— Crayola crayons and Play-doh and Legos and Slinkys. They shopped at Whole Foods for healthy stuff, and ate like there was no tomorrow. It was a little slice of Heaven built on quicksand, but Kai decided to eat the slice and paddle like hell. It seemed like the entire Earth was built on quicksand, these days, why not dance a little as you go under?

It was too short a time until Janie and the girls had to go back home. It was time for her to face her cracked marriage to her cheating husband and its probable demise. It was time for both sisters to face their own lives, right now, their broken parts that needed fixing, and the next step on each of their increasingly complicated, crooked roads.

The day Janie and her girls flew out of L.A. was exactly one week before Kai had to fly back to Salt Lake City for Fin's second cast, for his very first "cast change." Almost like clockwork, her nervous system kicked into high alert the moment she woke up that morning. All systems turned to fear.

She tried to explain it to Janie as she drove them to the airport, "The waiting...*ugh*, the hoping he won't get sick before he gets that next precious cast on...the not knowing how he'll handle having the cast being sawed off, removed for a whole day, and then how he'll react to going back to the hospital the next morning, and being put under anesthesia again, then waking up with a new cast back on..."

"You also don't know how you're gonna react, how *you'll* handle it," Janie added gently.

"Exactly," Kai said, exhaling, "I worry I'm not strong enough to do it again."

"You *are* strong enough, you've already done it. You're still standing, and your boy is thriving. Of course it's scary to face anesthesia for your child, it will be each and every time, of course, but you will do it, you'll do it for *him*."

Kai nodded, trying not to tear up, as she pulled the car into LAX airport, saying "Every time I do something new, I'm scared."

Janie turned to her, "It's almost too much to process, the whole journey you still have to go on. It's so...open ended; the end is not clearly in sight, right now. So you can't look at the whole thing, you can't look too far ahead. You'd go crazy. You just have to take it one moment at a time, one day at a time, one cast at a time."

Kai looked into her sister's eyes, "Do you realize we are at an airport, with children in the car, and not so long ago there were attempted terrorist attacks on this place being planned—there probably still are. And I can't even think about that. All I can think about is that I have to bring Fin back here in a week, and get on a plane to the Shriners Hospital, to try to keep straightening his spine, before Teddy abducts him."

Janie smiled sadly, "You're under a different kind of attack, but there is a lot of terror involved. This is big."

"Be like NEMO!" Janie's oldest girl, Micah, cried out suddenly. Both Janie and Kai spun around to look at her. "He was lost and scared, he lost his dad, and he just kept swimming."

Kai took in her little niece, who shrugged at her matter-of-factly. "Just keep swimming," Micah said. All three girls looked at Kai from the back seat, nodding, with the most innocent expressions on their small faces. Of course, it was so simple; Kai thought—keep swimming— they were right. Why couldn't the adults get it, why couldn't they really see it? When did life get so hard to see clearly?

Someone honked a car horn at them, annoyed that Kai was driving so slowly, and her mind was back to the hustle and bustle of the airport. She pulled into the parking lot for Janie's airline and found a space, turning off the engine and getting the bags out of the car, as Janie unstrapped and organized her girls.

Kai waited with them through the luggage check-in line, which wasn't so bad this time, and helped Janie get the checked bags to the right place, before saying goodbye. She hugged each one of her precious nieces, and then Janie and Kai hugged—a *real* hug— not like those forced ones they used to give each other. "*Just keep swimming, Kai,*" Janie whispered in her ear.

"You, too, sister," Kai whispered back, choking up.

She stroked Micah's hair, smiling, before beginning to walk towards the airport exit doors. "WE LOVE YOU, AUNT KAI!" she heard the girls yell, one last time.

Kai turned back, waving, as her sister and her girls did the same. It was hard to walk away, and then drive away from them, but Janie had insisted that she was used to handling her three girls alone. She said her husband chipped in very little, so she had learned to become self-sufficient with her kids. Kai knew she wouldn't have been

249

able to go past the security check with them, anyway—
still, she found herself fighting back tears again. *Crap.*

Self-pity was *not* her favorite emotion; she
considered it mostly a waste of time, but it kept creeping
into the edges of her mind, mixed with anxiety and fury.

The last nine weeks of Fin newly in the cast, as
well as the past few months, had been the most difficult of
her life, except for experiencing Fin's daily toddler joy.
She was also grateful for the chance to reconnect—really
to genuinely connect for the first time—with her sister.

Kai was so sad about Janie's impending divorce,
for the whole family, especially for Janie and the kids. To
put it mildly, divorce *sucked*. She had lost her father in a
different way, but loss of your parental unit, both Mama
and Papa Bear together, was painful, there was no way
around that. It would reverberate throughout their lives,
and their parents would have to work very hard to
maintain their girl's self-esteem and happy outlook on the
future, to allow them to still believe in love and its
possibilities.

All of the love she had felt with her sweet sister
and her nieces and Fin this past week, with all of the
warmth swirling around them—she wondered, how could
there still be so much beauty amidst so much pain? Did
one *ever* come without the other, would it *ever again*?

And then there was Jack. Part of her wished she
could just vanish, just die in his arms. She wasn't proud
of that emotion. It wasn't elegant or pretty, it wasn't nice,
it wasn't brave or courageous—she was a *mother*, and she
had to be here to fight for her child. She knew that, she
had to pull it together, she had to, and she *would*. She
wouldn't see Jack before the trip; she told herself, she had
to clear her mind. She didn't have to do it alone; she had
Doris to go with her, this time. Doris was family, now.

The waiting. The *waiting*. It was, again,
sometimes truly the hardest part, with the requisite nod to

Tom Petty and his Heartbreakers, because Kai's heart was breaking at all that her boy had yet to go through.

They would survive it, wouldn't they? Little Fishie Fin…just keep swimming. The wisdom of a movie classic, *Finding Nemo*, she could cling to that, she hoped. That and the ones who loved her, that would be enough. Fin's happiness was enough to weather any storm; she would gladly trade her life for his at any moment, without hesitation, with a grateful heart to God for giving her the choice. It was the brutal nature of the unknown that was so difficult, the not knowingness of this health crisis, the open ended fear. "False evidence appearing real," wasn't that what fear was?

She vowed to herself that she would look for wisdom and strength, she would pray, she would go on the online support group, she would take wisdom and advice from a child. As Shakespeare wrote, "Adversity's sweet gift…philosophy." She would cling to every ounce of philosophy that human consciousness had ever mustered, from all of the wise women and men in the history of the world. She would do whatever it takes to survive this pain, and to protect her baby.

But for now, this was the best advice she had ever been given:

Just. Keep. Swimming.

19
Cracking

Five days before she and Doris travelled back to Salt Lake City for the first cast change, Kai decided to venture out of the house alone with Fin on a stroll. She tried to semi-quarantine her little boy the week before the new cast—especially the last five days—but he was getting so stir crazy stuck in the house, that Kai decided they could at least go to the park.

It seemed like indoor places, like shopping malls and kid's playrooms, might have more children with winter colds and flus in an enclosed space; whereas the park was at least open aired. Kai figured she could see a virulent, runny nosed kid trying to share a slimy ball with her kiddo and steer him away, using anti-bacterial gel or wipes on Fin's small hands, if she needed to. She tried not to be a germaphobe, but it was hard not to be.

There was also the constant threat of legal action from Teddy hanging over them like an oncoming storm cloud, which made everything feel like a race against time, while the minutes to the casting date seemed to tick by ever slower.

At the sprawling, sunny green Clover Park, after a lovely twenty minute stroll from their rental house through charming, quiet suburban streets, Fin couldn't wait to get out of the stroller. Kai took him all the way to the tip end of the park, where there was the area with no sand to get down inside his cast. It was the closest spot to the Santa Monica Airport, and small planes kept taking off in the blue sky over their heads.

Fin kicked his legs excitedly and bounced out of his stroller on to the play area for ages two and up as soon as she unbuckled him. "YAY, MOMMY!" he shouted, delighted.

Doris had a part time nanny job for a few days that week, they were travelling to Salt Lake City on Sunday, so Kai was alone a lot with her toddler and her swirling thoughts; rife with anxiety and fear. Doris kept trying to calm her. "Think of his cast like a little crab shell," she said, "We will get to *crack that crab* and take out the soft, sweet baby inside of it for a *whole day!*"

She meant the day the cast would be sawed off. Kai had to smile, because the thought of hugging her sweet baby's naked skin made her so happy, she could burst. It was such a strange mix of emotions, and then there was the paranoia. Teddy's family was rich, powerful. Kai found herself suspiciously scanning the faces of the other parents and nannies in the play area where Fin was now picking up leaves and sticks under a nearby tree. He was collecting them, examining them like a botanist, as he loved to do. He was fully mobile, again, and it was just like before the first cast was applied.

Kai stood next to him and took in their surroundings: babies in strollers, a handful of other toddlers on ride-on toys and playing with bouncy balls, one or two other mothers, but mostly kids with their nannies. Some nannies were snacking on their lunches or chatting with each other near the play equipment with climbing areas and slides. Kai asked herself what she was really looking for, was she looking to see Teddy lurking near the edges, watching them? Or did she think he would actually hire someone to pose as a nanny and scoop Fin up and kidnap him?

She noticed, as usual, that most of the other kids and parents barely noticed Fin's cast under his long sleeved t-shirt. Most of them smiled sweetly at him, and only rarely did anyone give him a curious, sideways glance—wondering why he was bulked up near his neck, like shoulder pads on a football player. Kai didn't mind those looks, but if someone had implied she had hurt her child, she knew she might lose it.

Fin ran to the stairs that led to the slides, confidently climbing up on his own. Kai stayed right behind him, ready to catch him at any moment, but she was so proud to see him being active and independent. He smiled at a freckled little boy on top of the play equipment; then went for the small slide. Mama made sure he put both legs in front of him, and that he was sitting in the right position before letting him go— "WHEEEEEE!!!" he squealed, laughing and clapping when he reached the bottom. Kai slid down the slide right next to him and helped him off of the end, clapping along with him. "Yay! Great job!" she grinned, as he beamed back at his Mommy.

Then he took off running. Kai chased him, grabbing the stroller that was parked along the path and catching up to him without missing a beat. This kid was *fast*. He sped down the sidewalk behind the park's baseball field, and she was right next to him, urgently calling "*Slow down, wait for Mommy!*" They had just passed the metal bleacher area, when he suddenly turned to run down the grassy hill behind the baseball field.

Fin had turned into an inverted path in the ground. Kai's eyes widened in fear as she instantly let go of the stroller, leaving it behind, as she chased down the hill just a few feet behind him, reaching out her arms to grab him. It happened so fast, there was no time to think, and in an instant, she knew she couldn't stop him from falling. There were too many clumps of grass and bumps and rocks on the hill, and he was so top heavy and flying down it so fast, that he lost his footing and began to tumble to the bottom.

To Kai's horror, she saw that this inverted area in the earth ended in a heavy, permanent cement garbage can directly in front of Fin, just before the fence that surrounded the end of the baseball field. Her baby tumbled *end over end* towards it, her child with a spine already badly in need of saving, and her brain began running in slow motion, as she realized that he could be paralyzed or killed if his head struck the cement or his neck broke. *"NO!"* she screamed...it couldn't happen, not after all of this, it wasn't *possible*...not to her baby...

The world stopped turning. Fin's t-shirt caught on a large root, tearing his shirt open, just before he hit the unyielding surface of the cement obstacle—striking it against his back—bouncing horribly back a foot. The hideous cracking noise made people in the park turn to look, as Kai tumbled herself after him, landing next to him and feeling his body with her searching, desperate hands. His shirt had torn almost completely off, and she could now see that the cast had cracked *wide open*.

Fin began to cry hysterically, a good sign that he was not unconscious, she thought wildly. Kai carefully turned him over and delicately lifted him. His neck was clearly not broken, he was struggling and moving all of his limbs in a panic.

Strangers gathered around them, and she yelled, "HELP US!! CALL 911!!! *MY BABY IS HURT*!!!"

A stranger handed her a roll of tape and gauze, and she began desperately trying to tape the broken cast back together. It wasn't working, it continued to crack and fell off in her arms, and Fin screamed, as his spine began to CORKSCREW AND TWIST, RIGHT BEFORE HER EYES...

Kai woke up in her bed, sweating and crying. She grabbed the baby monitor on her nightstand and pressed the video button, seeing Fin sleeping peacefully in his crib.

She tried to catch her breath and stop
hyperventilating. It had been another nightmare, and there
were still five more days to go until they got on the plane.
The Undertoad was threatening to come back, her dark
and ugly, yellow eyed demon that wanted to pull her
under, and she wanted her own Mama to come and save
her.

She was starting to think of this Undertoad as
more and more of a *thing*, to visualize it as a greedy, soul
sucking creature that only she could see and only *she*
could fight—because it was inside her. Jack could hold
her in his arms all night long, Doris and Fadi could lift her
up and make her laugh, and Janie could hold her hand for
a lifetime, but no one could face this demon but her.

Maybe everyone had to crack up sometimes, Kai
thought, in order to stay sane. In order to cling to the
edges of the Earth, in order to live through the awful, the
most frightening moments, to get to the good stuff.

She glanced at the clock, it was 5 a.m. Kai didn't
sleep the rest of the night, but come morning, Fin was as
joyful as always, and he pulled her back from the ledge in
her mind.

The week dragged on, but on Sunday, she and
Doris were packed, and Fadi drove them to LAX airport
with Fin in his car seat and cast between them. The lines
were manageable, this time. Even the security check went
pretty smoothly, despite the fact that Kai had to tell them
about Fin's body cast for the second time—the first being
in the Utah airport, coming home—so that it could be
swabbed to determine that he didn't have a bomb strapped
on him. Kai still didn't mind that part, she would much
rather nicely explain it, than have them figure it out and
think she was trying to put something over on them. She
figured their jobs were hard enough, trying to protect
everyone from terrorists and crazies, and so far, they had
always been very kind to Fin and her. It was a huge help
to have Doris assist with getting restless little Fin in the

stroller, while they put on their shoes and gathered purses
and coats from those gray plastic bins.

The short flight to Salt Lake City was pretty easy
breezy, they were smart enough to bring snacks and books
and videos on a small portable DVD player for Fin,
including one cute "Dora the Explorer" video, with a tiny
singing frog named El Coqui. They splurged and bought
ten dollar deli sandwiches and chips in the airport for
themselves, turkey, provolone and bacon on a baguette for
Doris, and a huge caprese sub for Kai. There would be a
lot of stress eating on this trip, Kai figured, if she gained
five pounds in the next four days, she would not be
surprised.   "Calories don't count on casting trips,"
Doris declared grandly, as they inhaled their loot on the
flight.

Kai agreed, "I hear ya, Sista." She figured she had
to put her stress somewhere, why not on her stomach and
hips?

When other passengers coughed or sneezed, Kai
whipped her head around, praying the spittle wasn't
flying on to her child. As they hit a touch of turbulence—
always a little taste of death—Kai held both Doris' and
Fin's hands, as his big green eyes widened, concerned,
and Kai whispered soothing sweet nothings into his ear. It
was so cute how he stared intently out of the window at
the clouds, it was required by the airline that they put the
car seat next to the window. Fin would always have the
best view of the sky, on his way to being healed.

They got the rental car, this time a normal
midsized sedan, no unwieldy marshmallow SUV, and
they managed to get their butts safely to the hotel
relatively unscathed. As Kai drove, she remembered how
alone she felt on the first trip, and marveled at the fact
that she was actually happy to be in this now more
familiar, beautiful city. Snow still capped the glorious
mountains peaks, but there was none on the ground, now
that it was mid-April, so it wasn't as scary to navigate the

drive as the first time she came—only ten weeks ago! It
felt to Kai like only two days in some ways, and in other
ways it felt like ten years. Being *on the move* helped, at
least they were *in transit*, *doing* something, instead of just
that awful waiting game.

As they entered the spacious hotel room with the
discounted rate for their hospital visit, Kai locked the door
behind them and let Fin explore the room for a moment,
sinking on to one of the two queen beds. "Teddy hasn't
kidnapped him. He's not sick, at least not right now. We
just have to get him out of the cast tomorrow, and safely
back in it on Tuesday. Right?" She asked anxiously.

"Right, Sista. Hang in there," Doris replied, as she
began putting her folded clothes neatly in the dresser
drawers.

Doris was a creature of habit; Kai thought, as she
stopped Fin from pulling all of the facial tissues out from
the metal dispensers attached to the double sinks and
tossing them on the floor. *Hang in there* was an
expression she had always thought was a little bit cheesy
and trite, but she didn't think that anymore. It was exactly
what she needed to do, just survive this. Just *press on*.

They ate a meal of junk food from the
convenience store in the lobby, and slept in the two queen
beds, with Fin sleeping in the hotel's portable crib
between them. He seemed just fine with it; it was a little
like their set-up at The Four Seasons Hotel had been with
their trio, but a lot less fancy. Kai had a knot in her
stomach the whole trip, the one she was trying to feed
with giant subs and junk food, because what Fin didn't
know is that they were going to, as Doris had cutely put it,
"crack that crab" the next morning. Despite the
assurances that she would make it through from her new
friends in the online support group, she really had no idea
what to expect when she saw his little spine with her own
eyes, for the first time in over two months. She was afraid

of having the nightmares again, so she prayed and slept fitfully, but somehow the morning came.

Funny how that works; how the sun does still rise, even on the scariest of days. But this wasn't her worst day, this was not as bad as the day she found out what was really happening, and it wasn't as bad as the day of the first cast. Today, she would hold her soft, squishy baby from 10am until she sent him off to the surgical room again, first thing the next morning—*in theatre* as the Brits and Aussies call it. It was an apt term, Kai thought, there was certainly enough drama, but theatre, however excellent it could be, was still pretend.

As the three of them entered the Shriners Hospital's revolving glass front door for Fin's appointment, Kai felt a strange sense of calm wash over her. This place made her feel safe in some ways, the fact that they had finally made it to this day. They checked in and Fin ran around the lobby, exclaiming "FISH!" as he pointed to the large fish tank. Angie came down to greet them warmly a few minutes later, in person she was a pretty brunette woman with a bright smile and beautiful light eyes, and she took them all back to a medical room on the first floor, as they chatted. Angie told Kai that she could hold Fin on her lap, sitting on the hospital table with that thin white paper covering it, and she gave her a towel to protect her jeans from the cast dust that the saw would produce.

Kai and Doris tried to distract Fin by telling him the saw was just a "buzzy bee" and singing Bob Marley, but he still cried during the couple of minutes the saw was going. It was loud, not dangerously or deafeningly so, but scary for a little guy like him. Angie was super sweet and went as quickly and carefully as possible, sawing the cast down the back and literally using her hands and Doris' help to crack it open and pull it off of his arms. She then cut off the thin, stretchy gray medical t-shirt, revealing his naturally skinny body underneath.

It all happened so fast, Kai's brain could barely process how good his back looked. She was too focused on helping calm Fin and hugging him without the cast on. Angie and Doris both grabbed washcloths and began to gently wipe down his body; there was a small trail of dirt down the middle of his back.

"That's normal," Angie assured her.

Fin was a little "wasp waisted," as Kai had been told he might be by Matt, the Physician's Assistant, on the first casting day. The Mehta casts worked by being properly anchored at the hips, and so the kids often "went in" a little at that point on their waists, during the process of wearing the casts. Matt had said it would go back to normal, once the treatment was completed.

"His skin looks really good," Angie commented, as they finished wiping Fin off. "It's also normal for his skin to have some redness in areas that were under the cast—that should look better by tomorrow."

Fin was wriggling in Kai's lap, wanting to get down and walk around, so she put him on the floor to let him toddle uncertainly around the room, staying close behind as both she and Doris peered intently at his spine.

"It's definitely still curved," Kai exhaled, "but it's night and day from what it was ten weeks ago."

"The rib hump is a lot better, night and day," Doris agreed. Fin was gingerly walking forward; he was loose and a little wobbly, like a little turtle without his shell, standing on hind legs.

"It must feel so funny to suddenly have that heavy cast taken off," Kai said, following him around to make sure he didn't fall. He was exploring some sort of a large sink with a hose in it that was near the floor. This kid did not miss a beat.

"You'll want to watch him closely today, to make sure he doesn't have any bad falls. He's doing great, though. Casting is harder on the parent," Angie smiled sympathetically.

Angie was right; it was what Kai already knew to be true. She ran her hands over her toddler's fragile back, gently hugging him. It was as if she couldn't believe she was allowed to touch him without the cast on, almost like she was in a dream.

"Doris, would you mind handing me the calendula cream from the diaper bag?" she asked, suddenly remembering the advice from the C.A.S.T. group, a mom had said that Dr. Mehta recommends calendula baby cream, a homeopathic cream made from marigolds that helps with skin repair, itching, etc. She said to slather it on the parts of his skin that had been covered by the cast, to keep him from getting dry and itchy.

It would be bad to have him get any open sores from scratching, before they put a new cast on tomorrow—in fact, the hospital probably wouldn't even do it. Kai had also cut his nails very short to prevent that. Doris dug out the cream from the bag and Kai applied it liberally, putting Fin's long sleeved, regular cotton t-shirt back on. "So, we should go back to the hotel and give him a real bath!" she smiled.

"Absolutely," said Angie, "just remember to call us tonight to find out what time you should be here in the morning. They often do the youngest kids first, Fin might be the first up for the day."

"Thank you so much, Angie, we'll see you tomorrow!" Kai picked up her skinny, delicate feeling little guy, his arms wrapping around her neck and his legs around her waist. As Doris grabbed the diaper bag and followed her out, Kai was thinking that there would be a *lot* of yummy hugs today with her delicious boy, even more than usual.

Kai strapped Fin into his car seat, and they were already back at the hotel within ten minutes. She couldn't wait to give him a bath. Doris ran the tub and added a package of powered oatmeal bath to it, another tip Kai had gotten from the online support group to help sooth his skin. Kai was shocked to see that Fin cried through the whole bath, she thought he would love the sensation of the lukewarm water on his skin, but he seemed frightened at being wet and slippery in a big tub. He looked like he was scared he might slip and go under the water. Kai gently cleaned him as quickly as possible, and Doris held out a big towel for Kai to wrap him in as she pulled him out.

She laid him on the bed in the towel, using more of the calendula baby cream all over his skin. As soon as he was dry, the crying was over—he just wanted to stand up on the bed and look at himself in the big mirror that hung on the hotel wall. Doris and Kai laughed as he grinned at himself and touched his own bare belly. Seeing himself with a belly button was an experience he hadn't had in two months!

The next few hours were pure *bliss*. Fin loved playing in the warm hotel room in just a diaper for a while, and Kai and Doris both thought it was a good idea to let his bare skin breathe a little. He was still wobbly on his feet, and so Kai popped him in the portable crib with a super soft baby blanket, which he happily wrapped around himself and rubbed all over his skin, then he put the blankie over his own head, laughing and giggling in a game of peekaboo.

Kai took photos of his back, in case her memory failed her later on, so she'd have something to refer to. He was visibly better, but definitely a long way from a straight spine. Right before his first cast, he had the large rib hump on his right side, and he leaned over to his right, in a pronounced "C" shape. Now, the curve was much less pronounced, but *how* much less, she wondered? Without an X-ray machine and a doctor's measurements, she really couldn't say. All she could do was live in the moment, in his joy and delight.

As Buddhists say, all we ever have is the moment: this *current moment*, not the one before and not the one after. This is all we have for sure, *just this one*.

Doris went out to pick up some take out from a nearby chain restaurant, so that they could stay in the room to eat, and Kai spent the whole time Doris was gone just touching Fin and hugging him on the bed, the two of them rolling around and laughing as she cuddled him in blankets.

Heaven.

It felt like a little piece of Heaven on Earth, even in their current circumstances. It was a bubble of happiness, inside of the shaken up snow globe of their lives, and inside the bubble, they danced.

After they had lunch and Fin had organic baby fruit puree and a bottle of milk, he looked exhausted, and he took a nap curled up like a little pill bug under his soft blankets. It was a position he couldn't fully sleep in, when in the cast—the fetal position—and he slept deeply for two hours. Doris watched him while Kai went into the hallway to call Janie and Fadi and give them the update.

She thought about calling Jack, but she was too shy…maybe she would call him tomorrow, after the cast was successfully on. With Jack's sensitivity and kindness, she felt she might break down and cry, and she wanted to be strong today, for Fin.

She still kept asking herself what she was doing, getting entangled with a man while all of this was going on, while she was in the weeds of life, the thick of it. Why create even more of a tangle? A romantic relationship in the midst of all of this was sure to implode, part of her knew that. The other part of her struggled against those thoughts, like the two independent systems of the human brain, what psychologist Jonathan Haidt described as "the elephant and the rider"—the elephant being her raw emotions, and the rider being her good, common sense.

The rider was her rational side, but that damn elephant usually won, she was bigger and sometimes raged out of control, and she could trample the rider in a New York minute.

When Fin woke up at 3pm, they felt ambitious, and decided to take him to the Zoo. It was sunny out and cool, spring had *sprung*! They took turns pushing Fin around in the stroller, and both women were just as dazzled as he was by the park. It was laid out in such a way that they could see all of the animals in less than an hour and a half, with no skimping on the big ticket attractions.

"This is Fin's African Safari," Doris quipped, and it practically was. The Hogle Zoo had a rare male Siberian tiger name Kazak, who was lazily rolling and yawing six feet before their eyes, magnificent African elephants eating hay, including a mother with her baby, white rhinos, a Lowland gorilla named Tino, who appeared to be actually flirting with them, and giraffes with eyelashes thick enough to rival Fin's.

A group of penguins actually *sang* to them! Kai tried singing back, and they responded in kind with a new chorus, with Fin and Doris giggling each time. It was a near perfect day.

"Well, that didn't suck," Doris quipped, as they strolled to the car.

"No, it didn't," Kai smiled wearily. She was happy, though, they were still in the protective bubble, the sun globe of "cast off" day. "Just pray for good numbers tomorrow. *Low* numbers, because with spines, that's a good thing. "

"Low, LOW NUMBERS!!!" Doris cried out, holding her fist up in the air as they reached their rental car. Fin saw and copied her with a small fist to the sky.

"Fight the power, Fin!" Kai laughed, brightening.

"No justice, no peace!" Doris chimed in, as all three of them cracked up.

Kai wiped happy tears from her eyes as they climbed into the car. "As Lou Reed sang, "It's just a perfect day...I'm glad I spent it with you..." she trilled softly, as she clicked Fin's soft body into his car seat.

Fin fell asleep by 9pm that night, but both Kai and Doris were nervous, and only got about five hours of sleep each. They were up at 5am to get to the hospital by 6:30.

It was the hardest thing Kai ever had to do, to take her baby back to have him put under anesthesia again, and into another rigid, heavy cast. It was as simple as that, and it was irrational emotional logic, because without the cast, he would surely keep twisting, need horrible surgeries or die.

And yet, her emotional elephant struggled against her logical rider, threatening to trample her good common sense as she carried his small, sleepy body back into the beautiful modern Shriners hospital nestled in the mountains. His fragile, skinny arms and legs were clinging to his Mommy, who he trusted to keep him safe. It was still dark as they entered the front revolving glass door with the toy display, and Kai shoved her emotional elephant deep, deep down and choked back a sob.

She would *not* cry. She would *not* break down in front of him. She could *handle this*, goddammit.

That was the hardest part of Fin's second casting day. Everyone on the hospital staff was wonderful to them, just like the last time. It was like getting V.I.P. treatment, just superior medical care, and she had Doris there to hold her hand and squeeze her shoulder when she needed reassurance. Kai picked bright green this time, for the thin layer of fiberglass that went on top of the white plaster. Fin did great with the anesthesia again, and this time, when he woke up in the new cast, he didn't even cry. He was used to it; in fact, he almost seemed more comfortable in it than he did out of it. Right away, he saw Mommy and Auntie Doris and just wanted to play with

toys in the hospital bed and watch his favorite videos.
"Go, Diego, Go!" indeed. *Go Fin Go*, Kai thought, so
proud of her boy.

Doris joked that he was an environmentally
correct scoliosis patient, because he had a *green* cast.
"Yeah," Kai grinned, "next, I'm getting him a hybrid
car!"

Even though it went smoothly, it was still a long
day. They were at the hospital for almost ten hours, but
they filled the time up by getting Fin from liquids back to
solids (ice cream), grabbing some lunch in the cafeteria,
"petaling" the rough edges of the new cast with the soft
white medical moleskin tape, and having a lot of fun in
the large hospital playroom. At the end of the day, there
was a reward that made every single moment worth it. Dr.
D'Astous and Matt came into their hospital room
together, to tell them that Fin had gotten more correction
in his second cast.

Dr. D'Astous said, "Fin started at 63 degrees; then
went down to 34 degrees in the first cast, and now he is
measuring at 29 degrees, in this second cast."

It was *working*.

Kai and Doris beamed at each other and at Fin,
overcome. Kai hugged Dr. D'Astous and Matt, thanking
them profusely, and the three of them got to go back to
the hotel by 4:30pm, so that Fin could take his nap in the
hotel portable crib.

Back at the hotel, they turned out the lights in the
room and drew the curtains so that Fin could rest, and
Doris watched him as Kai went into the hall to make
excited, "YAY!" cell phone calls to Janie and to Fadi.

"Slow and steady *will* win this race!" Janie
shouted triumphantly, as Kai finally let the tears roll.
They were doing it. *One cast at a time*.

The next afternoon, Fadi picked them up at LAX
airport with a huge smile on his face. "I am *so* happy,

dearest Kai, and I am *proud* of you," Fadi exclaimed. "Fin is one *tough customer*!"

"Yes, he certainly is. He's my little Superhero," she said, brimming with emotion, "I'm the one who's proud."

"This baby is going to help change the world in some way, honey, he will." Doris said, beaming at Fin, who giggled back at her.

Kai was relieved to get back home and unpack, until she checked the messages on her phone from earlier that day, and she stopped breathing.

Teddy had called. He wanted to see Fin. *Crap.*

Doris walked into the living room, seeing Kai holding the phone, with her jaw dropped open. Fin was running around, excited to be in his familiar surroundings again, with all of his books and toys. Doris looked suddenly pale.

"It's *him*, isn't it?! What did he say? What does he want?!" Doris barked.

"He said he hasn't filed anything with the courts yet, but he has obtained a lawyer and he's been exploring his parental rights. He said he wants to see Fin, me and Fin, he wants us to meet him at Clover Park to talk."

"When?" Doris asked.

"Tomorrow," Kai closed her eyes, exhaling. "What do I do?"

Doris began to pace the room. "Don't go. It could be a trap. What if he grabs the baby? No, *wait*, go and tell him how well the casting is going. Maybe it will sway him, and the struggle will be over." Doris stopped walking, shaking her head. "What am I saying? This is *Douche Bag* we're talking about, we can never trust him. Lord, I wish we were back in Utah."

Kai covered her face in her hands. "We just got back. I can't deal with this right now."

"But if you don't, he may file the papers."

"You're right."

"I'm going with you, and we'll need to get a gun," Doris announced firmly.

Kai gasped, lowering her voice so that Fin couldn't hear. "A *gun*?! Are you *crazy*?!"

"Maybe, yes, I might be crazy," Doris muttered, nodding, "but how else do we defend ourselves if he pulls something? How do we defend *Fin*?"

"Doris, we can't even get a gun permit in 24 hours. Do you want me to bring an *illegal firearm* to a meeting with the biological father of my child?" Kai was incredulous; checking to make sure Fin wasn't overhearing them. He was still darting up and down the halls in his newly minted green cast, holding his Elmo doll.

"I know someone who has a gun," Doris rolled her eyes, "hand me the phone."

Fadi drove them to the park, with his handgun concealed under his right pant leg. His cab was off duty, but he still insisted on driving them, even though Kai had her own car now, and it was only a twenty minute walk from the house.

"We may need to make a quick getaway," Fadi had said, as he strapped Fin's car seat into the back seat of his cab.

It was the first time Kai and Fin had been back to this park, since she had the nightmare about the cast cracking open and falling off. That kind of freaked her out, but it was a play area Fin was familiar with, without sand he could throw and get down his cast, and it was close by.

They parked the cab in the nearby parking lot and Kai carried Fin in her arms to the climbing structure and play area for the younger kids. Doris and Fadi stayed a respectful distance behind her, letting her approach Teddy, who was already there, standing near the fence, as the small planes flew overhead and children played on the slides.

Kai had made Fadi promise not to have an itchy trigger finger, and he swore he would never use the gun at all, unless Fin was in true danger from Teddy. Kai had palpitations going off in her chest like fireworks, but she tried not to show him how nervous she was.

"DADDY!" Fin cried out excitedly, when they were six feet from Teddy. Kai couldn't believe it. Fin *remembered* him after all this time? *Imprinting*, she thought...wow.

Fin wriggled and kicked and Kai let him down, as he grinned at Teddy, who ruffled his son's hair as he ran up to him. Then Fin quickly darted to the climbing structure to play with the other kids. Doris chased Fin to keep him within a hugs reach, as Fadi stayed back, sitting on the bench of a picnic table and eyeing Teddy angrily.

"I see you brought *back up*," Teddy smirked.

"You aren't exactly the most trustworthy person I know," Kai replied, her eyes following Fin as he climbed the stairs to go down the slide.

Teddy shifted uncomfortably, shoving his hands into the pockets of his khaki pants. "I messed up. I know I've been a big disappointment as a father..."

"Big? How about *huge*? I thought you weren't sure if you *were* the father." Kai was just incredulous. *Really*?

Teddy sighed, "Listen, Kai, my Dad is sick. His heart is weak after the attack; we don't know how long he has."

"Uh-huh?" Kai didn't want to be heartless, but this was coming out of the blue—and how could she trust the guy, ever?

"I'm not filing for a DNA test; I know Fin's my son. And now that my own father may not be here much longer...it's dawning on me that what matters in life is family. Family is everything. My father wants to see his grandson, but he can't travel, Kai...he's too frail..."

Kai just looked at him, her mouth becoming dry.

"I know you hate me and I don't blame you, you have every right...but my Mom and Dad just want a visit with Fin. That's it. All expenses paid, we'll fly you by private plane to them. You can bring anyone you want...Doris, is that her name? Even...*that* guy," he gestured to Fadi, "the one who's glaring at me like he wants to shoot me, right now."

"He does want to shoot you," Kai stated plainly, "and so do I."

"Again, I don't blame you—but just think about it. It's lineage. It's Fin's heritage. Someday, the vineyards will be his. I just want to get a chance to be a part of his life."

Kai couldn't believe it, but Teddy somehow sounded sincere. Was this a situation where she would be cutting Fin off from his father and grandparents, without giving them a second chance? *She* didn't have to forgive him, but would her son forgive *her*, later when he was older, that she took such a hard line, that she was too angry and too hurt and too...stubborn...to open her heart to his father's side of the family, when his paternal grandfather might be on his deathbed?

She cleared her throat, facing him, "What about the casts? They're *working*, he's in his second one and he is getting better...it's going to take time, a year, maybe two, maybe longer...but he *is* getting better..." Kai felt the lump rising in her throat. She would *not* cry in front of Teddy.

"The cast is not an issue right now, for me or for my parents. The bigger issue is that time may be running out for my Dad." Teddy was getting choked up.

Kai felt her heart wavering...she knew she had to leave, to get her head on straight. "FIN, HONEY? DORIS, FADI! WE HAVE TO GO *SOON*!" she called out anxiously.

"Kai?" Teddy winced, "Say something...will you just think about it? He's my son..."

Kai looked him directly in the eyes. "You *don't deserve it!*" Her face was hot with anger. "You treated me like a *hooker*. You threw the *mother of your child* and your *baby son* out of the house and put us up in a *hotel*! And 'good luck, don't let the door hit you on the way out, you can keep the goddamn *ring*?!' What is WRONG with you?!"

"I know, I'm so sorry…" Teddy squinted, trying to look pathetic.

"No, you're not. You have no heart. You have a love gene missing, you're a *sociopath*," Kai spat.

"I was terrified and I ran. It's fight or flight, as simple as that. I'm here now. I'm trying to reach out to you, for Fin's future. Anger doesn't help anybody…" he argued.

"That's not true, Teddy, anger can *change the world,* if it's channeled properly! It was a mother's love and anger that got this treatment brought to the U.S. that is saving our child's spine!" she yelled.

"Okay, you're right…what can I say? I'm deeply ashamed of myself and my behavior." He looked as close to broken as she had ever seen him. If Kai didn't know better, she would have thought he was trembling. This was not the Teddy Verona she knew.

"My Dad is dead," she stately plainly. "I'm not sure why I even just told you that, not that you care."

"I do care, Kai, and I'm so sorry. That means Fin only has one grandfather left," Teddy said.

That was all that she could take right now, emotionally, but that fact stopped her in her tracks. She shot Doris and Fadi a pointed look, *we are leaving.*

Her friends had both been watching for her signal, now they went on red alert. Fadi stood up stiffly, and Doris swept Fin up from where he landed at the bottom of the slide, crying "WHHHEEEE!" and they both purposefully walked in step behind Kai, back to the cab in the parking lot.

Fin began crying and kicking, as he often did when he had to leave the park before he was done playing, but this time he cried "BYE, DADDDYYYYY! *BYE!*"

Wet tears streamed down Fin's cheeks, as Kai strapped him into his car seat. That split her Mama bear heart in two.

As Fadi drove them home, Fin stopped crying, and she found herself thinking about Jack—about calling him for advice. Did she want her son to grow up without his biological father in his life, when he appeared to, at least, want to be in it? Would she be a monster if she didn't allow it to happen, if she didn't go up to Northern California on the Verona private plane and let Fin and his paternal grandparents spend time together? Would she be taking away her child's heritage, his "lineage," as Teddy had said?

It's not like her own father had wanted to be a part of her life, let alone Fin's—and her own mom was not here. What price would her anger and her pride cost her child in the future? Forget about money, what *emotional* price would it cost him?

Back at the house on Ashland, Doris stepped outside to get the mail, and Fadi drank a cup of coffee at the kitchen table, as Fin drew with washable markers on a dry erase board. Kai couldn't drink or eat anything, and it was not lost on her that Fin was drawing happy faces as she paced in tense silence.

"Well, you're not going. That's final," Fadi announced.

Doris came in with the mail that had just been delivered, overhearing and handing Kai a letter. "He's right, you're not going—and if you are, I'm coming with you," Doris chimed in.

Kai took the letter from her, squinting at the return address, surprised.

"It's from Jack," Doris noted, watching Kai's expression change from tension, to surprise, to concern.

"Can I...?" Kai began asking, realizing she had to get out of Fin's air space, she didn't want to show him how upset and worried she was.

"Please," Doris replied, before Kai finished, "I'm watching him."

Kai nodded and took the letter back to her bedroom, closing the door and sitting on the bed. *Breathe*, she told herself. What was Jack writing her a letter about, what was too much to say on the phone? Was it a "Dear John" letter? Was he breaking up with her, when they hadn't really even been a couple? She realized she was probably too crazy for him, for anybody, she was too messed up, right now...she knew it.

She finally tore open the letter, reading it silently:

My Sweet Kai,

I think of you every moment, but I don't want to interrupt your life, when you're dealing with so much with Fin. I can't imagine the loneliness of going through a chronic, open ended health problem with your child, it must be as if the world itself is cracking under your feet and you're racing to mend the cracks before they envelop you. I see you holding on and I'm awed by the courage you're showing in fighting this fight, I believe nothing can truly triumph over a mother's love. Every child deserves that kind of devotion.

I hope you don't mind that I sent this note. Know that I am always here for you.

Yours,
-Jack

Kai slowly exhaled, tears rising to her eyes. "Yours?" What did he mean by that? Jack's simple words pierced her most vulnerable, aching heart. She felt skinless, lately—every nerve on edge; exposed to the world—flayed.

She set the letter down on the bed, and she knew that she would find a way to mend the cracks in the foundation of her life. She had to. She had to save more than one life, she had to save two. All she wanted to do was lie safely in Jack's arms, but it was mend or die, and she was more determined than ever to write a different ending to their story.

20
Fathers and Fireflies

Doris and Kai sat together on the Verona private plane, as Fin sat strapped in his car seat, in his own plane seat next to the window. He looked out calmly at the billowing clouds, unknowingly on his way to his family vineyards.

"Am I doing the right thing?" Kai winced at Doris.

"You're following your gut, and that hasn't steered you wrong yet, has it??

"Uh, yeah, it steered me to Teddy," Kai said wryly.

"But if you hadn't met Teddy, you wouldn't have Fin now, and you wouldn't give him back, would ya?" Doris smiled.

"No, no I sure wouldn't give him back. I can't imagine my life without my boy," she answered softly.

"Then your gut steered you right, chica. Just keep listening."

Kai wished that made her feel better. She really didn't know if she was doing the right thing, but if she didn't go to see Teddy's parents, at least this once, she would never know. She didn't want to be one of those people full of regrets later in life. She doubted all of those people set out to have deep regrets, so she figured she was going to have to steer this rocky path pretty carefully and try to keep her wits about her.

One thing Kai remembered about the first time she visited the Napa vineyards and Teddy took her on the tour of how their family wines were made, he showed her that the best wine came from grapevines that had to grow up through rocky soil. The simple soil made the wine thin and without character.

"Just like people," Kai had exclaimed, excited by the Ah-ha moment, and Teddy had smiled proudly at her.

Now that Kai was facing her child growing up through potentially very rocky soil, she wasn't sure that analogy was as comforting—and it wasn't just the casts and the scoliosis, although that was certainly enough—it was the relationship between his parents, she are Teddy. Divorce damages kids emotionally, everyone knew that, but it was much worse if your parents were at odds with each other, or fought viciously for custody, held grudges against the other parent or spoke ill of them. Divorce could be like a nuclear bomb going off in a child's world. Maybe the kids couldn't totally understand it when they were very young, but it surely came later, and it could wreak havoc on their sense of feeling loved, whole and safe. It could even make them not believe in love and its possibilities.

It was bad enough if a child's parents had the "perfect, cordial split," Kai thought to herself, just ask the kids a few years later how they felt about that. Ask them when they're teenagers, ask them when they're thirty years old. It would take almost super human effort for Fin to not be hurt by what had been going down between Kai and Teddy, especially if his father was completely absent from his life.

Kai pondered what would happen if she couldn't somehow find a way to make this better for everyone. *You can't hold on to anger*...she kept repeating to herself, trying to make it sink in.

She was still angry at Teddy, she kept feeling it rise up in her gut. If she held on to it, if she couldn't let it go somehow, would Fin later seek out his Dad and say he wanted to live with him? Would he blame her? Fathers and sons, they needed each other, didn't they?

Fin gazed at her lovingly as she put his bib on and gave him a bottle of milk. "Milk and Mommy," he smiled as he began to drink. Her heart soared up, up, up—higher than the plane they were in, with love.

"*Milk and Mommy*" was important, perhaps the most important loving relationship in most children's lives, but Daddy was a close second, if not an equal, depending—and in some cases much more important than Mom—especially if she had checked out physically or emotionally. She knew that every child would prefer their parents be a loving unit under one roof. That wasn't always possible, but it was something Kai knew was true, because she remembered how she had felt as a child, how her friends of divorced families had felt, how Janie had felt. The fallout reverberated for years, if not for the rest of their lives. Therapy could help, most everyone said so, but Kai wondered if therapy ever totally fixed the old childhood wounds, or was that just a human psychological fantasy? Nobody would want to be the person who says "Nothing works, not therapy, not drugs….nope, you're pretty much screwed, live with it."

We all walk around with our wounds, Kai thought, some of them have just been healed over better than others. She wanted to start to heal, that's why they were on this plane, flying into potential enemy territory.

A private driver met them at the airport with a sleek black town car, taking them to the Verona estate, where they entered the marble floored foyer with a hanging chandelier, and were greeted by Teddy, dressed casually and wearing a big smile for Fin. "Daahhh!" Fin cried excitedly; then he proceeded to run past Teddy into the living room and dart around the vast open space, filled with antiques.

"Thank you for coming," Teddy said to Kai, "and you also, Doris, thank you. Welcome."

Wow, Doris widened her eyes at Kai, as if to say, *that is a first.*

"My folks are outside on the patio. Lunch is about to be served. Please, follow me," Teddy said, walking towards the back of the house.

Kai chased after Fin and scooped him up into her arms, propping him on her hip. She and Doris followed Teddy, the two women exchanging a look, *here we go.*

They walked through the wide open back doors on to the vast stone patio, as Teddy's parents smiled at them graciously. Mr. Verona was in a wheelchair, with a sage green cashmere blanket thrown over his legs. He was a little thinner and frailer than before his heart attack, but he looked relaxed and happy. Both Mr. and Mrs. Verona were dressed in elegant casual attire, with a spread of wine and cheese, fruit and rustic breads, Italian meats and olives laid out before them. The vineyards provided the stunning backdrop to the layout, which could have come directly out of a designer clothes catalogue.

"Hello! Please join us!" Mr. Verona smiled, opening his arms like they were being welcomed to *Fantasy Island.* Kai had to admit to herself it was a pretty spectacular way to lunch.

Fin's t-shirt slid up a bit as he wriggled in Kai's arms and the bottom of the bright green cast was exposed. Both of Teddy's parents glanced at it and tried their best not to react, but his mother inadvertently gasped before purposefully closing her mouth.

Lunch went pretty well. Everyone gathered at the table, as waiters brought out salads and some grilled wild salmon, and Fin sat pretty patiently, eating fruit and bread and butter in the brand new high chair they provided. The Cadillac of high chairs, of course, nothing but the best. No one even asked about the cast, Kai could tell they were avoiding the subject.

After Kai excused herself to use the restroom, with Doris watching Fin as he played on the patio, she returned through the kitchen and was stopped short by Mrs. Verona. Mrs. Verona was standing by a large marble kitchen island with a wooden butcher block in the center. Kai saw the knives in her peripheral vision and tried to act casual, even though she felt like she was being sneak attacked.

"Kai...I wanted to take a moment to say how *mortified* Teddy's father and I were, about how he handled the news of Fin's condition. We've spoken at length to him about it; that is *not* how we raised him to behave." Mrs. Verona's mouth was tight and grimly set. She stood very close, a little too close, but Kai was afraid to back up and appear rude.

"Th...that's...well, it's not *okay*, obviously," Kai sputtered, "but you don't have to apologize for him. He's an adult, right?" She was taken aback; she hadn't had time to choose her words carefully.

Mrs. Verona took that in for a long moment. Kai felt lost in the conversational lull so large that semi-trucks could've driven through it, rubbing her arm self-consciously.   Finally, Teddy's mother continued. "I realize that, but I still wanted to say it. He is also a *father* now, and he should start *acting* like one. There are *sacrifices*."

It dawned on Kai that Mrs. Verona had been drinking a lot of wine at lunch...five or six glasses. Was that a whole bottle? *Crap*. Kai hoped she wasn't scary drunk.

Mrs. Verona put her hand with long, plum colored talons on Kai's shoulder. "We are Fin's *grandparents* and we want to be in his life. We can agree to disagree about this body cast business, for now."

"It's not a *business, it's a miracle*." Kai was startled by her easy dismissal of the subject. "Let me tell you about how Fin is being treated..."

279

Mrs. Verona cut her off, "Shhhhh...We're *family*. We have all the time in the world, let's keep this upbeat and positive. We moms have to do that, we have to lead by example." With that, Mrs. Verona patted Kai's shoulder condescendingly and sailed past her, back outside.

Kai blinked, not sure if she should follow her and demand that they listen to what their grandchild is going through, or if she should drop it. She sighed; she didn't want a confrontation, right now. She really didn't want a confrontation *ever*, and what if she caused Mr. Verona to have another heart attack? She didn't want to hurt anyone, especially not in front of Fin.

Kai gathered herself and walked back outside, where the waiter was pouring a small glass of dessert wine for everyone. The waiter handed one to Kai, as Mr. Verona raised his glass and announced, "Good, Kai, you're back. A *toast*! To my healthy, robust grandson! He runs and jumps around like a normal kid, even with that silly *brace* on!"

Doris glanced at Kai. They both bit their tongues as he continued his jolly toast. *Don't blow up, don't blow up*, Kai thought to herself...*we just got here...*

"Look at him: tall, confident...carrying on the Verona man tradition!" Mr. Verona exclaimed.

Fin squealed happily, raising his arms in the air, and Kai couldn't help but grin from ear to ear at the sight of her happy boy. In spite of his grandparent's insensitivity, his joy was contagious.

Doris and Kai were both given their own, luxurious guest rooms and a private bathroom to share. After lunch, they retreated to Kai's room, while Fin napped in a brand new, custom made designer crib they had bought for him to use at their house. It looked hand carved and probably cost them thousands of dollars, Kai figured. She wished they hadn't done it, but asked herself what could she do? Ask for the money in cash?

"These people are out of touch with reality, and believe me, it's *not* just the wine," Doris whispered in a hush, to avoid waking Fin.

Kai leaned back on the gigantic pillows on the bed. "I know. Maybe they're nervous?"

"Or just *plum crazy,*" Doris replied.

"I'm related to them, now," she said sadly, "By blood."

"Yeah," Doris nodded.

"Aren't all families a little crazy?" Kai was trying to give them the benefit of the doubt.

"Uh-huh. I'm afraid to dig any deeper with these two, though. I mean *three*." Doris shook her head in a *tsk, tsk* way.

Kai winced. She had ties, lifelong ties with the Veronas. She hoped they were just eccentric, her child shared genes with them, after all.

"Oooo, *sorry*, honey," Doris softened, "this is a very stressful situation, I shouldn't make light of it. I'm just feeling protective and defensive for you and Fin."

"It's okay; I've been touchy since the day he was diagnosed. If a complete stranger in the grocery store tells me I'm doing the wrong thing for my child, I will *flatten* them. But these are his grandparents. They may be nuts, but I'm just hoping we can get along."

A male voice came out of nowhere—"*Hey.*"

Kai and Doris both jumped—Teddy was peeking in the door, rapping a soft knock. "Sorry to disturb you," he said, "my folks want to have dinner at 7, then they said we could have some time alone to talk, Kai."

She gulped a little, hoping he didn't overhear what she said a second earlier. "Sure, Teddy...um...Fin's in bed by 7:30, so that should be okay."

"I'll be in the room watching Fin, don't worry," Doris chimed in. "I have a good book I'd like to get back into."

"Great." Teddy looked relieved, like she may have said no. "Drinks on the patio at 6," he smiled and ducked his head back out of the room, closing the door.

"Oh, good, have another drink, Mrs. Verona," Doris cracked.

Kai couldn't help but giggle. "We're gonna need a *lot* more wine to get through *this* trip." The truth was, Kai hadn't had much wine at lunch, just a small glass and a sip of the dessert wine for the toast. She would have a bit with dinner, but she knew she had to pace herself carefully, there was *no way* she was not gonna keep her mama bear wits about her.

Dinner was delicious, served in the main dining room of the house, filet steaks with a pink peppercorn butter sauce and a Verona petite Syrah. A very good year for the wine, unlike this one for me, Kai mused sadly. She let Fin watch a classic Sesame Street children's video when he couldn't sit still in the high chair, and he was happy as a clam learning how to count from one to ten as the adults conversed and broke bread. No one mentioned anything unpleasant or asked Kai about Fin's health or treatment. She was saddened and disappointed with them, but decided to bring it up at breakfast. They were heading out tomorrow afternoon to fly back to L.A., and if a blow up happened, God forbid, at least they wouldn't have to stay overnight in the house with that kind of tension hanging over them.

At 10pm, everyone else retired to their rooms, with Doris reading her book and watching the sleeping Fin, and Kai and Teddy were alone together on the patio.

"Come and take a walk with me," Teddy said.

"Okay," Kai replied, following him down the huge stone steps to the vineyard. It was pitch dark outside, save for the glow of the moon. It wasn't lost on Kai that it was a full moon, the kind of thing that affects tides, women and wolves. He led her down a walking path through the grapevines where tiny white lights were strung around fence posts and markers in the ground, which lit their path on either side. It was beautiful, like hundreds of dancing fireflies surrounding them.

"I've been thinking a lot, about what a terrible person I've been to you…" Teddy began.

"You did dump us on the lawn," she replied simply.

He winced. "I know. I was a…a douchebag of the highest order."

"King Douche Bag," Kai nodded, glancing at him as she shoved her fingers into the front pockets of her jeans.

"I didn't know I got to be royalty, but yeah, that sounds about right," he tried to joke, forcing a smile.

"No, that's actually what we call you now. Douche Bag, two words, both capitalized. It's your new name," she said.

"*Ah.* I guess that's well deserved," Teddy allowed.

"I'd say well *earned*," Kai replied briskly.

"Can Fin say Douche Bag?" he asked.

"Not yet, but if repetition is the key to learning, he'll be able to soon."

"*Ouch*," he winced.

"You don't know the *meaning* of ouch," she said.

"I hear you. I hope…I hope that we can be friends again, at some point…this trip, you coming up here and bringing Fin, it means a lot to my parents. Thank you."

"You're welcome," she kicked her toe in the dirt.

"You're being the bigger person, in all of this…I hope, with time, you can start to forgive me for what I did, for panicking and running from the situation. Children want both parents in their life, they need a father…"

"I thought so, too. Then you bailed in possibly the cruelest moment. It's hard to forgive that, to forget it ever happened. It's a wound…" Kai looked away, up at the moon.

He gently reached for her hand. She stopped walking, pulling it away. "I met someone. I'm seeing someone."

He stepped back, the news clearly struck him in the chest. "That…doesn't surprise me. You're beautiful, inside and out, who wouldn't want to be with you, Kai?"

"You didn't," she stated plainly. She wasn't letting him off that hook.

"Who is he?"

"Just…a guy. A friend."

"Does he know about what's going on with us, with Fin?"

"He doesn't know we came here, yet. We don't see each other every day. And if you're asking if I'm keeping Fin's condition a secret; that is offensive and hurtful. I would *never* not be proud of my boy."

"*Our* boy."

"You gave up some moral rights, Teddy."

"I'm still his Dad."

"No, you have to *earn* being a Dad."

"Don't you think you're being a little harsh?" Teddy whispered to her. He reached out to touch her face, and she recoiled.

"Why do you think it's okay to touch me?" her lip was trembling; her body was betraying her emotions. She hugged her arms around herself, feeling a chill.

"You tell me what's okay. Is this okay?" he took off his sport coat, putting it around her shoulders.

She let him. "Yeah…thanks."

"Is this okay?" he reached out his hand slowly, touching her hair like he used to when they were a couple, removing a rogue strand that fell across her face in the moonlight.

She froze, taking herself back to the time before all of this happened, when it was just the two of them. Now they had a child in this world who was part of both of them. Sure, Fin looked more like Kai, but he was taking on some of Teddy's features as he got older, and she couldn't ignore that they had a similar smell to their skin. It was a scent Kai had once fallen in love with, a sense memory of a happier time.

"Is this…?" he reached up and cupped her face in his hand, leaning in, their lips brushing in a near kiss…their noses grazing each other softly.

So much pain, Kai thought, *so much water under the bridge in such a short time*…there was a part of her that wanted all of the darkness and pain to disappear, to wash away with the tide. To burn off under the glow of the moon and the firefly lights.

"What if we could go back, pretend it never happened…?" he asked.

"I *can't*…" she swayed a little, unsteady on her feet.

"Fin will never remember anything, but his parents being together…he's only two…we can change this…it's up to us…" Teddy touched his whispering lips to hers and she relented. It was a beautiful dream, *if only…if only all of this hadn't happened…*

The white light fireflies danced around them as Kai's head swirled with the wine and with crazy, stupid hope…*Jack*, she thought, *this is a betrayal to him…what am I doing?*"

Kai abruptly pulled away from Teddy, murmuring "*No…*" just before Doris ran down the walking path in her pajamas and bare feet, her eyes wide with fear and panic.

"FIN IS *VERY SICK*!" Doris yelled, "I just took his temperature. He has a fever of a hundred and three!"

Kai took off running, full speed ahead towards the house, thinking *this can't be happening*. Not *here*, not *now*. She clenched her hands into fists and tried to anchor her heart for whatever was to come.

Fin was screaming and vomiting every ten minutes. He was burning up. Kai could feel his temperature was high just by holding his hand; she knew what her baby's skin normally felt like—this was not good. Teddy drove them to the hospital, speeding like a maniac. Kai and Doris had covered Fin in bibs and towels to try to keep the puke from soaking into the cast, sitting on either side of him in the back seat and repeatedly changing the wet mess with the horrible smell off of him, and replacing it with new bibs and wads of paper towels. They exploded into the E.R., where the people waiting for emergency care cleared a path for them. When the triage nurses saw the vomit and the body cast, they were rushed to a room immediately. It was mostly a blur—Kai hardly had time to think about being afraid—she had to try to calm her boy as best she could. She felt dizzy, but that was old hat by this point, her red alert panic system was on so much of the time that it was just who she was, now, a person with a crap storm of a life who had to learn to wade deep and brace herself for the next wave.

She told herself that she just had to hold that baby above the crap, so he could breathe. In moments like this, she didn't care if she died, except that Fin would need her arms to steady him.

The doctor came in, a young guy with red hair and pale skin, doing a quick assessment.

"His lungs are fine," the doctor said, "are you the parents?"

"Yes, I'm Fin's mother, Kai, and Teddy is his...father," she managed to say.

The doctor stepped aside with Teddy to get some basic information, talking under their breath, while Kai and Doris kept cleaning the vomit off of Fin. After a couple of minutes, the doctor left the room and Teddy walked back to them, saying, "It's probably a severe stomach virus, the doctor thinks, hopefully it's a 24 hour thing that's going around lately."

"Okay, okay, that makes sense…it can't be food poisoning, right Doris?" Kai asked frantically. "He hasn't eaten anything but bread and butter and his usual stuff."

"No, no, he hasn't," Doris replied, rattled.

"WE'RE CUTTING OFF THE CAST, NOW," a nurse loudly announced.

That snapped Kai back to reality. She turned to see the doctor standing there with a cast saw in his hand, as Teddy nodded, "Yes, please do."

Fin suddenly vomited again. Kai had been so distracted by cleaning and comforting him, she hadn't been able to pay any attention to the doctor's questions. Teddy had consulted with him and the decision was made before she was even asked.

"NO! IT'S SAVING HIS *LIFE!*" she shouted. "If you cut it off now, there's no way of knowing when we can have another cast put back on, we'd have to get back to Salt Lake City, and there could be a wait for an appointment…weeks, months……Fin could have a growth spurt in between, and lose the precious ground we've gained. *Continuous correction*, that's how this treatment *works!*"

"We're cutting it off," Teddy declared.

"I said *no*." Kai clutched Fin tighter. They were both covered in puke, he was still wailing.

Teddy looked at the doctor and the nurses who had entered the room, "I'm this child's father and I give permission to remove the cast. *Cut that thing off*, I insist!" Teddy was firm; he squared his jaw and locked eyes with Kai, challenging her.

She almost could not believe it. They came up for *one night*, and now, she suddenly realized, they were at a hospital that the Verona family had donated a *wing* to! She was backed into a corner. Security would hear the shouting and be there in a moment. Teddy's folks would get on the phone and get involved, they would make demands. She felt herself shrinking, like her own muscles and bones were twisting into knots. They were powerful, moneyed people, and there was *no way* she could win this fight.

Well, maybe only one.

"DORIS, *RUN!*" Kai yelled.

She grabbed her vomiting baby, covered in the stinky muck herself, and she and Doris and Fin bolted out of the hospital like bats out of hell.

Teddy was right behind them. Kai kept looking back, panting, as she ran down the hospital hallway holding Fin, heavy in his unyielding cast; she knew she couldn't out run Teddy.

Doris was behind her as they reached the E.R. waiting room, the prospective emergency patients all looking up, startled by the commotion. Doris suddenly screamed "DOMESTIC VIOLENCE!" as they ran past a Hell's Angel biker type guy with a thick salt and pepper beard and bloody gauze wrapped around his broken leg. The biker dude snarled and suddenly held his leg crutch out in the path, purposefully tripping Teddy, who flew forward and crumbled to the floor of the E.R., grabbing his knee and screaming "*AHHHHH!*"

Doris paused and smiled sweetly at the Hell's Angel who winked and tipped his head; then they shot through the exit doors, just as a cab was pulling up, with the passenger door swinging wildly open and a middle aged man stumbling out, clutching his middle and gasping in extreme pain. A triage nurse pulled up a wheelchair and, wheezing "burst appendix," the man collapsed into it, as he was hustled into the emergency room. Kai and Doris scrambled with Fin into the back of the open cab, slamming the doors, both yelling "GO! GO! PLEASE, DRIVE!" The driver widened his eyes, nodded and hit the gas, as Teddy limped outside and reached out for the windows of the cab, like one of the undead in the zombie videogames he plays, as they pulled away, eluding him.

It wasn't Fadi, but the middle aged cab driver was kind and he let them ride, even though they smelled horrifically. Puke was all over their clothes, it was in their hair. Once the cab was gunning down the road, Doris turned to Kai and said, "We're like Thelma and Louise with vomit."

Indeed, Kai laughed, amazed they could find any humor in this. That night, they stayed in a low rent motel, with all three of them up most of the night, which was *not* a lot of fun, but they got some fluids into Fin and his fever went down to normal by the morning. They paid in cash, so that their credit cards couldn't be traced, they didn't know what the Veronas might do.

The next day, they took another cab from the motel; first to buy a travel car seat and other toddler necessities at a nearby Target, as Fin's vomit coated car seat was still strapped into Teddy's BMW. Next, they headed to a rental car place, where they did put down Doris' credit card information as security, but again asked to pay cash. Finally, they began the long drive home to L.A.

Fin was fine by then, it had mercifully been a 24 hour virus, but they still didn't trust going through the airport, in case Teddy's family had put security men there or some kind of "rent-a-cop" to stop them. It wasn't worth the risk, the trust had been broken once again, and Kai seriously doubted now if it could ever be repaired.

The two women took turns driving, stopping a few times to use the restroom and get some snacks. Midafternoon, they munched on some junk food, sitting on top of a picnic table at a rest stop, gazing out at the highway with their feet on the bench, while Fin enjoyed a bottle of milk in his Mom's lap.

"Corn Nut?" Kai smiled at Doris wryly, offering her one.

Doris giggled, "Still a funny name for a food." She ate a Corn Nut; then crunched one of her onion flavored rings thoughtfully. "Not as funny as Funions, though."

"You know the Veronas donated a wing to that hospital we were in," Kai mentioned.

"I figured they had their tentacles everywhere," Doris muttered.

Kai nodded, thinking, "Does this mean we're on the lam? Did we break any laws?"

"I don't think so, no." Doris took a sip of Dr. Pepper, "You're the mother, you have physical custody, it's not like you abducted your own child."

"It sure felt like it," Kai sighed. She had been thinking about Jack a lot on the drive, now that things had quieted down. She felt like she should tell him that she almost, well, really *did* kiss her ex. Crap, had she cheated on Jack? What had come over her? The frickin' *moon*?

"I sort of brushed against Douche Bag's lips last night," Kai confessed, looking away from Doris.

"Why? Was he being less Douchey?" Doris smirked, raising a brow.

"A little. I think I wanted to believe for a minute that none of this had happened," Kai admitted, feeling some measure of shame.

Doris scrutinized her for a moment. "I get it, you're easy," she grinned, joking.

Kai smiled. "I must've gone temporarily insane. I fell in love with him once, he started to use the old moves on me…I'm in a weakened condition…"

"Oh, now he's Douchey Kryptonite?" Doris cracked.

Kai had to laugh. "I guess. *Never again*…I feel like such an *idiot*! So *stupid*. *Stupid*, trusting girl, he was totally *manipulating me*!"

"No sense beating yourself up. Some people are shape shifters, and they keep drawing us back into their twisted web. You're only human," Doris sympathized.

"We can't even really call him Douche Bag any more, he kind of owned it. It sorta takes the sting out of the insult," Kai frowned, wrinkling her nose.

Doris considered that. "Okay, then I'll call him by a *really* bad word: *Teddy*."

Kai threw her last few corn nuts to the nearby squirrels, sighing, "There is no prince on a white horse at the Verona estate, is there?"

"Nope," Doris shook her head, handing Fin a Funion, which he began to munch.

"There never was," Kai muttered.

"Yep, damn Cinderella!" Doris blurted, quickly covering Fin's ears.

"Yeah, lying old Cinderella, to hell with that bitch *and* her mice!" Kai yelled, releasing some tension.

"Whoa, earmuffs, we have a child here," Doris laughed.

"Hey, Ms. double standard!" Kai exclaimed.

"I'm black, black people can get away with some things you people can't."

"You people? When did I become you people?" Kai asked, amused.

"I don't make the rules. Nobody said life was fair, Princess," Doris said, fluffing Fin's hair.

"No, they sure didn't." Kai paused for a long time, as cars and trucks flew past them on the highway. "I guess I have to tell Jack about the kiss," she whispered, hanging her head.

"You don't have to tell Jack, you're not *married* to the man."

"No, but…"

"Have you made any promises to him, that you're exclusive?" Doris arched a brow.

"No, I guess I haven't…"

"Have you slept with him?"

"Not yet—not exactly—no." Kai felt her shame incrementally subsiding.

"Then maybe you shouldn't kiss and tell. Or *sort of brush lips* and tell. Are you in love with him?" Doris asked.

"Falling, I think I might be...*yes*," Kai admitted softly.

"Is he falling for you?"

Kai considered that. "I think so, I thought so...but he may feel differently after hearing this...it's a betrayal."

"Then don't tell the man," Doris said flatly, crumbling up her empty Funions bag as punctuation and tossing it in the nearby trash can. "Eat Funions and then he won't want to get near you. *Funion breath*, it's a natural repellant," she joked, smiling at Fin, who was still munching on his.

Kai rolled her eyes, "Good plan. *Seriously*, how do I explain to Jack that I got momentarily caught up in the dream of having a whole family for Fin, with both parents who love each other and act like grown-ups, instead of acting like mortal enemies?"

"Just tell him like that. Say the evil shape shifter used his voodoo on you," Doris cracked.

"But then he'll never know if Teddy might try to swoop back in, and I might fall for it again. I'll feel so guilty if I'm not honest with him, but how can he ever trust me after this?" Kai winced.

"He may not," Doris admitted.

Kai just looked at her, wanting a different answer.

Doris shrugged, "I'm being real.'"

Kai looked out at the highway, "I'm not asking for him to be Fin's Dad...it's so much to expect a man to take on. Part of me just feels like eventually he'll run from the pressure, and both Fin and I will get our hearts broken again. Fin may be older when it happens, and then he would know more, lose more. What is he going to feel if his own father isn't around, and then another father figure rejects him? I'm so afraid of damaging him, with my choices. He doesn't deserve that," Kai said softly, rubbing her arms.

"Whether or not Jack becomes Fin's father figure is yet to be written. One little step at a time. Maybe first, we can get home safely, and you can just *call* the man."

"You're right," Kai shook her head, riddled with exhaustion and confusion after their nearly sleepless night.

Doris reached for her friend's hand, "Honey. Loving anything or anyone is *nothing* if not a risk. If it wasn't worth it, nobody would bother teetering off the ledge all the time." Doris smiled at Fin warmly, as he smiled back at his beloved Aunt Doris. "Take a step back from the ledge just for today, my girl."

"Okay…okay…" Kai squeezed her boy.

"That's your Prince, right *there*," Doris grinned, nodding to Fin.

Kai burst into a smile. Of course. Of *course* Fin was her Prince.

Doris patted Kai's back. "It's worth it, honey. It's painful, it's messy, it's a sticky freakin' wicket, but loving people with your heart wide open is the most beautiful and painful way to go through life…and it is the *only* way to live."

21
Breathe

Once they were safely home, back into their
routine for a few days, with no attempts at contact from
the Veronas, Kai called Jack and asked him if he would
meet her for a walk on the beach. She had been carrying
around her guilt and shame from the lip brushing—well,
kiss with Teddy, and she had to get it off of her chest,
even if it meant Jack would run screaming in the other
direction. He probably would, she realized, but she felt
she had no choice but to lay it out there, warts and all.

Fadi came over to watch Fin with Doris while Kai
was gone, bringing his firearm tucked into his ankle
holster, just in case. Doris made them dinner and they
settled in for a couple hours of good, cherished Fin play
time together. With all of his gleeful jumping around and
dancing, he was better entertainment than any TV show.

Kai arrived early at the beach, as the sun was
about to set, and watched the waves alone for a few
minutes until she saw Jack approaching across the sand.
Her heart thumped loudly in her chest, and she fleetingly
thought of not telling him anything, just so she could be
enveloped in his arms again, without judgment or a sense
of betrayal pulling them apart.

Jack was wearing a pale blue, crew neck cotton
summer sweater over his broad chest, his sexy forelock of
hair flopping in his eye, as usual. *Lord, he was handsome*,
Kai thought—and those *eyes*. So kind, with the depth of

294

the ocean behind them, *what had she been thinking* when Teddy had tried to kiss her?? She was a damn fool; there was no way around it. Teddy had played her, but *she* was the dummy who fell for it, fell for his random acts of pretend kindness that hid his true intentions, which were to control her and to control Fin's treatment.

"Hey, you," Jack smiled at her, walking closer, reaching out to put his arms around her waist.

"Hey," she frowned, involuntarily glum.

"How is Fin? Is something wrong?" His smile dissipated and he was suddenly on alert, worried.

Kai crossed her arms, although it wasn't a bit cold. "Yeah...yes, Jack, I...I accepted an invitation to see Teddy, Fin's father, in Napa, where his parents live..."

Jack nodded, "How did it go?"

"His Dad, Teddy's father, is in ill health...his parents wanted to see Fin...Doris came with me...they had us as overnight...guests..." Kai didn't want to finish the story, looking away, pensive.

"Uh-huh," Jack was confused by her mood, slightly furrowing his brow.

"Teddy asked me to go for a walk; in the vineyard...he sort of kissed me. I kissed him back," she blurted, taking a deep breath. "I don't know why..."

Jack looked stunned.

"No, I *do* know why, it...it..." she stammered, "it was the wine, but it wasn't the wine, I hadn't had that much...so that's really B.S....I sort of... uh, *swooned*, to use an incredibly old fashioned word, at the thought of Fin having both parents together, loving him as a family, instead of being at each other's throats like wolves..." Kai looked at the sky, overcome with guilt at the thought of hurting Jack.

"I see," he was expressionless, now, just taking her words in. His face was white.

She forced herself to face him, "It wasn't real. I got lost in wanting everything to be okay for a few

moments. Then Fin got sick, with a hundred and three
degree fever, he was vomiting everywhere…"

"Oh, no…" Jack's hurt instantly turned to worry
for Fin.

"We had to rush to the emergency room, and
Teddy insisted they saw off the cast, even though it
wouldn't have made him better, only worse, probably
fast…"

"Kai…" he gently shook his head, pained.

The words began to tumble out of her, "So we ran.
We just ran as fast as we could, shot out of there like
criminals, and a biker dude in the waiting room tripped
Teddy with his leg crutch, and Fin is fine, now, it was just
a 24 hour virus…we stayed at a motel and drove home in
a rental car, and I am so, *so* sorry that I am such a *jerk* and
I betrayed you, your trust, it was *so, so stupid*…"

"No…" Jack reached for her and took her into his
arms, touching his fingers softly to her lips, her face…"I
won't listen to you say that about yourself. Stop it."

"He's going to try to take Fin away, now, through
the courts, I know it," she said, the fear seeping back in
through the shame.

"He won't win," Jack said.

"His family is powerful, I'm not. It's that simple,"
Kai looked up at him, her eyes haunted.

He met her gaze. "You're more powerful than you
know. You're a brave, strong mother with a *mighty heart*,
and they better not underestimate you any longer."

Kai felt her chest heave on his as she buried her
face into his strong arms, whispering "How can you
forgive me?"

"Well, I admit I'm a little hurt this very
moment…but that's just a bruised ego. That will pass, and
it doesn't really matter anyway."

"How can you be so selfless?" she pulled back,
confused.

"I'm not selfless. You don't owe me anything; you didn't owe me an explanation or an apology. You have been walking through Hell, and I just want to hold you right now, if you'll let me."

"I've never felt so ugly in my life, *how can you want me?*" she whispered, trembling. "You're somebody really...special...incredible, actually. You could be someone's...*someone*." Her head was swirling, her self-esteem was buried in the sand.

Jack took her in, their faces inches apart, his eyes intense with an open yearning, fearless and raw. "With every cell in my body, I want *you*. It's not selfless, because I've fallen for you. *I love you, Kai,* more than I ever imagined possible. When you told me just now, about Teddy...my heart stopped."

She heard herself softly gasp—this was not what she had expected at all, and she hadn't realized until that moment how desperately she wanted to hear those words from him.

"I love you," he said, "and I love your little boy. I love Fin."

"Oh, Jack...we're kind of a package deal..." her voice began to break.

"I hope so. My only fear is that I'll lose you and Fin before we've had a chance to even take the leap together. Into...whatever this can be. In my best, most hopeful dream, a *family*."

She blinked back blinding tears, "I want to...*yes, please*. We *three*," she murmured, and they kissed with an energy and force that blew the false fireflies above the Napa Valley sky, enveloping them into the billions of stars that make up the eternal unknown.

They held each other for a long time on the beach, listening to the waves crashing, no more words were needed.

Later, Jack followed her back to her little Santa Monica rental house in his car, to see her safely home. As

they walked up to the house together gently holding
hands, the menacing voice came out of the darkness near
the porch light.

"Where is my *SON*?!"

Jack let go of Kai's hand, his own hands
instinctually balling into fists.

"Teddy…you can't just show up here…" Kai said,
suddenly gripped with fear.

"Who is *this*?" Teddy snarled, stepping out of the
shadows and into the yellow glow of the porch light,
standing between them and the front door. Fin and Doris
and Fadi were inside. Her mind raced, *no no no, not
now…not like this…through the courts…no, Teddy…don't
do this…*

Jack let go of Kai's hand and faced Teddy,
unafraid. "I'm the man who's in love with your child's
mother. If you try to enter her house uninvited, I'm gonna
have to stop you."

Kai nodded, standing beside Jack, trying
desperately to appear as calm and measured as he
sounded. "Teddy, if you touch our child, *my* child, or try
to abduct my boy, make no mistake, I will *hunt you down*
and do anything in my power it takes to get him back.
Don't test me. You will *lose*. You will not take Fin from
me. *Ever*."

"Go to hell, Kai. My family will buy and sell you
before this is over."

"Try it." Kai stood her ground.

Teddy narrowed his eyes, hissing cruelly, "Your
father was a loser, an addict low life with no real job, and
you lived in that crappy shack on the beach like a
homeless person when I met you. You've always been
one step away from being *white trash*," he spat, turning
defiantly on his heels to head for the front door.

Jack threw the first punch, lunging forward and
connecting his large fist with the side of Teddy's jaw with
a crack that sounded like a giant redwood tree splitting

open. Teddy reeled back in astonishment, swinging around on the porch and diving at Jack with his fists flying.

Teddy's fist landed squarely on Jack's face, busting his lip open, as blood trickled down his chin.

"*STOP IT*!" Kai screamed, as Doris and Fadi exited the front door to the porch, seeing what was happening. Fadi drew his gun, holding it aimed directly at Teddy as Jack wiped the blood from his chin.

"Listen to the mother; she is the heart of the matter, here," Fadi said firmly.

"Fadi, put the gun away. This is a *neighborhood*; we have a small *child* inside." Kai was scared, with a gun involved, all bets were off…

Fadi's hands were trembling, but he kept the gun trained on Teddy. "If you do not obey the mother's wishes and leave us, I regret that I will have to force you to leave the premises."

Jack took a step closer to Teddy, a looming warning, "And I don't think you need to ask what I'll do," he added threateningly.

Teddy's face twisted up in anger, "Let me guess, *fuck the mother of my child*?"

"You're pathetic." Jack recoiled in revulsion, shaking his head, "If you hurt her, or lay a finger on Fin, I'll kill you with my bare hands. Or you can just head home right now. Your call."

Teddy grinned, "Empty threats. I'm going in to get my kid, and none of you are gonna do anything to stop me."

Fadi flicked his finger lightly on the trigger, preparing to fire.

"Fadi, don't shoot!" Doris screamed, reaching for the gun in Fadi's trembling hands, accidentally knocking it to the ground. Teddy dived for it, and it was in his possession before they could blink.

He trained it on each of them one by one, forcing himself to be able to circle around Doris and Fadi to the open front door. "Now, don't make me shoot anybody, my lawyers can prove any defense, especially since *Mohammed* here is probably a terrorist," Teddy said, glaring at Fadi as he nervously began backing up to the door.

Jack set his jaw grimly, "You'll have to kill me before you take that little boy."

"Then that will be a bonus," Teddy hissed, reaching for the door.

In the split second Teddy had to glance down to turn the knob, Jack bolted on to the porch and dove on top of him—both men crashing through the open doorway and into the house.

Kai, Doris and Fadi looked on as Jack grabbed the hand Teddy was holding the gun in and repeatedly smashed the butt of the firearm into his head until he knocked him out, slumping unconscious on the floor. Kai gasped as Teddy's body went limp and his head lolled back, blood trickling down from the gash in his skull.

Jack's chest heaved as he dragged himself off of Teddy's now still body, peeling the gun from his fingers. "Someone call 911. He may need an ambulance."

Kai glanced down at Teddy's chest rising and falling. He was still breathing, thank God.

Doris looked at Jack, confused, "Aren't you a doctor?"

"I'm a neurosurgeon, but trust me; he doesn't want me cutting his head open any more right now," Jack said. "I'd annihilate the son of a bitch."

"Doris, get the phone, I'll check on the baby!" Kai shouted, then sped to Fin's bedroom as Doris dashed for the phone, and the men who truly cared about Fin stood watch over his bleeding father.

Darting into Fin's nursery, Kai saw with palpable relief that Fin was still sleeping peacefully. He had always been a heavy sleeper, luckily. She steadied herself on the railing of his crib and said a quick prayer that he wouldn't have to know this happened for many, many years…hopefully he would never know. Just *breathe*, she told herself over and over, right now—*just breathe*.

The ambulance arrived, as did several police cars, and Teddy came to, before being taken to the hospital. They were questioned and Kai, Jack and Doris all reiterated that Fadi had drawn the gun in self-defense.

When the medical reports came in, they learned that Teddy's injuries weren't fatal or permanently damaging, and the most shocking thing of all was that Teddy didn't press charges, against Jack or any of them, but he did file with the court for joint custody. Kai was ready to take on that fight, because they was no way in heaven or hell she was going to let Fin be alone with his biological father, not after the last two frightening incidents. Teddy would have a *very* long road of repair work ahead, to prove if he was even worthy of being in his son's life.

But, Kai believed in miracles—after all, her son's spine was living proof. Two months later, Jack travelled with her to Salt Lake City for Fin's 3rd cast, and Dr. D'Astous happily informed them that Fin was now down from 63 degrees to 29 degrees in cast number 3. They were down from the sixties into the twenties! He was making steady, hopeful progress, and while they were still a long way away from the end of the treatment, each bit of correction in his curve was cause for true celebration. It was a slow and gentle process; Kai reminded herself of that many times over, *patience*.

Kai, Jack and Fin went to The Hogle Zoo like she and Doris had the last trip on "cast off" day, and Kai was actually starting to feel like this was their home away from home, this beautiful city with the hospital on the hill. The people who worked at Shriners Hospital were starting to feel like friends, and the three of them were beginning to feel exactly as Jack and Kai had both dreamed they could: like a family.

She had accepted that she wouldn't have a fairy tale ending, nothing was going to be neatly wrapped up in a bow with Teddy and his parents, and that Mehta Method casting was not a "get out of scoliosis free card" for every child with Fin's condition. Some children got the treatment too late to avoid beginning spinal surgeries at a young age, some children had other syndromes that created additional challenges, and in some very rare cases, a child's sensitive skin couldn't tolerate even properly applied casts, they developed dangerous sores underneath. In those rare cases, the casts had to be removed before they could be fully effective. Kai had become close to many of the other mothers and families on the online support group, and her heart was heavy with the knowledge that so many of their brave, precious children had such big mountains to climb.

But it was heart expanding for her to know these other mothers and their children. Kai truly loved every child with scoliosis, even the ones she had never met. These kids were warriors, each and every one of them, and their mothers and many fathers fought for their futures with everything they had. Kai realized she would now never have a life where she didn't personally know many kids with chronic and life threatening health problems. This was her life now, and it was both fuller and more heartbreaking.

But, what you must take on, you *must take on*— and she could never look away from children like Fin and other parents like herself, who found themselves frightened and lost and drowning in the confusion and fear of this diagnosis. She would try to paddle out and help pull them to shore when she could. She would offer them sustaining words of life and love and hope, she would support them with her own damaged emotional tools, and pray they would be the lucky ones, the kids who make it to the ocean, who face the ugly Undertoad of Progressive Scoliosis and still live joyful, beautiful lives. She prayed each one of them would thrive, and she hoped they danced.

More than one of the moms on the C.A.S.T. group had not one, but two kids with scoliosis—a younger child with the Progressive Infantile kind, and an older sibling who was diagnosed as an older child or preadolescent. The more Kai learned about adolescent scoliosis, which more commonly strikes girls than boys, it pained her to realize how it hits them at such a cruel time in life, just as they are starting to really notice boys and desperately want to fit in with their peers and just feel *normal*. It's bad enough that their body may be deformed to different degrees, depending on how bad their curve is, but then they have to wear a tight and bulky brace that sometimes makes them feel invisible or like a freak, and can even get them mocked or made fun of in school. More than one girl had thrown her brace down the stairs in tears; they put videos on YouTube about it with anger rock blasting in the background, talking about how emotionally painful it was for them. Many girls and boys also wore their scoliosis braces bravely and proudly, of course, and some even posted videos of themselves dancing in their brace, for all the world to see. They were all precious, beautiful souls, regardless of what the other kids said or didn't say.

Kai despised scoliosis and the pain that it caused in every form, and she knew she had her work cut out for her, to try to contribute some small part in helping to spread the word about Fin's treatment, and to get Progressive Infantile scoliosis on every pediatrician's "well baby" checklist. If she could help to save one child, who knew who that child would grow up to become?

Although she never would have chosen this path for Fin or herself, she knew in her cells that the hard won knowledge she had gained through this terrible journey was a gift. And in the name of every baby or young child

who had ever slipped through the cracks, as their mothers
helplessly watched them twist and even die from this
monster, when no proper treatment was available or
found…in the name of those angels who could not
breathe—she would pass the message *on and on and on*.

22
The Ocean

For Fin, the sky was the limit.

Actually, he had *no* limitations. At age five, he was now tall and skinny like a reed, but strong and healthy, with a completely normal body shape. He had no pain from his scoliosis, and he almost never got sick. When he did get a cold or flu, he fought off the pesky virus like the fighter he had always been.

He had worn a series of 10 casts for 2 and a half years, from 19 months old to age 4 and a half, and then wore a "Boston style" light, removable brace for a little over year, to make sure he was holding at the low degree curve they had gotten his spine down to. At that point it was around 11 degrees in the brace and 17-18 degrees out of it, no longer a dangerous curve at those numbers, but one to watch and keep an eye on.

Now Fin was wearing a "night time only brace" called a Providence brace, and he didn't have to wear any brace at all during the day! In this first night brace, his spine was down from the original 63 degrees curve to only 1.21 in the last "in brace" X ray. To put that in perspective, 0 to 6 degrees is medically considered *no scoliosis*. His curve bounced up slightly higher in numbers out of the brace, but still, the miraculous change in his back simply took Kai's breath away. And he still had the possibility of getting even straighter as he grew.

Her boy might never be "zero" degrees straight, never technically a hundred percent cured of scoliosis, but his syrinx cyst had not grown and it had caused him no problems, so far. They would stay on top of it for life, but Kai had a gut feeling it would never grow, the doctors agreed with her and her maternal instinct had not led her wrong, yet.

Fin had not had spinal surgery of any kind, and his doctor was confident he would never need it. His spinal "rotation" was gone, that terrible three dimensional corkscrewing, there was no visible rotation anymore on his X-rays. Their road wasn't over, but Kai still felt like they had won the heat of the battle. The greedy Undertoad had lost.

She stood alone on the sunny summer beach, wearing a navy blue and white striped bohemian sailor style bathing suit from her own new collection of designs, with real shells attached at her hips, and a big, floppy woven straw hat. She had begun creating her beachwear again, and even had a financial backer now, the famous romantic comedy actress who had been one of her first customers had called a year ago and asked about her designs, and a few magazines had photographed the actress wearing them. With Fin's health on the right path, Kai had taken her craft back up, and the doors began to open again as if it was meant to be. It was freeing to have a creative outlet, and while her business was still small, it was starting to help pay the bills, too.

She put her hands on her hip bones and exhaled with ease, watching her sweet boy flying a red, white and blue kite, high in the California sky. Kai dug her toes into the warm sand, as she drank in the sights and sounds of Fin dashing around with his cousins Micah, 7, Sarah, 6, and Ruth, 4. The young girls danced around him and giggled, playing, their small feet being tickled by the frothy surf. Fin was wearing funky island print swim trunks his mom had made for him; he was just about to go

306

in the water. He was already a strong swimmer, even though he hadn't learned how until he was four and out of the last cast.

Without his t-shirt on, he looked just like any other lean little boy on the beach, but maybe happier. Fin had a certain confidence around his peers and in the world in general. He had already been through more than most adults at his tender age, and it seemed to have wizened him, but it did not decrease his joy. If anything, it was the opposite, Kai mused, her little guy didn't seem to be afraid of *any* challenges, which can worry a mother at times. He was always the first to climb any hill, to take on any obstacle, and to protect the feelings of other kids.

He was good at all of the things that he had shown a natural talent for as a baby: art and music, and he still loved books, nature and the outdoors. He was very athletic and a fast runner, he loved all sports, the sports he wouldn't have been able to play if he had surgical growing rods in his back.

Kai looked on proudly as Fin handed her sister Janie the kite. She kept flying it high in the nearly cloudless blue sky for her three girls, all of them beaming and dancing around as they waved at their Aunt Kai.

Janie had moved back to California after her divorce, into a house right near her sister's. Doris had moved into her own place, but she was over visiting them all of the time. She and Fadi had developed a close bond over their love for Fin; they shared a beach umbrella nearby right now, watching the kids play.

Fin turned and looked up the beach at his mom, taking off running towards her with a big, gorgeous grin. He'd never really complained in all the years he'd had to wear the cumbersome casts and the tight braces, he just rose to the occasion and did what he had to do. Her child was her hero.

Today was the 4th of July, Independence Day. Kai tried not to get emotional as she watched her boy sprint to her, independent of his cast or brace. *Let freedom ring, indeed.*

A red Frisbee suddenly flew at Kai from her left side, spinning toward her in her peripheral vision. Her right hand instinctually shot out and caught it. She glanced down at the bright plastic disk, turning it over and seeing a hand written note taped to the underside of it. It read "MARRY ME," written in blue crayon.

She looked to her left, ten feet down the beach, and caught Jack grinning at her, as he carried a cooler of food and cold drinks across the sand, setting it down near Doris and Fadi. He touched his heart lightly with his left hand, the one with his simple platinum wedding band that matched hers, and she felt his love travel through the atoms or energy or whatever it was that connected people in love. He still made her flush with excitement, the small capillaries on her cheeks heating pink at the sight of him, as she dug her toes into the warm sand.

Her mirror was no longer cracked, she now could see herself as whole, the way Jack and Fin saw her. She had come home, to a place where she knew her soul was beautiful.

Jack had become her husband, and the Dad who Fin deserved, she couldn't have conjured or dreamed up a better man to love them. Teddy had changed considerably, and was already remarried with a new baby girl. They didn't see him often, but his relationship with Fin was improving. *Baby steps.* Fin was more of the adult in the relationship than Teddy was, but Kai was just grateful the court battle was now behind them; and that she had maintained Fin's proper medical treatment without letting Teddy's dangerous combination of ignorance and anger derail them.

Kai had long ago let her anger fly away. It wasn't worth holding on to in the long run, anger just *never was*. She closed her eyes and said a soft prayer of thanks:

Thank you God for this peace, love, and moment of grace.

She opened her eyes as Fin reached her. "Mom!" he said, grabbing her hand and pulling her towards the water, "*C'mon!* LET'S GO!"

"It's cold in the water today, isn't it?" she asked, hesitating as he pulled on her arm, leading her to the ocean, "Fin, be careful…" she heard her own Mama's voice coming out of her, "There may be an undertow…"

"Ahhh, Mom…" Fin grinned at her, "Like you're afraid of *anything*."

And with that, her child fearlessly led her onward.

ACKNOWLEDGMENTS

This book would not have been possible without the efforts of these heroes:

Dr. Min Mehta, Dr. Jacques D'Astous, Heather Montoya and her daughter Olivia and The Infantile Scoliosis Outreach Program (I.S.O.P.) founded by Heather. There are not enough thank yous for these four brilliant souls. You are bright lights in this world, I stand in awe of your courage and grace.

My deepest thanks also to the Shriners Hospital for Children in Salt Lake City, Utah (Shriners Intermountain Hospital), and their entire kind, generous staff, especially Mike Pond and Angie Livingston, the cheerful ladies in X-ray, the nurses and the anesthesiologists who kept our child breathing. We love you all.

There are not enough hugs for the brave children with Progressive Infantile Scoliosis and their amazing families we met on the C.A.S.T. Yahoo support group. Many of you helped steer our emotional ship back on course in terrifying waters, and by sharing your stories, you gave us the lifeboat of precious hope.

Some of our kids have had casts only, some casts and surgeries, and some just surgery, they are all inspiring. Although this book highlights the treatment I believe should be the first line of defense for IS when possible, there is no "us" and "them," there is only us.

310

I also owe a debt of immeasurable gratitude to the French doctors Cotrel and Morel who invented the EDF casting table, to Tim Berners-Lee, the inventor of the World Wide Web, and to Google search, without which we would not have found ISOP and this miraculous cure.

A special thank you to Bexon's entire family, including my own beautiful sisters who did not oppose casting like Kai's sister Janie did in this novel. Your love and support throughout my life has been one of the greatest gifts I could ever receive.

Thank you to our friends far and wide, including my wonderful and supportive readers on my blog **Girl to Mom.com**, and anyone and everyone who prayed, commented online, or sent good thoughts, positive energy and good healing vibes for our boy's spine. Your messages of love were heard and felt, it mattered.

As you can see, it took a village across continents to save Bexon. That gift is beyond any we could ever repay, but a portion of the profits from each sale of this book will go to I.S.O.P. and to Shriners.

Above all, thank you to God. Only we know the whole truth, you and I. In my darkest moments I couldn't see you or understand why this was happening, but you never deserted me. The fact that I'm even alive to publish this novel is a story for another book, coming soon. Thank you for loving me as I strive to "fail better," and for the chance to live this wild and precious life.

Love,

~ Heidi Ferrer, Los Angeles, 2012

www.ingramcontent.com/pod-product-compliance
Lightning Source LLC
Chambersburg PA
CBHW031549240626
47153CB00002B/436